For Princess Claire
A royally good agent,
and an even better friend

PRAISE FOR TWIN CROWNS

'TWIN CROWNS has all the charm of THE PRINCESS BRIDE
and all the stakes of GAME OF THRONES – but Wren and
Rose are in a league of their own. Addictive, swoony,
tender and vivid – I loved it with all my heart.'
Kiran Millwood Hargrave, bestselling author of
The Mercies and *The Girl of Ink and Stars*

'Riotously funny, fast-paced and dripping with romance, TWIN
CROWNS manages to deliver a tale as familiar and nostalgic in
the way of childhood blankets and fireflies in jars, while at the
same time wholly refreshing with its levity, charm and quirky
tale of sisterhood rediscovered. TWIN CROWNS is so
joyous that days after reading, I'm still grinning.'
Roshani Chokshi, *New York Times* bestselling author of
The Gilded Wolves and the Aru Shah series

'An absolute delight from start to finish. TWIN CROWNS is a
dazzling gem of a book. Magical, clever, surprising, and pure fun
from its captivating start to its spectacular finish. If you
love wicked kings, sexy bandits, and sister stories that are
full of heart, this is a must read.'
Stephanie Garber, *New York Times* and *Sunday Times*
bestselling author of *Caraval*

CURSED CROWNS

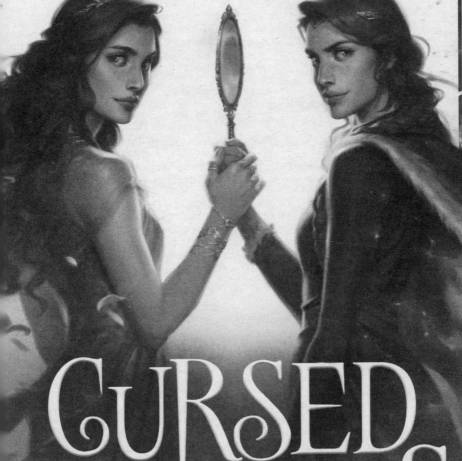

CATHERINE
DOYLE
&
KATHERINE
WEBBER

CURSED
CROWNS

First published in Great Britain in 2023
by Electric Monkey, part of Farshore
An imprint of HarperCollins*Publishers*
1 London Bridge Street, London SE1 9GF

farshore.co.uk

HarperCollins*Publishers*
Macken House, 39/40 Mayor Street Upper,
Dublin 1, D01 C9W8

Text copyright © Catherine Doyle and Katherine Webber 2023

The moral rights of the authors have been asserted
A CIP catalogue record of this title is available from the British Library

ISBN 978 0 0084 9223 6
'Wren' special edition ISBN 978 0 0086 1188 0
'Rose' special edition ISBN 978 0 0086 1189 7

Printed and bound in the UK using 100% renewable electricity at
CPI Group (UK) Ltd

1

Typeset by Avon DataSet Ltd, Alcester, Warwickshire

MIX
Paper from
responsible sources
FSC™ C007454

Break the ice to free the curse.
Kill one twin to save another.

Wren
CHAPTER 1

Wren Greenrock's crown was too tight. The band squeezed her temples, pressing into her skull. She tried not to wince as she stood on the balcony at Anadawn Palace beside her twin sister, looking out over the kingdom they had fought so hard to claim. Wren still couldn't quite believe it was hers. Or at least, half of it was. She and Rose had agreed to share it.

Still, her nerves were frayed. She had been worrying about this moment all morning, steeling herself for the worst. Given the events of the last few days, which had seen the unfortunate death of Rose's betrothed, Prince Ansel of Gevra, on their wedding day, followed swiftly by the welcome demise of Willem Rathborne, their traitorous Kingsbreath, Wren hadn't been expecting a big turnout, or even a positive one, but a jubilant sea of people had gathered just beyond the golden gates. Revellers from the nearby town of Eshlinn and beyond had come to wish the twins well on their coronation day. The crowd was so large it stretched all the way back to the woods. Thousands of grinning faces peered up at the white palace, their cheers rising on the summer breeze. They had come to celebrate Wren and Rose, the new twin queens of Eana.

The twins, for their part, stood on the balcony, bedecked in their finest gowns and brand-new crowns, absorbing their adoration like sunlight. Together, they glowed like a beacon – the promise of a new era, in which the witches and non-magical folk of Eana would live side by side in harmony, and all the old superstitions and festering mistrust would finally be laid to rest. It was a day of promise and possibility. Or at least, it would have been, if Wren's head hadn't been pounding like a drum.

'Stop scowling,' said Rose, out of the side of her mouth. 'They'll think you're unhappy.'

Wren glanced sidelong at her sister. Rose's smile was full and gleaming. It had been perfectly fixed in place for almost an hour. She had been waving for just as long, too, her hand raised high above her head, so every man, woman and child below could see it, and know they were welcome. Cherished. Rose was a natural at this. She had been born for it.

Wren had never felt more like a novice in her life. Her smile had come easily at first, her surprise at hearing the cheers as they opened the doors on to the balcony filling her with a rush of relief. But now her energy was waning. She had smiled and waved for so long her arm was exhausted. *She* was exhausted. It was no wonder. After all, she had grown up among the witches on the windswept beaches of Ortha in the west, far from the pomp and ceremony of Anadawn Palace and all the patience and decorum expected of a princess. 'How long do we have to stand out here for?' she hissed. 'All this waving is making me ravenous. And my head hurts.'

Rose grabbed Wren's free hand. She squeezed and a warm pulse travelled up Wren's arm. Healing magic. A heartbeat later, Wren's headache was gone.

'There.' Rose blew out a breath as she released her. 'No more complaining.'

Wren refixed her smile and returned to waving. Her head felt better but her chest was still tight. Despite her healing magic, Rose couldn't mend her sister's heartache. It bloomed like a dark flower inside Wren, reminding her of Banba. Barely a day had passed since her steel-eyed, fearless grandmother had been taken from the burning Protector's Vault by King Alarik and his ruthless Gevran soldiers. She had been hauled on to a ship before Wren could get to her. Her final moments plagued Wren's every waking thought now, the unfairness of it writhing inside her like a snake.

Wren had become queen, just as her grandmother had always wanted, but Banba wasn't here to see it. Wasn't here to help her. Instead, she was a prisoner of King Alarik, the young, feral king from the northern continent, who harboured a dark fascination with witches. But Wren intended to change that. She had made a vow to herself – and to Rose – that she was going to find a way to rescue her grandmother from the icy maw of Gevra.

Just as soon as she'd finished smiling and waving.

Wren caught the moment Rose's gaze flickered down to the courtyard, where Shen Lo was reclining along the edge of the fountain that marked the entryway to the inner palace. He had one arm slung over his forehead to keep the sun from his eyes, the other drifting in the crystalline water.

Wren could tell by his smirk that he wasn't sleeping. She didn't have to see his eyes to know he was enjoying the spectacle of Rose glowing in her natural habitat. And Wren squirming like a fish out of water.

'Wren, look!' squealed Rose, grabbing her sister's hand again. 'They're throwing flowers over the gates!'

Wren looked up just in time to see a bright red rose land in the courtyard. And then another, and another. There was an entire bouquet scattered along the stones – pinks and yellows and reds and purples – and still more sailing over the gates. 'Roses,' said Wren, with a chuckle. 'They really do love you.'

'They'll love you, too,' said Rose, blowing a kiss to the crowd. A cheer went up. Rose did an elaborate twirl, garnering another. 'Just as soon as they properly get to know you.'

'As long as they don't start flinging dead wrens over the walls.'

'Oh, don't be so morose.'

Wren made a show of blowing a kiss to the crowd. More whoops and hollers rang out. Down in the courtyard, Shen was laughing, his teeth winking in the afternoon sun.

'This really is too easy,' said Wren, blowing another kiss. 'Maybe I should do a cartwheel.'

Rose grabbed her sister's elbow. 'Don't you dare!'

Wren burst into laughter.

Just then, the crowd surged forward, causing the gates to

groan. Arms threaded through the golden railings, grasping for more space, as a single rotten tomato sailed over the spires. It soared as if in slow motion, getting bigger as it came towards them. Thankfully, it fell short of the balustrade and landed in the courtyard with a determined *splat*.

A ragged shout rose above the cheers. 'OUT WITH THE WITCHES!'

Down in the courtyard, Shen jolted upright.

Rose's smile faltered.

Wren stopped waving. 'I think we're done for the day.'

'Ignore it,' said Rose, quickly regaining her composure. 'It's one tomato.'

'Two,' said Wren, as another piece of rotten fruit vaulted over the gates. She watched Shen flit across the courtyard, trying to spot the protester among the masses, or perhaps to discern if there was more than one. The crowd was still surging forward, as though something – or someone – was pushing them.

When the second tomato landed in the fountain, Rose stepped back from the balcony. 'Very well,' she said, blowing one last theatrical kiss to the crowd. Another cheer went up, drowning out the next shout, but Wren swore she could hear the word 'witch' on the wind. The twins retreated from the balcony, both of them making a show of laughing gaily until they returned to the sanctity of the throne room, where the balcony doors slammed shut behind them.

They stopped laughing in the same breath.

'Well, that was concerning,' said Wren.

Rose wrinkled her nose. 'What a waste of perfectly good food.'

'I knew all those sheets were too good to be true.' Wren scraped her hands through her hair, dislodging her crown. There. *Much better*. 'Eana doesn't want to be ruled by witches, Rose. Even one they know.'

Rose waved her concerns away. 'Oh, please. That little protest wasn't even enough to make a bowl of soup. There's no need to be so dramatic.'

But Wren couldn't help it. Without Banba here, everything felt twisted, wrong. There was a pit in her stomach, and those four simple words – OUT WITH THE WITCHES – was only making it worse.

'I'm just trying to be realistic.' Wren's footsteps echoed after her as she marched to her throne. The room was the biggest in the entire palace, the ceiling covered in shining gold leaf. The walls were hung with gilded oil paintings and emerald drapes adding the barest sliver of warmth to the chamber. A couple of hours ago, it had been teeming with envoys and nobles from every corner of the country – as well as the Ortha witches – but it was empty now, save for the twins and the guards standing watch over them.

Wren sank on to the velvet seat and pinched the bridge of her nose, trying to calm her rioting thoughts. Willem Rathborne might be dead, but he had left them a legacy of problems. Their evil Kingsbreath had spent eighteen years preaching the same hate as the kingdom's long-dead Protector and poisoning the country against the witches. Wren and

Rose would have to do more than wave from a balcony for a few hours to hope to undo all of it. And until they did, the witches who had come from Ortha only days ago would have to remain at Anadawn, where they could be protected from those in the kingdom who still wished them harm.

Wren massaged the new ache in her temples. If their grandmother were here, she would know exactly what to do. She would lay her hand on Wren's shoulders and strengthen her with a few choice words, as only Banba could.

'You're thinking about Banba, aren't you?' Suddenly, Rose was before Wren, wearing the same look of concern. 'No wonder you're so anxious. I told you, we're going to get her back.'

'When?' said Wren, impatiently. '*How?*'

'I'm going to write a strategic letter to King Alarik. Monarch to monarch,' said Rose, with such sureness Wren dared to hope it might work. 'I imagine emotions are still running high after the death of poor Ansel.' Rose flinched at the mention of the prince, no doubt recalling how desperately she had tried to save him, only to fail. 'Perhaps a little diplomacy – and a well-worded apology – will do a world of good. I'll see if he's willing to open some kind of negotiation for Banba's release. Once the crowd disperses, I'll go down to the mews at once.'

'I'll come with you.'

'I'd rather you left the diplomacy to me.' Rose patted her sister's hand. 'A queen you might be, but it is going to take a while for you to learn what it means to be royal.'

Wren glared up at her sister. 'What is that supposed to mean?'

'It means I can see that dagger peeking out of your bodice and I know you've got another one fastened to your ankle,' said Rose, good-naturedly. 'And in this delicate negotiation, my darling sister, the quill will be *far* mightier than the sword.'

'Fine. But if you're wrong and something happens to Banba, I'm going to drive a big, shiny sword through Alarik Felsing's frosted heart.'

'Oh, Wren, I am never wrong.' Rose picked up her skirts and flounced away, tossing a winning smile over her shoulder.

Rose

CHAPTER 2

An hour or so later, after composing her letter to King Alarik, Rose held her head high as she strode through the palace corridors. She nodded and smiled at passing servants and soldiers, pretending everything was going perfectly to plan. Pretending her reign wasn't off to a truly terrible start.

Back in the throne room, she'd put on a brave face for Wren, whose temper was always flickering inside her, ready to erupt into a blaze. But as the day wore on, Rose could feel the cold tongue of her fear licking at her toes, and she knew if she let herself give in to it, it would devour her.

So, she would simply kick the fear away. As she had always done.

Now that the crowd had dispersed, she needed air and a moment to pull herself together. It was beginning to feel like the stone walls of Anadawn were closing in on her, like if she didn't get out of the palace immediately, she'd be trapped inside it forever.

She pushed on the door that led out to the courtyard, only for it to refuse to budge. Rose bit her tongue to stop herself from screaming out in frustration. She winced as she shoved it with her shoulder. With one strong push, it groaned open. And then, at last, she was outside, in the fresh afternoon air.

Rose wandered into her garden, at once calmed by the familiar sweetness of her roses. They were at their peak now, bursting into bloom all over, as if each one was trying to outdo the next. She lingered at a vibrant yellow rose bush and closed her eyes, inhaling its scent.

'Lucky flowers,' said a voice right behind her. 'I wish you'd smile at me like that.'

Rose yelped, lost her footing and nearly toppled into the thorns.

Strong hands caught her waist. 'Careful, Majesty.'

For a blissful moment, Rose allowed herself to lean into Shen Lo, resting her head on the hard planes of his chest, breathing him in as she had her roses. Then she came to her senses and stepped away from him.

'You shouldn't sneak up on people like that,' she chided.

'And you shouldn't close your eyes to your surroundings when you're out here all by yourself,' said Shen. 'Surely, I taught you better than that, Majesty.'

'Perhaps I need more lessons,' said Rose, coyly. 'And anyway, it's my rose garden. I'm as safe as can be out here.'

'Well, you are now.' Shen stuck his hands in his pockets, where Rose assumed he had stashed at least three daggers, and flashed a grin that made her knees weak. It was hard to forget they had shared their first kiss in this very place.

And then the following day, Shen had kissed her again, in

the heat of battle in the Protector's Vault, though they hadn't spoken of it since. They had built a wall around that morning, both of them dutifully pretending that Rose hadn't almost married Prince Ansel, that the dagger Willem Rathborne had thrown at Wren hadn't ended up in the prince's heart, causing him to bleed out in Rose's arms. Sometimes Rose wondered if she had imagined that brazen kiss. She had certainly allowed herself to imagine many others in the time since.

Shen's smile faded. 'Are you all right? The shouting in the crowd this morning . . .'

'I'm fine,' said Rose, the lie sour in her mouth. She turned from temptation and walked on into the garden. Better to look at her roses than into Shen's eyes. After all, she had come out here to gather herself, not unravel in his arms. He fell into step with her. 'What are you still doing out here anyway?'

'I was thinking about picking you a bouquet. Is it bad luck to gift a queen her own flowers on her coronation day?'

'Yes.' Rose chuckled as she looked up at him. 'Why do I feel like that isn't the full truth?'

'All right, maybe I was walking the ramparts. Scanning every face in that crowd to see who was out there throwing rotten fruit at you. I like to know who my enemies are.'

'Shen, really, it was just a tomato or two.'

'That's how it starts,' he said, darkly. 'Dissent is dangerous. A protestor today could be a rebel tomorrow.'

'It's early yet,' said Rose, as much to herself as to Shen. 'Wren and I will win them over.'

Shen huffed a sigh. He lifted one of her curls with his finger, settling it behind her ear. 'You are good at that,' he murmured.

Rose grinned. 'I know.'

'I just can't help—'

'Worrying?'

He winked. 'I'm not used to worrying, Rose. It doesn't suit me.'

'Nor me.' She took his hand in hers. 'Can't we set our worries aside and just enjoy today?'

'That's all I want.' Shen gently tugged her towards him. He was so close now she could see every shade of brown in his dark eyes, the freckle above his brow that she'd somehow never noticed before. 'To enjoy this.'

Rose bit her lip. Suddenly, she was feeling dangerously light-headed. 'It's the middle of the day,' she said, a little breathless. 'If people saw us together . . .'

'They would think we're . . . fond of each other.' He dipped his chin. 'Is that so bad, Rose?'

'Yes,' she whispered, but she couldn't quite remember why. All sensible thoughts eddied out of her mind until she could feel nothing but want pulsing between them, then Shen's arms around her waist, his breath warm on her cheek, his lips nearly brushing against hers—

The bell in the clock tower chimed and Rose jolted backwards. The world came crashing back in, and, with it, the swell of her duties. For goodness' sake, she was a queen now, not some love-struck desert-stranded princess. And she had made a promise to Wren. 'I'm afraid I have to visit the mews. It can't wait.'

Shen's shoulders slumped. 'Then I'll resume my patrol.'

'There are hundreds of soldiers at Anadawn,' Rose reminded him. 'You can take a rest, you know.'

He curled his fists. 'Not until every tomato in this land is hunted down and destroyed.'

They dissolved into laughter, Rose threading her arm through his as he walked her down to the mews, both of them pretending that the woes of the past were behind them, and the future was theirs for the taking.

Dear King Alarik,

I would like to convey my deepest condolences on the regrettable death of your brother, Prince Ansel, who was a dear friend to my sister and me, and to our country. As you must now be aware, our grandmother Banba was taken – mistakenly, I'm sure – by one of your soldiers in the kerfuffle, and she is very much missed here at Anadawn. Perhaps we can discuss the terms of her imminent return? Despite everything that has happened between our great countries, I believe there is a world in which Eana and Gevra can be allies once more. I hope very much that you agree.

Yours sincerely,

Her Majesty Queen Rose Valhart of Eana

Wren

CHAPTER 3

Thirteen days after the twins' coronation, when roses and rotten fruit had been hurled over the golden gates, Wren found herself back in the throne room, dressed no less finely in a sweeping violet dress embroidered with golden thread, and with her crown still digging into her scalp.

'You're slouching,' said Rose, who had been sitting ramrod straight all morning, and yet somehow still possessed the composure of a queen in an oil painting.

'I'm trying to take a subtle nap,' said Wren, without bothering to stifle her yawn. Last night, she had dreamed of Banba again. Her sleep had been fitful, her every thought haunted by visions of her grandmother, frail and suffering, all alone in Gevra. Back at Ortha, Banba had spent years teaching Wren to be brave in the face of danger, to be clever and resourceful, but she had never taught Wren how to face a world without her grandmother at her side. That was a fear Wren was not able to conquer. It plagued her even as she slept.

Rose pinched her hand, jolting her awake.

'Ow! Don't harm the queen,' snapped Wren.

'Then start acting like one,' said Rose. 'Today is important.'

Over the last two weeks, Wren had come to learn that every day as a queen was important. Especially as a queen of a new world that welcomed the witches, that saw them not just as equals, but as integral to the prosperity of the kingdom. There was much to do, and untangling the ancient tapestry of Eana from the threads of anti-witch sentiment that had mangled it under the legacy of the Great Protector was no easy task. The Kingsbreath, Willem Rathborne, although dead, had cast a long shadow over Anadawn. There were hundreds of laws to discard. Treaties to assess, territories to resettle and new edicts to sign. Proclamations to make. Governors to appoint.

Governors to fire.

Eana was home to the witches again. No. Eana *belonged* to the witches, and yet most of them were still sheltering at Anadawn Palace. It was Wren's and Rose's solemn duty to restore the kingdom to its former glory without the bloodshed and conflict that had once destroyed it, so that their kin could venture safely beyond the golden palace gates and make their lives in whatever part of the country they wished to. It was busy work. *Hard* work.

And then there was today.

As part of a monthly tradition established centuries ago by King Thormund Valhart and insisted upon by Chapman, the scurrying palace steward, the twin queens were holding their first-ever Kingdom's Call. An entire day dedicated to personally receiving visitors (and, more often than not, their complaints) from every corner of Eana.

Already the new queens had presided over a lengthy land dispute between rival farmers in the Errinwilde, had approved a delivery of six hundred barrels of grain for the sprawling town of Norbrook *and* had appointed no less than fourteen new governors to preside over the various provinces of Eana. They had also received formal banquet invitations from almost every noble family in the country and had even welcomed a missive from the neighbouring country of Caro, whose queen, Eliziana, had sent her warmest wishes, alongside three crates of summer wine and a beautiful olive tree, which now stood proudly on the throne room balcony.

And yet, despite such well-received gifts, the only royal Wren truly wished to hear from was continuing his infuriating silence. Despite Rose's diplomatic letter to King Alarik – and the further three that had followed it – the Gevran king had yet to respond. For all Wren knew, Banba was already dead. The very thought made her want to run all the way to Gevra and rip that feral king apart with her bare hands.

'It's almost lunchtime,' said Rose, encouragingly. 'I've asked Cam to make his delicious beef stew again. It's your favourite.'

Wren picked at her nails. 'So long as there's wine.'

Whoops and hollers reached her from the courtyard, the familiar trill of Rowena's laugh finding her through the open window. Over the last two weeks, the witches of Ortha had made themselves at home at Anadawn Palace, much to the chagrin of the servants and more than a few guards. Wren caught a glimpse of her friend's tempest magic now as Rose's favourite ball gown floated across the balcony, like a ghost.

A laugh sprang from Wren, earning her an admonishing glare from her sister.

'For the hundredth time, Wren, can you please tell Rowena to stop treating Anadawn as her personal fairground? And what is she doing in my closet? She shouldn't even be in my room!'

Thea, Banba's wife, who was attending the Kingdom's Call in her new role as the Queensbreath, sighed. 'I sent Rowena and Bryony to pick apples in the orchard hours ago. I thought if they could find a way of putting their magic to use around here, it would go a long way to helping them fit in.'

The ghostly dress began to cartwheel as the wind picked up. 'I don't think they care about fitting in,' said Wren, who desperately wanted to be outside cartwheeling, too. 'How many more people do we have to see before lunch?'

Rose looked to Chapman.

The steward's finely curated moustache twitched as he glanced at his never-ending scroll. 'Just twelve. Wait, no. Thirteen. The Morwell family have put in a last-minute request for an audience. They wish to raise a dispute with their farrier. They suspect he's been stealing horseshoes.'

Wren closed her eyes. 'Rose. I am losing the will to live.'

'Do try to salvage it,' said Chapman, pointedly. 'The Morwells have long been allies of the throne and are a family of considerable influence here in Eshlinn.'

'Archer Morwell,' said Wren, suddenly recalling the name.

She snapped her eyes open. 'I'm sure Celeste knows one of their sons. Rather well, if I remember correctly. Apparently, he has *very* impressive shoulders.'

'Wren!' hissed Rose. 'That is entirely improper throne room conversation!'

'Oh, calm down. No one cares.' Wren swept her hand around, indicating the ten bored-looking soldiers in their midst. Captain Davers, the stern-faced head of the royal guard, was standing sentry by the doorway, keeping a watchful eye over proceedings. And then there was only Thea, who was making a valiant effort to stifle her chuckle at the mention of Rose's best friend's dalliance.

Chapman cleared his throat, awkwardly. 'Onward.' He glanced at his scroll. 'Captain Davers, send in the messenger from Gallanth, please.' A moment later, the doors to the throne room swung open, and a boy with unkempt black hair and a paltry goatee was ushered in.

He bowed at the waist. 'Your Majesties,' he said, wiping his hands on his trousers. 'I, er, well, firstly, congratulations, on, um, well, there being two of you, I suppose, and, uh, well, we in the city of Gallanth are most honoured to—'

'Please get to the point,' Wren called out.

Rose swatted her hand.

'Sorry,' said Wren, quickly. 'I only meant that you can drop the pleasantries.'

Rose offered the nervous messenger a beatific smile. 'Though we do *so* appreciate the good wishes. Thank you, sir.'

'What of Gallanth?' prompted Wren, picturing in her

mind the sunset city that lay to the west of the desert, its mighty clock tower rising high above its sandstone walls.

'It's not Gallanth.' The boy swept the hair from his eyes. 'It's the desert. It's moving.'

'The desert is always moving,' said Wren. 'That's why we call it the Restless Sands.'

'Only it's not *just* restless,' the boy went on. 'It's more . . . um, angry?'

The twins exchanged a look. '*Angry?*' they chorused.

'It's the sand . . . it's started spilling over our walls,' the boy went on. 'Every so often, it comes like a wave and floods our city. It's buried half the Kerrcal trading route.'

'Goodness.' Rose pressed a hand to her chest. 'Has anyone been hurt?'

'We've lost camels. My father's best mule was swept away. And it's swallowed the huts closest to the border.'

Wren glanced at Thea. The healer was unusually grim-faced. 'Peculiar,' she muttered. 'The desert has always kept to its own rhythm, but it's never encroached on the Kerrcal Road before. Nor has it breached the border towns.'

'We must send someone out there to investigate,' said Rose.

Chapman frowned. 'The Ganyeve Desert is beyond Anadawn's reach. It's unsurvivable.'

'Not to everyone,' said Rose, and Wren knew she was thinking of Shen, who was somewhere close at hand. Drinking wine in the kitchens with Cam and Celeste, most likely, or perhaps he was training Tilda, the youngest warrior witch, out in the courtyard. In any case, they would have to tell him of this as soon as possible. After all, Shen was desert-born. He knew the currents of the sand better than anyone. If something was amiss in the Canyon, he would want to know of it.

'And in the meantime,' Rose went on, 'we'll send as many soldiers as we can spare back to Gallanth with you. You'll need to reinforce the town walls and erect new lodgings, as far from the desert boundary as you can.' She nodded to Captain Davers. 'See that the guards check on the town of Dearg as well. They're part of the desert trading route, after all, and if memory serves me, their walls are lower. Their risk is even greater.'

Davers dipped his chin. 'I'll see to it, Queen Rose.'

'Wise as ever,' said Chapman, approvingly.

Not for the first time that day, Wren felt woefully out of her depth. She was grateful for her sister, who was not only born to rule but had prepared for it. Committed her life to it. Wren had committed hers to Banba. Her grandmother had been preparing for this queendom for the last eighteen years, after all. Wren had only ever planned as far as her coronation day. She had always expected Banba to be there for that moment, and all the ones that came after, for her guiding hand to sit heavy on Wren's shoulder. Back at Ortha, they would talk about it most mornings when they walked the cliffs, tending to their vegetables. And sometimes late at night, when the beach fires burned low, and it felt like their dreams of the future were dancing in the smoke.

We will rule the new world together, little bird, Banba used to promise her. *We will bring our people home at last, and the great witch, Eana, will smile down on us from the skies.*

The longer Wren went on without her grandmother, the more her guilt grew. It gnawed at the very edges of her heart, whispered to her in the quiet of night. If King Alarik didn't respond to Rose soon, she would have to take matters into her own hands. To forsake the pen and use the sword instead.

After all, Banba would do the same for her.

There is no weapon sharp enough to keep us apart, little bird. No world cruel enough to deny our destinies.

The boy from Gallanth left, and, just as quickly, another messenger arrived. And after that, another, and another, and another. And then, finally, there was silence.

'*Ah*,' said Rose, smiling at the ornate grandfather clock. 'I believe it's time for lunch.'

'How about a working lunch?' said Chapman, who, to Wren's utter dismay, unfurled another scroll. 'I thought it might be prudent to discuss plans for the upcoming royal tour.'

'Can't it wait?' said Wren, who was already halfway to the door.

Rose blushed at her own grumbling stomach. 'I'm afraid I'm far too famished to even *think* about the royal tour right now, Chapman.'

Chapman opened his mouth to protest when the doors flew open and a harried-looking soldier rushed in. He went straight to Captain Davers, both of them muttering in low, urgent tones, until Rose interrupted the men to insist they address the entire room, and indeed the queens that stood within it.

'There's a protest in Eshlinn,' explained the soldier. 'They've set fire to the mill.' He glanced at Davers. 'We've had word it was organized by Barron. He was overheard spouting about it just yesterday in the Howling Wolf.'

Rose frowned. 'What kind of protest?'

The soldier gulped. 'A protest against the crown.'

'You mean a protest against the witches,' said Wren.

The soldier's eyes darted as he looked between them. Then at Thea. Wren got the sense he was uncomfortable, not because of the protest in Eshlinn, but by his presence here, among the very witches he had been taught his entire life to fear.

Coward, she thought, viciously.

'Well,' said Captain Davers, stepping into the conversation. 'These days, they are one and the same, are they not? It stands to reason that there would be some people in Eshlinn, and indeed throughout Eana, who wish to remain loyal to the *old* ways.'

'Of hating and harming defenceless witches, you mean?' said Wren.

Captain Davers raised his chin, meeting the challenge in her gaze. 'Witchcraft is as strong a weapon as any. That is simply the truth.'

'An unhelpful one,' said Wren, deciding in that moment that she disliked him, too.

'That's quite enough,' said Rose, impatiently. 'Who is

this Barron, and what precisely does he want?'

'That would be Sir Edgar Barron,' said Chapman, his frown deepening. 'You might recall he was the governor of Eshlinn, appointed by the Kingsbreath some years ago. Indeed, he trained under Captain Davers in the royal guard, before his promotion. It was his job to keep a wary eye out for signs of . . . well, witchcraft. He was, shall we say, *highly* devoted to his job.'

'And then we fired him,' said Wren, recalling the name, among many others, who had met with the same fate the day after their coronation. 'Mere days after we killed Rathborne, Barron's benefactor.'

Captain Davers stiffened. 'Succinctly put.'

Rose folded her arms. 'Why can't these men ever just go quietly? I mean, *truly*, take up candle-making or carpentry. There are plenty of honourable ways to make a living that don't involve killing innocent people.'

Wren was about to point out the irony of saying such a thing to Captain Davers, a man who had once supported a war against the witches, but was startled by a loud *crack!* from outside.

'Oh, that wayward Rowena,' Thea groaned, getting to her feet. 'I'll see to her.'

The old witch had barely taken a step when a scream rang out. Wren leaped up from her throne, just in time to see a flaming arrow vault over the gates. It landed in the courtyard, releasing a plume of acrid smoke. She rushed to the window.

'What's happening?' said Rose shrilly, as two more flaming arrows soared over the gates. Wren could see an angry crowd had gathered just beyond them.

'Goodness,' said Thea. 'I'd call this more than a protest.'

'Captain Davers!' cried Rose. 'Why on earth are you still standing there? Arrest those miscreants before one of their arrows strikes someone in my courtyard!'

'At once, Queen Rose.' The captain spun on his boot heel, barking orders to his soldiers as he left the throne room.

Wren frantically scanned the courtyard. The witches had retreated inside but she caught sight of Shen, who was running towards the commotion, rather than away from it. He had already scaled the outer wall and was treading along the ramparts. His head was low, his gaze fixed on the gathering below. They were yelling now, sending shouts of guttural fury along with each arrow.

Another flaming arrow sailed over the gate, this one higher and brighter than the one before it. The air turned hazy and grey as Davers and his soldiers rushed out of the palace, with their swords drawn.

The crowd began to disperse, but not before another arrow flew. This one sailed through the courtyard and struck the balcony window. Wren shouted in fury as it exploded in a shower of sparks, setting the olive tree ablaze. Smoke streamed in through the open window, making her cough.

'Get back!' Thea pulled her away from the glass, offering a quick pulse of healing magic to settle the spasm in her lungs. 'Keep your wits about you, Wren.'

Wren exhaled through her nose, trying to control her anger.

'CHAPMAN!' Rose's voice rang out as she stalked across the throne room. 'This Edgar Barron. Is he known to you?'

Chapman tore his gaze from the window, his eyes wide with horror. 'Yes, yes, of course,' he said, breathlessly. 'Or indeed he was.'

'Good. I want you to bring him to us,' she commanded. 'At once.'

Rose
CHAPTER 4

Rose sat by the window in the drawing room at Anadawn Palace and reminded herself that she was queen. That her people loved her. That she was a capable ruler. That everything was going to be fine. Better than fine. Everything was going to be *wonderful*. She had a vision for the future of her kingdom, a world in with the witches and non-magical folk lived side by side, in harmony, and she was not about to let a man like Edgar Barron – or *any* man for that matter – get in her way.

But a queen shouldn't have sweaty palms, whispered a voice in her head.

Or a racing heart.

Or a stomach tied up in knots.

Ping! An F-sharp interrupted her anxiety. She looked over her shoulder.

Wren was walking her fingers up and down the pianoforte, creating a clumsy melody. 'This stupid thing is out of tune.'

'You're the one out of tune,' said Rose. 'Perhaps you should take lessons.'

Shen, who was standing by the door, doing his best

impression of an official palace soldier, snorted. A lock of black hair had come loose from its leather strap, and there was a fresh graze on his cheek from when he had chased down the palace assailants three days ago, but apart from that, he looked completely fine. *Better than fine.* He looked irresistibly and irritatingly dashing. 'If you've ever tried to teach Wren anything, then you'll know she doesn't take kindly to instruction. Or rhythm.'

Wren stuck her tongue out. 'You're fired.'

'I don't work for you.' Shen must have sensed Rose staring at him, because he met her gaze and held it, the heat of it making her pulse race. She snapped her chin down and fiddled with the hem of her sleeve as he surrendered his post and crossed the room. Her heart hitched as he leaned against the window ledge, the warmth of his body easing the trembling in her bones. His smile was easy, but there was concern brewing in his dark eyes. 'I'm only here to make sure things don't go awry.'

Rose fought the urge to reach for his hand. It wouldn't be proper, here, where the guards were watching from their posts and servants were scurrying in and out, setting up the tea table. So she turned from him as though turning from the sun itself and looked to the gardens.

This was a game Rose found herself playing more and more. How late could she stay up whispering to Shen in the library, stealing kisses between the stacks? How many times could she allow herself to brush against him in the hallway, revelling in the fleeting heat of his skin against hers? What was allowed between them now that she was queen and he was still the warrior witch he always had been? Every time she lingered too long over his smile, or lost herself in those molten eyes, she felt the need to distance herself. After all, she had a kingdom to remake. A palace to run. A grandmother to rescue. And yet every one of those lingering kisses played on her mind, often driving her dizzy.

'I'm right here,' Wren piped up. 'Please stop salivating over each other.'

'We're not even touching,' Rose said, primly.

'I can't help it,' said Shen at the same time, his smile setting loose a flock of butterflies inside her.

'Ugh.' Wren went back to pounding the piano.

There was a rap at the door, and then Chapman appeared. 'Barron has arrived.'

Wren pushed herself away from the piano. 'Send the traitorous rat in.'

'Less of that language, please,' said Rose, rising from her perch at the window. She made for the couch, allowing her hand to brush against Shen's as she did so, the lingering touch allowing a brief, welcome distraction.

Shen flicked his wrist as he returned to his post by the door, and Rose caught a glint of silver as one of his daggers slid into his palm. She smiled, without meaning to. In a palace teeming with soldiers, she felt safest in a room with Shen Lo. After all, he was a seasoned warrior witch, the most skilled fighter she'd ever encountered, and she knew, deep in her bones, that he would do anything to protect her and

Wren. Even if Rose was more than capable of looking after herself these days, well, it was still nice to know Shen was there.

Rose sat down on the couch and smoothed her skirts. Wren leaned against the armrest, as though ready to pounce.

'Barron will be thoroughly searched,' Rose felt compelled to remind her twin sister. 'He wouldn't dream of trying anything here.'

'Oh, really?' said Wren, sarcastically. 'Then I must have imagined all those flaming arrows that were fired directly at our palace three days ago.'

'That was probably just a way to get our attention,' said Rose.

'Tell that to our olive tree.'

Chapman returned shortly with Edgar Barron and Captain Davers. The once-lauded governor of Eshlinn stalked into the room with infuriating ease, his presence filling the space like a storm cloud. He was taller than Rose had expected, lithe and narrow-shouldered, with coiffed brown hair, pale skin and deep blue eyes that flitted back and forth between the twins.

'Majesties,' he said, with no small amount of derision. 'You have clicked your fingers, and here I am.' He flashed a smile that contained far too many small, square teeth. 'Like magic. No?'

Of course, it had not been quite so simple to summon Barron to the palace. Captain Davers and his soldiers had spent two days searching for him, and another half day convincing him to sit down with the new queens, on the assurance that they would not have him arrested for his part – though it could not be proven – in the attack on the palace.

Rose gestured to the armchair opposite her. 'Please, sit.'

Barron fanned the end of his long black frock coat, as he did so. With reluctant appreciation, Rose noted its fine tailoring, and the crisp white shirt he wore underneath it. Barron possessed a surprising elegance. He was certainly less of a brute than Rose was expecting. He was refined, well dressed and soft-spoken, which of course made him all the more dangerous.

He looked between them. 'Which of you is the healer witch?'

'Why?' said Wren. 'Are you planning an assault?'

Barron curled his lip. 'I have heard she is the more reasonable of the two.'

Rose's gaze darted to Captain Davers, who was standing stone-faced by the window. Shen had moved to the pianoforte and was making no attempt to conceal his interest in their conversation.

'We will be entirely reasonable today, so long as you are reasonable in return,' said Rose. She gestured to a pot of peppermint tea and the plate of macarons Cam had prepared just that morning. 'May we offer you some tea? A macaron, perhaps?'

'I'd rather not.'

'Coward,' muttered Wren.

Rose shot her a warning glance. It did not go unnoticed by Barron. He leaned back in his chair, crossing one long leg over the other. His leather boots were impeccable, their gold buckles gleaming in the afternoon sunlight. Here was a man who did not get himself dirty, thought Rose. No wonder they did not spy him at the gates three days ago.

'Sir Barron,' she began, as politely as she could. 'The recent stirrings in Eshlinn are most troubling to my sister and me. We have reason to believe that *you* are the orchestrator of this discontent.'

'I'm afraid you mistake my intent.' Barron plucked a macaron from the table and twisted the top. 'For many years, I was in the business of peacekeeping. It was my solemn duty to keep watch over Eshlinn for any . . . *untoward* activity.'

'You mean witchcraft,' said Wren.

'And now, well . . . what could be more untoward than the present circumstances?' he went on, peeling the macaron apart with his fingers. 'The Kingsbreath himself has been murdered, our prosperous kingdom torn at the seams, its throne divided between two witches.'

'Eana is still prosperous,' said Wren. 'Despite *your* attempts to divide it.'

'Eana is suffering.' Barron crushed one half of the macaron between his fingers, letting the bright green dust fall and stain the carpet. 'The laws of our Great Protector have been stripped away, his land given over to the witches and their sordid ways. Tell me, Majesties, how can a kingdom respect that which it fears?'

'We are nothing to fear,' said Rose, straining to keep her temper.

Barron crushed the other half of the macaron. 'That is not for you to decide.'

'Stop wasting our macarons,' said Wren. 'Or I'll make you lick that carpet clean.'

Barron dusted his hands, then wiped them on a pristine velvet cushion. 'I trust you have called me here for a reason.'

Rose bristled at his tone. 'My sister and I want you to cease spreading your hateful lies and turning our own people against us. We demand a fair chance to rule this kingdom, as is our birthright.'

'At what price?' said Barron.

'Your immediate arrest,' said Wren.

Barron had the nerve to scoff. 'Captain Davers assured me that I would leave this palace unharmed.'

'That was before we knew how hideously infuriating you were,' said Wren. 'This is our first and final warning, Barron. No more protests. No more flaming arrows. No more treasonous town meetings. We're watching you.'

Barron's eyes gleamed with amusement. Rose had to pinch the back of her hand to stop herself from flinging a teacup at him. 'Surely, you are *both* aware that a pair of witch queens will *never* have the full backing of this kingdom. Not until you can prove that you do not see yourselves as above us. Not until you elevate one of us to sit alongside you.'

Rose frowned. 'What precisely is that supposed to mean?'

Barron flashed his too-wide smile. There wasn't an ounce

of warmth in it. 'It means you should have given the throne that sits next to you to someone known to your people. Someone they trust.'

'Let me guess,' Wren cut in. 'Someone like *you*.'

Barron's gaze was still on Rose. She hated how it sharpened, how she felt it like a pinprick at the base of her throat. 'You do not yet have a husband, Queen Rose.'

There was a stifled curse from somewhere near the pianoforte.

Shock and revulsion coursed through Rose. 'You cannot mean you,' she said, aghast. 'You're twice my age!'

'And more pressingly, you are an arrogant charmless creep,' said Wren, with equal disgust. 'Why would Rose marry the very man who seeks our destruction?'

'So you do not have to endure said destruction,' said Barron, simply.

'That sounds an awful lot like a threat,' warned Shen, who was suddenly beside Rose. 'I'd advise you to retract it. *Now.*'

Captain Davers stepped between the men. 'Stand down, Shen Lo,' he said, in a clipped voice. 'This is Anadawn Palace, not the lawless beaches of Ortha.'

'Lucky for Barron,' said Wren. 'Otherwise, he'd already be fish fodder.'

'Well, this has been a most illuminating afternoon,' said Barron, rising to his feet. 'Why don't I leave my suggestion with you for a week or so?'

'*Or,*' said Shen, through gritted teeth, 'why don't I shove it up your—'

'That's quite enough!' Rose clapped her hands, restoring some semblance of order as she leaped to her feet. 'Captain Davers will escort you out, Sir Barron. Our soldiers will be checking in on you most regularly from now on As a loyal subject of this kingdom, I expect you to heed our warning and keep yourself out of trouble.' She raised her chin, meeting his gaze with her own. 'You are familiar, I'm sure, with the full might of our army. My sister and I would hate for you to have to experience it, first-hand.'

'And in case it isn't already abundantly clear, we are *explicitly* threatening you,' Wren added.

Barron had the audacity to laugh. 'Threats are like arrows, Majesties. Anyone can fire them. But if you put enough thought and power behind one, it can cut a pathway through any great kingdom and pierce the very heart of its throne.'

In the blink of an eye, Shen had a knife to Barron's throat. 'I'm not letting that one slide.'

'Stop it!' said Rose, quickly. The last thing they needed was Barron's blood on their hands. They would have to play nice – or at least *appear* to – to get what they wanted. 'Sir Barron is a smart man. I'm sure he's quite understood our meaning.'

Slowly, and with great reluctance, Shen released Barron.

Barron dipped his chin, before promptly turning on his heel and stalking from the room. Captain Davers and his soldiers escorted him out, pulling the door shut behind them.

'Good,' said Wren. 'You scared him off.'

Shen was still glaring at the door. 'I should have cut his tongue out.'

'For those pathetic threats?' said Rose, as she wiped her sweating palms on her gown. 'They don't scare me.'

Shen turned back to her. 'No. For trying to marry you.'

'Oh.' Rose's cheeks erupted. 'Truly, what a laughable suggestion. Why are the most odious men always the most ambitious?'

'Well, it's not the worst idea I've ever heard,' said Chapman, who Rose had almost completely forgotten about.

She bristled now at his suggestion. 'You can't be serious.'

Shen went very still. Rose could almost feel the anger rolling off him.

Wren turned on Chapman. 'I've ruined one of Rose's weddings this year, Chapman. Don't think I won't ruin another.'

'Of course I don't mean Barron himself,' said Chapman, quickly. 'I simply meant the *idea* of a strategic royal marriage is not the worst I've ever heard.'

'Because it went so well before,' said Wren, dryly.

Chapman waved his hand around, as though to dispel the ugly memory of the Gevran wedding fiasco, and poor Prince Ansel's untimely death. 'An arranged marriage is the quickest way to an alliance. If some people in Eana are reluctant to put their trust in two witches, I believe a high-born, respectable husband would go a long way to alleviating some of that mistrust.' He ignored Wren's horrified expression and went on. 'Of course it would have to be someone known to Eana. With a pristine reputation.' He glanced meaningfully at Shen. 'Or indeed *any* kind of reputation. And of course, they *mustn't* be a witch.'

'Now you're just trying to annoy me,' muttered Shen.

Rose wrung her hands. She couldn't stomach the idea of another arranged marriage, but Barron's parting words had unsettled her more than she had let on. The protest was the spark of a movement that could twist and grow into something truly terrible if they didn't find a way to stop it.

She paced back and forth, her mind whirring with possibilities as Wren and Shen argued with Chapman about the suitability of the youngest Caro prince.

Then an idea struck. 'Oh, I know!' Rose burst out. 'What about presents? We can send gifts from the crown to every house in Eana!' Yes, that would work. Everyone loved presents. 'It's the perfect way to reassure them that they are valued subjects, who are most welcome in our new and improved kingdom.'

Wren grimaced. 'You want to bribe the *entire kingdom* into liking us?'

Rose was already wracking her brains. 'What about an artfully arranged fruit basket? Oh! Or scarves! After all, winter will be here before we know it.'

'I'm confused,' said Shen. 'Are you trying to woo them?'

'In a manner of speaking,' said Rose, defensively. 'You see, a queen is wed to her country first and foremost. Doesn't it make sense to woo them?'

Shen considered this a moment. 'As long as you're not wooing the prince of Caro.'

'We simply need to show our subjects that they are

cherished.' As she spoke, Rose's plan bloomed, even more. 'And we'll move up the royal tour! I'd like to expand it, too. We'll establish our foothold in the southern towns before Barron does.' She ignored her sister's souring expression, excitement quickening her voice. 'Think about it, Wren. We can shake hands with our people. Show them who we really are. You're an enchanter – perhaps you can make butterflies, or, or, or birds! And I can use my healing magic to help any townsperson who needs it!' Rose reeled through the other strands of witchcraft in her mind. Though displaying the power of a tempest would be quite the spectacle, Rose couldn't trust Rowena to behave herself, but perhaps they could come up with some kind of demonstration to showcase Shen's warrior talent. After all, that was a spectacle in itself.

Rose's thoughts flitted to her best friend. Celeste was still coming to grips with the possibility that she herself might be a seer, though both girls had grown up together at Anadawn, without knowing they were witches. Rose knew it wouldn't be fair to push her best friend on the issue, nor to parade Celeste up and down the streets of Eshlinn like a prize, offering prophecies wherever starcrest birds gathered. And in any case, when it came to seers, well, wasn't it their elusiveness that made them so special?

'When they see what our magic can do, they'll be assured that we can be trusted with the throne . . . with their future!' she went on, breathlessly. 'We can listen to their needs, their fears, and, more than that, we can promise them, eye to eye, that we will make Eana a better country for everyone.'

Wren folded her arms. 'And what if they fire arrows at us?'

'Wren's right,' Shen cut in. 'It's too dangerous for a royal tour right now. You need to let things settle.'

'Nonsense. If we do nothing, the resentment towards us will only grow,' said Rose, firmly. 'A leader must *lead*. I refuse to let Barron best us in the court of public opinion.' She looked between Wren and Shen. 'So, unless either of you two have any positive contributions to make, then I suggest you leave the planning—'

'I have a suggestion,' said Wren. Rose knew what it was before she voiced it. She could tell by the determined blaze in her sister's eyes. 'We take a tour to Gevra instead, so we can rescue Banba. She'll know exactly how to deal with Barron and his little rebellion.'

Rose frowned. 'Banba is all the way across the Sunless Sea.'

'I'm done waiting, Rose. It's time to act.'

Rose hesitated. In the space of a few days, everything had shifted. Danger had come to the gates of Anadawn Palace, and if Barron's parting words were to be believed, there would be more still to contend with. Surely, Wren wasn't suggesting that they divert their soldiers and launch an attack on Gevra, when rebellion was stirring under their very noses?

Wren's nostrils flared. 'I don't want to talk about frivolous fruit baskets and stupid royal tours before we talk about how we're going to bring our grandmother home.'

'Fruit baskets are *not* frivolous,' said Rose, her voice rising to match her sister's. 'And neither is our royal tour. You're not thinking clearly. Now is hardly the right time to go to Gevra.'

'I also hate that idea,' said Shen. 'In fact, I have yet to hear a good idea from either one of you.'

Wren folded her arms. 'You were wrong about the power of your quill, Rose. Your letters have failed.'

Rose sagged against the armrest, suddenly exhausted. 'Then we'll think of something else. I promise. But please, let's not argue, Wren. We're on the same side, remember?' Rose held out her hand, relieved when her sister took it. She hated fighting with Wren. Apart from anything else, it was unproductive. 'That horrid Barron has put me in a terrible mood. Why don't we go down to the kitchens and see what Cam is whipping up for dinner?'

'Finally. An idea I can get on board with,' said Shen.

Wren blew out a breath. 'Fine. But this isn't over.'

'No,' said Rose, quietly. 'I have a bad feeling it's only just begun.'

Wren
CHAPTER 5

The following days passed with the same infuriating silence from King Alarik. It quickly became clear that Rose had run out of 'diplomatic' ways to bring Banba home and, on the advice of Chapman, had turned her attention to problems closer to home. Every morning, she took her breakfast in the library with the bossy steward and Captain Davers, all three of them poring over plans for a royal tour that Wren had no intention of going on.

Her thoughts were still firmly on Gevra. So much so that two days ago, Wren had crept down to the mews and sent her own letter to King Alarik.

Listen here, you arrogant, unresponsive ass, if you
don't give me back my grandmother, I swear to that
stupid bear you worship that I'll sail over there and
smash every one of your teeth into your skull.
Don't test me. I'm a witch, remember?
Wren

Unsurprisingly, there had been no response.

Now Wren spent her mornings in the west tower of Anadawn, sifting through years of dust and grime and broken furniture. Mostly, it was an excuse to be alone while she came up with her own secret plan to save Banba, but there was a second purpose, too. Once it was decreed that the twins would rule Eana together, Wren had decided to turn the west tower into her bedroom.

To honour the memory of Glenna, the seer who had been trapped in the west tower for eighteen long years before being murdered by Willem Rathborne, Wren wanted to be the one to go through her things, but after days of trawling through moulding clothes, old birdcages and faded furniture, she was beginning to think there was nothing here worth salvaging.

Elske arrived in the early afternoon, nudging the door open with her snout.

'Clever girl,' said Wren, as she scratched the sweet spot between the enormous Gevran wolf's ears. 'I knew you'd sniff me out, sooner or later.'

The wolf snuffled her skirts in affection and Wren pressed her face into her shoulder, revelling in her alpine scent. It reminded her of Tor, who had sailed away from her over three weeks ago. The wolf had been the soldier's parting gift, a piece of his heart left behind in Eana. Wren's own heart panged at the memory of how Elske had saved her life on the banks of the Silvertongue, fiercely fighting off Princess Anika's snow leopard who had been intent on tearing Wren limb from limb. Afterwards, Elske had sat steadfastly by Wren's side as they watched the Gevran soldier sail away from them, into the mist.

Thoughts of Gevra made Wren's fingers itch. She would go right now if she could, but the day was bright and busy, and Anadawn was crawling with soldiers. She would have to be smart about her next move, patient.

Wren sifted through a pile of junk by the window, her gaze falling on a familiar cracked portrait. She turned it over, gazing down at two faces that looked so like her own. Two crowns that had destroyed a dynasty. The Starcrest twins, Wren and Rose's ancestors, had ruled Eana together over a thousand years ago, before one had turned against the other and brought about the ruin of the witches. In one fell swoop, Oonagh had managed to betray her sister, Ortha, and curse the witches, splintering their power into five different strands – healer, seer, tempest, enchanter and warrior – before drowning in the Silvertongue River.

Wren stared down at Oonagh's scowling face, as Glenna's warning echoed in her mind. *Beware the curse of Oonagh Starcrest, the lost witch queen. The curse runs in new blood. It lives in new bones.* It was a warning meant for Wren, one that she had not shared with Rose. Her sister had enough to worry about already, without questioning Wren's loyalty, or wondering what sinister flaw she might share with their cursed ancestor. Besides, Wren knew she would never betray her sister. Not for anything in the world.

'Nonsense,' muttered Wren, flinging the portrait into the growing pile of rubbish. 'We won't be like them.'

A low rumble jolted Wren from her excavation.

Elske was growling at an upturned chest of drawers. 'What is it, sweetling?' said Wren, scrambling to her feet.

The wolf backed away from the chest. Wren reached inside the drawer and found an old blue dress that had been rolled up and shoved right at the back. The material was plush and shimmering, and though the embroidery around the bodice was fraying, she could tell it was a dress fit for a princess.

Or, perhaps, a queen.

Elske growled at the balled-up dress.

'What's got into you?' said Wren, as she unfurled it. Something rolled out of the garment and clattered to the floor, making her jump.

Elske backed away from it.

Wren crouched to investigate and found her own emerald gaze peering up at her. The dress had been hiding an ornate hand mirror. It was made of silver and inlaid with a row of twelve sapphires that bordered the small, glass oval. She turned it over, marvelling at the fine craftsmanship.

'I knew if we looked hard enough, we'd find treasure in here.' When Wren looked up, Elske was standing at the door, with her tail tucked between her legs. Something about the mirror was frightening her, and Wren had a feeling it wasn't her snowy reflection. It was magic. She could feel its gentle hum against her fingers, a trickle of warmth that marked this treasure as a relic, not of the Valharts, but of the witches who had ruled long before them. A witch who had once lived in this very tower, perhaps.

Wren carefully laid the mirror down. A minute passed, her breath bound up in her chest as she waited for the glass to shatter, or something terrible to happen. But her own face looked back at her, her brow shiny with sweat, her chestnut-brown hair frizzing around her temples. Whatever magic the hand mirror might have once possessed was dormant. It was simply a mirror now, far too fancy for Wren's taste. But she resolved to keep it anyway. She didn't want it falling into anyone else's hands. Just in case.

She slipped the hand mirror into her satchel, just as a bird landed on the windowsill. Elske forgot her fear and bounded across the room to try to chase it, and for one hopeful heartbeat Wren thought it was a messenger falcon returning from across the Sunless Sea. But it wasn't a falcon at all.

It was a starcrest. The sight of the silver-breasted bird filled Wren with a sudden rush of anxiety. Starcrests only gathered near seers, witches who could divine patterns of the future from the birds' formations. But Glenna was dead. Why had this starcrest returned to her tower?

She eyed her satchel. Was this the mirror's doing? Had the enchanted bird been flying nearby and sensed the old magic she had awoken? Or was it simply a coincidence that it had come to rest on her windowsill?

Wren loosed a breath, trying to steady the rattle of her nerves. The bird took off just as quickly as it arrived, leaving her feeling like a fool for working herself up over it in the first place.

She scrunched her eyes shut. 'Stop being so bloody paranoid.'

The door creaked open and Wren jumped. 'Hello?' she called out. 'Who's there?'

A familiar laugh rang out like a wind chime. 'Don't act so spooked. It's only me.'

Celeste, Rose's best friend, swept inside wearing a flowing amber dress and a matching headband inlaid with pearls. 'I was bored so I thought I'd come and check on you.' She wrinkled her nose as she surveyed the mess. '*This* is where you want to sleep?'

'It's a work in progress.'

'Some progress.' Celeste snorted. 'It reeks.'

'Clearly, you've never been to Ortha. Trust me when I tell you it's an improvement.'

'Rose said I'd find you up here,' Celeste went on. 'I think she's hurt that you don't want to help her plan the tour.'

'I'm sure she's having more than enough fun for both of us,' said Wren, dryly.

'You're going to towns I've never even heard of.'

Wren groaned.

'Where are the guards, by the way?' said Celeste. 'There are none in the stairwell.'

'They're annoying. I sent them away.'

Celeste arched a slender brow. 'Are you sure that's a good idea? You know, given everything that's going on with Barron. Rose told me that his followers have given themselves a name.'

'The Protector's Arrows,' said Wren. They had received word of it yesterday morning. 'Not very catchy, is it?'

'He should have gone with Barron's Booze Hounds,' said Celeste. 'They meet twice weekly in the Howling Wolf.'

Wren let out a low whistle. 'Imagine that bar tab.'

'Glad to see you're taking this whole thing seriously.'

'A scary name does not a rebellion make.'

Celeste swept a discerning gaze over her. 'Have you decided what you're wearing to the farewell dinner tonight? You might want to comb your hair. And maybe burn that dress. Also, leave the wolf outside this time. Everyone's terrified of her.'

'Anything else, Chapman?' needled Wren.

'Just do as you're told, for once,' said Celeste. 'Tonight is important to Rose. She's trying to raise morale in the palace before you both leave for your tour.'

'Then dessert'd better be good.' Wren stood up and dusted off her skirts. She reached for her satchel, earning another warning growl from Elske.

Celeste stared at the wolf. 'What's got into her?'

Wren shrugged. For some reason, she felt compelled to keep the discovery of the hand mirror to herself. Perhaps it was because of how special it was. Or maybe it was because she felt vaguely like she was stealing it. 'She's still getting used to this place. She misses Gevra.'

A narrow dent appeared between Celeste's brows.

'Was there something else?' said Wren. 'You look like you need the loo.'

Celeste fiddled with one of her gold earrings, her frown deepening. 'Sort of. I don't know.'

'Celeste. The anticipation is killing me.'

'I had a dream about you last night,' Celeste blurted out. 'I wasn't going to say anything, but . . .' She pulled her arms around herself. 'Then you mentioned Gevra, and I suddenly felt like I should.'

Wren thought of the starcrest at the window, how it had arrived a moment before Celeste. She had raised the possibility of Celeste being a seer once before, but it hadn't gone down well, then. She wondered if she was ready to have the conversation again. 'What kind of dream?' she said, warily. 'What was I up to?'

Celeste hesitated. 'You were dead.'

Wren's stomach swooped.

Celeste's gaze darted to the window. 'It was just a dream. Not a proper vision. Nothing to do with the starcrests or the night sky. That's how it works, right? A dream could mean anything.' The more she talked, the less sure she sounded. 'And we don't *truly* know whether I even am a seer. I'm nineteen years old, for goodness' sake. If I was a witch, wouldn't I have figured that out long before now?'

Wren held her tongue instead of reminding her how long it had taken Rose to figure out she was a healer, or how difficult it would have been for Celeste to open herself up to her craft while living in the shadow of the Kingsbreath. He would have killed her for it.

'It was just an image,' Celeste went on. 'Your lips were blue, but your eyes were wide open . . . You were frozen.'

Wren tried to ignore the goosebumps prickling along

her skin. 'Like you said, it was just a dream.'

'Maybe so. But whatever happens, you can't go to Gevra, Wren.'

'What makes you think I would ever do something so reckless?'

'Everything I know about you so far,' said Celeste, flatly. 'I know how worried you are about Banba. How badly you want to save her. But you must know your first duty is to your sister. To your country.'

Wren's nostrils flared. Rescuing Banba wasn't just some half-baked plan cooked up by a heartbroken granddaughter. It was part of Wren's strategy to save Eana and ensure a prosperous future for the witches. Banba was the perfect advisor, the Queensbreath Wren and Rose needed to deal with the likes of Barron and his troublesome ilk. The sooner she came home, the better for everyone.

'Why have you gone quiet?' said Celeste, suspiciously.

'I'm just thinking about what we'll have for dinner.'

'No. You're changing the subject.' Celeste raised a warning finger. 'If you even *think* about setting foot on a ship—'

'What I *think* is that you love to boss me around even more than my sister does,' Wren interrupted. 'You're really very good at it.' She threaded her arm through Celeste's and steered her from the room, letting the door slam shut behind them. 'And besides, what makes you think you'd ever catch me in time?'

'You forget I have the benefit of foresight.'

'So, you're willing to admit it, then?' said Wren, as they

wound their way down the stairwell, Elske padding softly behind them. 'That you're a seer after all?'

'I suppose we won't know for sure unless your corpse winds up in Gevra.'

'It won't,' said Wren.

Celeste glanced at her uneasily in the dimness. 'We'll see,' she said.

Rose

CHAPTER 6

Rose believed there was very little that couldn't be solved by a well-executed dinner party. And the lingering mistrust between the guards at Anadawn and the boisterous Ortha witches was no exception.

At least she had believed that up until tonight.

Rose had made a special effort to brighten up the formal dining room by filling it with vases of fresh flowers, flinging open the dusty drapes to let the light in, and ordering the table to be set with lace tablecloths and gilded flatware.

She'd even gone as far as to take down all the tasteless battle paintings that usually adorned the walls, replacing them with a portrait of her parents on their wedding day and a breathtaking landscape of the Errinwilde that had once hung in their bedroom.

And yet the room still felt stuffy.

Worse than that. It felt haunted. She couldn't help picturing the ghost of Willem Rathborne looming behind her as she sat at the head of the table, waiting for the others to arrive. She swore she could even smell his rancid breath, as she imagined him correcting her posture.

When the clock chimed seven, Rose stood to welcome her guests. After another productive day of working on the royal tour together, Rose had decided to extend an invite to Captain Davers. He sat between Shen and Rowena, the sharp-tongued young tempest who had tried to kill Rose when she first met her in Ortha. She had since apologized for it, but her constant use of storm magic inside the halls of Anadawn had done little to bolster the guards' opinion of her.

Captain Davers, at least, was making an effort to hide his disdain. The head of the Anadawn Guard was stocky and pale, with a strong chin, cropped sandy-blond hair and a moustache to match. He was one of the longest-serving soldiers at Anadawn. He had watched over Rose since she was a little girl and would often slip her a caramel whenever he found her sulking in the rose garden.

Rose had seated Tilda on the other side of Shen, since the young witch was most likely to behave under his supervision. Then there was Celeste, who sat at Rose's left-hand side. And Thea, their new Queensbreath, on the other.

Wren arrived twenty minutes late with dust in her hair and Elske at her side.

Rose sighed. 'I asked you not to bring the wolf.'

'What wolf?' Wren feigned confusion as Elske crouched behind her skirts.

'Please just sit. Be merry.'

Wren sat at the other end of the table and took a large slug of wine. 'What've I missed?'

'We've received another report on Barron,' said Shen, by way of greeting. 'The swine's been travelling from village to village, preaching his hatred of the witches and whipping up supporters.'

'Shen,' chided Rose. 'This is hardly appropriate dinner conversation.'

'Not to mention it's privileged information,' said Davers, his moustache twitching in disapproval.

'Information that *I* found out by asking around Eshlinn,' said Shen. 'It was sitting right under your nose, Captain.'

'And what do you expect us to do with the information anyway?' interjected Rowena. 'We're not even allowed to leave this stupid palace.'

'Not yet,' said Rose. 'It's for your own safety.'

'And theirs,' muttered Captain Davers.

The first course was a welcome distraction. Rose couldn't help but beam at the whipped goat's cheese tartlets, drizzled in pomegranate sauce and garnished with crushed walnuts. Tilda shoved two in her mouth at the same time, then nicked one of Shen's for good measure.

Shen pretended not to notice, which made Tilda giggle in triumph.

Rowena chose that moment to launch into a thoroughly unsuitable tale of a flatulent goat who once lived at Ortha, which sent half the table into hysterics. Even Thea, who had grown increasingly forlorn these past few weeks, surrendered a chuckle. 'Banba hated that goat more than anything. Twice she blew him out to sea, only to find him back in our hut the next morning.'

Rose cleared her throat. 'Thank you for that, Rowena. Does anyone have a story that's not about goats?'

Shen raised his fork. 'I've got a good one about a farting donkey. I swear I've never met an angrier *or* smellier animal.'

Rose frowned at him. 'Shen!'

'Tell it!' squealed Tilda. 'Oh, *please* tell it.'

'Go on,' goaded Wren, who Rose was quite sure already knew the story.

'Oh, look, the next course!' said Rose, before Shen could launch into the tale. She had selected a duo of lobster and a perfect cut of beef, and was very pleased with how it had turned out. The shellfish was meant to represent the Ortha witches' home by the sea, while the meat symbolized the strength of the capital. For an accompaniment, she had chosen a generous helping of creamy mashed potatoes that she knew were Wren's favourite, and a medley of buttered green vegetables to showcase the bounty of the Errinwilde.

Much to her chagrin, nobody was focused on the food.

Wren kept glancing at the window as if she was hoping a falcon would crash through it at any moment, with a response from the Gevran king. Tilda was sneaking Elske pieces of meat under the table. Celeste wouldn't stop glaring at Rowena, who made a point of turning her nose up at every single dish. Thea was just as distracted as Wren. Rose didn't miss the way she kept twisting the simple silver wedding band on her finger, and knew she must be thinking of her wife, Banba.

Shen and Captain Davers seemed intent on outdoing each other in everything. It began with seeing who could crack open their lobster claws with their bare hands, before escalating into downing entire goblets of wine in one go, then seeing how many times they could spin their knives in the air before catching it by the blade. Thea had to lean over and intervene when Tilda tried to join the competition.

Exhausted, Rose finished her wine and poured another. She swirled the dregs in her glass, wishing the heady liquid held the secret to salvaging the chaotic evening. *A toast!* she realized suddenly. That's what the dinner was missing. She stood up, swaying a little on her feet. 'I wish to make a toast to the future of Eana!'

'To the witches,' said Rowena, holding her goblet aloft.

'To Anadawn,' countered Captain Davers, whose cheeks had turned rosy.

Celeste lifted her glass. 'And to the blossoming friendship between them.'

Tilda grabbed Shen's goblet. 'And to—'

'Not so fast!' said Shen, swiping it out of her hands.

She scowled at him.

'And to our new queens,' said Thea, deftly. 'Long may they reign.'

'I'll drink to that,' said Wren.

Rose smiled at her sister across the table as they raised their glasses.

For a short while after that, everyone behaved themselves, Cam's food working its own special kind of magic. For dessert, the head cook personally ushered in a glimmering tower of macarons. 'For the queens of Eana!' he said with a flourish, as two servants placed the precarious monument down in front of Rose. The macarons were green and gold, the tower so high she could barely see over it.

'Is that gold leaf?' Rowena leaned forward to inspect one. 'What a ridiculous waste.'

Celeste shot her a warning glance. 'If you can't think of anything appreciative to say, then maybe it's best you keep your mouth shut for the rest of the evening.'

Rowena glared at her. 'Excuse me?'

'If only you *would* excuse yourself,' said Celeste, crisply.

'Green and gold!' said Rose, loudly. 'What festive macarons to honour Eana! The country we all love.'

Rowena flicked her finger, sending out a gust of wind. The tower of macarons wobbled.

Celeste's hand shot out to steady it. 'Stop it!'

Across the table, Captain Davers stiffened.

'You're not afraid of a bit of magic, are you, Captain?' said Shen.

Davers visibly stifled a shudder. 'Of course not.'

'Good,' said Shen, with a wicked glint in his eye. 'Because I could take your sword from its scabbard before you even noticed it was gone.'

'That's enough, Shen,' scolded Rose. She raised her voice, calling an end to the clamour. 'Before Wren and I can bring harmony to Eana, we must first establish it at Anadawn Palace. That's why I have gathered you all here tonight . . .'

Just then, Rowena sent out another sharp gust. Elske was so startled she leaped up on to the table, causing a chorus of shrieks as she toppled the tower of macarons. The wolf looked around in alarm, before jumping down and hiding behind Wren's chair.

Tilda plucked a macaron from the floor and bit into it. 'They still taste good.'

'Something spooked her,' Wren said, leaning down to stroke Elske.

Celeste gave Rowena a pointed look. 'I'm sure I felt the wind pick up.'

Rowena smirked.

Rose dropped her head into her hands and sighed. 'There's tea in the drawing room if anyone would like it.'

Back in her room in the east tower, Rose sat on her bed in her favourite nightgown, with a pile of cracked macarons in her lap.

'How many of those have you had?' said Wren, who was unbraiding her hair at the dresser.

'Not enough,' said Rose, miserably eating another one. 'Eventually they have to make me feel better, right?'

'That, or you'll make yourself sick.'

Rose glowered at Elske, who was curled up at Wren's feet.

'Don't blame the wolf,' said Wren. 'She did us a favour. If that dinner didn't end soon, I was going to jump out of the window.'

Rose flung a macaron at her sister. 'That dinner had a purpose. And you could have done a lot more to help it go smoothly. You sulked through every course.'

Wren turned to face her sister. 'I'm sorry I'm finding it hard to be merry when our grandmother is probably being tortured.'

'I'm worried about her, too. But I'm choosing to be hopeful.'

'It's not the same,' said Wren, and Rose said nothing, because it was true. It wasn't the same. She wanted Banba to come home, but her mind didn't burn with that thought every second of every day. She was able to focus on other things, like the upcoming royal tour, and Barron's Arrows, and making sure the Ortha witches didn't ransack Anadawn Palace in her absence.

Rose knew that every day without Banba worsened the hole in her sister's heart. Wren could only fill it with worry, and the creeping fear that they might never again see their grandmother – the person who had raised Wren, *loved* her, and fought ceaselessly for a world that would one day welcome her home.

There was a knock at the door, and Thea bustled in, wearing her dressing gown. 'I hope it's all right to arrive unannounced at the queens' bedchamber.'

'You're always welcome here, Thea.' Rose scooped up the macarons and laid them on the bedside table, before rising to embrace her. 'It's late, why are you still up?'

'I couldn't sleep.' Thea worried the edge of her cloth eye patch between her fingers, and Rose noticed her nails were chewed down to nothing. 'I thought I'd come and check on you both. Dinner was certainly a boisterous affair, wasn't it?'

'The word you're looking for is "disastrous",' said Wren, as she disappeared into the bathing chamber to get ready for bed.

Rose groaned. 'I had planned it to perfection.'

'The food was wonderful,' said Thea, kindly. 'As was your company.'

'Thank you, Thea. Would you like a half-crushed macaron?' Rose plucked the best one from the table. Thea took it gratefully, then perched on the edge of the bed to nibble on it.

'Things will get easier. Transitions are always hard, but the important thing is you have each other.'

Rose looked towards the bathing chamber, then dropped her voice so Wren couldn't hear her. 'The truth is, right now, I feel like I'm in this by myself. How can we ever run a country if we can't even manage a dinner party?'

Thea laid her hand on Rose's shoulder, sending a pulse of warmth into her bloodstream. It eased the heaviness of her heart, if only a little. 'Let Wren be Wren for now. This is all new for her, too, remember? And she is trying to make sense of the world without Banba.'

Rose nodded. 'I'm sorry. I know you are, too.'

Thea smiled, but there was sadness in her gaze. 'All will be well.'

'Too bad you aren't a seer,' murmured Rose.

'I might not be a seer, but I know you and Wren will be all

right as long as you stick together.' Thea lumbered to her feet, her knees creaking in the silence. 'Now get some rest. Even queens need their sleep.'

Wren
CHAPTER 7

When Wren returned from the bathing chamber, washed and dressed for bed, her sister was already fast asleep. There was a bird sitting on the windowsill. Not just any bird, Wren realized with a start. It was a Gevran nighthawk. And in its beak, a note.

Wren,
Come and say that to my face. I dare you.
Alarik

Wren clutched the letter in her hands, seized by a rush of determination. These past weeks, she had been consumed with thoughts of Banba, *praying* for a sign like this, a spark of fire at her heels, that would propel her in the right direction. And now here it was – the push that she needed. King Alarik had practically invited her to Gevra.

She knew she had to go. She would address him in person. Face him, monarch to monarch. Fight him if she had to. She had her magic and her wits. Her charm. And if all else failed, she hoped Tor might help her, just as he had before.

Wren blew out a breath as her plan crystallized. She crushed the letter in her fist, hope hammering in her heart.

Hours later, when the residents of Anadawn Palace were deep in slumber, Wren sat up in bed. Rose was frowning in her sleep. She had been tossing and turning for hours. The royal tour was due to set off in the morning, and while Rose might have put on an eager face at dinner, in sleep, she couldn't outrun her anxiety.

Wren slipped her hand under her pillow and removed a pinch of Ortha sand from her drawstring pouch. Thankfully, the witches had brought plenty with them. Although Wren could use any kind of earth for her enchantments, the sands of Ortha, where the witches had lived in secret for the past eighteen years, was the most potent. She felt its power move between her fingers as she looked down on Rose, trying to ignore the guilt squirming inside her.

'Forgive me,' Wren whispered, as she cast the sand over her sister. *'From earth to dust and slumber deep, find peace and comfort in your sleep.'*

The sand turned to golden dust as it vanished. Rose's frown faded with a contented sigh. Wren was reminded of the first time she had used a spell like this on her sister. That night Shen had ridden away with her into the desert and Wren had taken her place.

Tonight it was Wren's turn to disappear.

She scribbled a quick goodbye and left it on her pillow, knowing Rose would be furious when she read it. Though Wren's heart clenched at leaving her sister this way – by midnight and betrayal – her guilt was surpassed by her loyalty to Banba. She owed her grandmother everything, and their efforts at negotiation had failed. Miserably. If she didn't rescue Banba soon, she would perish at the cruelty of King Alarik, a man who was already nursing a grudge against Eana and a dark fascination with the witches. In time, Rose would come to see that Wren had had no choice.

She got dressed in the dark and fetched her satchel from under the bed. It was already packed with a change of clothes, a flask of water, a hairbrush, a spare pouch of Ortha sand and the handful of stray coins she had managed to pilfer from her sister's dresser. It wouldn't be enough to barter safe passage to Gevra, but Wren was hoping the sapphire-encrusted mirror she'd found in the west tower might convince a merchant trader to take her on board.

Out in the stairwell, Elske's pale eyes shone in the darkness.

Wren sank to her knees. 'Please don't give me that look. I can't take you with me. You're far too conspicuous.'

The wolf released a low whine.

Wren cupped her large face. 'I need you to stay here and look after Rose. Can you do that for me, sweetling? Can you keep my sister safe until I get back?'

Elske dipped her head.

She patted it. 'Don't worry, I'll be home before you know it.'

Wren took care of the tower guards with a quick-tongued enchantment and two flicks of her wrist, before continuing down the east turret, where an ancient secret passageway was hidden inside a disused cupboard. The twins had made a promise to each other never to speak of it to anyone. It was their secret. Tonight it was Wren's tunnel to freedom.

She hurried down the stone passageway, ignoring the everlights that flickered after her. She could feel the breath of her ancestors on the back of her neck, their voices calling after her, telling her to turn back. To be patient. To be cautious.

But Wren had never been good at waiting, and the only advice she ever took was Banba's. She climbed out of the storm drain and crouched in the darkness to catch her breath. In the distance, the lights of Eshlinn flickered across the Silvertongue. Behind her, the white palace loomed like a ghost in the night, the spires of its gates glinting like sharp golden teeth.

She removed a pinch of sand and set to work on her appearance. She couldn't redesign her entire face, but she could change the parts that made her recognizable. She used an enchantment to twist her hair into ringlets then turned it a deep, rippling auburn. She scattered more freckles across her cheeks and dulled the emerald blaze in her eyes to a muted green. Lastly, she made her front teeth crooked.

'*Ouch*,' she hissed, as they bent inwards.

She fixed her cloak and set off across the bridge, her footsteps pounding in the dark. It was past midnight, and while the cobbled streets of Eshlinn were mostly deserted, the taverns were full to bursting. Music wafted through the narrow streets, mingling with the sound of laughter.

Wren rounded a street corner and barrelled into two young women, both red-faced and giggling.

'You must be mad, lass,' said one, the stench of cider heavy on her breath. 'Walking by yourself at this time of night.'

'There could be witches about,' said the other, while teetering unsteadily. 'Especially now the palace is crawling with them.'

'So what?' said Wren, taking a step back. 'The witches don't mean us any harm.'

'That ain't what they're saying down in the Howling Wolf,' said Cider-breath, gesturing to the tavern she had just spilled out of.

'Edgar Barron says the witches are gonna take over the whole country now they've got those witchy queens on the throne,' added Wobbles.

'And do what with it?' said Wren, unable to help herself.

The girls looked at her blankly.

'Um. Bad stuff?' said Wobbles.

Cider-breath nodded. '*Bad* magic.'

Wren narrowed her eyes. 'Elaborate.'

The girls shrugged.

'Well, I'm not afraid of the witches,' said Wren, as she arced around them. 'Try thinking for yourselves sometime,' she tossed over her shoulder. 'I promise it doesn't hurt.'

'Don't say we didn't warn you!' Cider-breath called after her.

'Mark your door if you know what's good for you,' added Wobbles. 'The Arrows will be out hunting for witches tonight!'

As Wren travelled deeper into the old town, she began to notice some of the houses were marked with arrows. She crossed the street to investigate one, tracing her finger along the dark paint.

The townspeople of Eshlinn were marking their doors to keep the Arrows from coming after them. Or maybe even to *help* them. Unease bloomed inside Wren. Rebellion truly was stirring in the heart of Eshlinn.

Wren thought of Rose slumbering back at the palace. In the morning, she would rise alone to face it. She winced as she imagined her sister's face when she read her letter, but Wren forced herself to go on, because imagining Banba alone in Gevra was far worse. And besides, Shen would look out for Rose. Thea would guide her. Elske would protect her. Celeste would support her. Chapman would advise her. Captain Davers and the witches would fight for her.

Rose would be fine. Eana would be fine.

When Wren reached the blacksmith's house on the outskirts of Eshlinn, she was relieved to find their door unmarked. The Morwells were still loyal to the crown.

Wren almost felt bad about stealing one of their horses. She used an enchantment to break into the stables and freed a brown mare from her stall. They set off into the night, leaving the twinkling lights of Eshlinn far behind them.

On a good horse, Wishbone Bay was half a night's ride away. The Morwells' mare kept a steady pace as they galloped along the north road, winding through farmland that yawned across Eana in fields of golden wheat and leafy vineyards in summer bloom. Everything glowed silver under the waning moon, the scent of lavender tickling Wren's nose as they strayed from the dirt road to pass through a meadow of wildflowers.

She revelled in the feeling of wind in her hair. For the first time in forever, she felt free. And though it was false and fleeting – this feeling of unbridled possibility – she held it to her like a prayer, until the rising scent of seaweed roused her from the illusion.

When Wren opened her eyes, Wishbone Bay was before her. The road twisted its way down to the dark water, where the bay arced in a perfect crescent, as though some terrible creature had risen from the deep and taken a bite out of it. The port lights flickered, beckoning her onward. Dawn was creeping over the horizon, breathing wisps of amber and pink across the sky.

Wren leaped off the horse and sent it home with an enchantment. She slipped the hand mirror from her satchel and quickly checked her spelled appearance before picking her way down to the bay.

The port was busier than she expected. Shouts and hollers filled the air as people rushed along the pier, dragging in nets and barrels heaving with freshly caught fish. They were carted off and dumped out just as quickly, the market traders setting out their stalls as the ships reloaded their supplies and prepared to sail again at first light. There were nine moored in the dock. Wren counted three fishing boats, two smaller sailings boats, one hulking galleon bearing the Eana Navy crest on its sails, and three large merchant ships.

Wren suspected the sturdiest-looking merchant ship at the far end of the port would be sailing the treacherous Gevran trading route, while the smaller two would probably journey south-west to Demarre, or perhaps Caro. Her suspicions were confirmed when she spied the barrels being unloaded from it; they all bore the Gevran crest – the terrifying ice bear, Bernhard, caught mid-roar.

Wren steeled herself and marched towards the merchant ship. It was a large, dark-wood vessel with three towering masts and twelve ivory sails. Its flag was green and gold, marking it as a local trading vessel, while *Siren's Secret* had been scrawled along its side. The prow bore a bronze carving of a mermaid wearing a crown of shells.

Wren grabbed a discarded length of rope from the dock and wound it around her shoulder. She kept her head down and tried to look busy as she carried it across the gangway and on to the *Siren's Secret*. She braced herself for an angry shout, or a hand yanking her backwards, but no one even glanced in her direction. The crew of the *Siren's Secret* were far too busy to notice the comings and goings of a scurrying lackey.

She hurried up the wooden steps at the back of the ship, spotted the captain's wheel and immediately turned around again. 'Idiot,' she scolded herself. She was halfway back down the stairs when a figure appeared before her, a hand braced on each railing to block her way.

Wren froze mid step, staring down at a pair of dark leather boots. 'Excuse me,' she squeaked. 'I've got to get this rope to the captain right quick.'

'Your captain is before you,' came a deep, plummy voice. 'And he has made no such demands.'

Wren flinched.

The captain took a step towards her. 'It appears I have a stowaway.'

Beneath the folds of her cloak, Wren reached for a pinch of sand. She raised her chin, studying the threat. First, the dark trousers and billowing white shirt. A mulberry frock coat embroidered with fine gold thread. Beneath it, a pair of wide shoulders and thick arms – easily strong enough to snap her in two. Not that he would need to with that sword fastened to his belt. His skin was dark brown, and under a grey tricorn hat his black hair was tightly curled, his strong chin shaded with matching stubble.

His brown eyes narrowed as he assessed her.

The crew had fallen out of their tasks to watch their exchange. Wren could feel several pairs of eyes on her, and more gathering. Her fingers twitched. She was about to throw caution to the wind and attempt a spell, when the captain did something unexpected. He chuckled.

Wren frowned. 'What's so funny?'

'You look like you want to run me through with a cutlass,'

he said, still laughing. 'What do you have inside that cloak of yours?'

'Nothing,' said Wren, letting the sand scatter to the floor. She showed him her hands. 'See?'

'Now your face,' said the captain, gesturing at her hood. 'Just in case you've got a dagger in your teeth.'

Wren tugged her hood down. She flashed her crooked smile. 'Just my charm.'

'I think I shall be the judge of that.' The captain's gaze roamed along her auburn curls. 'Does my stowaway have a name?'

'Tilda,' said Wren, the name spilling out before she could think on it.

'What are you doing on my ship, Tilda?'

'Admiring the carpentry.'

He laughed again. 'A stowaway who tells jokes. Maybe you do possess a measure of charm.' He wagged his finger, and Wren got the sense he was making fun of her. 'But I'm afraid charm won't be enough to barter free passage on my ship. I already possess an abundance of it, you see.'

Wren was beginning to believe it. The captain was proving to be remarkably good-natured, and the crinkles around his eyes told her he was used to smiling. She decided to try to reason with him. 'In that case, the truth is, I need to get to Gevra as soon as possible.'

The captain raised his eyebrows. 'In all my time sailing, I've never heard anyone say those words. Fleeing from Gevra is more of the done thing. Cursing it. Wailing at it.

Complaining about it. Shaking your first at it.' He rolled his hand. 'And so on.'

'My father's in Gevra,' lied Wren. 'His fishing boat washed up in a storm last month and he's been stranded there ever since. His leg is badly broken.' She wrung her hands. 'We're sick with worry about him. My dear mother hasn't slept in weeks.'

'Mercy,' muttered the captain. The amusement drained from his face. 'Gevra is no place for an Eanan right now. Especially after what happened to their prince on our shores. If I didn't have a trade to see through, I'm not sure I'd go myself.'

'I have an address,' said Wren, quickly. 'He wrote to me just last week. I know I can find him and bring him home.' She started rummaging around inside her satchel. 'I don't have any money, but I've got this—'

'Save your possessions.' The captain raised his hand. 'I'll take you to Gevra. I won't be staying long, mind. And I suggest you don't either.'

Wren was seized by such a rush of relief she nearly burst into giddy laughter. She dropped to her knees instead. 'May the stars bless you a thousand times, Captain! Yours is a heart of gold!'

The captain cleared his throat, embarrassed. 'On your feet, Tilda. There's no need to make such a fuss. I simply recognize the importance of family. I would do the same for mine.'

Wren smiled as she stood up. In another lifetime, she might have grabbed the young captain and kissed him for his kindness. And his handsomeness. Instead, she said, 'There's nothing in the world that matters more to me than family.'

And that, if nothing else, she truly meant.

'Go and find yourself a bunk below deck. I'll tell the crew not to bother you.' He stood back to let her pass. 'And fair warning, it'll be a long and choppy voyage.' He gestured to her satchel. 'I hope you've packed some ginger root in there.'

'Oh, I surely have!' Wren hugged the satchel to her chest as she skipped down the stairwell. She was lucky to have found her way on to a ship helmed by a soft-hearted merchant and not a pirate. The ones down at Braddack Bay would have chucked her in with the sharks for that sorry performance.

While the crew of the *Siren's Secret* hoisted the anchor and prepared to set sail for Gevra, Wren made her way to a storeroom full of wooden barrels and old sails for mending. She grabbed a tattered sheet and strung it up between two rafters, using the rope she had stolen to create a makeshift hammock.

She grinned as she rolled into it. She was just considering prising open a barrel of rum when the floorboards creaked behind her.

Wren shot up in the hammock.

A familiar pair of brown eyes glared at her from across the cabin. 'If you think that terrible disguise is going to fool me, *Tilda*, you're sorely mistaken.'

Wren's throat tightened. 'What in hissing hell are you doing here?'

'I was just about to ask you the same question,' said Celeste.

Rose

CHAPTER 8

Rose woke up as the sun was rising over Anadawn Palace, feeling like she had slept for an entire year. She stretched her arms above her head, then froze mid-yawn.

Wren was gone. Rose frowned. It wasn't like her sister to get up earlier than her. Usually, she woke to find Wren face down on her pillow and still snoring. She must have been more nervous for their royal tour than she was letting on. If only she had woken Rose, so they could be anxious about it together, but Rose knew her sister liked to be alone when something was bothering her. Wren was probably down in the kitchens making a mug of tea or walking Elske in the gardens.

Rose turned over to snatch a few more minutes of sleep when she heard a strange rustling on her sister's pillow. She patted around, finding a piece of parchment. She sat bolt upright, suddenly wide awake. With trembling fingers, she opened the note, somehow already knowing what it was going to say.

I'm going to Gevra. Don't come after me. I'll be back soon – with Banba.

'WREN!' Rose leaped out of bed. She bolted from the bedroom, and raced down the corridor, screaming her sister's name. 'WREN!'

She was still in her nightgown, her feet bare on cold stone. Maybe she wasn't too late, maybe she would catch her, stop her . . .

Just then, a white blur came bounding towards her. Elske reared up on her hind legs, nearly knocking Rose over as she licked the tears from her cheeks. Rose hushed the wolf as she came to her knees, pressing her face into Elske's soft snowy fur. A slant of light slipped through the hall windows, casting them in its warm glow. Rose knew it was too late. The sun had risen. The morning ships were already sailing. Wren was surely on her way to Gevra.

Rose was dimly aware of the servants poking their heads out of the nearby stairwell.

Rose couldn't muster any embarrassment. She simply sobbed as she held on to Elske. 'Did Wren leave you here to stop me or to comfort me?'

Elske blinked her big blue eyes.

Rose sniffed. 'I suppose she abandoned you, too. Oh, what a horrid thing to do.'

'Rose!' Rose looked up to find Shen running towards her. 'What is it? What's happened?'

'It's Wren,' she said, in a quivering voice. 'She's gone.'

'Why would she do this to me?' Rose fumed to Shen, after she had read Wren's paltry note a dozen times. 'And on the day our royal tour is supposed to begin!'

'I have a feeling that's not a coincidence,' said Shen, who had taken the news with quiet frustration. After Rose had thrust Wren's note into his hands, he had taken her down to the kitchens, away from prying eyes and ears, to make her a cup of hot tea.

The tea had helped to stay Rose's tears, as had Shen's steady hand in hers. The sun had risen in earnest, and the rest of the palace was finally waking up. Servants were moving to and fro, preparing for the twins' departure, while the stable hands were saddling the horses that would pull the golden tour carriage.

Rose couldn't focus on any of that right now. 'And how dare she tell me what to do! I'll go after her if I want to!'

'Don't do anything rash,' cautioned Shen. 'Let's not make two problems out of one.'

Rose threw him a withering look. Under her anger, there swirled another stronger emotion. Fear. She was *terrified* by that note. She'd only just found Wren. She couldn't lose her now. She needed her sister to help her rule, to bring the country together, to show her how to be a witch. But it was more than that. She needed Wren because she was her family. Her other half.

Or at least that was how Rose thought of Wren. She had

felt an instant recognition deep in her bones when she first saw Wren the night of the ball, but there was still so much she didn't know about her sister. So much she wanted to learn. She wanted them to be true sisters, not just bound by blood, but by experience and history. By their future. But more than anything, Rose wanted Wren to trust her, to *choose* her.

Wren's note said otherwise. She cared more about Banba than this entire kingdom, than her own sister, than her *own life*. The more Rose thought about it, the less she could stomach it. Her fear and hurt and anger were all merging into a furious torrent of emotion that she couldn't control. And she *hated* feeling out of control.

She stamped her foot. 'Oooh! When she gets back, I'm going to give her such a . . . a . . . stern talking-to!'

Shen raised a brow. 'You need to work on your threats.'

Rose stamped her foot again, accidentally spilling her tea. 'Queens do not run off to other countries on a whim without telling anyone. They do not leave their duties behind. Or their sisters!' Her voice broke, but Shen was there in an instant, wrapping his arms around her. She buried her face in his chest.

'What if something happens to her?' Rose instantly regretted speaking the words aloud, as if the mere act of saying them gave them power.

Shen pressed a kiss into her hair. 'Have faith in her. I'd bet on Wren against anyone. She wouldn't have gone to Gevra if she didn't have a plan.'

Rose snorted. 'What kind of plan could she possibly have?

Is she going to disguise herself as Bernhard the ice bear and waltz into Grinstad Palace?'

'I think you're wildly overestimating her magic,' said Shen.

The bells in the clock tower began to chime, once, twice . . . seven times. The sound snapped Rose back to reality. Wren was gone, and no one else knew it. The royal tour was about to begin, and they were a queen short. She pulled back from Shen, and to her horror saw that she'd left a trail of snot on his shirt.

Stars. Could this morning get any worse?

He pretended not to notice. 'What now, Majesty?' he said, brushing a wayward strand from her face.

Just then, came the shuffle of approaching footsteps. 'Rose, there you are! What on earth are you doing all the way down here in your nightgown?' cried Chapman. 'And with a man! Entirely unchaperoned!'

'You know my name is Shen,' said Shen, flatly. 'I see you every day.'

Chapman ignored him. He turned on Rose, his quill poised over his scroll. 'Never mind that now. I need your breakfast order. We'll take it on the road with us if it's not too uncivilized. And for lunch there's a suitable tavern at Glenbrook. We should make it there by—'

Rose raised her hand to interrupt him. 'We have a problem.'

'The Arrows won't get anywhere near your carriage,' Chapman assured her. 'We've sent out a troop to scout the route. They set off an hour ago.' He brandished his quill at her nightgown. 'Or were you referring to this attire? We have some time before we have to—'

'Wren is gone.'

Chapman's moustache twitched. 'Pardon me?'

'Wren. Is. Gone.' Rose thrust the crumpled letter at him. 'To Gevra.'

Chapman's face paled as he read the letter. He took out a handkerchief to wipe his brow. 'Right. Yes. Well, not to worry,' he said, more to himself than to her. 'At least we still have one queen. And arguably, the better one. Perhaps we can devise some sort of system to make you appear as two people . . . Ah! What about a dress with two different sleeves? You could wave out of one side of the carriage, then scoot across and wave out of the other?'

Shen stifled a chuckle.

Rose stared at the steward. 'You can't possibly be serious.'

'The tour must go on,' Chapman insisted. 'With or without your errant sister. Your people are expecting you. It's all been arranged.'

Rose massaged her temples, thinking . . . worrying. 'My sister needs me, Chapman. We have to go to Gevra and get her back.'

Shen dragged a hand across his jaw. 'You want to send a rescue mission for . . . the rescue mission?'

Chapman was shaking his head so vigorously his cheeks were jiggling. 'We simply cannot send our soldiers into such inhospitable territory. King Alarik would perceive their arrival as a threat and launch an immediate counterattack. We can only hope that your sister had the sense to don some sort of disguise before gallivanting off. I mean, the consequences of an uninvited sovereign arriving in Gevra from a country that has recently killed their crown prince at a wedding meant to *unite* the countries . . .' Chapman paused, meaningfully.

'Chapman, do get on with it,' said Rose.

'Untold consequences!' The steward threw his hands up. 'It could be seen as a declaration of war!'

'Everything in Gevra is seen as a declaration of war,' said Shen. 'They go to war for breakfast.'

'Exactly!' huffed Chapman. 'Which is why we cannot afford to worsen this situation by getting any further involved.'

'You want me to abandon my sister?' said Rose.

Chapman pressed his lips together. 'You must ask yourself, Rose, who here is abandoning whom?'

Rose chewed on the inside of her cheek, thinking of Wren sneaking out in the dead of night.

'And on the matter of abandonment,' Chapman went on. 'I'm afraid *you* simply cannot abandon your country at such a critical time to follow your sister on some kind of wild Gevran goose chase! Nor can you send your soldiers to bring her home. Their mere arrival on Gevran shores would be utterly catastrophic. And in any case, we need them here, where Edgar Barron and his followers are proving to be a very real threat.'

Rose glanced at Shen. She could tell by his sombre expression that he agreed with the steward.

'I know we haven't always seen eye to eye, and there is the

unpleasant memory of the former Kingsbreath lingering between us, but Rose, please know that my advice is true,' said Chapman, imploringly. 'I would not steer you wrong. My loyalty is to Eana. And *you* are Eana.'

'I am Eana, Eana is me,' said Rose quietly, the familiar words sending a whisper of warmth up her arms. They soothed her. Grounded her.

'Precisely. Which is why you must go out there and connect with your people. Charm them away from Barron and his ilk,' said Chapman. 'It is the only way forward for Eana.'

Rose nodded to herself. Chapman was right. The tour must go on, for the good of the kingdom. And in the meantime, she had to trust that her sister knew what she was doing. That Wren would be all right.

'I'd like to take Celeste with me,' said Rose, warming to the idea as soon as she voiced it. 'She's good with people. And she'll be excellent company.'

'No, no, don't worry about my feelings,' muttered Shen.

Rose was too busy settling into her new plan to hear him. Yes. Celeste was the answer. She'd ask her to ride in the carriage with her, to help her throw roses to the townspeople. If Rose couldn't have her sister by her side, she would have her best friend instead. After all, it had been just her and Celeste for years. They were like family to each other, too.

'Rose! There you are!' A new voice interrupted Rose's thoughts. Her maidservant, Agnes, rushed into the kitchen, red-faced and panting.

'Agnes, what on earth are you doing down here?'

Chapman threw his hands up. 'Shall we just dispense with the throne room entirely and hold court in the oven from now on?'

'I've been looking all over for you,' huffed Agnes. 'Lottie the chambermaid told me you were down here in the kitchens and I said, *Well, what in stars' name is she doing down there before I've dressed her in her tour gown?* I had to find you . . . I . . . Oh . . . let me catch my breath . . .'

'It's all right,' said Rose. 'I already know Wren is gone.'

Agnes frowned. 'Wren? But I've come to tell you about Celeste.' To Rose's horror, the maidservant reached into her pocket and withdrew another note. 'This just arrived from Wishbone Bay.'

Wren

CHAPTER 9

'I can't believe you followed me,' fumed Wren, as she tried, unsuccessfully, to roll out of the makeshift hammock for the third time. 'Really, Celeste, don't you have better things to do?'

'Actually, *you* followed *me*. I left the moment I saw that nighthawk fly past my window,' said Celeste, a hint of smugness in her voice. 'I knew you'd try something foolish. All I had to do was wait on the dock for you to show up.' She pointed at Wren's auburn hair, her crooked teeth. 'I'll admit I was expecting better than this pathetic disguise.'

'It got me this far, didn't it?'

Celeste folded her arms. 'This is where your journey ends, Wren.'

Below deck in the *Siren's Secret*, the air between them was too close, and it stunk of seaweed. 'Celeste, I'm going to Gevra.'

'You'll end up dead,' said Celeste, with unnerving certainty. 'And I can't let that happen.'

'What are you going to do, kidnap me?' Wren grunted as she launched herself free of the hammock, falling to her knees with a hard thud. She stood up, teetering on the floorboards. 'I'd like to see you try.'

'I'll leave the kidnapping to Shen.' Celeste had no trouble keeping her balance, despite the rocking of the ship. 'I've already sent a note to your sister. If you don't come with me right now, I'll cause the biggest scene this port has ever witnessed.'

Wren braced herself on a wooden pillar. 'Your sea legs are too good, Celeste. Can't you tell we've already set sail?'

Celeste's face fell. 'He wouldn't. He swore he'd wait.'

'Who?'

But Celeste was already stalking away from her.

'Celeste!' Wren yelled, as she stumbled after her. The last thing she needed was Celeste ruining her careful ruse. And how had she even managed to get on the bloody ship in the first place? 'Stop meddling in my business!'

Celeste ignored her protests as she climbed the rickety steps and jostled her way across deck, snapping at any sailor who dared get in her way. She made it all the way to the hull, where the captain was standing at the ship's wheel.

Wren lunged for Celeste's cloak, but she was already thundering up the stairs towards him. 'MARINO, YOU RUDDY CARP-BRAIN! I TOLD YOU NOT TO SET SAIL YET!'

'*Hissing seaweed.*' Wren's jaw fell open as she connected the siblings. The captain of the *Siren's Secret* was Marino Pegasi, Celeste's older brother. Suddenly, it was obvious – they shared the same strong cheekbones and warm brown eyes. Even now, he didn't look the least bit ruffled by his sister's outburst.

'No shouting on the sea, Lessie,' he said, calmly. 'You know the rules. I don't like to frighten the dolphins.'

'Turn this ship around right now! I don't want to go to bloody Gevra!'

Marino shook his head. 'There's a storm blowing in from the east. If we don't sail now, we'll never make it out of the bay.' He took out his compass and briefly studied it, before adjusting the wheel three notches to the left. 'Did you get a chance to speak to my stowaway, by the way? A real firecracker, isn't she?' He flicked his gaze to Celeste, and spotted Wren, hovering behind her. 'Ah, Tilda! There you are. Have you met my sister? Don't mind the foul mood. She's not a morning person.'

Wren flashed her crooked teeth. 'Oh, I know. Lessie and I are old friends.'

'Don't *ever* call me that again,' warned Celeste.

Marino broke into a pearly grin. 'What are the odds of that?'

'Extremely high, you dunderbrain!' Celeste swatted the tricorn off her brother's head. 'That's the queen of Eana! The one I told you to keep an eye out for!'

Marino turned to stare at Wren. 'Have you been on the rum, Lessie?' he said, passing a hand over his stubble. 'That is not Rose.'

'It's the other one,' said Celeste, impatiently.

Marino furrowed his brow, clearly trying to remember the name.

'Wren,' said Wren, as she picked up his hat and tried it on. 'The other queen is called *Wren*. It's not that hard to remember.'

Marino plucked his tricorn off her head, peering closer at her. 'But aren't you supposed to be identical?'

Celeste rolled her eyes. 'She's clearly in disguise.'

He cocked his head. 'Are you in disguise, Tilda?'

Wren hesitated. She really was enjoying being Tilda. Simple, pitiable, father-yearning Tilda. 'In a way, Marino, aren't we *all* in disguise?'

'She's an enchanter,' said Celeste. 'Sneaking around like this is second nature to her. Though I can see why she didn't bother using any of her magic on you. I've always said you're far too trusting for the spice trade.'

Marino frowned. 'But why would she lie to me?'

'Why does a squirrel hide nuts for winter?' Celeste pinched the bridge of her nose. 'It's what she does, Marino. And never mind the why of it. Just turn this ship around before you get thrown in the Anadawn dungeon for carting an Eanan royal off to Gevra.'

Wren watched Marino falter. His jaw twitched as he looked back towards Wishbone Bay. They had almost cleared the headland, the waves tugging them out into the open ocean, but he was folding under pressure from Celeste. She was a formidable influence, a sister bossy enough to rival Rose.

Wren removed a sprinkling of sand from her pouch, casting it over herself with a quick enchantment. Her teeth creaked as they reset, her hair unkinking as it returned to its original honey brown.

Marino gaped at her.

Wren put her hands on her hips. 'By order of the queen

of Eana, you are not to turn this ship around under any circumstances. Do you understand me?'

Marino looked between them.

'Marino,' said Celeste, in a low voice. 'Don't listen to her.'

'He has to listen to me,' said Wren. 'He's my subject.'

'Well, he's *my* brother.'

Wren stuck her tongue out at Celeste. 'Queen's orders come first.' To Marino, she said, 'In fact, technically speaking, you're supposed to bow to me now. But given the circumstances, I'll let you off.'

Wren's reveal had bought the ship enough time to clear the lip of the headland. The wind was picking up now, the ship skimming the grey water like a flat stone.

Marino tightened his knuckles around the wheel, staying the course. He relaxed his jaw, the shock finally leaving his face. When he spoke, it was not with the deference or respect Wren was expecting. '*May the stars bless you a thousand times, Captain,*' he said, raising his pitch to match her earlier performance. He even made his bottom lip tremble. '*Yours is a heart of gold.*'

Wren offered a brief applause. 'If the spice trade doesn't work out, then the theatre is for you, Marino.'

'I was just about to say the same thing to you, Your Majesty,' said Marino.

'Your good deed still stands,' Wren assured him. 'In fact, when I get back from Grinstad, I'll knight you for it.'

Marino's face lit up.

'You two are shameless!' said Celeste. 'Wren, you don't

even know how to knight someone, and *you*, brother, are as shallow as a puddle.'

'Don't be so hard on him, Lessie.' Wren nudged Celeste, trying to lighten her mood. But her face was like thunder, mimicking the clouds sweeping in above them. 'He's only doing his queen a favour.'

'And betraying his other one in the process,' snapped Celeste. 'I'm done with this conversation. Make your trade in Gevra, Marino, but Wren and I are staying on the ship. The second you're finished, we're turning back around and coming straight home. Through hail or rain or lightning or whatever else the sea throws at us!'

As she spoke, a creeping fog rolled in and swallowed the ship, releasing a sheet of freezing rain.

Celeste shrieked, pulling her hood up to protect her hair.

'Look at that, Lessie! Your bad mood has brought the storm down on us!' Marino had to shout over the thunder to be heard, but he didn't look one bit frightened by it; in fact, he looked giddy. He offered his hat to his sister, then tilted his face up to the rain.

'You are ridiculous!' Celeste jammed the tricorn over her hood. 'You've always been far too fond of storms!'

'You can have this one all to yourself, Marino!' yelled Wren, who was feeling dangerously seasick. Her moment of triumph would be embarrassingly short-lived if she ended up vomiting on herself. 'I'm going back to my hammock!' Then she pulled her cloak around her and hurried below deck.

The rum made Wren drowsy and the storm rocked her to sleep. Hours passed in the briny dimness, morning slipping seamlessly into afternoon before evening fell once more. When she woke up, the sea was eerily still and the sun was setting. There was no sign of Celeste, but after their argument on deck Wren hadn't been expecting her to join her as a cabin-mate. She was probably reclining in the captain's quarters, drinking all the good wine.

Wren ventured above deck, where her breath made filmy clouds in the air. The *Siren's Secret* had passed through the raging storm and emerged into a glassy sea, where an icy mist clung to the ship and the sky was the colour of a finely polished pearl. There was an eeriness about this water, as though it was filled not with living things but ghosts hiding in the ripples of long-dead waves.

Wren found Marino leaning over the bow of the ship.

'Looking for treasure?' she said, coming to stand beside him.

Their reflections stared up at them through the mist. 'Something better,' said Marino. 'Mermaids.'

Wren's eyebrows rose.

'Two years ago, I glimpsed one here on a starless night.' His lips twitched into a smile. 'She was floating like a blossom on the water. I thought she was sprung from a dream, at first. But then she sang to me.'

Wren leaned over the glassy water, searching for a shining tail in the waves. She had never seen a mermaid before, but a pirate that once washed up in Ortha had told her stories of them. How they glowed like jewels beneath the water and held the light of the stars in their eyes. How they sang with all the grace of a dawn chorus but swam where no sailor could hope to catch them. They were frightened of the world above the surface, of the famine and the greed and the wars, and those who stoked them.

'Did you speak to her?'

Marino shook his head. 'I couldn't summon the courage, Your Majesty.'

'Call me Wren. Or Tilda, if you like. I hate formality,' said Wren. 'And why don't you chuck some of your gold into the sea next time? You're rich. That might work.'

'Don't tease me.' Marino turned back to the misty water. 'If there's one thing this life has taught me, it's that you can buy almost anything in the world, except love. There is nothing you can trade for it. Only your heart.'

Wren looked out at the gentle water. It was a perfect mix of grey and blue, the same shade as Tor's eyes. Her heart clenched at the memory of him sailing away from her. She had tried to shut the moment away, to bury it in the back of her mind, but in the sudden stillness of her thoughts, it crept out again. A whisper of hope came with it, and she found herself wondering if she would see the Gevran soldier once she got to Grinstad . . . if she was a fool to think he might even help her rescue Banba. She knew she had no right to ask anything of him, not after he had sacrificed his prince to save her life. But hope was like a bird sprung from a cage. Once set free, it was hard to catch.

'I know that look.'

Wren blinked. 'What look?'

The captain smirked at her. 'You are in love.'

She barked a laugh. 'You're mistaking love with hunger.'

'If you say so.'

'Oh, shut up.' Wren swatted him. 'You're the one obsessed with a fancy flounder.'

They shared a chuckle as they turned back to the sea, the *Siren's Secret* gliding gracefully as a swan. For a long time, they were both silent, each lost in their own thoughts. Then the wind changed.

'Look,' said Marino, gesturing towards the horizon. 'Do you see that?'

Wren rose to her tiptoes. 'See what?'

'The famous ice cliffs of Gevra. We've made good time. The storm certainly helped.'

The mist curled as it parted, revealing a swathe of land so high and bright, it burned tears into Wren's eyes. She blinked them away, her heart pounding as she tried to make sense of what lay before them.

'*Stars above.*' The ice cliffs cut a jagged line across the horizon, jutting up from the sea like shards of shattered glass. The Gevran coast was a barrier so sharp and unforgiving that no man or woman could ever hope to conquer it. 'It's impenetrable.'

'Not quite.' Marino pointed to a gap in the cliffs, where two shards of icy rock bent away from each other. Between them lay a narrow fjord, where the sea rushed in.

Wren curled her fingers around the railings, suddenly aware of their numbness. 'Will we fit through there?' she asked, the words chattering through her teeth.

Marino nodded. 'To many sailors that fjord is known as the Death Crevasse. But I'm an accomplished captain of great skill. I have no cause to fear it.'

'Then please go and captain before you wreck us on those cliffs,' said Wren, a touch shrilly.

With a rippling laugh, Captain Marino Pegasi took off towards the wheel, hollering orders to the crew as he went. Wren stood rooted to the bow, watching the icy cliffs get bigger and sharper. A terrible shiver rippled up her spine and settled in her chest. For the first time since she had set out to rescue her grandmother, she felt truly afraid of what lay before her.

Rose
CHAPTER 10

Rose was determined not to let her worry for Wren ruin the tour. In a state of shock, she had gone back up to her room with Agnes to get ready, ensuring every ruffle on her pale blue dress was perfect. With the whole world seemingly falling apart around her, and everything spinning out of her control, at least Rose could still choose her outfit. Her armour. With Wren gone, she would have to be good enough, *queenly enough*, for both of them.

In the meantime, they would have to come up with an explanation for Wren's absence. Rose hoped that the townspeople of Eana would be so delighted to see her that they wouldn't care about her sister's absence. It might even be easier, really. Wren had been so grumpy about the tour, she probably would have made a terrible impression.

There was a knock at the door, and Thea entered, looking ashen. Agnes fastened the last delicate pearl button at the back of Rose's dress, before stepping away to give them privacy.

Rose sat at her dresser trying to wrangle her hair into submission while Thea perched on the end of her bed.

'Shen told me what happened.'

'I might have expected Wren to sneak off in the middle of the night, but I can't believe Celeste went after her without telling me,' she fumed. 'Is *everyone* in this palace determined to betray me?'

'I'm sure she'll be back before you know it,' said Thea, deftly taking the brush from Rose before she did any permanent damage. She combed her fingers through her hair, gently working out the tangles. 'And, with any luck, she'll have Wren with her.'

Rose closed her eyes, trying to take heart in Thea's words. Though she hadn't known the healer very long, there was no one inside the palace walls she trusted more. With the exception, perhaps, of Shen. Rose glanced out of the window towards the courtyard. She knew he was down there, watching the soldiers closely as they prepared for their departure.

Thea set the brush down with a sigh. 'I should have known Wren would go after Banba. It was only a matter of time . . .'

'Before she left me all alone,' said Rose, bitterly.

Thea braced a comforting hand on her shoulder. 'You are not alone, Rose. You have me.'

Rose reached for the healer's hand. 'And I need you now more than ever, Thea. You'll look after Anadawn while I'm gone. Truly, I couldn't imagine a better Queensbreath.'

'I'm not sure Wren would agree.' Thea's gaze found hers in the mirror. 'The plan was always for Banba to be Queensbreath.'

Rose wrinkled her nose. 'Wren certainly never discussed

that with me.' Though after the events of that morning, she was hardly surprised. 'And while I don't know my grandmother as well as either of you two do, I must say I think you have a better sense of diplomacy.'

Thea let out a wheezing laugh. 'That's one way of putting it.'

'In any case, it's a matter for another time.'

'A time I hope will come,' said Thea, quietly. 'How I wish Banba was here.'

'Me, too,' said Rose. 'What would she think of the tour?'

Thea laughed again as she drifted to the bedroom window, where she looked down on the preparations in the courtyard. 'She'd hate it at first, I'm sure, but she is cautious by nature. Upon reflection, I think she'd grudgingly admit it was a good idea. Though she would also tell you to make sure you know where the nearest witch settlement is, should you need their help on the road.'

'We're a long way from Ortha,' said Rose, with a frown. Not that there were many witches left there. And in any case, the tour was heading south, not west. Away from the Ganyeve Desert and everything that lay far beyond it, on the other side of the kingdom. 'And most of the witches live here now, at Anadawn. Don't they?'

Thea hmm'd. 'There are other settlements. Or, at least, there were. The Mishnick Mountains in the north-west. And another settlement in the south. Amarach Towers, the home of the seers.'

'Aren't the seers lost? Like the Sunkissed Kingdom?'

'The towers are hidden, not lost,' said Thea, turning back to her. 'As to whether there are seers still living there, I'm afraid I cannot say. But if you need to take refuge on the road, I know where you can find it.' A pause, then. 'Or at least I can point you in the direction of the towers. Even if the witches there are gone, the land will protect you.'

Rose offered a wry smile. 'If only it could tell me how to deal with Edgar Barron, too.'

'You have to trust yourself, Rose. You'll know how to handle Barron when the time comes.'

'I just hope this tour shows everyone that witches aren't to be feared. That we're all on the same side. Barron's been out there spreading lies and turning our people against us. Against me.' Rose wrung her hands, tugging at her delicate lace sleeves. 'I never thought my own people would hate me, Thea.'

Thea's brown eye softened. 'They don't hate you. They are simply afraid of what they do not know. But once they know you, once they see how much you love Eana, how much you love them, well, they will love you back.'

Rose blinked away tears. 'I hope so.'

'I know so. Now fetch me some parchment and I'll draw you a map.' She glanced towards the window, where outside the royal guard was starting to assemble. 'But best keep it to yourself. Just in case.'

By the time the tour was ready to depart, and all the trunks were packed and loaded, Rose was feeling optimistic about the weeks ahead. Shen nudged his horse Storm into formation beside the royal carriage, while she hugged Thea tightly, grateful to have her map tucked safely inside her bodice.

As Rose stepped into the golden carriage, with Elske at her heels, she looked back at Anadawn, at her palace, and swore to herself that when she returned, it would be as a queen beloved by her people. As a queen triumphant. She would charm the entire country, town by town, home by home, if she needed to.

Edgar Barron simply didn't know who he was up against.

Wren

CHAPTER 11

The ice fjords of Gevra loomed over Wren as the *Siren's Secret* drifted into the Death Crevasse. She could see her reflection in the sheer cliff face, a distorted dot peering out at the snow-swept world. The chill had settled in her bones now. Her toes were numb, and her teeth were chattering.

I'm almost there, Banba.

Marino Pegasi steered them through the winding inlet as if he had been doing it his whole life, and after a couple of painstaking hours, the fjords finally gave way to a frostbitten cove, upon which a bustling port was teeming with people. Wren counted at least forty ships, everything from battered fishing boats and tall sailing vessels to the hulking grey-sailed war boats that had sailed down the Silvertongue River a few weeks ago. She recognized the king's ship – the one Banba had been taken away on. Here it sat, moored and empty, save for the swabbies on deck and the soldiers guarding the gangplank.

Though evening had fallen, there were hundreds of merchants and sailors running about, and more market stalls than Wren had ever seen in one place. The shouts of their vendors carried on the wintry wind, reaching her all the way across the water.

Wren's fingers began to twitch. Back in Eshlinn getting to Gevra had felt like a fever dream, but suddenly it was before her, stealing the colour from her cheeks and the courage from her heart. She shook off her nerves, but the chill clung to her as she turned and stalked towards the hull. Marino was at the wheel, guiding the *Siren's Secret* into port.

'I'll need you to come back for me in three days,' said Wren. 'I know the timing isn't ideal.'

'You think I would knowingly leave a queen of Eana on hostile shores?' Marino shook his head. 'There are always other trades to make. I just hope you know what you're doing.'

Wren forced a laugh. 'You hardly think I bartered my way on to your ship without a plan, do you?'

'Your lips are turning blue,' said Marino. 'Didn't you pack a warm stole? Or is getting immediate frostbite part of your plan, too?'

'I may have underestimated the weather.'

'Lessie told me why you've come.' He turned his face west, his expression grim. 'The mountain palace is a fortress, cut into the heart of the Fovarr Mountains. I hope you're not planning on scaling a wall.'

'Believe it or not, that's worked for me before.'

'You're not in Anadawn now, Wren,' warned Marino. 'Gevra doesn't give second chances. To queens or peasants.' He dropped his voice, as though he was afraid the wind was listening in. 'Soldiers *and* beasts patrol the mountain palace.

And if they don't get you, the frost will.'

Wren folded her arms to hide her trembling hands. 'I have an invitation from the king himself.'

Marino made a noise of disbelief. 'What if it's a trap?'

'I'm a queen of Eana. I'm sure even Alarik Felsing would have more sense than that.'

'I wouldn't be so sure,' said Marino. 'When the young prince of Radask paid a diplomatic visit to the palace last year, he lost three toenails and a front tooth. They say he fled the palace in tattered robes.'

Wren quailed. 'What happened to him?'

Marino shrugged. 'A tussle with the king's bear, most likely. Or maybe the king himself. All I know is, invitation or not, I wouldn't count on Alarik Felsing's hospitality. Especially not after what happened to his brother on our shores.'

Wren's hand flew to her drawstring pouch, suddenly rethinking her entire plan. Marino was right. She would be a fool to simply stroll into Grinstad Palace, thinking her crown would protect her. Alarik Felsing did not play by the rules.

'There are several fur-lined coats in my cabin below deck,' added Marino. 'Take one.'

Wren dipped her chin in thanks. 'I don't suppose you know of an ancient secret tunnel that leads directly into the palace?'

Marino chuckled. 'Now that's what I call a long shot.'

'You'd be surprised,' muttered Wren. She turned to go, when he stopped her.

'Wait. What if there *was* another way to get inside the

palace?' Marino's eyes darted towards the port. 'Last week, I picked up a shipment of saffron in Caro. I'm trading it with an envoy from the palace. The new cook, Harald, is an adventurous sort. He wants to expand the tastebuds of the royal family. He's going to meet me at the market.'

Wren turned her gaze to the teeming shore. 'Aha! You're going to stuff me into one of your spice barrels.'

Marino laughed, awkwardly. 'That's a joke, right?'

'Oh. So, that's a no?'

'Only if you want to actually survive the journey,' said the captain. 'But there may be room enough *between* the barrels if you wait for the right moment.'

Despite the cold, a smile twitched on Wren's lips. 'I am a master at finding the right moment.'

While the crew of the *Siren's Secret* prepared to dock, Wren hurried below deck. Mercifully, Celeste was still snoring in the captain's quarters. Ignoring the ever-rising tide of her guilt, Wren withdrew a pinch of sand and spelled her into an even deeper sleep. 'This *barely* counts as magic,' she whispered, before grabbing a fur-lined frock coat from Marino's closet.

By the time Wren set foot on the shores of Gevra, the last rays of sunlight had long melted across the distant mountains. The port remained a hive of activity, market vendors hollering back and forth as they manned stalls that sold everything from fresh crab and lobster, to bloodied slabs of beef and lamb. There were cheeses and loaves, too, pastries smothered in almonds and chocolate and berry jams, all of it creating a strange symphony of smells that lingered in the cold night air. Wren meandered between the lantern-lit stalls, keeping a wary eye on Marino as he unloaded his spices and carted them down to the marketplace.

There were beasts everywhere, but they didn't startle Wren as they once might have. She had Elske to thank for that. She barely batted an eyelid at the snow tigers and leopards that prowled the marketplace, hardly noticing the Arctic foxes that slumbered atop the awning. Most of the animals were tame, roaming freely by the sides of their fur-clad masters. Wren supposed they had Tor's family of wranglers to thank for that. Her heart clenched at the thought of seeing him again. She wondered what she would say – how she might thank him for saving her life. Or, if the moment allowed, whether she would just fling herself into his arms and kiss him senseless.

Stop that, she scolded herself. There was no time for that now.

Nearby, a tiger growled, banishing all thoughts of Tor entirely. These particular beasts were on chains. They had been bred for war and belonged to the soldiers who were patrolling the port. They snapped at the other animals as they went by, occasionally growling at anyone who was talking too loudly or gesticulating too much.

Wren made sure to keep her head down. She had manipulated her appearance again, turning her hair red and, as much as it pained her, bending her teeth inwards. She had even doused herself in Marino's cologne to try to mask her scent, but the beasts in Gevra were as clever as their masters, and for all she knew, some of them could have been at Rose's ill-fated wedding, when the twins had killed Rathborne and accidentally burned the Protector's Vault to the ground.

A sudden waft of freshly baked bread made Wren's stomach grumble. She withdrew a pinch of sand and sprinkled it over a passing wolf, warping the chain around its neck. It leaped at a wandering snow leopard, causing the marketplace to descend into momentary chaos. Vendors yelled as they cowered behind their stalls, while panicked customers tried to drag their own beasts away from the fight.

Wren used the distraction to pilfer a slice of rye bread smothered in fresh salmon. She devoured it in three bites, before nicking some battered cod and shoving it into her pocket for later. She hurried away, just as the harried soldier rechained his wolf.

At the other end of the marketplace, Wren spied who she was sure must be Marino's palace envoy, Harald. He had arrived in a hulking iron sled, emblazoned on both sides with the Gevran crest. It was being pulled by eight grey wolves. Harald was accompanied by two palace soldiers; a tall, black-haired woman with fishtail braids and a stocky bald man with a wide jaw were already loading the spice barrels into the back of the sled. Harald himself was tall and thin, with pale skin, a wide mouth and a shock of bright red hair. Even though he was dressed in a heavy brown coat with a huge furry hood, he was speaking to Marino through chattering teeth.

Wren left the flickering marketplace and ducked behind a nearby stack of crates. When the last barrel of spice had been loaded on to the sled and covered with a black tarp, she flung a piece of cod into the middle of the wolves. They descended on it in a tornado of grey fur, growling and snapping at each other for first claim.

The guards lumbered around to investigate the sudden fuss, and Wren darted out from behind the crates and crept under the tarp. She squeezed herself between the spice barrels until she was tucked away at the very back of the sled, with her legs squished to her chest and her arms pulled tight around them.

She listened as the soldiers returned to their seats atop the sled, the wood above her creaking as they sat down. A moment later, Harald came back. He hopped up on to the sled and called a warm goodbye to Marino. The male soldier barked a command and the wolves settled into formation. And then, all at once, they were off, the barrels jostling against each other as the sled pulled away from the marketplace.

Wren sat stiffly, mindful not to breathe too loudly. For a long time, there was only the sound of gravel shifting beneath them, and the howl of the wind as it slipped through the gaps in the tarp. Then the ground turned whisper-soft as the wolves tugged them onward, into the snow-swept countryside.

When Wren dared to peek out, night had fallen in earnest, the silvery landscape the same colour as the waning moon. There were no lights for miles around, and for a long while it felt to Wren that theirs was the only sled in the entire country, and on it, the only people.

Sometimes, when the snow gave way to gravel, she heard the sound of horses clopping by, but there were few carriages on these twisting roads. She supposed the ice was too treacherous. Even the wolves had to slow occasionally to navigate it.

The ache in Wren's back slowly spread into her legs. The rye bread had made her thirsty, but she was too scared to reach for the flask in her satchel. Up above her, the soldiers were silent as they rode, but every so often she would hear the cook attempt to make conversation.

It always went unanswered.

Wren kept her pouch of sand at the ready. She had come to realize that the ice in Gevra was not just treacherous to travellers, but to enchanters, too. If she ran out of her earth, where would she find more? There was nothing living here that hadn't been smothered in inches of snow or covered in a layer of frost. She would have to use her sand cleverly and sparingly.

Finally, the sled began to slow. Wren peered out from under the tarp to find that dawn was breaking. There were no birds to announce it, nothing in the paling sky, but heavy white clouds. All around them were glassy mountain peaks climbing up to touch the clouds.

Wren suspected they were in the heart of the Fovarr Mountains, but from her place at the back of the sled, she couldn't see Grinstad Palace. She could sense it, though, like a ghost looming over her. The wind had died. In its place came the sound of roaring beasts. Their growls got closer. Louder. Then there were gates, groaning as they opened, and the voices of more soldiers as the sled journeyed onwards into the grounds of Grinstad Palace.

Wren caught a glimpse of it through the rippling tarp. It was an enormous sculpture of limestone and glass, cut into the jagged mountain range, so it was hard to tell where Grinstad began and the landscape ended. It was every bit as impenetrable as Wren imagined, its narrow turrets glistening like fangs as they pierced the low-hanging clouds. The sled took a wide berth of the palace, arcing through snow-laden gardens punctuated with thorn bushes. Wren assumed they were heading to the servants' entrance at the back of the palace. All the better for her, she thought, as she flexed her toes, restoring feeling to them.

At last, the sled stopped.

She pulled her hood up and readied her sand, waiting to strike . . .

The soldiers hopped off and the cook clambered down after them. The tarp was folded back on itself, revealing the first six barrels. Wren crouched at the back of the sled as the guards set about lifting them off and carrying them into the kitchens, one by one.

She was waiting for their return when a wolf appeared out of nowhere and came bounding up on to the sled. Wren dropped the sand in a fright, barely swallowing back her shriek as the beast began to sniff at her coat. Suddenly, she remembered the battered fish in her pocket. She flung the rest of it on to the ground, and the wolf bounded after it, devouring the fish in one bite. Wren barely had time to grab another pinch of sand before he came back for more. She flung it at his snarling mouth, hissing a hurried sleep enchantment. The wolf slumped on to its side, just as two more came sniffing around the back of sled.

When they spotted Wren, they began to howl.

Wren reached back into her cloak, grabbing a fistful of sand just as a sword appeared at her throat. She looked up, into the hostile gaze of a Gevran soldier.

'One more move, and I'll gut you,' he growled.

Rose
CHAPTER 12

Tucked away in the plush surrounds of her tour carriage, with Elske snoozing at her feet and flanked by the entire royal guard, Rose should have felt safe. But Wren's absence still unsettled her. They had been almost inseparable these last few weeks, sharing dinner together every evening and whispering late into the night, catching up on their childhoods, their dreams, their fears, until their lids grew heavy and sleep finally claimed them. Now Rose was alone, and afraid for her sister.

A sharp whistle from outside roused her from her worry. She drew back the curtain to find Shen grinning at her. Unlike the rest of the regiment, he was riding bareback, in a loose black shirt, dark trousers and sturdy boots. He looked more like a bandit than a soldier, and yet the sight of his rough cloak and easy smile conjured memories of their time together in the desert that set Rose's pulse racing.

She tried not to show it. 'Did you just *whistle* at me?'

'I was trying to be discreet.'

Rose scowled, which only made him chuckle.

'I wondered if you wanted some company?' he said,

leaning closer. 'It's a long ride to Glenbrook. You'll get bored in there all by yourself.'

'You are incorrigible!' said Rose, but she couldn't fight her smile. In truth, she would like nothing more than to welcome Shen into the royal carriage.

'You're blushing,' said Shen, his voice low. 'I love it when you blush.'

'Shen Lo!' barked Captain Davers. 'Straighten up! Fall in line!'

Shen bristled. 'I really wish that bossy oaf would stop trying to command me.'

'Careful,' teased Rose, quite enjoying the reprimand. 'You don't want to get in trouble.'

Shen's gaze lingered on hers. 'Depends on the trouble.'

Another violent blush stole up her cheeks. Curse this boy and his indomitable charm. They had barely crossed the Silvertongue Bridge and she was already losing focus. 'Stop distracting me,' she scolded.

'From what? Sitting inside there all by yourself?'

'I'm not by myself,' said Rose, primly. 'I have Elske.'

Shen's face fell. 'And now I'm jealous of a wolf. This is a new low for me.'

Rose giggled as she flopped back against the seat, letting the privacy curtain fall between them. She might not have Wren or Celeste by her side, but she was fiercely glad of Shen's company. She closed her eyes, lulled by the reassuring thrum of Storm's hooves as they rode on through the bustling capital of Eshlinn, and continued south. To buy time, they had already sent out word that Wren was travelling north to Norbrook, to personally oversee the delivery of rations, before returning to be by her sister's side.

On and on they journeyed, over rivers and fields and glorious green hills, towards towns that Rose had only ever known by name – first Glenbrook, where she meandered down winding streets teaming with people. She flung roses from her carriage, waving and smiling until her cheeks vibrated. She made a stop at the infirmary on the edge of town, offering her healing magic to those in need of it. After hours of using her craft without pause, Rose was so exhausted she had to be escorted back to her carriage by two guards, where she promptly curled up and fell asleep.

The royal tour left Glenbrook to a chorus of cheers, but Rose was too deep in slumber to hear them. After a brief stop to feed and water the horses, they pressed onward to Horseleap. Here the weather was so fine, Rose left the carriage for a lengthy walkabout before visiting the local orphanage, where she spent all evening with the children, reading storybooks. She even introduced them to Elske, the friendly white wolf rolling on to her back and snuffling with delight as they all rushed to pet her.

When Rose finally returned to her carriage, it was much later than she thought, but her heart was so full she almost burst into tears. All her life she had studied the vast plains of Eana and its many bustling towns, but nothing could have prepared her for the vibrancy of visiting these places in person, or the wonder in reaching out to the people who lived there, touching them, *knowing* them.

'You were incredible back there,' said Shen, who had managed to slip, unnoticed into the back of the carriage, and was looking at her now with such wonder it cast starlight in his eyes. 'You *are* incredible.'

Rose startled. 'What on earth are you doing in here? This is entirely improper!'

'Then tell me to leave.'

Rose pursed her lips. '*Shen.*'

'I love it when you say my name.'

'I can't imagine why. I only do it when I'm scolding you.'

'Maybe that's it,' he said, with a wink. 'Let me ride with you to Millis. I promise I'll be good.'

Rose surrendered her resolve as it crumbled. She sat down on the bench beside him, a shiver rushing through her as his leg brushed against hers. Oh, it truly was such a glorious feeling. 'Well, don't be *too* good,' she murmured. 'I am happy that you're here.'

Shen turned his face to hers, trailing a finger along her jaw. 'As you like, Your Majesty.'

Rose closed her eyes and pressed her lips to his. He groaned as his mouth opened, deepening the kiss. Rose relaxed into it, knowing that this moment was not only fleeting but against all sorts of rules she had made for herself before setting out. But in Shen's embrace, none of that seemed to matter.

At last, Rose pulled back from him. She was heady with exhaustion, her lids impossibly heavy.

Shen curled his arm around her, pressed a kiss to the crown of her head. 'Go to sleep, Rose. I'll hold you.'

Rose sighed as she laid her head against his shoulder. Cradled in his arms, sleep came swiftly, whisking her far away from her worries.

When she woke, it was almost midnight, and Shen was gone.

The carriage was slowing. They must have reached the town of Millis. They would stop here for the night, just enough time for Rose to bathe and eat and sleep on a real pillow, before setting off again at first light. The royal entourage crowded into the biggest inn in town until there was barely space enough to move. Agnes went up to ready her room and unpack some of Rose's things, leaving her to speak with Chapman over a late supper of chicken and leek stew.

So far, the tour was proving to be a success, with little sign of Barron and his Arrows. Rose knew she should be pleased – relieved, even – but as she looked around the crowded dining room, she found herself preoccupied. 'Have you seen Shen?'

The steward sighed. 'Must you turn your thoughts to that troublesome boy? I ask you, Queen Rose, how a warrior witch with no official training or indeed allegiance to the royal guard can mean to get away with commanding Captain Davers and his soldiers all day long.'

Rose took a swig of wine from her goblet. 'You know well he's the finest warrior in Eana.'

'With the arrogance to prove it.' Chapman tutted. 'And to answer your question, he is, at this very moment, patrolling the outer walls of Millis. At his own insistence.'

Rose grinned into her goblet. 'You must at least admire his thoroughness.'

'Indeed,' said Chapman, with no small amount of disapproval.

After supper, Rose set off for her lodgings on the third floor, which was a large, well-lit room with a huge canopy bed and adjacent bathing chamber. It was the grandest room the inn had to offer, and came complete with an accompanying cot for Agnes, who opened the door to welcome her.

Rose undressed and got ready for bed, then sat at the dresser while Agnes brushed her hair out.

'You did well today, Queen Rose. Everyone's been sayin' it.'

Rose smiled at her maidservant in the mirror. 'I've never spoken to so many people in my life, Agnes. I think I'm in danger of losing my voice.'

'We'll get it back right quick,' said Agnes. 'I'll go down to the kitchen and fetch a cuppa ginger tea with honey and lemon. You'll be right as rain by morning.'

'You are a treasure, Agnes. I don't know what I'd do with you.'

Agnes had barely left the room when there was a knock at the window. Rose spun on her heel, startling at Shen's face in the darkness. She rushed to the window and heaved it open.

'What on earth are you doing?' she hissed, as he clambered inside. 'We're three floors up!'

Shen swept a loose hair from his eyes as he straightened. 'Nothing I can't handle.'

'You can't stay here. Agnes will be back any moment.'

Shen's dark eyes glittered. 'So, you're saying Agnes is our only obstacle?'

'What? No! Of course not. I just mean—' Rose groaned. 'Oh, don't tease me I'm far too tired.'

'I wouldn't dare,' said Shen, even as he smiled. 'I only came to say goodnight. And to give you this.' He reached into his pocket and removed a carefully wrapped heart-shaped tart.

Rose stared at the treat in disbelief. 'Please don't tell me you sneaked off to bake that for me?'

'I'm a man of many talents, but not that one, Rose.' Shen laughed. 'Thea told me the bakery in Millis is famous for its jam tarts. I thought I'd see for myself.'

Rose looked up at him. 'But it's midnight. Where did you find an open bakery?'

'Did I say open?' Shen flashed his dimple. 'I'm sure I didn't say open.'

Rose took the jam tart. 'Thief,' she whispered. 'Is that why you left the troop? To bring me a jam tart?'

Shen's smile faltered. 'I thought someone might be tracking us. I saw a rider following us through the pass just outside Millis. I'm sure I spotted him back at Glenbrook, too.'

Rose startled. 'Goodness. Could it be Barron? Or his wretched Arrows?'

Shen shook his head. 'The rider was alone. And far quicker than I was expecting. When I doubled back, he was gone.'

'A curious onlooker, perhaps,' said Rose. 'It might be nothing.'

'Maybe,' said Shen. 'Though in my experience, people

don't hide unless they're up to no good.'

'I suppose not,' she muttered.

Shen cast aside his worry, stepping into the space between them. 'Which reminds me. Shouldn't we make use of this stolen moment?'

Rose took a step before she could stop herself, folding herself into his embrace. 'What did you have in mind?

His dark eyes drank her in. 'I am yours to command, Rose.'

She tilted her chin up, until their noses brushed. 'Shen,' she whispered against his lips. 'We really shouldn't.'

He combed his hand through her hair. 'Say my name,' he murmured. 'Just one more time.'

She felt him smile against her.

There came a sudden cry of alarm. 'Oh, mercy! Not another kidnapping!'

Rose leaped away from Shen with such a fright that she dropped the jam tart. She scrabbled to pick it up. 'Oh, Agnes. You're back! Ah, and there's my tea. Thank you!'

Agnes wagged her finger at Shen. 'You know good and well you're not supposed to be in here.'

Shen splayed his hands as he backed towards the window. 'I was just on my way out, Agnes.'

'For goodness' sake, Shen, take the door!' called Rose, but he was already gone, leaping through the window and disappearing into the night, leaving only the echo of his laugh behind.

Agnes shut the window at once. 'He should know better than that.'

Rose sighed. 'I know.'

'And so should you, Queen Rose.'

'I know that, too.' Rose slumped on to the bed, smiling at the crumbling tart in her hands. She laid it on the bedside table, careful to keep its shape, before licking the jam from her fingers. It tasted almost as good as Shen's kisses. But not quite. 'Goodnight, Agnes.'

'Goodnight, Rose. Here's hoping tomorrow goes as well as today.'

Rose closed her eyes, making that same wish. Not just for herself, but for Wren, too. Wherever her sister was, Rose hoped she was safe.

Wren
CHAPTER 13

Wren was marched through the kitchens of Grinstad Palace at sword-point by a pair of Gevran soldiers. The scullery servants fell out of their tasks to watch her go, muttering furiously among themselves.

'I don't remember a girl being part of the order.' Harald cast a wary glance at his shipment of spice barrels as though he was expecting more to leap out. 'Where in Great Bernhard's name did she come from?'

'Must have sneaked on to the sled back at the port,' said the female soldier, Marit, who was currently pointing her sword against Wren's spine.

'Foolish little ship rat,' sneered the male soldier, Vidar, who had been the one to confiscate her dagger, and was now pointing a blade at her chin. 'Bartering her life for a look inside the palace.'

The cook surveyed Wren with pity, taking in her frizzy auburn hair and crooked teeth. 'Where will you take her?'

'To the courtyard,' said Vidar, darkly. 'Where all trespassers go.'

Wren didn't miss the way the servants flinched. Even the kitchen tabby cat, who was slumbering underneath the stove, looked at her dolefully. The cook couldn't look at her at all. 'Bernhard save her,' he muttered, before turning back to his workbench. 'Come now, you shameless gawkers, there's work to be done. Nina, it's time to roast the boar. Didrik, fetch the leeks.' He clapped his hands, drawing the servants' attention away from Wren as she was dragged through the kitchen and up a winding iron staircase that seemed to go on forever.

Wren's panic reeled with every step. She had been a fool to think this would be easy, that relying solely on her magic would keep her safe in this sunless land. She should have prepared herself for those wolves, been smarter with the food in her pocket. The sand in her pouch. She had no choice now but to use the only plan she had left – the one she had been hoping to avoid.

'There's been a misunderstanding,' she said, her voice lifting in the stairwell. 'I came to Grinstad to see Tor Iversen.' She wracked her brains for the name of the soldier's hometown. 'I'm a messenger from the isle of Carrig. I need to speak to him at once.'

The soldier in front of her – Vidar – stopped walking. 'You know Captain Iversen?'

'Yes,' said Wren, all too conscious of his sword at her throat.

'How?' demanded Marit.

Wren was seized by a memory of their heady kiss in the library at Anadawn, how Tor had pressed himself against her with abandon, whispering her name against her lips like a spell. 'We're . . . neighbours.'

Vidar lowered his dark unibrow. 'You do not speak like someone from Carrig.'

'And you look like a thief. Dressed up in a man's coat and reeking of brine.' Marit twisted the sword at Wren's back. 'Where on Carrig are you from?'

Wren ignored the question, since answering it would reveal her lie. 'Take me to Tor and I'll explain everything,' she said, instead. 'He'll know exactly who I am.'

The soldiers exchanged a bemused glance. 'I think our little thief is a liar, too,' said Marit.

'She thinks we came down in the last fall of snow,' snorted Vidar. 'All that spice must have gone to her head.'

Wren wished for a sword of her own to knock these sneering soldiers down the stairs. She leashed her temper before it unravelled, fighting to keep her voice steady. 'I want to be heard.'

'You will be heard,' Marit assured her. 'We will take you somewhere you can scream at the top of your lungs.'

The soldiers continued onward, climbing up and up and up, until they reached a bright hallway punctured with huge glass windows and lined with life-sized statues. Wren let her gaze roam along the proud-faced kings and queens of Gevra, each one expertly chiselled in ivory stone. She searched for Alarik's likeness among them, but the row ended with the statue of a man, who shared the same sharp cheekbones and hooded gaze as the king – Alarik's father, the late King Soren, who had perished in a hailstorm some years ago.

The hallway led to an enormous atrium domed with glittering windows. It was bigger than the ballroom at Anadawn Palace, with a magnificent split staircase bordered by a balustrade of glass icicles that led to the upper levels of the inner palace. The floor was made of exquisite white marble threaded with strands of blue and green, and in the centre of the atrium a glass pianoforte sat on a sprawling bear-skin rug. Above it dangled the most decadent chandelier Wren had ever seen, each crystal droplet casting its own rainbow along the pale stone walls. It provided the only whisper of colour in this strange and soulless place.

There were soldiers everywhere. Two at each doorway that branched off the atrium, and more lurking in the alcoves. Their wolves prowled about the atrium at their leisure, while the largest curled up on the rug underneath the piano.

'Tor!' Wren called out, in a fit of desperation. 'Tor Iversen!'

She scanned the soldiers' faces, but none of them broke their stony composure to glance in her direction. If Tor was somewhere in Grinstad Palace, it was not here. That didn't stop Wren from screaming his name, louder and louder, as she was dragged through the atrium at sword-point. Her voice echoed back at her from the glass dome, where the silver peaks of the Fovarr Mountains glistened high above her.

The soldiers marched Wren out of the back of the atrium and into a walled courtyard that had been cut into the icy heart of Grinstad Palace. They cast her satchel aside, then shoved her forward.

Wren's heart thundered in the sudden silence. She looked around, nervously. Vidar and Marit were backing away. They slammed the gate, sealing her in.

More soldiers gathered around the periphery. Some climbed the high wall, their boots dangling as they looked down on her. Wren had acquired an audience, but she had a feeling the true spectacle had yet to begin. Then she spotted the iron hatch to her right. She took a cautious step, and then another, until she was close enough to hear the growls rumbling behind it.

Rotting carp.

This wasn't a courtyard. It was an arena. Built for beasts, not humans.

Wren tried to make a run for it, but the gate was too high. She reached into her cloak, fumbling for a fistful of sand. She cast it over herself, restoring her appearance with a quick enchantment. The soldiers erupted in shouts as her hair unfurled into honey-brown waves. Her teeth reset, her eyes blazing emerald green once more. She rolled her shoulders back, casting off Marino's frock coat as she announced herself. 'I am Queen Wren Greenrock, of Eana, and I demand an audience with your king.'

'Witch!' yelled a voice behind her. 'She's trying to trick us!'

'Raise the hatch, Vidar!'

Wren readied her sand as a roaring snow tiger leaped from the open hatch and bounded towards her. Its maw was stained crimson, and she could tell from the bloodlust in its eyes that it was untamed.

The tiger reached Wren in three strides. She leaped from its path, but not fast enough. It slammed into her side and she rolled over, inhaling dirt as she cast the sand over her shoulder. She choked an enchantment out just as the tiger pounced on her. It opened its mouth, revealing its long pink tongue and sharp teeth, but its roar died quickly in its throat. It slumped to the ground, and in the next breath was snoring.

Wren scrabbled out from under it. Her cloak had come undone in the scuffle and was trapped underneath the slumbering beast. She yanked her pouch free and grabbed another fistful of sand.

'I'm the queen of Eana!' she screamed, as the hatch opened again. 'Let me out!'

'Another trick!' yelled Marit. 'Don't listen to her, Vidar!'

Wren backed away from the hatch as more growls filled the air. There were three tigers this time and five wolves. Eight beasts, in total, with nowhere to run. How on earth could she spell all of them at once?

She wracked her brains for another enchantment – something to buy her time – but there was nothing strong enough to cheat this death. Nothing to save her from the fate Celeste had promised her. Wren had risked it all for a violent demise inside a fighting yard, where no one she loved could hear her scream.

The first tiger pounced. Wren cast it to sleep. The next one knocked her off her feet. Her head hit the ground with a hard thud. Stars exploded in the sides of her vision as a mouth full of fangs appeared above her. Wren punched it, hissing as the skin on her hand broke open.

She made it back to her feet before the next attack. She tugged her cloak out from under the sleeping tiger and flung it over a snapping wolf to momentarily blind him. She made to run for the gate but three more wolves stood in her way, ready to pounce. Behind her, the tigers circled ever closer. Not for the first time, Wren wished she were a tempest, blessed with the power of a storm that could blow them all away.

The high wall was packed with soldiers now, onlookers who had abandoned their posts to watch the spectacle of her death. Another wolf leaped at Wren and knocked her on her back. It stood on her chest, crushing her into the earth.

Wren covered her face and screamed one last time, sending Tor's name up to the winter sky.

This time, Tor roared back. Wren heard his voice in the chaos of her panic and swore she had imagined it. But it came again – the addled shout of a man charging out from the palace at full speed. The gate was flung open and the wolf thrown off her, Tor's command ripping through the air like thunder. 'HEEL!'

The beasts fell back, all at once.

A new face appeared above Wren. A jaw slack with shock, and eyes the colour of storm clouds. Suddenly, the rest of the world melted away, the beasts and the soldiers and the frosted windows of Grinstad Palace all paling to nothing as Wren stared up at Tor, thanking the stars for this moment. This reprieve.

Wren. Her name was silent on his lips, as though he

couldn't believe what he was seeing, couldn't speak the truth of it out loud.

Wren took a shuddering breath – pain and relief mingling together at the sight of him, so real and so close again. Her own lips trembled as she reached for that whisper of familiarity that once existed between them. 'Hello, stranger.'

Tor stared down at her in horror. When his words came, they were sharp as glass. 'What in freezing hell are you doing here?'

'You know why I'm here,' said Wren, as she sat up.

His expression darkened, silver streaks cutting through the storm in his eyes. 'I can't take you to your grandmother, Wren.'

'Fine. Then take me to King Alarik.'

Rose
CHAPTER 14

The following morning, Rose awoke feeling refreshed. Outside, the birds were singing, the rising sun flooding the room with golden warmth. It made her feel hopeful about the tour, about Wren. With any luck, her sister would rejoin her soon, and they would conquer the far-flung reaches of their land together, charming everyone with their magic and their personality.

Rose bathed and dressed in a bright pink dress trimmed with ivory lace, pairing it with her favourite white shoes. She sat at the dresser then, munching on fresh bread with poached eggs and thin slivers of ham, while Agnes corralled her hair into a long braid wrought with a beautiful floral vine.

'You are the very picture of elegance, Rose,' said the maidservant, as she gently settled the royal crown atop her head. A skill she had perfected over the last few weeks. 'The people of Ellendale will fall over themselves just to shake your hand. I'm sure of it.'

Rose beamed at her reflection. 'I confess I have a good feeling about today, Agnes.'

'So do I, Queen Rose. So do I.'

Rose had been sorely mistaken. Although they left the town of Millis to a boisterous crowd of well-wishers, the journey to Ellendale was dusty and quiet. There were few banners lining the road, and no sign at all that the southern town was expecting a royal tour.

When they approached the outer wall of Ellendale, Rose's stomach twisted. She couldn't hear any cheers. In fact, she couldn't hear anything at all, save for the sound of clomping hooves and the grinding carriage wheels. She pulled back the privacy curtain to find Shen scowling at something over his shoulder.

'What is it?' she said, anxiously.

'I think it's that rider again,' he said, squinting at something in the distance.

'Forget about that,' said Rose, urgently. 'What's going on in front? I can't hear anyone.'

Shen turned around, rising in his seat to see over the regiment of soldiers. His frown only deepened. 'That's because there's no one there.'

Rose flushed. Did the people of Ellendale truly not care to welcome her? Not even enough to wave from their windows? Unless, of course, Ellendale had got the timing wrong. Perhaps the royal tour was simply ahead of schedule . . .

'Something isn't right,' muttered Shen. 'The town isn't just quiet. It's *silent*. We should wait here. Find out what's going on.'

Rose was inclined to agree. If nothing else, it would save her the embarrassment of parading through all those empty streets, waving at her own reflection in the shops' windows. But Captain Davers was ploughing ahead.

Shen bit off a curse. 'What is that trumped-up buffoon doing?'

Before Rose could say another word, Shen nudged Storm out of line and cantered off towards Captain Davers. Rose flopped back in her seat. At her feet, Elske woke from her slumber and rose to all fours, her ears drawing back as though she sensed the strangeness, too. It wasn't long before Rose heard the distant rumble of Shen's argument with Captain Davers. When it stopped just as abruptly, she leaned out of her window, craning her neck to catch a glimpse of them. Shen was galloping ahead, through the empty streets of Ellendale – no doubt trying to figure out what was going on – while Captain Davers was leading the procession onward, entirely unperturbed by the ghost town.

'Well, I'm not waving just for the sake of it,' grumbled Rose. 'I've got to retain *some* dignity.'

Even so, she kept her curtain open, scanning the windows as they passed through the main street. Every now and then, she glimpsed a face behind one.

Rose's stomach was so tight, she was nauseous. What on earth was going on?

The procession slowed unexpectedly, the carriage grinding to a stop. Up ahead, Rose heard voices. *Angry* voices. She tried to see out of her window, but there were horses in the way. There was no sign of Shen either.

She sat back and waited. And waited. And *waited*.

A ragged shout rang out, and Rose's heart stuttered in her chest. What if Shen had got into another argument with Captain Davers? His smart mouth was bound to get him in trouble sooner or later, and Captain Davers had made no secret of his disdain for the warrior witch.

When another shout erupted, Rose hopped out of her carriage, ignoring the guards yelling at her as she marched to the front of the procession. She would have to defend Shen before he argued himself into any more trouble, or indeed drew his sword on Captain Davers. That would be an unmitigated disaster, and she simply couldn't allow such a thing to—

Rose stopped short, her heart leaping into her throat as she ducked behind a nearby horse. Shen and Captain Davers weren't arguing at all. In fact, they were standing side by side, their swords drawn, as they faced off with what appeared to be an angry group of local townsfolk. Rose's gaze darted, counting at least forty of them. Not enough to threaten the might of her army, but certainly enough to cause a stir. She noted, with growing dread, that they carried weapons, too. Swords, mostly, but a man on the end was holding a mace, and another was wielding a pair of battle axes.

Goodness.

It was then that she noticed where they had congregated – outside the local Vault, a place where followers of Rose's long-dead ancestor, the Great Protector, still gathered in worship. A place that had been built on the hatred of the witches. Her hands trembled at the sight of the scrawled arrow on the door.

These men were Arrows. She might have got the jump on Barron back in Millis, but he had beaten her to Ellendale. Though she could glimpse no sign of him in the crowd.

'I'll only say this one last time,' Captain Davers was saying. 'You will stand aside at once, or face the might of Anadawn's army.'

'And the witches,' said Shen, with a precise spin of his sword.

'It's the witch we've come to see,' snarled a red-cheeked man near the front. He had a black thorny beard and cruel eyes that flickered like firelight. 'We want to acquaint ourselves with your cursed queen.'

Rose didn't miss the way he said *your*, not *our*. Nor the way he spat on the ground afterwards. These people had already disowned her.

'I've got a better idea,' drawled Shen. 'Why don't you acquaint yourself with the sharp end of my sword instead?'

'Easy,' warned Davers.

'No,' hissed Shen. 'Do your job, Davers.'

Just then, the Vault doors swung open, and more men poured out, surrounding them on all sides. They were edging down the procession, towards the golden carriage. Rose looked for a place to hide, just as the lead Arrow spotted her.

'*Majesty.*' The word was a rumble in his throat. 'What an *honour* this is.'

Shen spun around, spotting Rose in the same instant. Before he could get a word out, the Arrows lunged and Rose screamed.

The Anadawn guards sprang into action, Rose's foot soldiers surrounding her in a protective arc as they drew their own swords, pushing back against the advancing rebels. Shen leaped from Storm, moving in a blur of shadow and steel as he fought his way towards her.

The street echoed with the clash of sword-fighting as flaming arrows rained down from above. *Stars*, there were Arrows on the roof, too! Barron had prepared an ambush for Rose, and Captain Davers had been foolish enough to walk right into it. The Anadawn soldiers broke apart, diving for cover, as the rebels rammed the tour carriage, toppling it to one side.

Elske bounded out of it with a furious growl, sending a group of Arrows running. She snapped at their heels, chasing them back into the Vault.

Shen had been set upon by another group. They were no match for his strength and speed, but flaming arrows accosted him from above, one grazing his left shoulder and setting his sleeve alight. He dropped to the ground, trying to smother the flames. Rose screamed as she tried to battle her way towards him, but the guards shoved her back. Chaos had descended upon Ellendale, the horses rearing up and scattering as hundreds of oil-soaked flaming arrows set the street alight.

A man grabbed Rose by the waist. 'I've got her!' he yelled, in triumph. 'I've got the bloody queen!'

Rose kicked out, sending her shoe flying skyward. It plummeted back down, landing with a *thunk!* on the man's head. He swayed on his feet, but two more men swept in, grabbing her arms and hauling her off the street.

Rose cried out, but Shen was surrounded. The Arrows had clearly marked him as a threat and were keeping him as far from Rose as possible. Captain Davers was just as preoccupied, caught in the midst of the fray. Elske, too. There was no one left to help Rose, just the sound of her own feeble shouts as the Arrows carted her away from her people.

'Edgar Barron sends his regards,' came a wet growl, close to her ear. 'He'll be along soon, witch. Don't worry.'

Rose bucked violently, slamming her head into the man's teeth. She winced as he slumped to the ground, freeing her for a half-second. The other man caught her before she ran, swinging her around and shoving her towards an abandoned-looking house at the end of the street. Rose knew with sudden, sickening clarity that once she went through that doorway, she would not come back out.

Somewhere in the distance, Rose swore she heard the determined thrum of hooves. Had Shen fought his way through the crowds? She tried to free herself but it was no use. The street was on fire, her screams lost to the crackle of the blaze around her. The doorway loomed, like a dark mouth. She closed her eyes, praying for a miracle.

It came in the guise of a shadow, bursting through the flames. There was a loud *crrrrack!* as a whip came down, lashing her assailant in the cheek. He leaped back, as blood poured from the gaping wound in his cheek. Another *craaaaack!* and he was on the ground, unconscious, leaving Rose alone to face the man cloaked in shadow.

He was riding the fastest horse she had ever seen, its sleek coat the exact shade of the restless sands. To run from him would be futile, but she tried anyway. The whip came again. Only this time, it didn't crack. Rather, it twisted around her waist, taut as a noose, and yanked her backwards.

She shrieked as she hurtled towards the horse. An arm reached down, plucking her from the ground as though she was no lighter than a feather. Rose was hoisted up on to the horse, that same arm coming around her waist and stilling her protest as she was whisked through the burning streets of Ellendale.

Rose whipped her head around, catching a glimpse of Shen. He was still trapped in the belly of the baying Arrows, kicking and slashing his way to freedom. He snapped his chin up at the sound of those thundering hooves, his eyes growing wide as she galloped past, cradled in the vice-like grip of its cloaked rider.

After the first twenty minutes or so, Rose stopped struggling. It was entirely useless. Her strength was no match for her kidnapper, and she was spending the last of it unwisely. Aside from a few grunts of amusement, the rider had done little to reassure her that he wasn't about to kill her, but she had resolved that she couldn't do anything about that until they stopped. She could not believe she was being carried away on horseback by some sort of bandit, *again*.

Eventually, they stopped, the horse slowing as they came to a river about ten miles south of Ellendale. The rider released Rose. She leaped from the horse and ran to the riverbank, where she grabbed the biggest stick she could find and hoisted it like a sword.

When she spun around, he was standing beside his horse, his leather whip curled around his forearm, like a snake waiting to strike. 'Is that twig supposed to frighten me?'

'I've been kidnapped once in my life already,' huffed Rose. 'I refuse to let it happen again.'

He barked a laugh. 'That wasn't a kidnapping, Queenie. That was a rescue.' He rolled his hand, expectantly. 'You're welcome, by the way.'

Rose prodded the air with her stick. 'Who are you? Throw off your cloak and reveal yourself.'

To her surprise, the rider did as he was asked. He removed his black cloak and tossed it on to the grass.

Rose gaped. The cloaked rider was now a man. A *shirtless*, barefoot man.

She quickly covered her eyes. 'Goodness! Where is your shirt?'

'I don't like shirts.'

Rose swallowed. 'What about your shoes?'

'I have a hard time finding ones big enough.'

Rose blew out a breath. 'Oh dear.'

'You're not wearing shoes either, but you don't see me

making a big song and dance about it.'

Rose looked at her feet and flinched. They were indeed bare and positively filthy. She must have lost her other shoe in the getaway. No matter, she was still a queen and she would act like it.

She raised her chin, doing her best to ignore his bare chest, as she cut her gaze at her mysterious rescuer. The first thing she noticed – apart from his obvious impudence – was how handsome he was. He had golden-brown skin and dark eyes, and his lips were naturally quirked as though he was teetering on the edge of a smirk. He was impossibly tall and broad, every part of him corded with muscle. His dark wavy hair fell past his shoulders, and it was wind-whipped and dappled with sand.

The second thing Rose noticed was that he looked disconcertingly like Shen, if perhaps a little older. No wonder she thought he was handsome. And yet how peculiar.

She cleared her throat. 'Shoes or not, you are expected to bow to me. And I'll have your name, too.'

The man grinned, revealing a pair of pronounced dimples that momentarily stole her breath. Then he crossed his arm over his stomach and bowed low at the waist. Rose got the sense he was mocking her, but she was distracted by a familiar black horse, thundering across the bridge towards them.

Shen's sword was drawn long before he reached them, but the shirtless rider struck first, unfurling his whip with such speed, Rose only noticed it when it yanked the sword from

Shen's grip. She scolded herself for missing earlier what was now apparent: the rider was a witch, too.

A warrior witch.

More peculiar still.

Shen didn't miss a beat. He leaped from Storm and vaulted through the air, drawing his daggers in twin blurs of silver. He landed in a crouch in front of Rose, ready to strike.

And then, to her surprise, he froze.

The rider had fallen still, too, his whip slack at his side.

'Shen Lo?' he said, in barely more than a whisper. He took a step towards them, blinking in disbelief. 'I swore I was hallucinating when I saw you outside Millis yesterday. I thought it was a trick of the shadows.'

Shen inhaled sharply at the sound of his name in this stranger's mouth. 'Who are you?' he said, warily. 'Why do you seem so familiar to me?'

The rider simply shook his head. 'We thought you were dead.'

'What on earth is going on?' Rose demanded. 'Why were you following us?'

The man looked to Rose. 'They say you're a witch. That your sister is a witch, too.' He took another step, slow and cautious. 'I heard the whisperings in Gallanth on my way here. I knew, then, that you could help me.' He returned his gaze to Shen. 'But no one spoke of you, Shen Lo. I couldn't have known . . . I wouldn't have believed—'

'Say your name.' Shen kept his daggers high, his body positioned like a shield in front of Rose. 'Now.'

The man flashed his teeth. 'Don't you recognize your own cousin?' he said, pressing closer. 'Don't you remember your childhood in the desert? All those times I bested you at horse racing. All those mornings we sparred in the training hall, until you were winded, flat on your back, begging me to stop.'

Shen stiffened, the name bursting from him in a half shout. '*Kai?*'

'Ah!' The rider – Kai – barked a laugh. 'I knew I was unforgettable.'

'Shen?' said Rose, uncertainly. 'Who is this man?'

It was not Shen who answered her. 'My name is Kai Lo. And I come from the Sunkissed Kingdom in the desert.'

Rose frowned. 'The Sunkissed Kingdom is gone,' she said, remembering what Shen had told her about it. Eighteen years ago, the desert had spat him out. He was the only survivor. Banba had found him wandering alone in the desert, all traces of his kingdom gone from this world. His people along with it. 'It was buried long ago.'

'Buried it may be. But it is still living,' said Kai, looking between them. 'And we need your help.'

The silence swelled. Rose felt like her heart was swelling, too. It didn't sound like a lie, but then, how could such a thing be true? She looked to Shen. His hands were slack at his sides, his breath punching out of him in sharp bursts.

'I looked for it,' he said, more to himself than to Kai. 'I've been searching for the Sunkissed Kingdom for eighteen years. It's gone.'

'Things are changing,' said Kai, evenly. 'The desert is stirring again.'

Rose recalled then what the messenger from Gallanth had told her about the roiling desert. She had passed on his message to Shen, too, both of them wondering what on earth it could mean. If it meant anything at all. But never in their wildest imaginings could they have guessed at this.

'Is it possible, Shen?' she whispered. 'Is your home still out there somewhere?'

Kai spread his arms wide. 'You are looking at the proof of it. Three days ago, I managed to claw my way out.'

Rose's mind reeled. How badly she wished Wren was here, to help her navigate the enormity of what she was hearing. She reached for Shen, but he went to his cousin.

'Who else is down there?' he said, his voice hungry. Rose could tell that in that moment she had disappeared for him entirely, that the events in Ellendale had been forgotten. All Shen could see was Kai, standing in front of him, holding the answers to his past. 'Is my mother—'

Kai shook his head.

Shen closed his eyes – and his fists – weathering the news. 'And my father?'

Kai's expression was grim. 'The loss of your mother was too much for him to bear. He passed not long after.' He raised his finger, as if tracing Shen's face. 'You look so much like him.'

Shen dropped his head and drew a shuddering breath. Rose's heart clenched painfully for him. It was one thing to wonder if your family had perished, but another thing to *know* it. To let go of that last kernel of hope inside you. And yet to know that your home had survived, that there were people within it who still remembered you – who *needed* you – well, there was some comfort in that. For Shen, and for her.

'Where exactly is your kingdom buried?' she asked Kai.

Kai's smile turned rueful. 'When the desert spat me out, it was still moving. It hides the kingdom, with every crest, every quake. But with a witch on the throne and the resources of Anadawn Palace, we can track the currents of the sand. We can dig for it. We can finally unbury the Sunkissed Kingdom, and let it shine once again in the sun.' He reached for his whip, winding it around his forearm as he spoke. 'In return, we can help you defend your throne.' His dark eyes flashed. 'My offer couldn't come at a better time, Queenie. From the looks of things back there, you could use all the help you can get.'

In a small clearing, not far from the road, Rose sat with her back against a tree, watching Shen pace back and forth. Kai was down by the river with the horses, allowing them time to discuss his request.

On the one hand, it was madness to consider riding into the endless, arid desert with nothing but a hunch about its lost kingdom. But on the other, Rose could not stomach the idea of going back to Ellendale to face the army who had failed to protect her. According to Shen, Captain Davers had managed to regain control, chasing off most of the Arrows and arresting the ones who couldn't get away in time. But Rose knew word would soon spread of Barron's ambush, and his movement would gain momentum.

After all, he had made Anadawn look weak. He had made *her* look weak.

Rose had never seen Shen so agitated. He wouldn't stop moving, grinding his jaw and flipping his dagger as he paced. 'We have to help him, Rose. There's an entire kingdom of witches trapped in the desert.'

'It's not that I don't want to rescue them,' said Rose, for the tenth time in as many minutes. 'But we don't know *how*, Shen. We don't even know where to begin.'

Shen jerked. 'So, that's it? You're just going to give up and go back to your golden carriage?'

Rose reminded herself that Shen was hurting. 'I'm saying I want to help,' she said, gently. 'I just don't know how.'

He slumped to the ground. The look of pain on his face was so raw, Rose's heart clenched. She pressed a hand to the ache in her chest. Something crumpled beneath her touch. She sat bolt upright. 'I think I have an idea.' With trembling fingers, Rose withdrew the map that Thea had sketched for her from inside her dress. She had carried it with her all this time, keeping her solemn promise to the Queensbreath. 'It's not a map of the desert. But it could be something.'

Shen was on his feet in half a heartbeat. 'The Amarach Towers,' he breathed. 'You have a way to the seers.'

'We don't even know if there *are* any seers left,' Rose cautioned him. 'But we're not far from their valley.' She traced the winding route. 'It's a day's ride south from here. Maybe two.'

Shen came to his knees, touching his head against hers as he studied the map. 'This is it, Rose. If there's anyone in Eana who can help us find the lost kingdom, this is where they'll be.'

Rose's mind whirled. How badly she wished Wren was here, but then, she knew already what her sister would do. She'd have already left for the Amarach Towers by now, and probably stolen Kai's fancy horse to get there.

Shen's voice interrupted her reverie. 'This isn't just about my home. The sooner we find the Sunkissed Kingdom, the stronger we'll be against Barron and whatever else he has in store. And we'll have a fighting chance against Gevra. You saw what Kai can do. There are warriors trapped down there. Seasoned witches. People with powers unlike anything your soldiers have to offer. And you need them, Rose. Just as badly as they need you.'

Shen was right. Kai's request was as much a favour as it was a lifeline. After all, a lost kingdom of witches was a kingdom of allies. And after Captain Davers had walked her into Barron's trap earlier, she could do with as many of those as possible.

'This rediscovery would certainly be a wonderful thing for all of Eana,' she murmured. 'It might just be the thing to unite everyone.'

'Better than a tour,' said Shen. 'If you do this, it will go down in history.'

Excitement tingled in Rose's fingertips as she tucked the

map away. This was the perfect way to prove to everyone, dissenters and supporters alike, that she was the queen Eana needed. The kind not to be trifled with. The kind who ventured into the unknown, at great risk to herself, for the good of her people. She would be Queen Rose the Brave. No, the *Glorious*.

Oh, she did like the sound of that.

Rose pressed a hand to her hip as she stood up, relieved at the jangle of coins there. Clever Agnes. She always warned Rose to keep her coin purse close, just in case. Now she would truly need it. After all, Kai had dragged himself out of the Ganyeve Desert without so much as a shirt, and all Shen's worldly wealth was contained in the golden dagger in his boot and the ruby ring that hung from his neck, which Rose knew he would never part with. Not that she would ever ask him to.

'Of course, it will be dangerous travelling so far south without my guards,' said Rose, more to herself than to Shen. 'I'm currently the only queen Eana has to offer.'

'Rose,' said Shen, with such seriousness she turned to face him. He curled her hand in his. 'You know I'll protect you with my life.'

Suddenly, a whip cracked between them. It sheered a line in the dirt, and nicked the hem of her dress. 'As will I,' said Kai, stepping out from between the trees. Rose could tell by the huge grin on his face that he had heard every word.

Shen glowered at him. 'This was a private conversation.'

'Privacy is for losers, cousin. Now can we go?'

'Very well,' said Rose, as she stood. 'First point of order, I insist you find a shirt.'

Wren
CHAPTER 15

Wren's heart pounded as she was ushered through the glittering halls of Grinstad Palace. Every step brought her closer to King Alarik, a ruler whose fearsome reputation stretched far beyond the Sunless Sea, and whose hatred for Wren – and Rose – ran so deep, he might well kill her on sight.

Tor was silent at Wren's side, but she could hear the whistle of his quickened breath as he marched her away from the courtyard of beasts. From one danger, into another. But Wren had begged him for an audience with the king, and with the eyes of his fellow soldiers on him in that bloodied arena, Tor had no choice but to take her. Unlike Vidar, Tor kept his sword in its scabbard and walked alongside her, allowing her the brief illusion that she was not his prisoner.

His hands were clenched so tight his knuckles were white. Wren's fingers itched to reach out to them, to kiss those hands for saving her – three times now, but she had cost him enough already.

'I know you're angry at me.' She kept her voice low, mindful of the soldiers who watched them go by. 'But I had to come, Tor. Alarik took my grandmother.'

Tor only shook his head, his jaw so hard it looked like marble.

Wren hated his silence. 'Did you expect me to stay at Anadawn and doom Banba to the obsession of your terrible king?'

Finally, he looked at her. 'I expected you to stay alive, Wren.'

'I *am* alive.'

'For now.'

Wren wrung her hands. She couldn't afford to worry about herself. 'Have you seen Banba? Is she still alive?'

A new shadow crossed his face. 'She's not making it easy on herself. You are alike in that way. Stubborn. Hot-headed.'

Wren relaxed her shoulders. 'That means she hasn't lost hope yet. She must know I'm coming for her.'

Tor bit off a curse. 'Hang your hope, Wren. I can't protect you outside the arena.'

Wren knew that well enough already. The beasts in Gevra might bow to Tor, but the king and his men did not. 'I don't expect you to protect me. You don't owe me anything.'

Tor ran a hand through his hair, unsettling the wavy strands. 'Not everything is a transaction, Wren.'

'Maybe not. But you've already risked enough for me.'

He was silent, then. He couldn't find a way to deny it.

'I'm sorry for what happened to Ansel,' said Wren. 'For taking Elske. For all of it.'

'I know,' he said, and for the briefest heartbeat, his hand brushed against hers. Wren didn't know if it was deliberate, but the barest touch of his skin made her heart hitch. They came to the end of the hallway, only to turn down another, the winter sun pouring in through the arched windows and threading strands of copper through Tor's hair. Wren guessed by the number of guards stationed along the corridor that Alarik Felsing was close at hand.

Her stomach twisted, her desire lost in the sudden swell of her fear. 'Tor,' she whispered.

'I'll stay with you,' he said.

Wren was embarrassed for wanting it. For needing it. And yet, the relief at those four words flooded her like morning sunlight.

Presently, they arrived at a pair of iron doors. They were intricately carved with Gevran beasts, everything from nighthawks and silverjays to snow leopards and reindeer. In the centre, along the seam, the Great Bear, Bernhard of Gevra, stood mid-roar, his mighty paws curled into two silver handles. Wren's breath shallowed as Tor took hold of one. She imagined the bear opening its dripping mouth and swallowing her up as the doors swung open.

An icy wind swept over her, casting goosebumps along her arms. She stalled in the doorway, blinking into the sudden dimness.

Tor's hand was warm against her back. 'Wren.'

She tried to trap that heat inside her as she stepped over the threshold and on to a marble floor so polished, she could see her own refection in it.

The throne room at Grinstad Palace yawned around Wren like a glacial cavern, cold and hollow and absent of any natural light. Huge white columns climbed up to an arched ceiling that depicted the great wars of Gevra, a sprawling mural of sparring beasts and bloodied soldiers that looked even more dramatic in the flickering sconce light.

Wren snapped her chin down before fear got the better of her. Tor nudged her onward, his voice feathering the shell of her ear. 'Mind your temper. And your tongue.'

They passed endless white pillars, where soldiers and their beasts looked on dispassionately. Snow tigers skulked in the shadows, while two wolves, one grey and one black, prowled alongside Wren, matching her step for step. If she wasn't so terrified, she might have complimented Tor on their impeccable training.

They came at last to a marble dais, upon which sat a formidable crystal throne. The shards were so sharp, it looked like cut glass, but Wren didn't linger over the impressive carpentry nor the ice bear slumbering to one side of it. Her gaze fell on the king, who was reclining on his throne.

In a room full of beasts, Alarik Felsing was the most ferocious creature of all. He was dressed in black, his high-collared frock coat embroidered with delicate threads of silver that shimmered faintly in the candlelight. His hair was as blond as summer wheat, save for the black streak that cut into it like a line of spilled ink, and his skin was as pale as ivory. Shadows pooled under his cheekbones and beneath his pale blue eyes, which were fixed firmly on Wren.

'So, my soldiers have spoken true. A queen of Eana walks the halls of Grinstad Palace.' His voice echoed back at her from every corner of the cavernous room. 'I'm surprised you didn't swing in from the chandelier.'

'I'm nothing if not unpredictable.' Wren summoned the ghost of a smile. 'I got your invitation.'

'I was hoping you'd take it literally.' The king pitched forward in his seat. 'Go on, Wren. Say those hateful things to my face.'

Tor looked between them with obvious confusion. The king's note was a game, but clearly Alarik liked to play alone.

'Let's not waste time on well-trodden ground,' said Wren. 'Now that I'm here, why don't we talk?'

Alarik's face darkened. 'I don't do casual conversation.'

'Well, that's one thing we have in common.'

Alarik flicked his gaze to Tor. 'Search her. Thoroughly.'

Wren bristled as Tor turned on her. 'Don't be ridiculous,' she protested. 'You hardly think I came in here armed?'

'And you hardly think I'd take you at your word?' countered Alarik.

Tor didn't look at Wren as he searched her. He was the perfect Gevran soldier, stone-faced as he patted her down, his hands sliding over her shoulders, and then her waist. She closed her eyes, trying to distract herself from his touch, the memories conjured by his alpine scent.

'You look like you're enjoying that,' mused Alarik.

Wren snapped her eyes open. *Mind your temper.* It took every ounce of her self-control not to tell Alarik exactly what she thought of him.

Tor moved down to her trousers.

'Don't,' she hissed, trying to push him off, but he was too quick. Too good. He found her drawstring pouch and held it up to King Alarik.

'Sand,' he said, as he stepped away from her. The betrayal was small, but Wren felt it like a slap in the face.

Alarik's eyes gleamed. 'What was that you were saying just now about trust?'

Wren snorted. 'Sand is hardly a weapon.'

'Unless, of course, you use it for your spells.'

Wren folded her arms. 'I didn't know you knew about that.'

'You'd be surprised at the things I know,' he said, darkly.

Wren cleared her throat. 'I feel like we've got off to a bad start.'

'We can trace our bad start to the day you killed my brother,' said the king, so casually Wren thought she had misheard him. He went on, without pause. 'You are the one my longest-serving captain saved over Prince Ansel.' He flicked his gaze to Tor. 'But of course you already knew that, Tor. You can tell the enchanter and the healer apart, can you not?' He didn't wait for Tor's response. 'What I want to know is why you didn't confiscate that sand before you brought her before your king.'

'Forgive my oversight, Your Majesty.' Tor dipped his head in shame, and not for the first time, Wren wanted to launch herself on to the dais and pummel the king in his perfectly sculpted face.

'Willem Rathborne is the reason your brother's dead,' she said, instead. 'And, as it happens, I have already taken care of that problem for you. He went up in smoke, like the rest of the Vault.'

Alarik's smirk was mirthless. 'Have you come for a reward?'

'I've come for my grandmother. But since you got my letter, you already know that.'

'Every beast in my palace knows that,' said Alarik, drolly. He gestured to the hulking white bear slumbering by his throne. 'Even Borvil, and he's in hibernation.'

'How much do you want for her freedom?' said Wren. 'Name your price.'

Alarik's smirk grew, revealing the pearly glint of his canines. 'There isn't enough money in the world, Wren.'

'There must be something you want,' she pressed. 'Everyone has a price.'

Alarik stood up, his tallness exaggerated by the dais as he looked down on her. 'I want my brother back.'

Wren shifted, uncomfortably. He had chosen the one thing she couldn't grant him, just to watch her squirm. 'I'm sorry about what happened to Ansel. If I could go back—'

'But you can't, can you?' said Alarik, a strange hunger glowing in his eyes. The ice bear stirred in his sleep, as if alerted to the shift in his master's mood. 'There is no witch that possesses such power. Is there?'

'No,' said Wren, slowly.

He came down the steps towards her. 'But you are an enchanter. A *manipulator*. You can change things.'

'Yes . . .' Wren had a bad feeling about that ravenous look in his eyes, the sudden urgency in his voice.

Alarik stopped on the step above her. There was nothing between them now, no soldiers or beasts, just the clouds of their breath. 'The old witch hasn't said a word since we set sail from your country. She won't speak. Will barely eat. The only time she opens her mouth is to spit on my soldiers.'

Wren bit back her smile. 'Banba can be a little cantankerous.'

'And what are you? Impulsive. Reckless. Loyal to a fault.' Alarik cocked his head, snaring her in his bright gaze. 'Your note revealed you, Wren. And now here you are, confirming my suspicions.'

The accuracy in the king's descriptions stung – not to mention the way he fired them at her like arrows – but Wren was careful not to show her hurt. 'Loyalty has no limit,' she said, steadily. 'Not the truest kind.'

The hardness in Alarik's face softened and, for the briefest moment, he looked just like Ansel. Human, almost. 'That is another thing on which we agree.'

'My grandmother will only get worse with time,' said Wren. 'You're better off releasing her before she starts biting the soldiers. That's when the real trouble starts.'

'I can't release her,' said Alarik. 'You see, I need a witch.'

'What for?' asked Wren, warily.

'King's business.' He fixed his sleeve, lingering over a cufflink shaped like a wolf's fang. 'However, an uncooperative witch is as useful to me as a rotten barrel of meat. I admit I have been considering feeding your grandmother to my tigers for her insolence. At least to make use of all that grisliness.'

Wren froze. 'You wouldn't.'

Alarik quirked a brow. 'Wouldn't I?'

She looked to Tor. His expression was grim.

'And since you say she'll only get worse with time . . .' Alarik went on.

'Trade with me, then,' said Wren, seized by a sudden fit of desperation. 'I propose a switch.'

Alarik stilled. 'A switch.'

'Wren,' said Tor, breaking his stony silence.

Alarik raised his hand, restoring it.

It was too late to take it back now. Wren had been swept up by an idea so wild it had leaped out of her before she could stop it. But Alarik had made it seem like the only way forward, the only way to save her grandmother. 'If you want a cooperative witch, you can have one,' said Wren. She paused then, the colour prickling from her cheeks as the fullness of his plan came into focus. 'That's why you sent that note, isn't it?'

Alarik smiled. 'You see right through me, Wren.'

Wren tried not to think of her sister in that moment. If Rose was here, she'd strangle her for making such a stupid suggestion. But Rose would never be foolish enough to come to Gevra on a whim, to risk everything. To lose everything. If this was Wren's only hope, then it would be her penance, too. After all, everything came at a price. And her sister was a better queen than Wren was anyway, a smarter ruler. Rose *wanted* to rule. But the throne meant nothing to Wren without Banba. Rose could take care of Eana in her absence. With Shen Lo by her side, and an entire army to command, she could face down Barron and his Arrows. And soon, Banba would be with her. Banba would help her.

But first Wren had to free her.

'You can have me,' said Wren.

Tor's voice rang out. 'No.'

Alarik turned on him. 'Remind me, Tor. Which of us is king?'

'Wren is a queen of Eana,' said Tor. 'You cannot keep her here, under lock and key. Not without consequences.'

Alarik narrowed his eyes. 'Would you prefer I kill her for her crimes and be done with it?' He whistled through his teeth and his two wolves came prowling out from the shadows. 'Luna, Nova. Who wants breakfast?'

Tor raised his hand, stopping the beasts in their tracks. 'Alarik,' he said, in a low voice. 'Be reasonable.'

The king flashed his teeth. 'Careful, Tor. Your composure is slipping.'

Wren looked between the men. She was losing her footing, caught in some twisted game of power and possession. The king was angry at Tor for what had happened to Ansel – that much was clear. Now he was using Wren to test him. To break him. If she didn't seize control of the conversation, it would unravel completely.

'I'll help you with whatever your secret mission is,' she said, climbing on to Alarik's step, using herself as a distraction. 'I'll teach you everything you wish to know about magic. All I ask is that you let my grandmother go.'

'And if I don't?' said Alarik.

'Then you'll have two uncooperative witches on your hands.'

'Or two dead ones.'

Wren smiled, thinly. 'And a war. With a great many more witches. The kind that *will* cooperate. To kill you.'

Alarik swallowed hard.

A swell of triumph rose inside Wren. Her threat had landed. As much as the Gevran king was fascinated by the witches, he was terrified of them, too.

So, what, then, did he need one for?

The doors to the throne room swung open, startling them from their negotiation. Princess Anika Felsing arrived in a fury, her crimson hair flying after her as she stomped towards them. Her long black dress billowed around her like the wings of a butterfly.

'What is that traitorous bitch doing here?' she cried, the cavernous room turning her anger operatic. 'And why in freezing hell is she still alive?'

Alarik sighed. 'Darling Anika, you must learn to knock.'

The last time Wren had seen the crimson-haired princess of Gevra, Anika had sent her snow leopard to devour Wren on the banks of the Silvertongue, only to be thwarted at the last second by Elske. For all the fury Anika felt towards Wren, Wren possessed just as much for her. But she was on foreign soil and without a weapon, so she banked her temper and waggled her fingers at the fuming princess. 'Nice to see you, too, Anika.'

'It won't be nice when I jam the heel of my shoe into your skull.'

Alarik rolled his eyes. 'Charming. Tor, restrain her.'

Tor caught Anika before she could fling herself at Wren. He swung her around, clamping his arms around her until she stopped flailing. Wren hated the hum of jealousy she felt at watching them tussle.

'Easy, Anika.' Alarik addressed his sister like one of his beasts. 'Remember Father's rule? We don't make scenes in the throne room.'

'She killed Ansel!' hissed Anika. 'She's the reason our brother is dead!' Anika turned her seething rage back to Wren. 'You're an arrogant fool for setting foot in Gevra. I don't care how many witches you have back in Eana. I'll have your head before you leave here. You won't get away with what you did!'

Tor tightened his grip on the princess, until her kicking feet dangled three inches above the floor. At Alarik's insistence, he hauled her away, until only the echo of her wails remained.

Wren fought the urge to run out of the throne room after them. She would take Tor and the tantrum-throwing Gevran princess any day over the singular presence of King Alarik.

Alarik waited until the doors were closed before he spoke again. 'Grief has made my dear sister rabid,' he said, with something remarkably close to concern. 'She's not usually so . . .'

'Murderous?'

Alarik paused. 'I suppose so.'

The king's black suit took on a new significance, as did

the dark shadows under his eyes. Grinstad Palace was in mourning. And there was part of Wren – just the barest sliver – that felt bad for him.

He tucked his hands behind his back as he stepped down off the dais. 'Won't your country miss you if you stay here?' he said, as though they were discussing the weather and not the total surrender of Wren's freedom. 'You are, after all, a new queen.'

'I suppose that's the benefit of having two of us,' she said, with a shrug. 'One to rule. And one to—'

'Break into foreign palaces.' Alarik walked on, and Wren got the sense she was to follow. 'How reckless you are, Wren.'

Wren hated her name in his mouth. 'I prefer the term "proactive".'

The king snorted. 'You could have died in my courtyard today.'

'But crucially, I didn't.'

'Luckily Captain Iversen was close enough to hear your screams. He does have a certain knack for keeping you alive. Which is fortuitous, since you seem to lack that ability yourself.'

'You speak like I'm some kind of dimwit,' muttered Wren.

'The facts are speaking. I am merely listening.'

Wren had to fight the urge to shove him into a pillar. 'Is this the part where you welcome me to Gevra with open arms?'

'This is the part where I decide whether or not I want to tolerate you in Gevra,' Alarik corrected. 'I am still considering your offer.'

Wren's fingers twitched. The sooner Banba was safely out of Gevra and back with Rose at Anadawn, the sooner she could find a way to trick the king and follow her home. 'How long does it take you to make a decision?'

'As long as I please.'

'Great. Who doesn't love an indecisive king?'

'Or indeed a flighty queen,' he shot back.

Wren glared at him.

'Tell me, Queen Wren,' said Alarik. 'Why did you so readily abandon your own kingdom to sneak into my palace on the back of a sled, dressed like an unkempt peasant?' He gestured to her tunic, then the messy strands around her face. 'Why not arrive in your crown and full regalia to discuss the terms of your bargain? Or did you think I'd be more receptive to a common kitchen thief than a queen from the country that killed my brother?'

Wren weighed her answer. 'Honestly, I was hoping not to cross paths with you at all.'

'Well, now I'm offended.' Alarik swept a stray strand from his eyes, drawing her attention to the black streak in his hair. 'I'm an excellent host.'

'Oh, so you don't always maul your guests to death in your own personal killing arena, then?'

'Only the thieves.' Alarik stopped walking. He turned towards Wren until she stood alone in the spotlight of his glare. 'In truth, it's your recklessness that appeals to me. The way in which you barrel through the world, without thought for consequence or regret.' He dropped his voice, so even the soldiers couldn't listen in. 'You see, I need a witch to do something reckless for me.'

Unease churned in Wren's gut She felt suddenly that she had made a terrible mistake by coming here.

Alarik stepped back. 'If you stay here, you will help me with what I need. If this is another one of your schemes, you won't fool me. And if you try, you will meet the full wrath of Gevra.' He pointed to the ceiling, and Wren looked up at the art that covered it, at a hundred different wars depicted in rivers of crimson – bloodshed and victory and death, bodies broken on frozen ground, beasts roaring in their chains. 'Believe me, witch. You will not like it.'

Wren swallowed, thickly. 'I'm not afraid of you.'

'Not yet.' Alarik snapped his fingers, and a pair of stern-faced soldiers stepped out of the shadows. 'Take her away. You'll have my answer by nightfall.'

Wren was hauled out of the throne room, no longer a queen of her own country, but a prisoner of another.

Rose

CHAPTER 16

Before they set off in earnest, Rose insisted on stopping in the town of Bridge End to write two hasty letters.

The first, to Thea, back at Anadawn. And the other, to Chapman, who was probably still on the road in Ellendale. Rose didn't include any details, only word that she was safe, and that they were not to come after her. She would be back soon. It was not lost on her that she was sending the very same sort of infuriating letter that Wren had left on her pillow. And Rose's resentment towards her sister softened, if only a little.

Rose hid with Kai and the horses while Shen tied the first letter to a carrier pigeon he had liberated from the local postal house, and entrusted the other to a young courier, paying the girl a full gold coin to ride back towards Ellendale, in search of the royal retinue.

With the letters safely dispatched, Shen slipped into a nearby boarding house to pilfer a satchel, which he stuffed with a homespun servant's dress, a pair of shoes, a hairbrush and a nightgown, as well as some food for the journey.

Blushing furiously, Rose changed into the dress behind a tree on the outskirts of town, while Shen and Kai watched the crossroads for passers-by.

With great reluctance, Rose removed her crown. 'What should we do with this? I can hardly take it with me. It's far too conspicuous'

'Give it here, Queenie. I have an idea.' Rose watched in abject horror as Kai flung her crown into the river. 'Some lucky trout is about to become very rich.'

Shen glared at his cousin. 'What is wrong with you?'

'The design was poor,' said Kai, with a snort. 'You'll see true craftsmanship when we reach the Sunkissed Kingdom. There are rubies there as big as my head.'

'Hopefully they're not as hollow,' said Rose, as she prodded him in the chest. 'You owe me a crown, Kai Lo.'

After Bridge End, they rode south, only stopping for a brief snack of sourdough bread smothered with cheese and chutney. Rose noticed Shen sneaking glances at Kai as they ate, as if he was afraid that if he lost sight of his cousin, he might disappear again. Her heart ached for him, and for everything she knew he wanted to ask Kai about the Sunkissed Kindgom, his home, his past.

Late that evening, they came to a small town. 'Perhaps we can stay here for the night. They must have an inn of some sort.' She slid off Storm and dusted her skirts off, leading the way. 'Come.'

'Careful. This might be an Arrow stronghold.' Shen nodded at the domed building at the entrance to the town. 'They have a Vault.'

'Almost every town in Eana has a Vault. That doesn't mean anything,' said Rose, just as the door swung open and three men stumbled out. The old man in front was holding a lantern, and the two behind him were younger. They looked like brothers. One had long black hair and an unruly beard, while the other was nearly bald.

'What are you three gawking at?' said the bearded brother, his hand going to the knife at his waist.

'I wouldn't do that if I was you,' warned Kai.

'Pardon us,' Rose cut in, deftly. 'We're merely a troupe of travelling musicians passing through your darling little town.'

'You talk awful fancy,' said the other brother, suspiciously.

'Thank you,' said Rose, subtly fixing her hood. 'I had elocution lessons as a child.'

'Sing us a song,' slurred the old man, stumbling as he came down the steps. 'Do you know "Tell the Wolves I'm Coming"?'

The bearded one circled Storm. 'I'd bet my best belt that's a desert horse.' He reached out to touch her, but Shen reacted lightning fast, slapping his hand away. Beard moved in front of Storm, blocking their way. 'Tell me, traveller. Do you shoot the arrow straight and true?'

Shen didn't even blink. 'I'm an excellent archer if that's what you mean.'

'It's not,' he said, raising his palm to reveal the raised

inking of an arrow. 'Are you telling me you've never come across our kind on your travels?'

'No,' said Shen, tersely. 'Please move out of our way.'

Beard bent down and picked up a rock. Without warning, he flung it straight at Rose.

Shen reacted in a blur, one hand braced on his horse as he kicked it away. It whizzed through the air and embedded in the Vault door. He bit off a curse, but it was too late.

'Witches,' sneered Bald. 'I could smell 'em.'

The old man brandished his knife. 'We've been preparing for your kind.'

'Not well enough,' said Shen, who knocked him out with a single, spinning kick. His lantern fell to the ground with a clatter, the oil inside it spilling out. Flames licked the cobblestones as the bald man lunged, but Shen struck again, cracking his nose with the palm of his hand. He fell backwards, dazed.

Rose winced at the crunching sound.

Beard grabbed the lantern and flung it at Kai. 'Burn, witch!'

Kai stepped out of the way. The lantern landed in a nearby bush, where, with a hiss and crackle, the entire shrub burst into flame.

'My turn.' Kai knocked Beard out with one swift punch.

'Time to go!' said Rose, clambering on to the nearest horse, which happened to belong to Kai, just as the doors to the Vault opened and more people came pouring out. They raced down the dusty street, alongside Shen and Storm.

Rose glanced over her shoulder. 'They're following us!'

Kai winked at Shen. 'Time to put your desert horse to the test, cousin.'

'Storm's been riding under the sky her whole life,' scoffed Shen. 'Your horse is the one out of practice.'

'Pah! Victory's been waiting years to stretch his legs.'

'Are you two really bickering over which horse is faster?' said Rose. 'Surely, now is not the time.'

They both ignored her.

'A name doesn't make a winner,' said Shen. 'There's no horse under the sun as fast as Storm.'

'We'll see about that.' Kai whacked Victory's rump, who somehow began to gallop *even* faster.

'Kai!' shrieked Rose. 'Slow this horse, at once!'

Behind them, Shen let out a shout, and soon Storm was matching Victory stride for stride, both men laughing so hard, Rose could barely hear herself shout. 'It looks like it's a tie! Well done, everyone!'

'The race has only just begun,' yelled Kai. 'My horse can ride all night.'

'I'm not riding Storm to her death to prove her worth,' Shen yelled back. 'We'll race to the next bridge, and when I win, you can bow to Storm and kiss her hooves.'

With that, he took off in a whip of cool wind.

'No chance!' said Kai, laughing as he chased him. And even as the wind howled in Rose's ears and she clung on to Victory for dear life, she found herself laughing, too.

After an hour of thunderous horse racing, Shen and Storm pulled ahead, arriving at the next bridge in swirling plumes of dust. Seconds later, Victory, carrying Kai and Rose on his back, barrelled into them, and nearly knocked Storm into the river.

'Watch yourself!' shouted Shen. 'You lost. At least be a dignified loser.'

'There's no such thing as a dignified loser,' said Kai. 'And this race was rigged from the start. Victory had to carry an extra person. Next time, I'll win.'

'Next time, I'll throw you in the river, Kai.'

'Give it a rest, you two,' said Rose, wearily. 'It's dark. Let's keep going.'

The men stewed in silence as the moon rose overhead, dappling them in silvery light. They journeyed onward, into the town of Hollyfort.

'We can stay here for the night,' said Shen, who was scouring the doors for painted arrows. 'It looks like a safe spot. And the horses need a rest.'

'As do I,' said Kai, through a sprawling yawn. 'And I could eat an entire boar.'

Rose eyed the dark streets, warily. 'Just be careful not to cause any trouble this time. The doors might be unmarked but there could be Arrows here.'

Something rustled nearby. 'Look!' she said, her voice hitching. 'There's something moving in those bushes!'

Kai tensed.

Shen had a dagger in hand, ready to leap.

The bush let out a low growl, and then a huge white blur shot out of it and bounded straight at Victory. The horse reared up with a whinny, nearly throwing Rose and Kai off. The blur – which had become a beast – snapped at Kai's ankles.

'Rotting hell,' cursed Kai. 'It's a wolf!'

Shen began to laugh. 'I think we're good,' he said, pocketing the dagger. 'Unless Elske also has a twin.'

'Elske?' Rose gasped. 'Is that you?'

Elske was far too busy snarling at Kai to acknowledge Rose.

'Since you two know this rabid beast, can you please call it off,' he hissed. 'Or else I'm going down there and taking a dagger to it.'

'Don't you dare!' Rose slid off Victory. 'Shh, shh, darling,' she said, coming to her knees. 'It's all right now. You found me.'

The wolf stopped snarling and nuzzled into Rose's skirt, smearing it with even more dirt. Rose smiled as she stroked the spot between the wolf's ears, seized by a new wave of affection for her. Having Elske here made her feel closer to Wren. 'Why did you follow me all the way down here?'

'Wren probably told her to keep an eye you,' said Shen. 'She's protecting you.'

'By trying to kill me?' said Kai, eyeing the beast uneasily.

Shen smirked. 'Maybe.'

'Her disdain for you merely proves that she is an excellent judge of character.' Rose stood up and shook out her skirts, trying not to dismay at the dirt that cascaded from them. 'We'll be much safer travelling with Elske . . . if a bit more conspicuous.'

'A bit!' scoffed Kai. 'Send her back right now.'

'No,' said Shen and Rose, in perfect unison.

'The wolf stays,' added Rose. 'If you have a problem with that, then you may leave.'

Kai pouted but said nothing. The matter was settled.

'There's an inn just up ahead.' Shen pointed towards a tall building at the end of the street. Candlelight glowed faintly from its windows and the sign above the door said *The Straggler's Rest*. 'Elske will have to hide outside while we go in, but we can see about sneaking her in later.'

As it turned out, getting a room at the Straggler's Rest proved to be somewhat of a headache.

'Late summer is our busiest time, I'm afraid,' said the burly innkeeper, his pearly smile shining against his brown skin. 'But I might be able to scrounge something up.' He whistled to get the attention of another man, who appeared to be doubling as both the barkeep and the cook. 'Todrick, is the attic room in any condition for guests?'

Todrick wrinkled his nose. 'We got the bats out this morning. Or at least most of them. I'll send Marianna up to open the window. Air it out a bit.'

The innkeeper clapped his hands, turning back to them. 'It'll be a tight squeeze.' He gestured at Kai's formidable build. 'Especially with him. But it's the best I can do.'

'We appreciate it,' said Shen.

'Isn't there another room?' Rose flushed. 'I'm sure those two won't mind sharing, but a qu— *lady* really does need her space.'

The innkeeper simply shrugged. 'It's all I've got, miss.

We're the last inn for miles. There's a fancier inn back in Ellendale, if you want to try your luck—'

'Ellendale?' Rose's voice rose an entire octave. 'No, no. I think we'll stay here. We'll be pressing on in the morning. We're travelling musicians, you see, and we've got a job with . . .' She wracked her brain, grasping for a noble family that lived down south. 'Lord Shannon and his family. Down in Golders Glen.'

'If you get an early start tomorrow, you'll reach the Glen by nightfall,' said Todrick, helpfully. 'But bring a fair luncheon. There's nothing between here and there.'

'Except the Poisonweed Valley,' muttered the innkeeper. 'But you'd be best to avoid it. Folks who trek through there don't come out the same.'

'If they come out at all,' added Todrick, ominously. 'The air down there addles the mind.'

Rose and Shen exchanged a look.

'Never mind about that now,' said the innkeeper. 'Will you be wanting the attic room or not? I'll throw in a free supper for the trouble.'

Kai rubbed his hands together. 'Let's eat.'

Rose blew out a breath. It was just for one night. And she was not a queen here in Hollyfort, but a travelling musician. Safe from prying eyes and wagging tongues. And besides, she'd much rather sleep in a bed, protected by two seasoned warriors, than sleep outside where who knows what might stumble upon them.

'We'll take it,' she said, summoning a smile. 'With gratitude.'

After a supper of lamb stew and soggy carrots, Todrick showed them to their room at the top of a creaking staircase. 'You three go on in,' he said, at the door. 'I don't think we'll all fit in there.'

'Oh!' exclaimed Rose as she stepped through the door and nearly banged her head on a low beam. The attic room was tucked into the eaves of the building and was so cramped that Kai's head brushed against the ceiling.

There was a small window overlooking the town square and a stained wash basin in the corner. The rest of the meagre space was occupied by the bed.

Todrick waved at them from the doorway. 'If you need to relieve yourselves in the night, there are buckets under the bed, and the privy is out back.'

'Delightful,' said Rose, in a strained voice. 'Thank you for your hospitality.'

Todrick eyed the three of them curiously. 'Well . . . have a good night, then.' As soon as he closed the door, Kai tossed his whip aside and flopped on to the bed. The springs groaned as he splayed out, his fingers brushing both sides of the mattress.

'Claiming it now!' he said, with his face in a pillow.

'You may certainly not!' said Rose, grabbing the other pillow to thwack the back of his head.

Kai chuckled, as he turned over. 'I'd like to see you make me move with those little hairpin arms.'

Rose gasped in affront.

'Allow me.' Shen folded himself into a ball and leaped on to the bed. The mattress rebounded, jostling Kai over the other side, where he landed on the floor with a resounding thud.

Rose collapsed into peals of laughter.

Kai sprang up, whip in hand. He pulled it taut, cracking it between his fists. 'Little cousin, you are going to regret that.'

Shen sidestepped Kai's advance. 'Too slow, cousin.'

Kai smirked as he drew his whip back. 'We'll see.'

'Stop it!' Rose leaped between them. 'Behave, both of you! We can't afford to draw any more attention to ourselves.' She cleared her throat. 'I will be taking the bed. With Elske. You may each have a pillow.'

'How generous of you, Queenie.' Kai grabbed a pillow and stretched out on the floor at the end of the bed. 'The desert would be more comfortable than this,' he grumbled, kicking his boots off in two determined thunks.

'Speaking of Elske,' said Shen, going to the window. 'I should fetch her.'

Rose came to stand next to him, all too aware of how close their faces were in the narrow frame.

'I'll go down and wait for the coast to clear. Then I'll sneak the wolf back up.' He pinned Kai with a warning look. 'You stay there. On the floor.'

Kai waved him off. 'Don't worry about your queen's virtue. If she was my type, I would already have seduced her.'

'Excuse me?' Rose tossed her hair, frustrated by the tangles. 'What is that supposed to mean?'

'Nothing personal.' Kai gave her a wolfish grin, 'I wouldn't assume to be your type either, but I've seen how you look at my cousin, and, let's be honest, I'm just a better-looking, bigger version of him.'

Shen stood over Kai, his boot dangling just above his crotch. 'What was that?'

Kai chuckled as he rolled over. 'You two are so highly strung. Must be all that repressed desire.' He smirked into his pillow. 'Anyone with eyes can see how you lust after each other. Don't let my being here stop you from finally doing something about it.'

Rose spluttered at Kai's words, but she had momentarily lost the power of speech.

Shen was looking anywhere but at her, his cheeks redder than she'd ever seen them.

'Elske,' Rose managed finally. 'You should—'

'Right. I'll go now.' Shen bolted from the room like he was fleeing a fire.

Rose sagged against the window ledge as Kai broke out into laughter. 'That was so much more fun than sparring with him,' he crowed. 'You really should put my cousin out of his misery. Either let him in your bed or tell him it's never going to happen. You can't keep him at arm's length forever.'

Rose stiffened. 'You have no idea what you're talking about. And I'll remind you, *yet again*, that I am your queen.'

'Then I'll save my advice for someone who appreciates it,' Kai mumbled, as he closed his eyes. 'Goodnight, Queenie.' In a matter of moments, he was fast asleep, the rattle of his snores thundering throughout the little room.

When Shen returned a few minutes later, he was cradling Elske to his chest, the snowy wolf wrapped up in his cloak until only her snout and tail stuck out.

'You *carried* her up here?' said Rose.

Shen shut the door with his foot. 'I figured if anyone stopped me, I'd just pretend she was you.'

Rose stared at the cloaked wolf as he set her down. '*Me?*'

Elske immediately bounded on to the bed and curled up. 'Well, my plan was to say you had twisted your ankle on the way to the privy and . . .' He trailed off.

'Grew a tail?' teased Rose.

Shen rubbed the back of his neck. 'Anyway, it's done now.' He eyed his snoring cousin. 'He sounds like a dying donkey.'

'He really must have been exhausted.' Rose yawned as she sat down on the bed. 'It's been a very long day.'

'How are you feeling about Barron? And Wren? And, well, everything?' Shen gingerly sat down next to her, only to stiffen when the springs groaned.

Rose desperately wished there wasn't a wolf in her bed. Or an annoying warrior witch on the floor. Or a whole chasm of things unsaid – undone – between them.

'I think I'm still in shock,' she admitted. 'I can't think about Wren too much or dwell on what she might be facing in Gevra because it makes me too scared. And I can't afford to be scared right now, Shen. I have to be strong.'

Shen turned his body towards her, lifting her chin with his finger. 'Rose, you are the strongest person I know.'

Rose gazed into his night-dark eyes. Before she could second-guess herself, she pitched forward and pressed her lips against his. Shen froze, surprise stilling the muscles in his body for an agonizing moment. Then he leaned in, his lips parting as he kissed her back. He grew bolder, hungrier, sliding his fingers into her hair as he pulled her against him, sending a delicious shock of heat through Rose's body.

Rose sighed with pleasure as he slid his tongue into her mouth, feeling like she might burst into flames—

Then Elske growled, and the moment shattered.

Rose pulled away, suddenly all too aware of their surroundings. There was a wolf on the bed and a man on the floor! Snoring! No, wait. Not snoring. He was *chuckling*.

'Is that it?' said Kai, who was sitting up now, and unabashedly staring at them. 'Don't let me stop you.'

Rose buried her face in her hands. Thank goodness for Elske.

'*Rose, you are the strongest person I know,*' mimicked Kai. 'That's a line if I ever heard one.'

In a flash, Shen's knee was on Kai's chest, his dagger at his throat. 'Cousin or not, I will spill your blood all over this floor.'

Kai cocked a brow. 'For what? You were the one with your tongue in her mouth.'

'Shen, it's all right,' said Rose, through her fingers. This was her fault. She shouldn't have kissed him. Not now, not here. 'Please put the dagger away.'

Shen leaned back on his heels and stood up. 'I don't

remember you being this annoying,' he said, sliding his dagger back into his boot.

Kai's eyes danced in the moonlit dark. 'A lot has changed since you were home, little cousin.' With that he turned over, and within seconds, was snoring again.

Rose stared down at him. 'I've never known anyone to fall asleep so quickly.'

'We should get some sleep, too,' said Shen, scrubbing a hand through his hair. 'Tomorrow's going to be a big day.' He stepped over Kai, and rounded the other side of the bed, where he kicked off his boots and stretched out on the floor.

'Here. Take a pillow, at least,' said Rose, tossing him one before crawling under the covers and settling in the middle of the bed, with Elske curled up at her feet.

'Goodnight, Rose,' said Shen, quietly.

'Goodnight, Shen.'

Rose slowly inched her way across the bed, and casually let her hand drop, as if she had done it by accident. It hung limply for a moment, and then she felt the warm touch of Shen's fingers as they threaded through hers. He pressed a kiss against them. The heat of it rushed through her body, until she wanted nothing more than to tug him up on to the bed and let him kiss her properly. Endlessly.

But if she couldn't have that, then she would have this. Her hand in Shen's and the gentle rhythm of his breath as he fell asleep right next to her.

When his grip loosened and his hand fell, and Rose was sure he was asleep, she leaned over the edge of the bed and peered down at him, grateful for the moonlight that slipped in through the window.

In his sleep, Shen looked peaceful. Rose let herself admire his features, the strong line of his jaw and the soft curve of his lips, the shadow of his lashes against his cheeks.

Then Elske farted, the thunder of it startling Rose so much she nearly rolled out of bed on top of Shen. She scrambled back to the middle and squeezed her eyes shut, willing herself to fall asleep. Shen was right. Tomorrow was a big day.

Wren

CHAPTER 17

Night fell in the capital city of Grinstad, and still, Wren received no word from King Alarik about her proposed bargain. His soldiers had locked her in a room on the fourth floor of the palace, where she had been waiting impatiently since morning. She may have been a prisoner of Gevra, but her cell was a surprisingly luxurious one.

The bedchamber was almost the same size as Rose's room back at Anadawn. A crystal chandelier dangled from the corniced ceiling, the walls adorned with navy wallpaper that shimmered faintly in the flickering light. The gold furniture was so ornate Wren had hesitated to sit down at first, the couch and matching chairs piled with tasselled cushions of ivory and silver. The bed sat squarely in the middle of the room, framed in gold and covered with a sweeping canopy. The duvet was as tufty as a summer cloud, scattered with at least ten matching pillows and a fur throw, for good measure.

Wren had rifled through the armoire in the corner to find it filled with expensive outfits, fur-lined cloaks and soft winter scarves, plus an entire rack of velvet and lace dresses that would make Rose squirm with envy. Now who on earth did they belong to?

A large window looked out over the snow-capped Fovarr Mountains, where jagged peaks pierced the low-hanging clouds and valleys fell away in yawning shadows. Roaming beasts howled at the waning moon, while nighthawks flitted across the indigo sky. And yet, despite the icy mist that clung to the spires of Grinstad Palace, the bedroom itself was surprisingly warm. It was a shame there was nothing to do in it. Wren's boots marred the white rug as she paced back and forth, waiting for Alarik's decision.

She wasn't foolish enough to think Banba was close by, enjoying the same luxury as her. She needed to get out of this room and see her. Her patience frayed with each passing hour, her gaze pinned to the door handle, willing it to open. But the soldier on the other side was silent. She wouldn't have known he was there at all if his wolf wasn't snoring so loudly.

Wren's fingers began to itch, but without the root of her magic, she was powerless. Tor had confiscated her pouch of sand, and the rest of it was in her satchel, which had been discarded in the courtyard. She had searched the room for something to use – a new kind of earth – but the king was two steps ahead of her. There were no flowers on the dresser. No wood in the fireplace. She opened the window and stuck her head out into the chill. The palace walls were smooth to touch, no ivy inching up the stonework, and not a trellis in sight.

'Would it kill them to try to plant something in this giant

ice block,' she muttered, as she slammed the window shut. She turned her attention to the wardrobe, rifling through dress after dress, looking in vain for an iron button, or even a pin. 'That clever brute.'

She crossed the room and banged her fists against the door. The wolf yelped, startled from its slumber. 'If you're not going to let me out, at least feed me for goodness' sake. I'm famished!'

She sank down to the floor and kicked her legs out. To her surprise, dinner arrived shortly. Perhaps she had some power here after all. The kitchens had delivered a rich beef stew, with a child-sized spoon. No knife.

Wren knocked on the door again. 'This stew is as dull as dishwater. Could you at least bring a little seasoning?'

A few minutes later, after Wren had practically licked her plate clean, the door creaked open and a small jar of salt was rolled inside. Wren snatched it up, grinning at its pink hue. Fools. This was rock salt, pure as the day it was mined. Here, in her pampered cell, it was more precious than gold dust.

She set aside her new morsel of earth as she got changed. Her tunic was ragged, and her trousers were filthy from her brief time in the courtyard of beasts. If she was going to snoop around Grinstad Palace, it was in her best interests to try to blend in. Better to look like a noblewoman than a thief. She chose a teal dress with pockets from the armoire, admiring the silver beading along the neckline as she shrugged it on. It was simple, yet beautiful. But who on earth was it for? It wouldn't fit Princess Anika's generous curves, and, even if it did, Wren highly doubted the prickly princess would share her clothes with her guests. Or indeed prisoners.

She wrangled her hair into a fishtail braid and scrubbed the dirt from her cheeks. Then she stuck the jar of salt into her pocket and knocked once more on the door.

'What now?' said the soldier, wearily.

'You may clear my plate,' said Wren, haughtily. 'You hardly expect me to sleep in a room stinking of stew?'

The soldier muttered a Gevran curse.

'I *heard* that,' said Wren. 'It's no way to speak to an esteemed guest. I am a queen, you know.'

'You're a prisoner,' the guard corrected her.

'Actually, that's still up for debate.' No response. 'If you don't take this plate away this instant, I'm going to stick my head out of the window and shriek until everyone in this palace wakes up, and they'll have *you* to blame for it. For goodness' sake, I'm hardly asking for a prancing pony! Just stick your hand in and take it away.'

The key turned in the lock. The second the door creaked open, Wren blew the salt from her palm, sending a hurried incantation after it. The soldier slumped to the floor. His wolf woke with a start, but Wren was ready for the beast. Within seconds, it was curled up beside its master, both of them snoring in perfect harmony.

She dusted her hands as she stepped out of the room. 'Really, that was too easy.'

Wren was relieved to find the rest of the hallway empty. She skulked to the end of it, making her way to the back of the palace, where she found the servants' stairwell. She followed it down one flight and then another, her footsteps featherlight on the stone. Beastly snores echoed through the palace, growing louder as she descended. Wren didn't know where the dungeons were, but she sensed if she ventured down deep enough, she'd find them.

When the patter of footsteps echoed up the stairwell towards her, Wren turned around and ducked out on to the first floor. She stuck to the wall, inching through the shadows as she searched for another way downstairs. More footsteps sounded somewhere behind her, only these ones were accompanied by the click-clack of claws on marble.

She scurried away from the patrolling soldier and his beast, swinging around the next corner at such a speed she nearly lost her balance. She skidded to a stop, a hand pressed to her chest to calm her racing heart. Moonlight cascaded over her in rivers of molten silver, casting a dreamlike glow about the palace. Wren looked up, to where a familiar glass dome revealed the starlit sky.

Oh.

She was standing at the top of the split staircase, looking out over the same atrium she had marvelled at hours earlier. Something shifted in the half-light and she dipped her chin, a breath catching in her throat. There was a woman sitting at the piano. She was much older than Wren, with sinewy limbs and a gaunt face, and wearing a black nightgown, her long blond hair glowing like a pearl. Her fingers rested lightly on the keys, but she didn't play a single note. She was staring vacantly at the piano, wearing a look so haunted, it made the hairs on the back of Wren's neck stand up.

It was like she was frozen.

And stranger still . . . although Alarik's soldiers were stationed throughout the atrium, not a single one was looking at the woman. Even the beasts didn't seem to notice her. Was she a ghost, sprung from Wren's addled imagination? It suddenly occurred to her – this must be Alarik's mother, the reclusive Queen Valeska.

Wren tried to creep a little closer, but a hand closed around her arm.

'What in freezing hell are you doing down here?' said Tor's voice close to her ear. Wren swallowed her gasp as he pulled her away from the banister and spun her into an alcove.

'Who is that woman sitting at the—'

'Wren, this isn't Anadawn,' Tor whispered, furiously. 'If you get caught sneaking around like this, it will cost you your head.'

Wren blinked up at the soldier. He filled the alcove, the heat of his anger pressing her back against the wall. 'Well, I wasn't planning on getting caught.' She looked at his hands on her waist, feeling every searing inch of his touch. 'How did you even know I was down here?'

Tor snapped his hands away, returning one to the pommel of his sword. 'I found your satchel in the courtyard. I was bringing it to you when I found Ulrich lying in a heap.'

Wren bit her lip. 'He must have been tired.'

'What are you playing at, Wren? Are you trying to

bait Alarik? Or is it me you're toying with?'

'*Stars*, Tor, I'm trying to see if my grandmother is still alive,' snapped Wren. 'What did you expect me to do? Wait in that room like some mindless idiot while that arrogant lout wastes my time and just . . . *ignores* me?'

'Yes,' said Tor, through his teeth. '*Yes.*'

Wren blew out a breath. 'Then you clearly don't know me very well.'

'I found you quick enough, didn't I?'

'You win at hide-and-seek, Tor,' said Wren, dryly. 'Why don't we play again?'

Tor braced himself against the wall, trapping her inside the alcove.

Wren pushed against his chest. It was rock solid, as immovable as the stone at their feet. '*Move.*'

'The dungeon is crawling with beasts.'

'I've got my magic.'

Tor raked his gaze along her body.

Wren folded her arms. 'You'll never find—'

He slipped his hand into her left pocket, curling his fingers around the jar. 'Well,' he breathed. 'This feels familiar.'

Wren pressed her hand against his, trapping it in her pocket. 'Don't.'

His gaze flicked to her eyes, then her lips.

But Wren had caught his moment of weakness. She rose to her tiptoes, brushing her nose against his.

Tor's free hand found hers. He gently pushed her away. 'This is not a game we can play in Gevra.'

Wren dropped her hand. 'When was it ever a game?'

'You tell me.' He held her gaze as he removed the jar of salt from her clothes. 'I never did learn the rules.'

Wren watched him pocket the salt and wanted to slap him for it. 'I suppose they're your rules now.'

They were interrupted by a low growl. Then the sound of approaching footsteps. Wren reeled backwards, flattening herself against the stone. Tor stepped into the alcove, covering her body with his, as he sealed them in. The soldier drew closer. Wren closed her eyes and laid her head against Tor's chest listening to the drumbeat of his heart. He rested his chin on her, the ghost of his lips brushing the crown of her head.

They stayed like that until the footsteps faded. Wren could have lingered far longer, listening to the steady rise and fall of Tor's breath, but he pulled back from her and the truce was broken. 'Go to bed, Wren. For both our sakes.'

The fight seeped out of Wren, a wave of exhaustion sweeping over her as she stepped out of the alcove. She frowned as she looked left. Then right. 'I've lost my way.'

Tor sighed. 'I know.'

He escorted her back to the fourth floor, where they found Ulrich and his wolf still slumbering outside her door. Wren deftly stepped over them, then paused in the doorway. 'Tor,' she said, holding on to the frame. 'When will he make his decision?'

Tor gestured past her to the confines of her opulent bedroom. 'Can't you see? He's already made it.' He looked back at her, a terrible shadow moving in his eyes. 'When he comes to you and asks for your help, I hope for your sake – and his – that you refuse him.'

'Why?' said Wren, warily.

Tor's face shuttered as he pulled the door shut. 'Just trust me,' he said, through the wood. 'If you can do nothing else, do that.'

The key turned in the lock, and his footsteps faded, leaving Wren pondering his final words. Her satchel had been left on the chair by her dresser. She rifled through it, searching for her sand. It was gone, every last morsel of earth taken from her by Captain Tor Iversen. The rest of her stuff remained, even that ridiculous bejewelled mirror. Wren pulled it out, catching a glimpse of her haggard reflection.

'Some queen you are,' she muttered, as she set it down on the dresser. Not for the first time that day, she thought of Rose across the Sunless Sea, and wondered how her sister had taken the news of her desertion. Would she send a troop of soldiers to fetch Wren or trust her sister to work out this new wrinkle in their destiny? Wren hoped Rose would keep her focus on Barron, and the trouble brewing closer to home.

She crawled into bed, trying to ignore the prickle of guilt at abandoning her sister. In the midnight darkness, with the winter wind howling at the window, Wren felt more foolish than ever. Tor was right. The second she had offered herself to Alarik Felsing in the throne room, his eyes had lit up, like the stars of Polaris. This fancy bedroom wasn't a gesture of goodwill, it was a message. He was telling her to get comfortable.

Alarik was going to keep Wren now that he had her. But what was he planning to do with Banba? The uncertainty around the old witch's fate rocked Wren to sleep. It followed her deep into her nightmares, where she screamed for her grandmother, until a bitter frost crawled over her, freezing her bone by bone, breath by breath.

Rose
CHAPTER 18

Rose stood high in the west tower of Anadawn, staring at a pool of Glenna's blood. The seer was dead, but there were faces peering up at her from the crimson puddle. *No, not faces.* A portrait. Rose picked it up, cleaning away the blood with her sleeve. An oil painting of her ancestors, Ortha and Oonagh, stared back at her, their emerald gazes so like her own. Only Oonagh looked angry. Vengeful.

Rose traced her finger along the portrait, causing a crack against the glass. 'We won't be like you,' she heard herself say. 'Wren and I will be different.'

A floorboard creaked behind her. She turned to find her sister standing in the darkness. The walls groaned as they crumbled around them, the tower cracking open like an egg. The sky stretched over them in a mass of dark thunderclouds. A drop of rain landed on Wren's cheek, turning to blood.

'Wren?' said Rose, uncertainly. 'Are you well?'

Wren lunged, shoving Rose from the tower and sending her plummeting towards the ground.

Rose screamed as she fell, the world spinning faster

and faster, as the courtyard rose to meet her. Blackness exploded in her mind, and from deep within it, came the urgent whisper of a familiar voice. *Break the ice to free the curse . . .*

'Wakey, wakey, Queenie.'

Rose sat bolt upright, smacking her head against something hard. There came a muttered curse, and, as her eyes adjusted to the morning sunlight, she realized she'd headbutted Kai in the nose.

On the other side of the bed, where he was pulling on his boots, Shen wheezed with laughter. 'Some warrior witch you are,' he said. 'Nearly got yourself knocked out by a slumbering royal. I did tell you not to wake her.'

Rose rubbed her forehead, trying to cast off the horror of her nightmare. She frowned at both of them. 'How long have you two been awake?'

'Hours,' said Kai, his voice stuffy as he held his nose. 'Ever since that damned wolf started chewing on my hair.' He glared pointedly at Elske, who was curled up by the door. 'But *someone –*' he jerked his head in Shen's direction – 'insisted we let you sleep.'

'What?' Rose scrambled out of bed. 'What time is it?'

'It's barely an hour after sunrise. You needed rest,' said Shen, as he retied his hair in its leather strap. 'And you were talking in your sleep,' he added, with a wink. 'We wanted to eavesdrop.'

'Oh no.' Rose felt herself pale. 'What was I saying?'

'*Oh, Shen!*' cried Kai in falsetto. '*Why didn't you tell me you*

*were cousins with the most handsome man in Eana? I wish I could
kiss him instead.'*

Shen crossed the room in a blur to punch his cousin in the
shoulder. 'I can't believe I'm related to you.'

'What was I really saying?' she asked, praying she hadn't
screamed in her sleep. Or, worse, fawned over Shen. Oh,
she'd die of embarrassment.

'You said Wren's name a few times, but mostly you were
talking about food,' said Shen, and Rose could hear the
laughter in his voice. 'At one point, it sounded like you were
listing all your favourite things to eat. Chocolate, cheese, jam,
bread, gooseberry tarts . . .'

'I am rather hungry,' Rose admitted, with great relief. 'Do
you think we could also have some tea before we set off?'

'By all means, Queenie, have your tea.' Kai rolled his eyes.
'Why rush ourselves to uncover an entire kingdom of people
trapped beneath the desert?'

'A good cup of tea sets the day in motion,' said Rose, as
she scooted out of bed, stopping to pet Elske before she
sought out her hairbrush. 'Everyone likes tea. I bet even *you*
like tea.'

'Can't stand the stuff,' said Kai. 'Unless it's been spiked
with whisky.'

'I'm sure.' A thought occurred to Rose, then. She set the
brush down. 'How has the Sunkissed Kingdom lasted this
long without provisions?'

'Because it knows how to survive,' he said, simply. 'The
Sunkissed Kingdom is thousands of years old, Queenie.

As old as Eana, the first witch. It was built by ancient magic.'
He stalked to the window, his eyes straining as if he could see
the lost kingdom shimmering just beyond the horizon. 'It's
always been able to disappear at will. To hide when it needs
to. From desert storms. From enemies.'

'From me,' muttered Shen, who was idly fingering the
ruby ring that hung from his neck.

Kai frowned. 'Eighteen years ago, something went wrong.
The kingdom hid but we couldn't undo it. We couldn't be
found. We lost the wind, the sun, the horizon. The desert
became our sky. Our earth. Our world.' His voice turned
distant, and Rose saw in Kai the same glassy-eyed wistfulness
that came over Shen whenever he spoke of his childhood in
the desert. 'But the magic that kept us trapped beneath the
sands provided for us, too. In the Sunkissed Kingdom, there's
a place called the Hall of Bounty, a chamber that offers us
whatever we need – water, food, weapons, *whisky* . . .' He
rolled his hand.

'What about sunlight?' said Shen. 'Didn't you need it
to train?'

Rose was just about to ask the same thing. She knew
warriors were charged by the sun. It was the source of their
magic, the very root of their energy.

'It gave us that, too,' said Kai. 'On training days, when I
visited the hall, it would fill with streaming sunlight. The
walls themselves would shine, the ceiling glittering so brightly
it would burn tears in my eyes. But I didn't care. I would
stand in the middle of that room, with my arms flung out,

gathering the energy to me.' He turned from the window. 'But it was never the same. Our people deserve to feel the true sun on their faces again.'

Shen tucked the ring back under his shirt. 'We'll find them.'

Kai nodded at Rose. 'Just as soon as the queen has had her tea, right?'

'I'll forgo my tea,' said Rose, quickly. 'We'll take our breakfast on the road.'

Shen managed to charm the kitchen staff into giving them a parcel of bread, cheese and jam for the road. They were in the middle of sneaking Elske out of the room, when a maid caught sight of the massive wolf in the stairwell and let out a scream loud enough to wake the entire town.

'Big dog, isn't she?' said Rose, cheerfully patting Elske's head. 'She's as friendly as anything.'

Elske growled at the maid, sending her scurrying past them.

Outside, the wolf stalked back and forth between Victory and Storm, as if daring the horses to gallop off without her.

'That beast is going to slow us down,' said Kai, glaring at her. 'And she's not riding with me.'

'She might well outpace you,' said Rose, who was sitting in front of Shen, astride Storm. After the wildness of yesterday, it felt both familiar and comforting to be on a horse with him again. And she'd rather walk in her bare feet than ride with

Kai again. 'Elske caught up with us, after all. And even if she does fall behind, she's an expert at tracking people.'

Kai rolled his eyes as he nudged Victory into a canter. 'Fine. As long as we get moving, I don't care what wild creature comes with us.'

They rode in companiable silence, the morning sun beating down on them as they left Hollyfort behind, winding deeper into the southern plains of Eana. After several hours, Rose heard the sound of rushing water and spotted the Whitestone Bridge up ahead. 'We're almost there. According to Thea's map, we take a left at the river and follow the water down into the Poisonweed Valley.'

'Ah yes, the valley of *poison weeds*,' said Kai. 'That sounds like a great idea.'

'Never mind those tall tales,' said Rose, as she folded up her map. 'Thea would never send us into danger.'

Leafy trees peered over them as they strayed from the road, following the river down into fields where long grass brushed against their knees and tall-stalked flowers grew up to meet them, each one bigger and brighter than the last.

'Why was that innkeeper so skittish about this place?' Rose frowned as she looked around. 'I know it has a funny name, but it doesn't look very poisonous to me.'

'Looks can be deceiving,' warned Shen. 'Stay on your guard.'

Rose kept her eyes trained on the distant treetops, searching for a tower among them, but there was nothing but the grass and the flowers and the wind whispering in her ear. She thought of her nightmare again, her thoughts drifting to Wren across the Sunless Sea. Rose hoped her sister was all right, and that her dream was simply an expression of her anxiety and nothing more. Sweat dripped down the back of her neck, and her legs began to ache.

'How much longer?' demanded Kai. 'We've been down here for hours and everything looks the same.' His voice vibrated with agitation, reminding Rose of an angry wasp. 'Every step we take away from the desert is a step in the wrong direction.'

'Hush now. I'm sure we're almost there.' Rose rubbed her eyes, trying to see straight, but the air was getting hazy. Or was that her vision? She blinked and her lids grew heavy.

'What was it the innkeeper said?' asked Shen, his voice slurring. 'Something about the air in the Poisonweed Valley?'

Rose was struggling to remember. 'Did he say anything at all?'

Shen's head lolled against her shoulder. 'My head hurts . . .'

Rose twisted to find Kai half slumped on his horse, too, muttering to himself. 'One whisky, two whisky, three whisky more . . .'

'Oh no,' she said, as the world began to spin. She scrunched her eyes shut. 'We're being poisoned.'

But the men were both slipping from consciousness. In a panic, Rose grabbed Shen's hands from where they rested on her waist. She squeezed them, tightly, sending a burst of healing magic into his bloodstream.

Shen stiffened, coming back to himself. 'Whoa,' he said, blowing out a breath. 'I felt like I was drunk.'

'Kai,' said Rose, catching the name before it escaped her. 'We need to help Kai.'

Shen nudged Storm closer to Victory, until Rose was able to reach across the space between the horses and grab the warrior's hand, which was hanging limply. She sent out another burst of healing magic, as her own body began to sway.

Kai sat up again, the colour rushing back into his cheeks as he grinned at Rose. 'I knew you wanted to hold my hand.'

Rose flopped back against Shen's chest.

His arms tightened around her waist. 'Rose?' he said, worry straining his voice. 'Are you all right?'

'I just . . . need . . . a moment . . .' she said, gazing up at the bright blue sky. They rode on, the gentle clip-clop of hooves lulling her into a trance. She felt like she was floating in a lake, the wind tickling her ears and making her smile. 'Ooh . . . look at all the pretty birds.'

'Sounds like she's going loopy,' said Kai. 'Shame she can't heal herself.'

Rose began to laugh. 'They're so shiny,' she said, feebly reaching up to catch one of the birds in the sky.

Deep in the haze of her addled mind, Rose knew there was something special about these birds, but she couldn't remember what it was. She closed her eyes, thinking, *thinking*.

And then it came to her – and she shouted it at the world. 'STARCRESTS!'

She sat bolt upright, trying to shake off the poisonweed. The fields had shed their flowers for spindly trees that grew to make a leafy wood, where silver-breasted birds were diving and swooping between the branches. 'There's a whole flock of them,' she said, breathlessly. 'Look!'

'Rose, you're right,' said Shen, gasping as he looked past her. 'If the forest is full of starcrests then there must be seers nearby.'

Rose tried to smile but her lids were drooping again, and it was taking every ounce of her energy to keep them open.

'Follow those birds!' said Kai, urging Victory into a gallop.

The birds swarmed overhead, leading them deeper into the wood, where the trill of their song hung like wind chimes. They followed it through the trees. Rose was so tired now; she wanted nothing more than to slide off Storm and curl up on the springy moss. It looked so warm and welcoming. *So soft* . . .

'Stay awake, Rose,' said Shen's voice in her ear. 'We're almost there.'

'*Mmm*,' she murmured. 'You smell good.'

Shen chuckled. 'I doubt that. We've been on the road for two days.'

'You always smell good to me,' said Rose, with a giggle.

'Yeah, she's definitely poisoned,' said Kai.

After a while, Shen's voice came again. 'Sit up, Rose. Look. We're at the edge of the wood.'

With great effort, Rose cracked an eye open. They were far beyond the Poisonweed Valley now. The trees had parted to reveal a stony basin cut deep into the earth. All around it, trickling waterfalls flowed down into crystalline pools, casting a creeping silver mist. Inside it, nine stone towers hung with trailing ivy climbed up towards the sky, where hundreds of starcrests soared in a murmuration.

Rose's heart lifted at the sight. 'We *found* it.'

'Something's spooking the horses,' said Kai, cutting through the shining sense of wonder. The horses had stopped at the treeline and were refusing to go any further.

'Then leave them.' Suddenly, Rose couldn't wait a moment longer. She wanted to feel the spray of those waterfalls on her cheeks, to dive into one of the crystal pools and let it wash the clinging poisonweed off her skin. She rolled off Storm and stumbled towards the towers.

'Rose! Wait!' Shen jumped off Storm and ran after her.

'For the love of Eana,' muttered Kai, as he leaped off his horse and followed them.

Rose had barely taken ten steps before the ground gave way beneath her. One minute she was wading through a pile of leaves, and the next she was plummeting into a dark hole in the earth. Shen lunged, flinging his hand out to catch her, but the hole widened to swallow him, too. They landed on the hard ground with a thud, just as Kai came tumbling after them.

'Oh!' said Rose, as she sat up. She knew she should have been worried, but she couldn't help the giggle that sprang from her. 'We've been caught!'

There came a rustle from above. She looked up to find an

old man in a midnight-blue cloak staring down at them.

Rose waggled her fingers. 'Hello.'

The man scowled at her. 'You're late.'

Wren

CHAPTER 19

It was snowing when Wren woke up. Overnight, a thick layer of frost had settled over her window, sealing it shut. The world outside was hazy and white, the morning chill seeping through the walls and turning her nose numb. She pulled the fur blanket up to her chin, thinking of Banba freezing somewhere far below her. Her grandmother was hardy – life in Ortha had made her that way – but her bones had grown brittle with age, and her knees often ached in the cold.

Wren *had* to free her; there was no time to waste.

A maidservant arrived presently, carrying a breakfast tray of rye toast, smoked salmon and scrambled eggs. No salt. Wren wondered if Tor had warned the kitchen of her subterfuge last night and was annoyed at the way the thought instantly stung her. She had to remind herself that the Gevran soldier didn't owe her his loyalty, and yet she had hoped, at the very least, that he wouldn't go out of his way to thwart her. The maid set the tray down on the dresser, leaving Wren to eat in peace as she readied a bath in the adjacent bathing chamber.

Wren demolished her breakfast in less than ten bites. Then she wandered into the bathing chamber, which smelled of cinnamon and clove, and surveyed the mountain of bubbles with some surprise.

'I'd advise you to dress warmly today, Your Majesty,' said the maidservant, as she laid out a fluffy white towel. 'We're expecting a blizzard. You're welcome to any of the furs and dresses in the armoire. And there are some warm boots in there, too. If you'd like me to help you to pick out something—'

'What's your name?' said Wren.

The maidservant blinked. 'Klara.'

'Why are you being so kind to me, Klara?'

Klara smiled, sheepishly. 'I was only told to help you get ready.'

'I see,' said Wren, slowly. If she didn't know better, she'd swear she was a guest, rather than a prisoner at Grinstad Palace. Alarik was being nice to her, which only worsened the unease stirring inside her. She stood back to let the maid pass. 'I can take it from here. Thank you, Klara.'

Klara scurried away, collecting the empty tray on her way out of the room. The door closed with a click, the key turning in its lock, leaving Wren alone with her suspicion.

She sank into the bath, trying to ignore the distant cacophony of growls as the kingdom's beasts rose to face the day. She scrubbed every inch of her body until her skin was pink and her hair smelled of cinnamon. Afterwards, she dressed in a red velvet dress with a narrow waist and lightly flared sleeves, pairing it with a matching cloak lined with fur, the hood so large she could hide her entire face in it. As she tied it at her neck, she stared at herself in the mirror.

Wren was unnerved by how Gevran she looked. She was draped in fur, her face too pale in the biting cold, her wet hair darker than usual. 'Another palace,' she muttered. 'Another part to play.'

A knock at the door made her jump. She turned to find a towering blond soldier standing in the doorway. She was about Wren's age, with wide shoulders, a round face and darting grey eyes. She was gripping the pommel of her sword so tight her knuckles were stark white.

'Careful with that thing,' said Wren, gesturing to her glittering sword. 'Enchanters aren't that scary, you know. Especially ones without earth.'

The soldier swallowed, thickly. 'The king has sent for you.'

Wren picked up her skirts and marched across the room. 'It's about damn time.'

The soldier led Wren down one flight of stairs after another, winding deeper and deeper into the recesses of Grinstad Palace, until they reached a tunnel that stretched underneath the mountain itself. Stone soon turned to rock, stalactites dripping from the ceiling like icy tears, while stalagmites crawled up from the uneven ground to meet them. The air beneath the palace was so frigid Wren had to wrap her arms around herself to keep warm. Snow leopards prowled alongside them, patrolling the network of narrow cells where frostbitten prisoners cowered, looking half frozen to death.

Wren's stomach twisted every time she peered into a cell

searching for Banba. A prisoner lurched for her as she passed, and a leopard lunged from the shadows, snapping at his bony fingers.

Wren hissed at the beast, shooing him with her cloak. 'Get back, you wicked thing!'

The leopard bared its teeth as it slunk away. The prisoner whimpered as he withdrew into the corner of his cell, cradling his hand to his chest.

They walked on, the mountain creaking as ice water dripped into pools at their feet. Finally, after what felt like an eternity, Wren spotted her grandmother huddled at the back of a cell. Her cropped white hair flickered in the low sconce light, and Wren's fingertips tingled, the magic inside her recognizing another of its kind. Banba's hands were chained behind her back to keep her tempest magic at bay. The sight of her, small and shivering, sent a bolt of fresh rage through Wren, but it was desperation that made her fling herself at the bars.

'Banba!' she cried, the sound echoing all the way down the tunnel. 'Are you all right?'

The old woman looked up, her green eyes bright in the dimness. She blinked once, then twice, as if Wren was an apparition come to haunt her. 'Wren?' she croaked. 'But it can't be my little bird . . .'

'It's me, Banba. It's Wren.' Emotion thickened Wren's voice. Her grandmother might be freezing, but she was alive. She was *here*, mere feet from Wren. 'I've come to rescue you.'

'No, it must be a trick . . .' Banba stood on trembling legs.

She was still wearing her brown tunic and trousers, with only a paltry woollen cloak to cover her. She shuffled towards Wren, her bound hands making her lumber to one side.

Wren reached for her through the bars.

A sword shot out so close to Wren it almost nicked her arm. She glared at the soldier over her shoulder. 'Get that thing away from me.'

The soldier raised her sword, until the point hovered at Wren's chin. 'Look, but don't touch.'

'Says who?' snapped Wren.

'King Alarik,' said the soldier.

Wren gritted her teeth. 'Where is that frost-hearted bastard?'

'He's waiting for you. Come.' The soldier inclined her chin back the way they had come, towards a darker tunnel that branched off, deeper under the mountain. Dread prickled in Wren's cheeks. Banba wasn't the destination; she was simply part of the journey – a cruel stopover along the way to Alarik. He had wanted Wren to see her imprisoned grandmother first. To know what was at stake.

'You have seen the witch,' said the soldier, impatiently. 'Now we must go.'

But Wren was rooted to the spot, her heart clenching so tightly it ached.

'Wren, listen to me!' Banba pressed her forehead against the bars, spittle foaming at the edges of her cracked lips. 'I don't know what possessed you to come here, or how you survived it, but don't strike any deals with the Gevran king. Better if you don't speak to him at all.'

'It's all right, Banba. I'm here now. I'm going to save you.' Wren ignored the soldier's warning and threaded her arms through the cell, rubbing warmth into her grandmother's shoulders. They were stiff and as cold as ice. 'We've already come to an arrangement.' Wren's voice cracked, but she held her smile. She didn't want Banba to worry about her. 'I'm getting you out of here.'

'Foolish child.' Banba shook her head fiercely, her eyes so wide Wren could count the red veins inside them. 'You must leave at once. Forget about me, little bird. Go home to your throne. Your sister needs you.'

Wren balked at the harshness in her grandmother's voice. Suddenly, she felt like an unruly child, who had been caught pinching honey from the Ortha hives. 'It's *our* throne, Banba. It means nothing to me without you.' She laid her forehead against the bars until they were almost nose to nose. 'Rose and I can't do this without you. We need *you*. I need you.'

'The price of my freedom is too high,' said Banba; her breath was cold on Wren's cheeks. 'I won't pay it. And neither should you.' Her shoulders began to shake, and Wren realized with dawning horror that her grandmother was afraid. In all her life, she had never known Banba – fierce in all she did – to cower from anything, to tremble as she was trembling now. 'Listen to me well, little bird. There is a darkness that moves in Gevra. The wind is heavy with it. It feels like old magic. *Tainted* magic.' Her gaze darted, the rest of her warning chattering through her teeth. 'I feel it when I sleep, Wren.

I hear it when I wake. It's in the mountain. It rattles against my feet.'

'It's just the frost, Banba.' Wren desperately tried to rub some warmth into her grandmother, to give her a morsel of the comfort she had given Wren when she was a child who had nightmares on dark windy nights. 'It's toying with your mind. There are no witches in Gevra. That's why the king took you here in the first place. He wants to learn about magic; he wants it for himself.'

The soldier's hand fell heavily on Wren's shoulder. *'Move.'*

'The king is toying with things he doesn't understand,' said Banba, urgently. 'Things that should stay buried. You can't stay here, Wren. You have to run!'

Wren shook the soldier off. She unhooked her cloak and passed it through the bars. The soldier drew her sword, but Wren shot her a look so withering it froze in mid-air. 'It's just a cloak, for goodness' sake. She needs warmth.'

Wren worked the cloak around Banba's shoulders and tied it loosely at her throat. 'Try to stay warm,' she said, as she was yanked away from the bars. 'I'll be back for you as soon as I can.'

Banba called after her, telling her to turn around, to run and never look back, but Wren shut out her ragged pleas and kept her eyes on her feet, shivering violently as she ventured deeper into the mountain. Now that she knew Banba was still alive, and utterly petrified, she was more determined than ever to get her out of here. Fast.

The sconce light grew few and far between, the world

growing darker and colder with every step. Wren's teeth were clacking noisily, her toes so numb she began to stumble.

'H-h-h-how m-m-m-much f-f-further?' she eked out.

The soldier pointed up ahead, to where a pair of golden-eyed wolves peered out of the dimness.

'You're late.' Alarik's crisp voice echoed down the tunnel. A few more steps and Wren could see him standing behind his wolves, flanked by a soldier on either side. Neither of whom were Tor. The king was wearing black again, the high collar of his coat trimmed with dark grey fur. 'I summoned you an hour ago.'

Wren cut her eyes at him. 'I'm not a dog that can be called to heel.'

'If only you were,' he said, drolly. 'I could have Captain Iversen wrangle you.' He raked his pale gaze over her dress, then looked accusingly at her chaperone. 'Why isn't she wearing a cloak?'

The soldier's throat bobbed. 'She gave it away, Your Majesty. I tried to stop her.'

Alarik cocked his head. 'Which of you possesses the sword, Inga?'

'I have a better question,' Wren cut in, deftly stepping in front of the quivering guard before he could flay her alive. 'Where did all those fancy dresses and fur cloaks in my room come from?'

Alarik turned on Wren. 'Unwanted gifts. Don't spare them another thought.'

Wren was intrigued, despite herself. 'So, you've been

rejected by a sweetheart, then? I can't say I'm surprised.'

'I have no interest in sweethearts, I assure you,' said the king.

Wren hmm'd. 'Must be hard to love anything with that block of ice in your chest.'

He raised a slender brow. 'Just as it is for you to behave yourself with that snake's tongue in your mouth.'

Wren folded her arms. She didn't care for the king, but their sparring had warmed her up nicely. 'Now that we've got the pleasantries out of the way, what the hell are we doing down here?'

Alarik stood aside, revealing a narrow door with rusted hinges. 'You and I will enter alone. Then we will discuss the particulars of our arrangement.' He pressed his palm against the wood, looking at her over his shoulder. 'Unless, of course, you wish to renege on our bargain.'

'Well, that depends,' said Wren, hesitantly. 'Are you planning to kill me in there?'

He chuckled, darkly. 'I assure you, Wren. I would treat your death with the utmost spectacle.'

'Is that your idea of a compliment?'

'In fact, it is.'

'No wonder you got rejected by your sweetheart.'

'I didn't get rejected.'

Wren swished her velvet skirts. 'If you say so.'

Alarik turned back to the door and closed his eyes for a moment, as though he was steeling himself for whatever was behind it. Then he pushed it open and stepped inside.

Wren followed him, leaving the soldiers out in the tunnel. The door closed behind her, sealing them in. The room was small and dark, a single candle flame illuminating a low ceiling dripping with icicles. Beneath it, laid out on a thick stone slab, was a dead body.

Wren clapped a hand over her mouth.

The body belonged to Prince Ansel. The corpse of the young royal lay before her, his expression placid, as if he was only sleeping. But the wound above his heart betrayed the awful truth. Wren had seen him take his dying breath with her own eyes, had watched the blood spurt from his mouth like a fountain when Willem Rathborne had thrown his dagger at him. Ansel was dead. He had been dead for a while. She stumbled away from him.

Alarik caught her by the shoulders, holding her still.

'What is this?' breathed Wren. She couldn't take her eyes off the dead prince, his porcelain cheeks and fair eyelashes, the gentle sweep of his golden hair. 'Why have you summoned me here?'

The king brought his lips close to her ear, his breath as cold as the ice that wept from the ceiling. 'Here is the new bargain, witch. You will perform the spell your grandmother refused. If you succeed, then I will free her, and you may journey home to Eana together.'

Wren turned to stare at the king in horror. 'Have you lost your hissing mind? Your brother is *dead*, Alarik.'

'I know,' he said, calmly. 'I want you to bring him back to life.'

Rose

CHAPTER 20

'Let us out of here, you withered old fool!' Kai took a running leap at the earthen wall.

Rose watched him with mild curiosity. 'You know we can't get out until they let us out, right?'

'Nobody traps Kai!' he roared, as he leaped again.

Shen, who had kicked his legs out beside her, sighed. 'Just let him get it out of his system.'

Rose dusted herself off as she stood. Now that the Poisonweed Valley was behind them, its effects were wearing off. Her head was clearing, and the absurd urge to laugh at their predicament had passed. 'Excuse me,' she called out in her most polite voice. 'Can you please let us out? I think you'll find I'm rather important.'

'Nice try,' Kai scoffed.

A moment later, a rope ladder unfurled in front of Rose's nose. She tossed a smirk at Kai before grabbing hold of it. She climbed back up, marvelling at the view.

Above her, dozens of starcrests perched in the leafy trees, adding their dulcet chirps to the distant tinkle of the waterfalls.

Beyond the mist, Rose could see the crumbling towers more clearly now. They seemed to grow up from the stony valley as if they had always been there.

The old man was waiting for her up on the grass. Beneath the hood of his blue robe, Rose could see that his skin was pale and deeply wrinkled, his tumbling grey hair bleeding into a long, wiry beard. He had a sharp nose and keen eyes that matched the silvery mist around them.

'It is her!' he cried to the woman, beside him. 'Queen Rose is here. I foresaw the queen's visit and she came! And *you* had the nerve to doubt me, Meredia.'

The woman wore the same midnight-blue robe. She had brown skin, hazel eyes and a strong jaw, her long white hair tucked away beneath her hood. Even though her face was unlined, there was something ancient about her. 'There is always doubt among the skies, Fathom,' she said, with serene calmness. 'You know that just as I do.'

A pale-faced boy dressed in a simple white robe lingered behind them. He appeared to be a year or so older than Tilda, but his shorn blond hair and huge blue eyes made him look like a giant baby. 'And you did say there would be *two* queens.'

'Details,' said Fathom, waving his hand.

The boy frowned. 'And shouldn't we bow to the one who is here?'

'Oh, yes!' said Fathom. 'Good idea, Pog!'

'Thank you, Pog,' said Rose, primly.

The seers bowed, just as Shen and Kai emerged from the hole in the ground.

Meredia picked up a stick and prodded Shen. 'And what of the queen's companions, Fathom? I don't recall you mentioning them.'

'Hey!' Shen snatched the stick and broke it in two.

'They're warrior witches.' Pog gestured at Kai, who was making a show of unwinding his whip. 'Isn't it obvious?'

Fathom frowned. 'The birds are keeping secrets from me again.'

'It's because you forget to feed them.'

Fathom glared at the boy. 'Yes, thank you, Pog, that's quite enough out of you.'

'Hmm.' Meredia closed her eyes. When she opened them again, they were cloudy white, as if a fog was passing over her irises. She turned on Kai, her voice deepening as though she had fallen into a trance. *'Kai Lo of the Sunkissed Kingdom, you hold great power in your fist. But inside you lies a darkness you must fight to resist.'*

She blinked and the mist was gone.

Kai wheezed an uneasy laugh. 'I think someone's been inhaling a little too much poisonweed.'

Meredia pursed her lips, and Rose made a note to find out exactly what she had meant by those words and why they were making Kai squirm.

'What about me?' said Shen, stepping forward. 'Don't I get a welcome rhyme?'

'We try not to make a habit of it,' said Fathom, pointedly. 'But sometimes, Meredia does like to show off.'

'Well, you started it,' said Pog.

He glowered at the boy. 'Don't you have a bed to turn down somewhere? A privy to clean?'

Meredia cocked her head as she came towards Shen. 'Shen Lo . . .' she said slowly, as though plucking his name from the ether. 'Your heart is split in two.'

Kai raised his brows. 'So, he *is* in love with the other twin!'

Shen elbowed him in the stomach.

'Your home is your heart,' Meredia clarified. Her frown deepened, as the strange fog returned to her eyes. 'But I see a foot in two worlds. A future that forks, where both paths are hazy. It's hard to see . . .'

'Then stop looking,' said Kai, impatiently. 'No one cares about his future.'

Meredia quirked a brow. 'Is that really so, Kai Lo?'

'Stop rhyming at me.' Kai turned on Rose. 'Can we get to the point now?'

'I think we'd better,' said Rose. 'I'm afraid time is of the essence. We've come here to ask for your help.'

Meredia dipped her chin, offering Rose a tentative smile. 'Our promised witch queen has at last returned. We are honoured to welcome you to Amarach, Your Majesty. And of course, we are at your disposal.'

'Come inside,' said Fathom. 'Pog will see to your horses.'

'What about the wolf?' said Pog.

'What wolf?' said Fathom, looking to the treeline, where Victory and Storm were grazing.

'The one in my head.' Pog's eyes darted fearfully. 'I can *see* it.'

Fathom sighed, wearily. 'Remember what we talked about in your lesson last week, Pog? Regarding the difference between imagination and prognostication?'

'But—'

'Pog,' snapped Fathom. 'If you want to be a trained seer, you must let yourself *be* trained.'

'Actually, there is a wolf,' Rose cut in, feeling sorry for the boy. 'Her name is Elske, and she won't eat you, Pog. Just give her some food when she arrives and then bring her to me.'

Meredia smirked. 'So, you didn't see the wolf either, Fathom?'

'Oh, hush, Meredia. You know very well the first rule of Seeing: *no gloating*.' Fathom extended his hand to Rose. 'Watch the leaves, Your Majesty. The treeline is rife with traps.'

Rose took the old man's hand, but the moment they touched, he stiffened. Where Meredia's gaze had turned to fog, Fathom's frosted over. '*Break the ice to free the curse. Kill one twin to save another.*'

Rose snatched her hand away as Glenna's words came hurtling back to her. She still had no idea what they truly meant but with Wren now in Gevra, plus her strange nightmare last night, Fathom's words only deepened her worry.

The frost in the seer's gaze cleared, but he looked unsettled now. 'But that's not it,' he muttered, to himself. 'That's not why you've come.'

'We're here to find the lost Sunkissed Kingdom,' said Rose, before another vision could rise up and threaten to sweep them all away in a tide of panic. Better to get what they came for, and deal with one problem at a time. 'Can you help us?'

The seers exchanged a look. 'Come,' said Fathom. 'We will do our best.'

While Pog went to fetch the horses, Rose, Shen and Kai followed the seers through the valley of crumbling towers. The ground was bursting with leafy bushes, creeping vines and springy moss, the starcrests flitting between the waterfalls and casting droplets over them as they went. The towers themselves were impossibly tall, but Rose couldn't help noticing how most of them had fallen into disrepair.

'How many of you are living down here?' she asked, as she traced an orange wallflower growing from the grooves of a tower.

'There used to be hundreds of us,' said Meredia. 'More than enough to fill every tower, and the surrounding woods, too. But now we are less than twenty. The rest are sleeping. We prefer to rise at dusk, so we may read the patterns of the starcrests at night. That is when they are most potent.'

'And I suppose you use the Poisonweed Valley to avoid being discovered,' said Kai.

Meredia smiled. 'Most wanderers never make it to the woods.'

He puffed his chest up. 'Well, you clearly didn't account for this pair of brave desert warriors.'

'Or the healer who saw fit to help them when they passed out,' said the seer, her hazel eyes twinkling.

'And yet they still haven't thanked me,' said Rose, as they came to a stop at one of the towers. It was here that Meredia left them, journeying on to the next one to alert the cook of their arrival.

Fathom pushed on the wooden door, and it opened with a groaning creak. The room at the bottom of the tower was warm and smelled of sage. A threadbare rug sprawled across the stone floor, which was lined with more bookshelves – and books – than Rose had ever seen before. A spiralling staircase hugged the stone wall, winding up and out of view, where silvery-blue lights flickered from faraway alcoves, lighting their way towards the sky. *Everlights.* Rose smiled, thinking of Wren. She wished her sister was here to see this place, too.

Fathom paused with his foot on the bottom step. 'Follow me,' he said. 'We must visit the Moonlit Menagerie.'

The Moonlit Menagerie was well named. The room at the top of the tower had been painted to resemble the night sky, with each tiny sparkling star marked by a gemstone. Up here, the walls were lined with more shelves, brimming with all manner of items, including ticking clocks in the shape of trees and mountains, crystalline birds that chirped when touched, cracked vases and dusty goblets, ancient tea sets, an entire row of giant conch shells, boxes upon boxes of ornate hairpins and unpaired earrings, hourglasses filled with sand of every colour, and hundreds of dusty parchment scrolls.

The floor was covered in a patchwork of rugs and strewn with oversized pillows. While Rose examined Fathom's bizarre collection of treasures, the seer shuffled over to a clock by the window – which lorded over the room, like a second moon – and adjusted the hands on its face. There was a faint ticking noise as the clock resettled. 'There now,' he muttered. 'That should do it.'

Fathom reclined on one of the pillows, gazing up at the imaginary sky. 'And now we seek the Sunkissed Kingdom. A place long lost to the sands of Eana.'

'Does he think those are real stars?' said Shen, in a low voice.

'Probably,' said Kai, without bothering to whisper. 'The old man's mind is decaying, just like these towers. We should never have come here.'

Fathom traced a constellation with his finger. 'To know how to find the kingdom, we must first discover how it became lost.' His hand got faster, his frown deepening. 'This ceiling presents the movements of starcrests from years past. And oftentimes, we need the past to see the future.'

It was only then that Rose noticed the ceiling was moving. The gemstones were drifting back and forth, creating new patterns in the sky.

'Time is a slippery thing.' Fathom pointed to the giant moon clock. 'That is why, to find what it is we seek, we often have to adjust it.'

Rose and Shen exchanged a dubious glance. But this time

no one interrupted the old seer. They simply waited, watching the stars just as keenly, until, after what seemed like an eternity, Fathom sat bolt upright. 'A map!' he burst out. 'Yes, that's exactly what you need!'

Kai folded his arms. 'That was not worth the suspense, old man. The desert cannot be mapped.'

Fathom tsked. 'Not a map of the terrain. A map of the heart.' He scrambled to his feet and scurried towards the shelves.

'No, no. Not this,' he said, as he rummaged through his vast collection of scrolls. 'Not that either. Hmmm. Oh! I forgot I even had this! Ugh, is that *mould?* Never mind. Where *is* this blasted thing?' He tossed a glass orb over his shoulder, and Shen lunged to catch it before it shattered.

'Nice catch,' said Fathom, without looking back. 'Of course I knew that would happen.'

Shen glared at the back of his head.

Rose could tell by Kai's crouch that he was preparing to tackle the old man.

'Be patient,' she chided them, even though she was running low on patience herself.

Finally, Fathom jumped back. 'Ah! But of course! The map isn't in the Moonlit Menagerie at all.' He chuckled to himself. 'It's downstairs in the cartography section of the Lunar Library!' He waved at them as he shuffled out of the room. 'I won't be a moment!'

Kai flopped down on one of the pillows. 'I say we steal everything in here and see what we can get for it at the market.'

'We're not stealing from the seers,' said Rose, as she idly trailed her fingers along the shelves. She stopped suddenly, as they began to tingle. She picked up a gold comb to inspect it.

'But if Fathom knew we were going to rob him, he would have already stopped us,' said Shen.

Rose threw him a warning look. 'Your cousin is a bad influence on you.'

Kai snorted. 'I've never met a seer before. Are they all like him?'

'My grandmother's sister was a seer.' Rose shuddered as she remembered poor Glenna, the seer Rathborne had kept trapped in the west tower of Anadawn. How he'd slit her throat and left her to bleed out in Rose's arms. 'She wasn't like the seers here, but she was close to madness in a different way.'

Celeste came to her mind, unbidden. Wren was convinced that Celeste was a seer, too. Celeste herself had always denied it, but recently her nightmares had been getting more vivid. And Rose had begun to notice more starcrests at Anadawn, flocking to the roof above Celeste's bedroom. If there *was* any truth to Wren's suspicions, Rose hoped this wouldn't become Celeste's future. Living in a far-off tower, surrounded by poison, falling so far into visions that you couldn't tell the past from the future, or the present.

Rose set the comb down. She walked on, but the tingling in her fingers got stronger. She stopped again, this time drawn to a hand mirror. It was silver and bordered with a delicate row of sapphires. As soon as her fingers closed around the handle, the mirror sparked, sending a jolt of power into her hand. She yelped.

'What is it?' said Shen, spinning around.

'Nothing, I just . . . pricked my finger.' Rose didn't want to tell Shen about the strange jolt, in case he thought her mind was slipping, too.

Just then, the door swung open and Fathom returned. Rose jumped back from the shelf.

The seer wagged his finger. 'Be careful what you touch, Your Majesty. Some of those trinkets bite.'

'Did you find what you were looking for?' she asked.

Fathom held up a roll of yellowed parchment. 'Come and see for yourselves.'

Shen spun from the window and was across the room in four strides. Kai sprang to his feet and reached for the parchment.

Fathom yanked it out of reach. 'I think the queen should be the one to unroll it.'

Rose took the parchment and did so, her heart climbing into her throat until she could taste her hope. She held her breath . . . and then blew it out in one big sigh.

The parchment was blank, save for a single black squiggle in the middle.

'There's nothing here.'

'Listen to me, you old prune,' said Kai, grabbing Fathom by the collar and lifting him off the ground. 'This isn't a game to us. Stop giving us riddles and start talking sense.'

Rose handed the parchment to Shen. 'Kai! Put him down

at once!' she said, railing her fists against his arm. 'That is an order from your queen!'

Kai flung Fathom to the floor. With remarkable grace, the seer stood up and dusted himself off. 'Your temper will be the end of you, Kai Lo,' he said, raising a finger in warning.

'I'm so sorry,' said Rose, as she fixed the old man's robe. 'We're all just so exhausted and coming here was our only . . .' She trailed off as the parchment began to glow in Shen's hands.

'Rose?' he said, as his fingers trembled. 'Are you seeing this?'

'Yes,' breathed Rose. 'Yes, I see it.'

The squiggle of ink was spreading, sketching a map of the desert before their eyes. 'That's Balor's Eye!' said Shen, in amazement. 'And . . . look. There's the Golden Caves!'

Rose and Kai crowded next to Shen as the map continued to show itself, the lines bleeding across the parchment until every inch of it was filled in. The map glowed brighter, and suddenly, in the dead centre, a large ruby-red beetle appeared.

Rose gasped. 'What on earth it that?'

Shen clutched his chest, as though something inside him was trying to hammer its way out. 'That's it,' he said, his voice hoarse. 'That's where the Sunkissed Kingdom is.'

Fathom snapped his chin up, staring at Shen like he was just now seeing him for the first time. 'Ah!' he said, as he rubbed his eyes. 'Why didn't I see it before? *You're* the key to finding the desert.'

Shen stared at the seer. 'Me?'

Kai reeled. '*Him?*'

'Shen?' whispered Rose, in disbelief.

The old man nodded. Then he threw his head back and laughed.

Wren

CHAPTER 21

Deep in the snowy mountains, Wren stood outside the chamber that held Prince Ansel's body and tried to catch her breath. She had only been in the room for five minutes, but it had felt like a lifetime. She could still see Ansel's lifeless face behind her eyes, hear the rest of Alarik's bargain echoing in her head. *You have three days to bring my brother back. Three days to fix what you destroyed in Anadawn.*

Wren had no idea if it could even be done – if it had ever been done before. And yet, as the possibility of Banba's freedom floated between them in breathy clouds, she had looked King Alarik dead in the eye, and said, *Yes, I'll do it.*

Yes, I'll save your brother.

Hope had sparked in Alarik's gaze. Or perhaps it was desperation that made his eyes shine brighter, bluer. *Until tomorrow then, witch.* With a curt nod, the king had swept from the room, leaving Wren alone with his brother's body, wondering what on earth she had just promised.

Alarik and his guards were long gone now. It was just Wren and Inga hovering in the dark tunnel.

'The king has ordered me to take you back to your room,' said the soldier. Perhaps it was Wren's imagination, but her tone was gentler now. 'You'll freeze down here.'

Wren stepped away from the door, conscious of the numbness in her fingers, how she had lost feeling in the tip of her nose. And then there was the matter of the *very dead* prince lying on the other side, mere feet from both of them. 'Let's get out of here.'

They hurried back the way they had come, Wren's footsteps quickening as she made a beeline for her grand-mother's cell. Banba was sitting cross-legged on the ground, the crimson cloak cascading around her like a pool of blood. A wash of colour had returned to her cheeks, and she was no longer shivering.

Wren came to her knees at the bars. 'I know what the king wants from me, Banba.'

Banba looked up. 'You can't give it to him.'

'Is it possible?' said Wren, ignoring the warning in her grandmother's voice. 'Is there a way to bring Ansel back? I've heard tales of such things. When I was a child, you told me once of a—'

'Enough!' The old witch pitched forward, knocking against the bars with such force, the entire cell shuddered. 'The question is not *can it be done*, the question is *should* it be done. If I have raised you at all, little bird, then you already know the answer.'

'Three days,' Wren pressed on. 'I have three days to bring Ansel back. Just tell me if there's a way. Please.'

But Banba was stone-faced. 'The witches of Ortha do not dabble in death. That is a door that must remain forever closed, for once it is opened, you cannot stop the darkness from seeping out. It will take from you until there is nothing left,' she said, gravely. 'What use is your body, once you've bartered your soul?'

Wren didn't care about her soul. She cared about the frost that clung to her grandmother's eyelashes, the tinge of blue that lingered around her lips. 'So, it can be done,' she said, reading between the lines of her grandmother's warning. 'There is a way.'

Banba's gaze flitted to Inga who was hovering over Wren's shoulder. She dropped her voice, until Wren had to strain to hear her over the drip-dripping of ice water. 'Some things aren't worth the price, little bird. Or the blood. Take your three days and use them to escape this infernal place.'

Banba pulled back from the bars. She raised her chin, signalling to Inga. 'My granddaughter is shivering. Take her back upstairs before she gets frostbite. I don't imagine your king would take kindly to you letting her fall into such a condition.'

'Banba!' said Wren, but her grandmother was already lumbering away from her, retreating to the dark recesses of her cell.

'I've said all I have to say to you, Wren. I don't want to see you down here again.'

Inga, who had been startled into action by the old witch's

warning, tugged Wren away from the bars.

'You will see me again!' shouted Wren. 'I'm going to free you! And then we're going home!'

Wren wrapped her arms around herself, seething at her stubborn grandmother as Inga marched her out of the dungeons. She was certain now that Banba held the secret she needed to bring Ansel back, just as surely as she knew her grandmother would never utter it to her. She would sooner freeze to death under the mountain than put Wren's soul in danger.

'It's *my* soul,' muttered Wren, as she plodded up the stairwell. 'I can do whatever I want with it.'

Back in her chamber, Wren was surprised to find a fire crackling in the grate. A delicious heat swirled about the room, restoring the feeling in her nose. She inhaled the warmth, hoping it might ease the ache blooming in her chest. But as the snow-swept morning roared into a stormy afternoon, Wren's uncertainty continued to gnaw at her.

Back in Ortha, there was nothing Banba wouldn't do for Wren. In the winter, when food was scarce, she filled Wren's dinner plate before her own, offering her the best vegetables from their meagre stock, the biggest cut of mutton. Sometimes the only cut. At night, she swaddled Wren in her warmest cloak, her laughter chattering through her teeth as she threatened to fight the wind that howled through the cracks of their little hut.

Someday, these winters will be long behind us, little bird, she promised Wren. *And you will have all the warmth and luxury that you deserve.*

With her grandmother's guiding hand on her shoulder, Wren had found her way to that luxury, but now Banba wasn't here to enjoy it. She was still shivering, still fighting to take up her place in the world.

It wasn't right. Wren couldn't stand it.

If Banba wasn't going to help her raise Prince Ansel from the dead, then she would have to find another way. She sat at her dresser and raked her fingers through her hair. 'Ancestors, please help me come up with something, so we can get out of this wretched place.'

But the room was silent, save for the wind howling at the windows. Wren had left her ancestors back in Eana, along with her sister. And her good sense.

By the time dinner arrived, she was ravenous. It was a bowl of chicken stew, flavoured with a medley of winter vegetables soft enough to melt on her tongue. To Wren's surprise, the cook had sent up dessert, too, the stew arriving with a thick slice of carrot cake and a generous glass of frostfizz.

She downed the frostfizz in one go, hoping it would dull the sharp edge of her anxiety. The bubbles went straight to her head, the drink stronger than any she had tried in Eana. Feeling lazy and heavy-limbed, she sank down in front of the fire and devoured the cake, eating it with her fingers and licking them clean so as not to miss a single crumb.

Wren was so enthralled by sugar and flame – not to mention by the frostfizz dancing in her head – that she didn't notice Tor until he was standing over her, repeating her name. 'Wren. Wren? *Wren.*'

Wren snapped her chin up, blinking out of her daze. The soldier shifted into focus, his shoulders broad under the crisp lines of his navy uniform, the hard edge of his jaw clenched.

'Tor,' she said, on a breath of confusion. 'What are you doing here?'

'You said yes. Why did you say yes?'

Wren staggered to her feet. 'Yes?' she said, wobbling a little. 'Yes to what?'

Tor's hand shot out. He caught her by the elbow, pulling her into the heat of his body. 'You said yes to Alarik.'

'Oh.' Wren understood then. He was referring to the bargain she had made over Ansel's corpse, the unthinkable promise that Banba had refused to make. That explained the harrowed look on his face, his mouth pressed into a hard line, like she had already done something unforgivable. 'He has my grandmother in chains,' she said, taking a step backwards to glare at him. 'Of course I said yes.'

Tor dragged a hand across his jaw. 'Stars, Wren. What were you thinking?'

'I was thinking that I don't want my grandmother to die in Gevra.' Wren folded her arms, steel-eyed in the face of his judgement. 'I was thinking that I would do anything to save her life. And I will.'

Tor was shaking his head. 'You can't play with the dead, Wren. I'm no witch, and even I know that.'

'It's Ansel,' said Wren, using the name to calm the squall

of nerves in her stomach. If she personalized the king's request – thought of the spell in terms of the prince, rather than the darkness of the deed itself – then it didn't seem so scary. So unforgivable. 'It's only Ansel.'

Tor frowned. 'Ansel is dead.'

'For now.'

'No, Wren.' He turned to the fire, staring into the flames like he was watching the memory of the prince's death play out all over again. 'It's too late.'

Wren studied the shadows on Tor's face and felt the distance between them as though it were an ice chasm. How different things had been back in the library at Anadawn, when they couldn't keep their hands off each other. Now it felt like Tor was a world away, the ghost of the fallen prince filling up the space between them.

Wren wanted desperately to cast it out. To turn back the moment of Ansel's death, and banish the pain that lingered in Tor's eyes. Just one more reason to find the spell.

'Don't you want to bring him back?' she asked. 'If there was a way to do it, wouldn't it make everything better?'

Firelight danced along their skin, illuminating Tor's face as it crumpled. Wren felt his longing, sensed the deep wound of his regret, and hated her part in it.

She reached for his hand. 'Let me try to fix it. I can—'

'You can't.' He looked down at his fingers, limp between hers. 'I didn't even think about him, Wren. When Rathborne let that dagger fly, all I thought about was you.'

'I'm sorry.'

He pulled away from her. 'A Gevran soldier relies on their instincts.'

It was Tor's instincts that had killed Prince Ansel. They had made him leap in front of Wren without hesitation, mere moments after her showboating had put Ansel in danger.

'I know it should have been me. The dagger was meant for me.' Wren drifted to the fire, turning her face to the flames to hide the shame in her cheeks. 'I know you wish you had saved him.'

'I don't wish it.' The bed creaked as Tor slumped on to it. 'Even now, I don't wish it.'

Surprise stilled Wren's tongue.

'I think perhaps that makes it worse,' Tor went on. 'I carry Prince Ansel's death with me every moment of every day. But I can't bring myself to . . .' He trailed off, shook his head. 'The alternative . . . I can't bring myself to think about it . . . It was to be my undoing either way.'

Wren's heart clenched. She crossed the room and sat down beside him, relieved when he didn't move away. She touched her head against his shoulder. 'I don't want to argue with you, Tor.'

He turned to look at her, the storm in his eyes so violent, Wren felt like she might fall into it. 'Then tell me you won't do it.'

'Don't make me lie to you.'

Tor closed his eyes. 'It will be *your* undoing, Wren.'

'Then we'll both be undone,' she murmured. 'It's my choice, Tor. I'm going to try.'

Tor's throat bobbed as he swallowed his anger. He nodded, then stood up. He walked back to the door and picked up a bag, dropping it with a *thunk!* on the dresser. 'This is from the king,' he said, stiffly. 'I'd wish you luck, but I don't want to lie to you either.'

In the next moment he was gone, the key turning in the lock and sealing Wren in once more. She stood by the fire, listening to his fading footfall. The room was colder without him, but she couldn't afford to dwell on his disapproval. She had to rely on her own instincts. And whether he meant to or not, Tor had given her another reason to go through with her plan. If she could bring back the prince, not only would she save her grandmother from death, but she would save Tor from the regret that festered inside him, devouring his goodness day by day. And if the price of such freedom was a sliver of her own soul, then that was another bargain Wren was prepared to make.

She drifted to the dresser, where her bejewelled hand mirror glittered faintly in the firelight. Wren opened the bag Alarik had delivered, expecting to find a gift of some kind, but a rancid smell seeped out, making her gag. She pinched her nose as she peered into the satchel, spying a pale pink tail curled up on itself.

Ugh. A dead mouse.

What in rotting hell was Alarik playing at?

Wren grimaced as she turned the bag upside down and shook out the rest. There were six dead mice in total. And a handwritten note.

Practice makes perfect.
Alarik

Rose
CHAPTER 22

As soon as Shen passed the map to Rose, the shapes began to disappear. In a panic, she'd thrust it back to him, only for them to return.

'Should we try to copy it on to something more permanent?' she suggested. But that wasn't possible either, because to Rose's amazement, the ruby beetle that Shen was sure represented the Sunkissed Kingdom kept moving. It may have been lost, but it certainly wasn't staying put.

'It must be because you're from the desert,' said Rose, trying to make sense of it. 'That's why the map responds to you.'

But that was wasn't right either, because when Kai snatched the map from his cousin, it went blank again. Rose caught the flash of rage that crossed his face as he stared at the yellowing parchment, willing it to work for him. 'Temperamental thing, eh?' he said, through his teeth. 'It's lucky I found you on the road, little cousin.' He forced a laugh, but Rose didn't miss the stiffness in his shoulders nor the coldness in his eyes.

She tried not to linger over Meredia's warning. *Kai Lo of the Sunkissed Kingdom, you hold great power in your fist. But inside you lies a darkness you must fight to resist.*

After dramatically declaring that Shen was the key to the lost desert kingdom, Fathom offered no more clarity on the subject. 'You have the map and the key. What more do you need?'

He had fiddled with his beard then, growing cagey, and Rose suspected Fathom had rather exhausted his knowledge of anything to do with the map, or indeed Shen. Still, it was more than enough to help them on their way. By the time they left the Moonlit Menagerie, the valley languished in darkness, the starcrests flitting overhead like shooting stars. They decided to stay the night and depart at first light, cheered by Fathom's promise of a special herbal tea that would counteract the poisonous fumes of the valley.

They ate with Meredia and Fathom in a small, candlelit room beneath the Moonlit Menagerie, the stone walls hung with beautiful woven tapestries that showcased the towers at their full glory, while Pog scurried off to make up their rooms for the night. Dinner was bland but filling – a hearty soup made from bitter greens, served with brown bread and thick slabs of cheese. Kai asked for whisky and was told there was nothing of the sort at Amarach. The seers abstained from alcohol so as not to impede their craft.

'Nobody tell Celeste,' said Shen, between mouthfuls. 'Or she'll never embrace her destiny.'

Rose's gaze drifted to the window. She watched the top of

each tower flicker to life, as the seers arrived by candlelight to read the skies.

'But what's the point of future-gazing if you're all cloistered here?' asked Rose. 'Can you even help people?'

'When there are people to be helped,' said Meredia. 'In such cases, we send out messages and pray they are heeded. And of course, the starcrests will always find their way to new seers to guide them in their craft. Now that the throne of Eana has returned to the witches, I expect we will see more of them.'

Fathom set down his spoon. 'Once the country settles, that is,' he said, ominously. 'We have seen rebellion stirring in the skies.'

'We've seen it on the streets,' said Kai, reaching for more cheese. 'Nothing a little warfare can't handle.'

Rose shot him a warning look. 'I'm afraid what you've seen is true. Edgar Barron is succeeding in building a movement. One that seeks to remove my sister and me from the throne.' She felt a pang of guilt at leaving Thea back at Anadawn to face the growing rebellion, but Rose would rejoin her soon enough.

'Barron has made a weapon out of people's fear,' said Meredia, uneasily. 'There is nothing more dangerous than a hateful man with a clever tongue.'

'Which is why we mustn't tarry too long on our quest,' said Rose, gravely. 'Once we recover the Sunkissed Kingdom and garner a new army of witches, I must return at once to Anadawn to show Edgar Barron the true might of the throne.

And when my sister returns from Gevra, we will embark on a new royal tour together.' She looked around the table. 'I'm sure you've seen her safe return?'

The silence that followed was as stony as the seers' faces, but they offered up nothing about Wren. When Rose prodded for an answer about her sister, Meredia simply frowned and said she had strayed too far from their gazes.

Unlike the Straggler's Rest, the Amarach Towers had plenty of rooms.

And while that meant that Rose, Shen and Kai each had their own, nestled side by side in the largest of the towers, Rose hated seeing all the empty ones they passed as they climbed the winding stairwell. Once, long ago, before the war named for her mother, all these rooms had been full of witches and seers, young and old, who had looked out at the same promising future.

Rose hoped one day soon the Amarach Towers would be full once more, and all talk of rebellion and darkness would be confined to the past.

Still sour over the lack of whisky, Kai offered a curt goodnight before stalking into his room, leaving Shen and Rose alone in the hall.

'Do you think he's all right?' said Rose, as his door slammed shut in their faces. 'He didn't mock us once over dinner. He just kept scowling into his soup.'

Shen shrugged. 'Maybe he's always been moody.'

'Or maybe it's the map,' Rose whispered. She couldn't shake the memory of Kai's face when he realized it didn't answer to him. 'I think he might be jealous of you.'

Shen pressed a hand to his waistband, where the scroll was safely stowed. 'Let him stew in his jealousy, then. He'll move past it eventually.'

Rose chewed on her lip.

'You worry too much.' Shen reached out and tucked a strand of hair behind her ear. His fingers lingered on her cheek. 'Get some sleep. I'll be right next door if you need anything.'

Rose leaned into his touch. For a wild moment, she wanted to invite Shen into her room and spend the rest of the night kissing him senseless. But in a valley full of seers, Rose wouldn't dare risk her reputation by doing something so royally inappropriate right under their noses. And anyway, she was filthy. As much as she wanted Shen, she also desperately wanted to have a bath. And Pog had promised to have one bubbling in her bedroom when she arrived.

'I should go inside before my bath gets cold,' she said, as she stepped away from him. 'Goodnight, Shen.'

'Enjoy your bath.' His gaze lingered on hers. 'I bet it won't be as nice as a soak in Balor's Eye.'

Rose flushed at the memory of them bathing together in the desert. 'Keep your map close, and perhaps we might visit it again,' she said, before she could stop herself.

Shen smiled as he turned for his room. 'Now I know what I'll be dreaming of tonight.'

The tub wasn't nearly as luxurious as her one back in Anadawn, but the water was warm and bubbly and lightly perfumed. Soon, all the dirt and grime from the past two days had sloughed off her, and Rose felt like herself again. Or at least as close to a queen as she could hope to feel so far from her throne.

When the water was cold, she clambered out. Pog had left a fluffy towel on the dresser, beside a pot of face cream and a hand mirror. Rose smiled, heartened by his thoughtfulness. She dried herself and put on her nightgown, before fetching her hairbrush.

She picked up the mirror and startled at the jolt in her fingers. It was only then that she noticed the sapphires around the rim. It was the same one from the Moonlit Menagerie! But the glass was cloudy now. She blew on it, then used her sleeve to wipe it clean. Suddenly, the glass began to glow, casting a faint blue light across the room. Rose gasped as a reflection flickered to life.

But the face in the mirror didn't belong to her.

It belonged to Wren.

Wren

CHAPTER 23

Wren stared at the dead mice with mild revulsion. There was no earth to accompany them. Alarik might be pleased with her, but that didn't mean he trusted her.

She frowned as she picked up the first mouse. It was stiff and cold, its tail flopping over the edge of her palm. With no idea where to begin and no earth to assist her, she curled her fingers around the rodent and reached for an enchantment anyway. The words filled her mind at once, before tingling on the tip of her tongue.

'*From death to life, heed my request, and wake from your eternal rest.*'

The fire crackled in the grate. Outside, the rising storm howled. Wren scowled at the mouse. 'Come on, you little bastard. Wakey, wakey.'

No use. It was an entirely new spell. She had never tried anything like this before with her enchantment magic, and she had nothing to trade for it anyway. She picked up another mouse and held one in each hand. She summoned a new spell, offering one corpse for another, but neither mouse stirred. They were as dead now as they were when the kitchen tabby cat had caught them.

Wren went to the door and told Inga to bring her some bloody salt. And some more frostfizz, while she was at it. No response. Wren fumed in silence. She would have to have words with the king tomorrow.

Exhausted by her own frustration – and ten more failed enchantments – Wren flung a mouse into the fire and watched it sizzle. In a fit of desperation, she sank to her knees and gathered up a pile of ash. She returned to the other mice, offering the ash in exchange for her spell.

Another failure. 'What am I supposed to do with six bloodless corpses?' she muttered, as she paced the room. What could an enchanter do without earth? Alarik would have had better luck bargaining with a healer.

Wren thought of Rose, and her stomach twisted with guilt. She would never dabble with dark magic, and certainly not against Banba's wishes. Then again, Rose would never have come to Gevra in the first place. She was far too cautious, too—

A blue light flashed in Wren's periphery. She spun around, scouring the dresser for a twitching mouse. But the five remaining rodents were still very much dead. Wren was about to turn away from them, when she glimpsed another blue spark. Her fingertips began to tingle, the magic in her bones waking up in recognition of another.

She froze mid-step.

The light wasn't coming from the mice at all.

The hand mirror was shimmering. A gasp swelled in Wren's throat as she peered over it. Inside its jewelled frame, someone else was looking back at her.

'Wren?' said Rose's face in the mirror. 'Is that really you?'

'Rose? Where *are* you?' Wren pressed her fingers against the glass, trying to make sense of what she was seeing. The mirror began to tremble, her sister's reflection warping under her touch. A rush of wind whipped up, casting Rose's hair askew. It seemed to be coming from inside the mirror.

'Oh no!' said Wren, as the wind broke free from the glass and reached out for her, too. It threw its arms around Wren, tugging her into a howling tunnel. One minute, she was standing in her bedroom in Gevra, and the next she was seized by the horrible sensation of falling – no, *plummeting* – through the earth. The room whipped around her in a blur, her breath shallowing as the snow-swept mountains of Gevra slipped out from under her, and a new world slid into place.

The wind stopped, abruptly, and Wren found herself kneeling on hard ground. The mirror was at her feet. No, not her mirror, but its twin. The sapphires were still glowing, but faintly now. She stood up on trembling legs, taking in the small, candlelit bedroom. 'Rose?' she called out, tentatively. 'Are you here somewhere?'

'Wren? Where did you go?' came Rose's voice from the mirror. 'Wait. Oh no. Is that *snow*?' She gasped as she whipped her head around. 'Am I in Gevra? I'd better not be in Gevra!'

Wren picked up the mirror. 'Well, at least you know where you are. This isn't Anadawn.' She glanced once more at her meagre surroundings. 'Are you on the royal tour?'

'In a manner of speaking.' Rose paused. 'I'm in Amarach. Or, at least, I *was*.'

'What?' Wren clutched the hand mirror, listening in stunned silence as her sister filled her in on the events of the past few days, how the desert had spat out Shen's cousin and how his sudden appearance at Anadawn had set in motion a journey that had led them south, through a poisonous valley and all the way to the Amarach Towers. Where Wren now found herself.

She hurried to the window, straining to make out the valley of lost seers, but in the darkness she could only see the top of the towers flickering like tapered candles. And above them the starcrests arcing across the sky like a magnificent meteor shower.

'Wren! Are you even listening?'

'Sorry,' said Wren, holding up the mirror so they could see each other again. 'I want to see what it looks like. Nobody's been here for years.'

'Wren! Focus! For stars' sake, I thought you might be dead. First, you disappear in the middle of the night—'

'I left a note,' Wren cut in. 'And Elske.'

'Will you please just tell me what your plan is?' Rose glanced around the room. 'I see you made it to Grinstad Palace. But how on earth did you charm your way into such a nice room? I mean, just *look* at those furs. And that chandelier!'

'Now who's losing focus?' said Wren. 'It might be pretty, Rose, but it's still a prison.' She briefly explained how she had made it all the way to Grinstad in one piece. But, unlike Rose, Wren was deliberately hazy on the details. 'So, Alarik and I made a bargain,' she finished, vaguely. 'I just have to help him with . . . something . . . and then he'll let me and Banba go.'

Rose frowned. 'Since when are you on first-name terms with King Alarik? And what exactly is the bargain?'

Wren swished her hand about. 'It's just a little enchantment . . . thing.'

'Go on . . .'

'It's complicated,' said Wren, shortly. 'But don't worry. It's all in hand.' Above her, a flock of starcrests twirled in tandem, moving across the sky like a silver spinning top. She let out a low whistle. 'I still can't believe you found this place.'

'Of course I did. And I'm going to find the Sunkissed Kingdom, too. Which is why we have to switch back,' said Rose, frantically. 'As much I appreciate this charming decor, I don't want to spend another minute in Gevra.' She started prodding the glass with her fingers. 'How does this stupid thing work?'

'Wait!' said Wren, as a thought occurred to her. 'Give me two minutes. I need earth.'

'Wren—' Rose's voice rang out from the mirror as Wren tossed it on to the bed.

'Don't worry! I'll be right back!' She bolted through the door and made for the stairwell, following a row of flickering everlights down to the bottom of the tower. She wrenched the door open, breathing in a generous lungful of fresh air. The night was dewy and scented faintly with moss – a far cry from the glacial prison of Grinstad Palace and the ghostly Fovarr Mountains that loomed over it.

Wren stepped over the threshold and bumped into an old man wearing a trailing blue robe. He was holding a jar of dirt.

'There you are,' he said, offering it to Wren in greeting. 'I knew Pog would give her the mirror. And that you would have its twin.'

Wren stared at the jar. Then the man. 'Who are you?'

'Fathom.' His smile winked beneath his grey beard. 'I've been expecting you.'

'I'm not staying.'

'I know,' he said, mildly.

Wren took the jar, rotating it in front of her nose. 'Earth,' she muttered.

'The very best of it,' said the man, proudly. 'Mined from the silt beneath our waterfalls.'

Wren frowned. 'How did you— Oh, right. Seer.'

The man tapped his nose. 'Twelve sapphires for twelve minutes.'

'Huh?'

'The mirror,' he said. 'When the last sapphire stops glowing, the switch is reversed.'

'Oh.' Wren hugged the dirt to her. 'Where did they come from anyway?'

The man stood back and in the fractured moonlight, his eyes were just as bright as the starcrests. 'The mirrors belonged to the Starcrest sisters, another lifetime ago,' he said. 'Ortha had them made during a time when magic was not so . . . limited.' His beard twitched with the beginnings of a frown. 'Even when they travelled far from one another, the twin queens were never apart. Until . . .'

'Oonagh broke them apart,' said Wren. She didn't like to be reminded of Oonagh Starcrest, the twin who had succumbed to the darkness and betrayed her sister. 'I know the story.'

'A travelling witch brought the mirror to Amarach many years ago, alongside other magical treasures that once resided at Anadawn.'

'Isn't that stealing?'

Fathom chuckled. 'I prefer to think of it as rescuing.'

'Twelve minutes,' said Wren, stepping back into the tower. 'I should head back.'

The seer dipped his chin. 'Tread carefully, Queen Wren. Both outside, and in.' At Wren's look of confusion, he tapped the space above his heart. 'There are some journeys we can never come back from.'

Caught in the unnerving brightness of his gaze, Wren found herself lost for words, but in the end it didn't matter. The seer turned on his heel and was gone, his blue robe fading into the night.

Wren tried to shake off his warning, but it squirmed inside her. She was about to close the door behind her, when she caught sight of a familiar white blur moving in the bushes.

'Elske!' She clicked her teeth. 'Is that you, sweetling?'

The wolf bounded out of the shrubs and barrelled straight into Wren, knocking her to the ground so she could lick her face. Wren burst into laughter, then sat up to scratch behind her ears. 'What are you doing out here?' she said, as she shooed the wolf inside. 'You're a princess. You deserve a proper bed.'

The wolf kept pace with Wren as she hurried back up the stairwell. She slowed at the sound of a door creaking, squinting at a figure in the dimness. A growl rumbled in Elske's throat. The man had his hand on the doorknob next to Rose's room, his ear pressed to the wood like he was eavesdropping.

'Who the hell are you?' said Wren.

He spun around, lightning fast. 'Queenie,' he said, forcing a chuckle. 'I thought you'd be asleep by now.'

'Oh,' said Wren, letting her shoulders relax. 'You're Shen's idiot cousin.'

Elske growled again.

The man – Kai, Wren recalled – blinked. Then fell back against the door. 'Wait. You're the other one.' His gaze darted. 'What are you doing here?'

'Just passing through,' said Wren, waggling the jar of dirt as she returned to Rose's door. She paused, then, turning back to Kai. 'The better question is, why are you skulking around out here in the dark?'

'I was just checking on my cousin.'

'Why?' said Wren. 'I've never known Shen to have nightmares.'

Kai flashed a grin – and what a grin it was. 'I'm the protective sort.'

Wren narrowed her eyes. 'So am I.'

'Right, well . . . good,' said Kai.

'Indeed.' Wren waited for him to retreat. Eventually, he stepped away from Shen's room and returned to his own.

Once Kai was gone, she turned back to Elske. 'I was going to tuck you into bed, sweetling, but I think it might be better if you slept out here tonight and kept an eye on things.' She glanced at Shen's door, listening to the light rumble of his snores behind it. 'I don't know what Kai was doing just now, but I've got a strange feeling about him.'

Elske dipped her chin, growling softly in agreement.

Wren cupped the wolf's mighty head and kissed it. 'Clever girl.'

Rose

CHAPTER 24

Rose stood in the middle of Wren's bedroom at Grinstad Palace, glaring at the mirror in her hand.

'Wren?' she hissed. 'Wren! Where are you?'

Rose's panic echoed around her. A moment ago, her sister had been inside the mirror, looking back at her – *talking* to her – and now she had disappeared, leaving Rose all by herself. In Gevra!

'Why must you be so infuriating?' she fumed, as she placed the mirror on the desk. It was then that she noticed the dead mice. She bit back a shriek as she stumbled away from them.

Is this what King Alarik was sending Wren to eat? He was even worse than Rose thought!

Her stomach churned. The mice were starting to make her feel ill. In a bid to distract herself, she explored the decadent bedroom. She grabbed the mirror, in case Wren returned, and made a beeline for the armoire. 'Now what do we have in here?' she murmured, as she swung the doors open. Her eyes went wide as she gazed upon the finest collection of dresses she had ever seen. 'Oh my.'

She trailed her fingers along a sumptuous silver stole, before yanking it out. She draped it around her shoulders, luxuriating in its softness. *How peculiar*, she thought, as she twirled in front of the full-length mirror. *The king feeds Wren dead mice but dresses her like a queen.*

For a moment, Rose wondered what her life would have been like if she had married Ansel and come to live at Grinstad Palace. Full of beautiful clothes and terrible food, by the looks of it. But surely as her husband, Ansel would have treated her better than this. She drifted to the window and pressed her palm against the frosted glass. She wondered where the poor prince was buried, and was stung by the regret that she could not lay a rose at his grave and pay her respects. She was glad, at least, that Ansel had been brought home to rest among his beloved mountains.

A knock at the door startled Rose from her thoughts.

'Wren? Are you in there?'

Rose leaped behind the curtain, fearfully peering out at the door handle. *Please don't open, please don't open, please don't open.*

Another knock. 'It's Tor. Can I come in?'

Rose gasped. Wren hadn't mentioned a thing about Captain Iversen! What was he doing knocking on her door in the middle of the night? What else was her sister keeping from her? It occurred to Rose that she should say something before he barrelled in. 'One moment! I'm changing for dinner!' She glanced at the clock and winced.

'Dinner?' said Tor. 'At midnight?'

'Bed!' said Rose, in a fluster. 'I meant, changing for bed! Don't come in! I'm not decent!'

Tor was silent for a long time. Then there was a soft thud, as he pressed his forehead against the door. 'Wren, I can tell you're not yourself.'

Oh no. He *knew*. The blood drained from Rose's face as she cowered in the curtains. She glared down at the mirror. What was taking Wren so long? She was going to murder her sister. Gingerly, Rose stepped out from behind the drapes and took a deep breath, preparing to face the Gevran soldier. 'Tor—'

'I know you're upset about earlier,' he went on, earnestly. 'I don't want to fight with you.'

Rose sagged against the window ledge. He *didn't* know. Yet.

'But I can't just stand aside and let you do this. I shouldn't have given you those mice.' He cursed under his breath. 'It's not right. It's not *natural*. Alarik's not thinking straight, Wren. He's clouded by grief.'

Rose went perfectly still. This must be the bargain Wren had mentioned. But what could be so terrible that it had unsettled Tor this much? She waited for him to go on.

'Ansel's dead. If you bring him back, it won't be the end of Alarik's fascination with you, it will be the beginning. He'll never let you go.'

Rose blanched. *That* was the bargain? Wren had promised to bring Ansel back from the dead? She shook the mirror, desperately trying to summon her sister. Was Wren out of her mind? Could she even *do* that? The only witch who had ever toyed with forbidden magic was Oonagh Starcrest. It was her use of human and animal sacrifice – *blood magic* – that had ended up twisting her soul and the entire fate of the witches.

Rose glanced at the dead mice, a new shiver of dread walking up her spine. They suddenly made a lot more sense.

'I know you don't want to hear this right now, but I care about you too much to see you go down this path.' Tor's voice was quiet with resignation. 'When you're ready to talk, I'll be here. We can figure this out. Together.'

Finally, he turned from the door. Rose stared at the handle with her breath bound up in her chest, listening to the sound of his fading footsteps. A moment later, Wren's voice rang out from the mirror.

'Good news! I spoke to Fathom,' she said, by way of greeting. 'He says we'll switch back when the final sapphire goes out.'

Rose glanced at the last shimmering gemstone, then glared at her sister's reflection. 'Then I'll make this quick. You are NOT under ANY circumstances to attempt a resurrection spell.'

Wren's face fell. 'Did the dead mice tip you off?'

Rose ploughed on. 'Don't you remember what happened to Oonagh Starcrest when she turned to human sacrifice? You can't play with death, Wren. It's forbidden.'

Wren squeezed her eyes shut. 'I really don't need this lecture right now.'

'Well, you just missed a rather stirring one from Tor.'

The last sapphire was winking out. 'Promise me you won't

try to do this,' said Rose, desperately. 'There has to be another way to save Banba. Please, Wren.'

Wren opened her mouth to respond just as the wind rushed back in. Rose yelped as it burst from the mirror and swirled around her. The world tilted, turning to blurs of blue and white and silver, the fur rug at her feet giving way to hard stone, as she landed back in Amarach.

'Wren?' She grasped the hand mirror, but her sister was gone. There was only her own panicked reflection staring back at her, bordered by twelve sapphires no longer aglow.

Wren
CHAPTER 25

Once Wren returned to her bedroom in Grinstad Palace, she swept the hair out of her eyes and tucked the hand mirror safely back inside her satchel. She grinned as she set her jar of dirt on the table. 'Well, that was an adventure.'

Even after eighteen years of living as a witch, she still marvelled at the boundless possibilities of magic. Sometimes she could forget just how long it had lived – no, *thrived* – in Eana, how powerful the witches had been before Oonagh Starcrest had cursed her sister Ortha and shattered their craft into five different strands.

Wren blew out a breath, the knot of her anxiety uncoiling in her stomach. She was grateful for the chance to speak to her sister, though she could have done without her warning at the end. Of course Tor had meddled and tipped Rose off. But Wren couldn't think about Tor right now. Or her sister. She had been relieved when the sapphires winked out, saving her from making a promise to Rose that she would only have to break.

Still, part of Wren wished she could have stayed with Rose

in Amarach and woken in the morning to watch the sun rise over the lost towers before journeying to find the Sunkissed Kingdom together. But the strands of her destiny had tugged her north, and, right now, she had to concentrate on getting herself – and Banba – out of Gevra in one piece. And whether Rose approved of it or not, there was only one way to do that.

Wren had vowed to resurrect Prince Ansel, and *that* was a promise she intended to keep.

She sat at her dresser and removed a fistful of dirt. The earth glinted amber in the firelight, a whisper of ancient magic tingling against her skin. Wren smiled. This was good earth, *powerful* earth – watered by the falls of Amarach.

She positioned a dead mouse in front of her and scattered a pinch of dirt over its lifeless body. She conjured a new enchantment, willing the creature to come back to life. The earth shimmered as it disappeared, but the mouse didn't so much as twitch.

Wren huffed as she reached for more. 'Rise, you useless rodent!' Another spell – tighter, shorter. Nothing. She bit off a curse as she worked on another. And then another, and another. Minutes turned to hours, the fire slowly dwindling in its grate. Wren's patience was wearing thin, and, to make matters worse, a blistering cold had started to seep in from outside.

'This is a waste of time,' she muttered, as she slumped in her chair. She should have known it wasn't going to be easy. It would take more than a handful of silt and a crafty rhyme to prise a spirit from the jaws of death and reanimate its stiffened corpse. If she couldn't wake one measly mouse from the dead, how was she ever going to resurrect Ansel?

Wren tipped her head back with a groan. Once Alarik figured out she had no idea what she was doing, he would take his anger out on Banba. She had made an impossible deal with an impossible man, and the longer she sat in her room, staring at those dead mice, the tighter his noose felt around her neck. She rolled to her feet, pacing the room to keep warm. Outside, a blizzard raged in the starless dark. The wind moaned and the mountain creaked, like an old house.

There is a darkness that moves in Gevra, echoed Banba's voice in her head. *The wind is heavy with it. It feels like old magic.* Tainted *magic*.

Wren's stomach twisted. Maybe it was the dead mice or the howling blizzard, but fear was taking root in her. She knew that if she let it grow, it would douse the flame of her magic, and enchantments of any kind would soon prove impossible. She needed to see Banba again, to beg the secret of death magic from her grandmother before Wren's incompetence destroyed them both.

She grabbed a white fur stole from the wardrobe and threw it around her shoulders to keep warm, then removed another fistful of dirt from her jar, carefully folding most of it inside a handkerchief. She knocked on the door urgently, and when it opened the earth flew from her palm and sent Inga slumping to the ground in a heap.

Wren stepped over the soldier's body and out on to the fourth floor of Grinstad Palace.

She retraced her journey to the dungeons from earlier that day, winding down one flight of stairs and then another, the echo of her footsteps lost in the ragged cry of the blizzard as it pounded its icy fists against the windows. They were packed with snow, the flickering hallways eerily silent. The soldiers on duty were half asleep at their posts, their beasts slumbering at their feet. It was later than Wren thought.

Before long she made it to the top of the grand atrium staircase. She paused to take in the magnificent glass dome and the sky, white and whirling, beyond it. Wren felt for a moment like she was trapped between a fairy tale and a nightmare, the glacial beauty of this faraway world howling as it loomed ever closer, threatening to suffocate her. She dipped her chin to assess the lower floor of the atrium and froze with her foot on the topmost stair.

The woman in white was back. Queen Valeska. Just as before she was sitting at the glass piano, as still and marbled as a statue. Pale, slender fingers rested on the keys, too light to make a sound. Wren placed a hand on the crystal banister and tiptoed to the next stair, her eyes straining to make out the woman's face.

Why did she come here, night after night, to brood at that glass piano? Wren moved to the next stair. And then the next. She was planning to sneak around her on her way to the dungeon, but as she drew closer, she couldn't look away from the pain on her face. Her strange stillness. Her—

The woman snapped her chin up, snaring Wren in her pale gaze. Wren froze. She raised one long, spindly arm, as though to skewer Wren with the point of her finger.

Alerted to the sudden stir of movement, a slumbering snow tiger poked his head out of a nearby alcove. Wren turned on her heel and tried to bolt back up the staircase, but her foot caught on the step and she stumbled, her arm flying out to stop her fall. She grabbed on to the crystal balustrade, hissing as its jagged edge cut into her palm. She quickly hauled herself up, her blood leaving behind a crimson stain as she hurried back up to the landing.

If the queen screamed or the snow tiger decided to chase Wren, she wouldn't just lose her newly acquired dirt but possibly her life. She sprinted back to her bedroom, her breath bulleting out of her as she leaped over Inga and deftly sealed herself inside. She closed her eyes and waited, but no one came. The snow tiger hadn't followed her.

Wren's bedroom was darker now; the fire was nearing its last embers. She shrugged off her stole to find her blood all over it. She flung it into the corner of the room and stood beneath a sconce to examine her palm. The wound was deep, about the size of an almond and bleeding badly. Wren winced as she pictured the incriminating trail of blood that now led from the atrium stairwell all the way up to her bedroom. She slumped on to her bed.

Wren wished Rose was with her. Not just because she missed her sister more than she thought she would, but because Rose was a healer. Now she would have to make do with her own wits. She returned to the dresser in search of cloth to bind her wound. The dead mice looked eerie in the dimness, their white fur matted with dirt. *Wasted dirt*, thought Wren sourly. And they were beginning to reek. She wrinkled her nose as she rifled through the top drawer, leaving her left hand palm up and still bleeding on the dresser. Her pinkie finger absently brushed against a mouse, sending a sudden shock of heat through her.

Wren froze. The fingers on her injured hand were tingling. And the blood itself . . . Wren blinked, just to be sure, but there was no denying it. Her blood was *glowing*. Her stomach lurched as she tried to make sense of the soft red glimmer that now emanated from her skin. Her eyes focused on the dead mouse lying beside it; its fine white whiskers, its curling pink tail, but her mind was miles away, back in the Amarach Towers, and the voice in her head was not her own. It belonged to Rose.

Don't you remember what happened to Oonagh Starcrest when she turned to human sacrifice? You cannot play with death, Wren. It's forbidden.

Wren stared at her bleeding palm, feeling magic tingle beneath it. If human sacrifice resulted in the most potent magic – the kind that had toppled an entire empire of witches, then what could a single drop of blood do? Not just human blood but witch blood.

Her blood.

Suddenly, the answer was obvious.

'Blood magic,' whispered Wren, recalling what the old seer, Glenna, had told her before her death. One thousand years ago, Oonagh Starcrest had turned to blood magic to become more powerful than her sister Ortha. She began with animal blood, but in time she had turned to human blood. *Human sacrifice.*

Wren sat bolt upright, remembering that Banba had said something similar down in the dungeons.

Some things aren't worth the price, little bird. Or the blood.

Or the blood.

Wren looked between the dead mouse and her own mangled hand. Was it truly possible? Could she really use her own blood?

She knew it must be. That's why her grandmother had looked so scared. Even Banba wouldn't dare dabble in the same magic that had twisted Oonagh's soul. She had chosen to perish rather than attempt a forbidden craft.

'Stubborn old woman,' muttered Wren. 'One time won't hurt.' And it wasn't as if Wren was planning to follow in Oonagh's footsteps and sacrifice living things. She'd just use a bit of her own blood and see if it worked. There was no harm in that, surely. It already belonged to her.

Outside, the blizzard raged on. The window rattled in its frame, cowering against the angry whorls of snow. It felt as if the mountains themselves were trembling in fear. Wren was trembling, too. She made a fist of her mangled hand and raised it above the mouse, watching the blood drip through her fingers. It landed on the snow-white fur, staining it red.

'From death to life, heed my request, and wake from your eternal rest.'

For a moment, the wind stopped keening, as though to

listen in. Wren could feel the slow thud of her heartbeat in her chest, a strange calmness spreading through her until she felt deliciously drunk. She watched her blood fall, one drop and then another, but felt no pain. The mouse's fur began to glow.

Wren's throat tightened. 'Wakey, wakey, little one.'

She didn't realize she was holding her breath until her lungs began to burn. Outside, the wind kicked up again, thrashing restlessly against the window. The mountains groaned, like they were in pain, and the last embers of firelight flickered in the grate. As darkness crawled over the room like a shroud, something impossible happened – the moment so small and fleeting, Wren almost missed it.

The mouse's tail twitched. Once. And then again. The blood on its fur disappeared, revealing its white undercoat. A heartbeat passed, and then it opened its beady eyes.

Wren stared into them. 'Get up,' she whispered.

The mouse rolled to its feet, zigzagging across the dresser as though it had drunk too much frostfizz. Carefully, Wren lowered it down on to the floor and watched it stagger across the rug. She tiptoed after it, ignoring the blood still dripping from her hand. Her magic fizzed inside her, pulsing like a second heartbeat. It was awake. It was *triumphant*.

Wren was triumphant.

Until, suddenly, she wasn't. The mouse collapsed in the middle of the rug, twitched once, and was dead all over again. Wren sank to her knees as the flood of her magic rushed out of her. It left a strange hollow behind, as though some innate part of Wren – her heart, her lungs – had gone with it. Her stomach roiled and she lunged for the grate, vomiting her dinner back up. She wretched and wretched, waiting for the discomfort to ease. When it finally did, she looked down to find that instead of food, the grate was full of ash.

Beware the curse of Oonagh Starcrest, the lost witch queen, whispered the wind. *The curse lives in new bones . . . new blood.*

Wren examined her hand in the darkness. The wound was clotting over, and her palm was starting to sting. The hollow feeling was still there, but it was more manageable now, like the soreness that comes with a bruise. Was this the curse taking root inside her? Or was it simply the queasiness that came from using forbidden magic? From seeing it work before your own eyes?

Yes, thought Wren, trying to convince herself. *That must be what it is.*

Seized by a new wave of determination, she stood up and returned to the other mice, still laid out on her dresser.

She had done it once. All she had to do was do it again, but better. Practice makes perfect, after all. She didn't give herself time to second-guess her decision as she dragged her fingernail across her wound, drawing fresh blood. When she spoke again, her voice was clear and strong. The enchantment filled the room like a fierce wind, rivalling the blizzard raging through the mountains.

The next mouse woke up with a determined squeak.

Wren's lips curled. 'Welcome back to the world of the living, little one.'

Rose
CHAPTER 26

Rose slept in her silver fur stole with the mirror clutched in her fist just in case Wren tried to contact her again. But the sapphires never glowed. She tossed and turned all night, plagued by nightmares of those disgusting dead mice floating in rivers of Wren's blood. Surely, her sister wouldn't do what Alarik was asking.

She wouldn't.

She *couldn't*.

Wren had to know how risky it would be. After all, Oonagh had lost everything when she had dabbled in that kind of magic. And she had cursed all the witches, too, fracturing their power into five separate strands.

By the time the sun peered over the horizon, flooding her chamber with golden light, Rose had convinced herself that Wren would do the right thing. She'd figure out another way to save Banba and come home. The fact that she was not only alive but staying in such luxurious quarters spoke to her sister's innate ability to charm her way into getting what she needed, even without her magic. And now that she had earth from Amarach to help her, she would be fine. All would be well.

But still, Rose decided to keep the mirror close.

Over a hearty breakfast of porridge drizzled with honey and sprinkled with walnuts, Rose told Shen what had happened with the mirrors, and how she and Wren had switched places.

'I told you she'd be fine,' he said, after weathering the news with surprising calm. 'Although I'm offended she didn't think to say hello to me while she was here. We're supposed to be best friends.'

Rose wrinkled her nose. 'I wouldn't call *promising to bring back the dead brother of the iron-fisted king who wants to kill you* "fine", but at least she's alive.'

Kai quirked a brow.

'What are you smirking at?' snapped Rose, catching his eye.

'You witch queens sure like to get yourselves into trouble.'

Rose's nostrils flared. 'I think you'll find that *you* are the only trouble I'm currently dealing with.'

'I've been on my best behaviour, Queenie,' said Kai. 'But you've still got Barron and his Arrows to worry about. And a buried kingdom to find. Your sister's off in Gevra dabbling in forbidden magic, and then, of course, there's the question of who you're going to marry if you want to ally yourself with a stronger nation before King Alarik openly declares war on—'

'That's enough out of you,' interrupted Shen.

'One thing at a time,' said Rose. 'Today we find the Sunkissed Kingdom.'

Kai held up his cup of untouched tea. 'I'll drink to that. Even if it is this hot horse piss you people are so fond of.'

Rose thanked the seers for their hospitality while Shen and Kai fetched the horses from the stables. Elske padded after her, staying close. The wolf must have arrived late last night; Rose had found her in the stairwell outside her room before breakfast, her pale gaze trained on Kai's door.

'I hope to see you all again,' said Rose, smiling at each seer in turn. 'You are always welcome at Anadawn.'

Fathom took her hands in his own. Rose tensed, waiting for him to spout another dire warning, but his eyes remained warm, present. 'Should you need anything else, now you know where to find us.'

'I trust you'll see me coming,' said Rose.

'Of course,' said Pog, with a grin. 'And the wolf. I was right about her in the end.'

'Hush, Pog,' said Fathom. 'No one likes a show-off.'

Meredia chuckled. 'We hope you find what you're looking for, Queen Rose.'

Rose unfurled the silver stole she'd taken from Grinstad Palace. She'd desperately wanted to keep it, but Shen had put his foot down. For one thing, it would be far too warm for the desert, and for another, it was much too conspicuous. *Goodbye, sweet luxury*, she thought as she held it out to Fathom. 'I thought you might like to add this to your menagerie.'

'Ah, a silver ermine!' He took the stole and buried his face in it. 'It's just what I've been missing.'

Meredia and Pog exchanged a look, both of them stifling a giggle as Fathom tossed the fur around his shoulders and did a twirl.

'What was that you were saying about show-offs just now?' needled Meredia.

Fathom tickled her nose with the end of his stole. 'Jealousy doesn't suit you.'

'Do you have to take the wolf with you?' said Pog, crouching next to Elske to scratch behind her ears. 'We'd take good care of her here, you know. I've always wanted a best friend.'

Fathom stopped twirling to scowl at the boy. 'And what am I? An old boot?'

'I'd leave her with you if I could, Pog. The desert is no place for a Gevran wolf,' said Rose. 'But I don't think she'd stay. She's very loyal.'

'Keep the wolf,' said Meredia. 'The way ahead is fraught with danger.'

Rose swallowed, thickly. 'Do you mean the Arrows?'

'Barron. And others.' Meredia's frown deepened as she studied Rose, her eyes darting as though she was tracing an invisible aura. 'It is hazy.'

Rose wanted to ask more, but at that very moment, Shen and Kai arrived on their horses. Shen held his hand out to

Rose, and she climbed up, settling herself in front of him. Elske leaped to her feet and howled, as if to say she was ready to go, too.

Rose nodded at the seers. 'Thank you again.'

They bowed in unison. 'Safe travels, Queen Rose.'

They picked their way back through the Poisonweed Valley, Fathom's special herbal tea keeping them safe from its mind-addling effects. It was almost noon by the time they reached the Whitestone Bridge. Rose removed Thea's map, while Shen's fingers flew to his waistband, checking – as he had done every ten minutes since they set off – that his own map was still there.

Rose frowned, trying to trace a route to the Ganyeve Desert, which lay at the heart of Eana, coiled up like a snake. She didn't want to return to Bridge End, but the southern tip of Eana was so narrow she could see no way around it.

'We could ride wild,' said Shen, leaning forward to look over her shoulder. 'Let's break from the road and go through the hills. We have food to last us.'

'And horses to race,' Kai piped up. 'I want a do-over.'

'Very well,' said Rose, carefully folding up her map. 'But wait until I'm— SHEN!'

The horses bolted across the bridge and off the road, galloping across the grassy plains at such a breakneck pace, Rose had to gasp for breath. The land unfurled around them, untamed and wild-flowered, and they went with it, their laughter mingling with the wind as they rode north, towards the desert.

After hours of riding, when the sun was surrendering to the evening sky, they reached the trading town of Thornhaven, which marked the crossroads between east and west Eana, and the valleys to the south. A hundred miles or so beyond it, the Ganyeve Desert began its golden sprawl.

Once inside the walls of Thornhaven, they slowed to a trot, wary of drawing too much attention to themselves. Elske had long since fallen behind, but Rose knew she'd turn up soon, a little dusty and travel-worn from the journey.

She was just about to suggest they stop in Thornhaven to rest and wait for her when she caught sight of something that made her heart lurch. An arrow painted on the tavern door. And then another on the blacksmith's. And the wheeler's. On and on they went, all the way down the cobbled street.

There were arrows on almost every single door.

Shen tensed behind her. 'Thornhaven is an Arrow stronghold. I wasn't expecting another one so soon.'

'Or in a place so central,' said Rose, uneasily. She felt the prick of every single arrow as if they were piercing her own skin. Each one represented someone, or perhaps an entire family, who hated her and her sister, and what they stood for. Edgar Barron was gaining ground. His followers were enticing others to his cause, which made every step away from Anadawn Palace feel greater than the one before.

Hold fast, Thea. I'll be home soon.

'Should we kick their doors in?' suggested Kai.

Rose glared at him. 'Keep your head down and don't draw any attention to yourself,' she said, pulling up her hood. Something had hardened in her heart at the sight of all those arrows. All that hatred. 'And when we get back to Anadawn, with our new army of desert witches, we will remember the name of every single town that chose to rise up against us.'

'Vengeance suits you, Queenie,' said Kai, approvingly. 'I knew you had some fire in you.'

Shen tightened his grip around her waist as they journeyed through the streets of Thornhaven. Even when they were back on the road, with night yawning over them in dusty strands of grey and blue, he didn't let go.

They rode until long after midnight, when they stopped to rest at the edge of a forest, far from the glare of the Arrows – and anyone else for that matter. They fed and watered the horses, before sharing the bread and cheese Pog had packed for them.

'We'll rise at dawn,' said Shen, checking his map in a shard of moonlight. The Sunkissed Kingdom was moving again. He traced the red orb with his finger. 'It's drifting south. If all goes well, we should find it by noon tomorrow.'

Rose lowered herself to the ground and curled up on a mound of moss, trying to get comfortable. The accommodation was far too rural for her taste, but she didn't see the sense in complaining about it. She used her satchel as a pillow, which offered some improvement, but the night air had grown chilly and she couldn't keep her teeth from chattering. It was times like this that reminded her of just how far she had strayed from her home at Anadawn and her duty on its throne. She hoped with all her heart it would be worth it.

'I'm sorry,' said Shen, dropping to a crouch beside her. 'I should have let you take that stole.'

'Is this when you offer to sleep next to her to keep her warm?' called Kai, who was doing pull-ups on a nearby tree branch.

Shen stiffened.

'Don't,' said Rose, bracing a hand on his arm. 'It's not worth it.'

Shen swallowed his anger. His gaze slid to hers, his voice turning husky. 'He does have a point. If you want, I can sleep—'

He was interrupted by a triumphant howl, as Elske bounded into the clearing and came straight for Rose. The wolf licked her face in greeting, then curled up next to her, nudging Shen out of the way.

'How wonderful!' said Rose, through a giggle. 'My blanket has arrived. I think I'll sleep rather soundly after all.'

Kai chuckled as he dropped from the tree branch. 'How does it feel to lose out to a wolf, cousin?'

Shen leaped at his cousin, tackling him at the waist. They fell to the ground, kicking and punching each other, and, this time, Rose let them. She turned over, snuggling into Elske's warmth. 'Men,' she said, with a sigh.

The wolf whined in agreement, and, almost at once, they both fell asleep.

The next morning, not long after sunrise, they crossed the edge of the Ganyeve. Shen unfurled the map, his gaze trained on the ruby beetle as they journeyed into the desert. Rose hadn't thought it was possible for the desert horses to go any faster, but once their hooves touched the sand, it was as if they'd sprouted wings and begun to fly.

Hours passed in the sweltering heat, the beetle zigzagging across the map as though it was trying to avoid them. And then, finally, when they found themselves close to the very heart of the desert, it stopped moving.

'We're close,' said Shen, lifting his head and pointing west. 'It's that way.'

'What are we waiting for?' said Kai, walloping Victory until the horse quickened.

'What about Elske?' cried Rose, searching the dunes for the white wolf. 'She's fallen behind again!'

'She'll catch up,' said Shen. 'We can't stop now, Rose. We're almost there!'

They galloped onward, exhilaration bursting from them in rippling laughter. When Shen pulled Storm to a stop in the middle of a brassy dune, Rose glanced over her shoulder and saw hope shining out of his face, as pure and bright as the sun above them. 'It's here,' he said, frantically looking around. 'The map says we're here.'

Kai swung off his horse, landing easily in the hot sand. 'Well, what now, wonder boy?'

There was an edge to his voice – something more than just impatience – that Rose didn't like.

Shen slid off Storm. 'I don't understand,' he said, shaking the map. 'How are we supposed to get to it?'

'Give it here,' said Kai, snatching it off him.

Shen lunged for it, but Kai kicked his feet out from under him. Shen fell to his knees, cursing. The ruby ring around his neck slipped free.

Rose gasped, pointing at it. 'Shen! Your ring is glowing!'

Shen clasped the ring in his fist, the red glow spreading across his skin, until it looked lit from within. 'It's enchanted,' he breathed. 'I can feel it.'

Suddenly, the sands began to hum. The lilting chime rose up like an aria, until the wind itself joined in. It sounded like it was beckoning them, *welcoming* them.

Shen shot his free hand out. 'Give me the map.'

This time, Kai relinquished it.

Rose hopped off the horse, joining them as they crowded around the parchment. As the sands chimed ever louder, new words appeared across the top.

A heart in the blade of a desert hand
Will unearth its kingdom from the sand.

Rose frowned. 'I've heard of a blade in a heart, but never a heart in a blade.'

'Witches and their bloody rhymes,' muttered Kai.

'The blade of a desert hand,' muttered Shen, as he withdrew his dagger from his boot. 'When Banba found me wandering in the desert, I had a dagger and a ring . . .' he said, more to himself than to them. He flipped the dagger, revealing a small hole in the base of the hilt.

'The ruby,' said Rose, catching his meaning. The ruby must be the heart. Just like it is on the map. And your dagger – that's the blade!'

'I'm still lost,' said Kai.

Shen ignored him, as he freed the ring from its necklace and slotted it, ruby first, into the hole at the base of the dagger. 'It fits.'

The sand began to tremble, its song rising around them until Rose could barely hear herself. 'What now?' she shouted.

As if possessed by an ancient magical spirit, Shen fell to his knees and drove the dagger into the sand, right up to the hilt.

There was a moment of utter stillness, all three of them looking at each other in anticipation. And then the sand shifted so violently that Rose was thrown on to her back.

'Move!' said Shen, stowing the dagger and pulling her up.

They leaped on to the horses, rearing back from the chasm that opened before them. The sand was churning so fast, it spat out in every direction, burning their skin and stinging their eyes. The ground groaned as it cleaved apart, the hole getting bigger and bigger. They galloped along the edges of it, the horses whinnying in alarm as the sand collapsed in on itself.

Rose cried out as a huge shimmering dome emerged from the chasm, rising up from the sand like an iridescent bubble. It glimmered in the sun, so brightly, it took her a moment to realize there was an entire *city* inside it.

No, not a city.

A kingdom.

Golden waterfalls of sand sluiced off the sides of the mighty dome as it rose, before settling atop the desert as though it had been there all along. The dome shimmered out of sight, revealing a high stone wall and a pair of towering scarlet gates. Beyond them, Rose glimpsed hundreds of red and gold roofs, glittering in the sun.

Finally, the sands stopped churning. The music melted away, and all was still.

Rose was so struck with wonder, she couldn't speak. Behind her, Shen was breathing heavily. She grabbed his hand, squeezing it in hers.

'Home sweet home,' said Kai, with a triumphant grin. He nudged the horses onward. 'Let's go, slowpokes.'

To Rose's mounting surprise, the red gates swung open by themselves. Just beyond them, she glimpsed beautiful sandstone buildings and winding pathways, lush with desert shrubs and blooming white flowers. And in the middle of it all, at the top of a pale stone staircase, stood a huge golden palace.

Before they could make their way towards it, they were beset by people.

'I can feel the wind on my face!'

'Look at the sun! The sky!'

'At last! At last!'

They poured out of their homes, crying with joy as they lifted their faces to the sun. Children whooped and hollered as they made for the gates, while people threw their hands to the sky and wept.

One by one, the people of the Sunkissed Kingdom spotted Rose, hovering just inside the gates. And as they did, they fell to their knees and pressed their foreheads to the earth.

Rose blushed. 'Oh, there's really no need for that,' she said, hastily. 'Please, do get up.'

Behind her, Kai snorted. 'I'm going to enjoy this.'

An old woman lumbered to her feet. 'Praise the skies!' she cried out. 'The crown prince has returned!'

All around her, others joined in. 'The crown prince has saved us!'

'All hail the crown prince!'

Rose frowned. 'I think all that time under the sand has confused them,' she muttered to Shen. 'I'm a queen, not a prince.'

Just then, the doors to the golden palace opened, and a regal-looking man in a red silk shirt and flowing black trousers came sauntering down the steps. He was tall and lithe, with tanned skin and long black hair pulled away from his face and coiled on the top of his head. He wore a thin gold band above his stern brow, and though Rose had never seen him before, there was a certain familiarity in the hard edge of his jaw. His eyes were brown and discerning, and they were trained on Shen.

'Behold, the crown prince!' he called out, opening his arms in greeting. 'I never thought I'd see this day.'

Rose whipped her head around, the heat draining from her cheeks. 'Who on earth are they talking about?'

The crowd parted for the man, and he came to stand before

them. He smiled up at Shen, revealing a dimple in his left cheek. 'Welcome home, Shen Lo. You have been missed.'

Rose nearly fell off Storm.

Behind her, Shen had gone so still, she wondered if he was still breathing.

'Oh,' said Kai, leaning forward on his horse. 'That's right. I forgot to mention that you're the heir to the Sunkissed Kingdom.'

Rose turned to stare at Shen's cousin. '*What?*'

The man turned to Kai, then, and for the briefest moment his smile faltered. 'Welcome home, son. You have done well.'

'Thank you, Father,' said Kai, dipping his chin. Perhaps it was Rose's imagination, but she could have sworn she watched a shadow cross his face as he did, and thought it looked an awful lot like fear.

Wren

CHAPTER 27

The following morning, after a sumptuous breakfast of cinnamon-dusted pastries, honey bacon and perfectly poached eggs, Wren chose a violet dress trimmed with soft grey fur from the wardrobe. The blizzard had blown itself out around dawn, not long after she had collapsed into bed, bug-eyed with exhaustion after a night of spells.

Blood spells.

A mouse squeaked at her from under the dresser as she fastened the buttons in her bodice. Her magic flared in answer, sending a current of heat through her body. 'Good morning, my little miracle.'

The mouse cheeped, merrily. Wren grinned. He was perfect, except for a little stiffness in his hind quarters. More importantly, however, he was still alive. The other mice had only lasted a handful of minutes after Wren's enchantment, but this one had survived the entire night. A good omen indeed.

She unravelled the cloth from around her hand and examined her palm. The cut had scabbed over. Her stomach had welcomed breakfast, the honey bacon doing wonders to banish the taste of ash from her mouth, and as she stood before the mirror braiding her hair, she realized she felt better than ever.

If this was the cost of a little blood sacrifice, then she would gladly pay it.

A short while later, Inga poked her head inside. 'I see you survived your first blizzard, Your Majesty,' she said, with uncharacteristic warmth. 'Would you like to go for a morning walk?'

Wren stared at her. 'Is this some kind of trick?'

To her surprise, the soldier smiled. 'I think you have fallen into the king's favour. He has ordered me to take you out for some fresh air.'

'Just like one of his wolves,' mused Wren, but she didn't pass up the chance to stretch her legs. If agreeing to help Alarik had somehow softened his disdain for her, then she would gladly take advantage of the perks that came with it. She fetched a trailing fur cloak from the wardrobe and waved her mouse goodbye. 'I'll check on you later, little one.'

Wren fell into step with Inga, enjoying the feeling of walking, rather than being marched somewhere against her will. It helped that Inga had no memory of the sleeping enchantment Wren had cast on her last night. 'So, what is there to see around here? And don't say the courtyard of beasts. I've already had a tour of that attraction.'

Inga glanced sidelong at her, and up close Wren was struck by how young the girl was. Perhaps even younger than her.

She wondered if, like Tor, she had come here to train when she was just twelve years old. 'We could take a stroll around the lake,' suggested Inga. 'The beasts don't go there.' She flinched at a memory. 'Not since Anika tried to teach Borvil to ice-skate. She nearly killed the bear and herself. The king was livid.'

Wren raised her eyebrows, trying to picture a giant ice bear lumbering across the frozen pond. She couldn't help it – she laughed. Inga chuckled, too. 'I'm afraid it was not so funny at the time.'

They passed through the atrium, where beasts napped in streams of morning sunlight, exhausted from last night's blizzard. Outside, the wind was biting, but swaddled in her decadent dress and cloak, Wren barely felt it. There was a crispness to the Gevran air that she liked. It made her feel alert, focused. They walked the perimeter of the sprawling lake, where white hares darted in and out of winterberry shrubs, helping to dust off the freshly fallen snow. Out here, Wren could barely hear the growls from the palace. There was only the wind keening through the mountains, their jagged peaks rising around her like glistening fangs.

'It's beautiful here,' said Wren, her breath making clouds in the air. 'And I say that as a prisoner.'

'With any luck, you won't be a prisoner for long,' said Inga. 'King Alarik does not make a habit of it.'

'Taking prisoners or keeping them alive?' said Wren.

The young soldier shrugged. 'Both.'

'Great.' Wren rubbed her hands together, wishing she had

thought to wear gloves. They came to a wrought-iron bench heaped in powdery snow. Beneath it, she spied a discarded pair of ice skates. She lifted them by their laces, admiring the silver blades on the bottom. 'You could take an eye out with these.'

Inga stiffened, a hand coming to the pommel of her sword.

'Not *your* eye,' said Wren, quickly. 'Can I try them on? They look about my size.'

The soldier raised her eyebrows. 'I believe they belong to Princess Anika.'

'I'm sure she won't mind if I borrow them,' Wren lied. 'She seems the type who likes to share, doesn't she?'

Inga's lips twitched. 'Have you ever even skated before?'

'No, but I'm familiar with the concept,' said Wren, breezily. 'A little momentum. A little balance. How hard can it be?'

Inga's silence was answer enough. Wren took it as a challenge. She sank on to the bench and kicked off her boots, deftly replacing them with the ice skates. They were a little snug, pinching her toes together, but they would do well enough.

She stood up, wobbling precariously as she trekked through the frosty grass.

Inga shot a hand out to help her.

'I can do it,' said Wren, waving it away. 'It's just like walking. Well, plodding really.'

'But the ice—'

'Will be conquered,' said Wren, as she gingerly stepped out on to the frozen lake. 'Don't worry, Inga. I'm a fast learner.'

The soldier hmm'd, unconvinced. 'Make sure to take your time. The ice can be tricky at first .'

But Wren was already gliding away from her. The ice hissed as her blades bit into it. She had to concentrate on not lifting her feet, pressing the nose of her skates down as she lengthened her strides, leaning one way, and then the other. She flung her arms out, teetering as she fought for balance.

'See?' she called over her shoulder, to where Inga was hovering at the edge of the pond. 'I told you I'd be a natural!'

'Be careful of the middle!' Inga called back. 'That's where the ice is thinnest!'

'Don't worry,' said Wren, making a poor attempt at a twirl and nearly face-planting on the ice. 'I'm as light as a feather!'

She crouched a little as she quickened her strides, the ice crunching beneath her as she raced around the pond. The wind whipped her face, stealing the feeling from the tip of her nose, but Wren didn't care. For the first time since she had set foot in Gevra, she felt free.

She twirled and fell, laughing as she dragged herself back to her feet. Her knees stung, but she ignored the pain, losing herself to the *swish* and *crunch* of each stride.

'That's enough!' shouted Inga, after a while. 'We must return to the palace!'

'One more lap!' said Wren, skating away from the soldier in case she tried to catch her. 'I'm just getting the hang of it.'

She twirled again, her blades arcing in a perfect crescent. Wren whooped in triumph, then did another, and another, drifting ever closer to the middle of the lake. By the time the ice cracked beneath her, it was already too late. She looked down at the fissure spider-webbing around her, and then back at Inga.

The soldier froze, her face ashen.

'HELP!' screamed Wren, as the ice gave way. She stole one last breath as she plunged into the freezing water. The lake was so cold it paralysed her – her legs went limp, then leaden, the skates like two weights around her ankles. She sank deeper into the glacial abyss, a single spot of light marking the hole through which she had fallen. It drifted further and further away, the bottom of the pond quickly rising to meet her.

With her lungs burning in her chest, Wren crouched against the silt and stone, and pushed herself off the bottom. She rose once more, straining for the surface, her hands out, as though to catch that single sliver of light. It was too far, and suddenly she was falling again. Flailing. She kicked out, fighting the heaviness of her own feet, desperately propelling herself towards the surface.

And then a hand found hers in the darkness. Strong and sure, it dragged her up, towards sunlight. Salvation.

Wren broke the surface in a shuddering gasp, her face covered in reams of sopping hair. The hands moved quickly, from her wrist to under her shoulders. She clawed at the ice as she was dragged back on to its glassy surface. They released her then, and she crouched, quivering, on all fours.

Through a tangle of hair, she could just make out a pair of black boots. She crawled towards them, terrified of falling again. They moved backwards, one step and then another, leading her away from the middle of the lake. Back to the edge, to safety.

Only when her fingers met frosty grass, did Wren fall back on her heels and peel the hair from her face.

Alarik Felsing stared down at her, his gaze as glaring as the sun above him. His hands were faintly blue, and the sleeves of his black coat were soaking wet. When he spoke, it was not to her. 'I told you to take her for a walk, Inga, not drown her.'

'I did, Your Majesty. I tried, but she wanted to skate, and she fell, and then I—'

'You froze,' said Alarik, crisply. 'At a crucial moment.'

Wren stared at him, in utter disbelief. '*You* pulled me out?'

He cocked his head. 'Would you prefer that I left you down there?'

'No. I . . .' Wren shook her head. Her teeth were chattering awfully, and her mind had yet to thaw. 'I'm . . . surprised, that's all.'

'You made me a promise,' Alarik reminded her. 'And I intend for you to keep it.'

Wren raised her chin. 'So do I.'

'Good.' He flashed his canines in a quick smile as he stood back, revealing Inga, red-faced and crying, behind him. 'The queen is turning blue. Go inside and warm her up. This is your last warning, Inga. Don't let me down again.' He walked away, without looking back, his parting words to Wren floating over his shoulder. 'I'll send for you tomorrow. Be ready, witch.'

Rose
CHAPTER 28

Rose couldn't stop staring at Shen.

Shen Lo, a prince? Her Shen Lo, who dressed like a bandit and laughed like a pirate, who broke into palaces and kissed another person's bride on her wedding day, was heir to an entire kingdom? How could it be?

Shen had no answer for her. No answer for himself. His jaw was slack with shock, the warrior struck silent for once.

After Kai's father's dramatic pronouncement, they were ushered away from the ruby gates and into the heart of the city. For a place that had been trapped beneath the sand for eighteen years, the Sunkissed Kingdom was remarkably verdant. The labyrinth of narrow streets and copper-stone pathways was lined with trellises of vibrant yellow and red flowers the size of Rose's palm, as well as hearty desert shrubs pinpricked with small white blooms. The buildings were made of sandstone that shimmered softly in the sun and topped with peaked red-slate roofs that curved upwards at their gilded edges.

Rose could feel magic thrumming in the very bones of the

city. It was ancient and powerful, stronger than anything she'd ever felt at Anadawn. Even Ortha. It brushed against her cheeks like an invisible wind. She took heart in its presence, letting it steady her nerves as they journeyed through the gathering crowd.

They dismounted Storm at the bottom of the palace steps. The moment Shen slid to the ground, Kai's father threw his arm around his shoulders, pulling him ahead of Rose so he could whisper in his ear. Kai leaped off Victory and trailed behind them with his hands in his pockets, while onlookers clustered around the steps, craning their necks to catch a glimpse of the crown prince.

Rose eyed Kai's father with mounting resentment, noting the gold band around his head. He might well be the ruler of the Sunkissed Kingdom, but this territory resided inside *her* desert, and as a queen of Eana she deserved more respect than this.

So far, she hadn't got so much as a greeting.

She swept her hand through her hair, wishing she was wearing her crown. Or at least something other than her sand-stained dress. Then everyone would know exactly who she was.

'That's quite a scowl, Queenie,' came Kai's drawl from behind her.

She tossed him a withering look. 'This wasn't what I was expecting.'

'Just wait until we get inside the Palace of Eternal Sunlight.' A shadow flitted across Kai's face, gone as quickly as it came. 'Or, should I say, *Shen's* Palace of Eternal Sunlight.'

'Now who's scowling?' muttered Rose.

They stewed in silence as they trudged up the rest of the steps. The stairwell was bordered on both sides by intricate golden statues, including a beetle with jade eyes, a giant scorpion, a dragon caught mid-roar and eight desert horses rearing up on their hind legs. Each one looked like it was about to spring to life, and Rose wondered if, with the right kind of magic, they could.

Kai's father stopped at the top of the steps and turned to face the crowds below. He lifted his arm, raising Shen's, too. Shen was still in a daze, staring out at the city as though he couldn't believe it was here, at last, before them. That after all these years, he had finally found his way home.

'Not only has our crown prince returned to unbury us, but he has just informed me that the woman at his side is none other than the queen of Eana,' announced Kai's father. 'She has come to welcome us back to the sun!'

Only then, did his gaze fall on Rose, his lips spreading into a wide smile. He did not bow to her. Rose tried not to let her irritation show as she made her way to join them, climbing the last few steps to thunderous applause. She turned to the people of the Sunkissed Kingdom, who were running and leaping about with joy, and offered them a queenly wave. Thousands waved back at her.

She glanced sidelong at Shen. 'Are you all right?'

He swallowed, thickly. 'I . . . I don't know.'

Kai lingered on the step below them. 'Well, Prince? Aren't

you going to say something to your adoring subjects?'

Shen's eyes went wide with panic. He turned to Rose. 'What do I say?'

'Nothing,' said Rose, relieved to be taking charge once more. 'I will address my subjects here.'

She cleared her throat. 'Greetings, people of the Sunkissed Kingdom,' she called out. 'My name is Queen Rose Valhart, and I have journeyed from my seat at Anadawn Palace, on behalf of my fellow queen and twin sister Wren, to welcome you back to our land. I am overjoyed that we have found you alive and well after all these years. In the days and weeks to come, you will find this country changed for the better. Witches now sit on the throne of Anadawn and under our reign magic is welcome throughout the country.'

'Except in Arrow territory,' Kai interjected under his breath.

Rose ignored him. 'Together we will restore the former glory of our ancestors and return all witches to the sunlight, not just here but everywhere in Eana.'

The crowd broke into applause again.

'Thank you, Queen Rose,' said Shen's uncle, dipping his chin. 'It is an honour to host you here in our kingdom.' Rose didn't miss the way he lingered over the word 'our', his voice a little crisper than before.

He flicked his wrist, and as a pinch of sand fell from his fingers, the statue of the golden dragon opened its mouth and released a thunderous roar. The crowd erupted in cheers. So, Shen's uncle was an enchanter, and quite a skilled one, Rose noted, as the palace doors swung open behind him.

She paused, waiting for Shen, but he brushed past her, falling into step with his uncle.

'Come on, Queenie,' said Kai, slinging his arm around her. 'Time to show you what a real palace looks like.'

As much as Rose hated to admit it, the Palace of Eternal Sunlight outshone the dated grandeur of Anadawn.

The entrance hall was smaller in size, but far more extravagant. The walls were gilded and brushed with gemstones, while the ceiling was hung with the largest chandeliers she had ever seen. The floor tiles were made from sparkling desert quartz, which made her feel as if she was treading on rare treasure. Everywhere she looked, something was shining or glittering. Huge porcelain vases of desert orchids graced the entryway, which was lined with even more statues of desert beasts. In the middle of the grand hall stood a golden fountain, where clear water gathered in a mirrored pool.

Shen stopped to admire it.

'Those who follow the Protector may have their eternal flame, but the desert kingdom is built around our Forever Fountain. It was one of many gifts given to our people long ago, to ensure we could survive the harshness of the desert,' said Shen's uncle, proudly. 'In all its years, it has never run dry. Its waters flow through the entire city.'

Shen trailed his hand in the water, watching the beads slip between his fingers. 'I remember playing in this fountain.'

Rose leaned down for a closer look and was immediately splashed with a faceful of water. She yelped as she leaped away from it.

A musical laugh rang out. 'I hope you remember more than just the fountain, Shen Lo!' A girl about Shen's age came skipping around the fountain. She was wearing a sleek indigo tunic, and matching trousers, her waist-length black hair swept away from her face by two jade pins. A gust of wind came with her, marking her as a tempest.

'Lei Fan, you know we do not use magic in the entrance hall,' said Shen's uncle, sternly.

Rose's heart dropped as she peeled the sopping hair from her face. Who was this beautiful Lei Fan? And why did she look so happy to see Shen?

'You really need to get better at hiding your emotions,' said Kai, nudging her in the side. 'That's my younger sister. Shen's cousin. Nothing for you to worry about.'

Rose's cheeks prickled with relief. 'I don't know what you're talking about.'

Kai laughed. 'I saw your face, Queenie.' He turned his lips down in an exaggerated pout. 'Boohoo-*hoo*.'

Rose glowered at Kai as Shen rose from the fountain and threw his arms open. 'Lei Fan! Is that really you?'

'Don't you remember my dazzling beauty?' Lei Fan laughed as Shen picked her up and swung her around. 'We've missed you, Shen!'

Rose hovered on the edge of their reunion, trying to smile. She felt peculiar, as though she was outside a bubble of glass looking in at a place she didn't belong, at a person she only half knew. But then, she supposed, Shen Lo had only ever known half himself, too.

'I've missed all of you,' he said, as he set his cousin down, and Rose's heart clenched at the yearning in his voice. 'I'd forgotten so much . . . but I remember your faces.' He turned to his uncle. 'Your voice, Uncle Feng.' And then back to Lei Fan. 'Your laugh, Lei Fan.' He winked at Kai. 'Your ego, cousin.' He laughed, and the sound soared all the way to the ceiling. 'I remember running through the streets of this city, trying to track a jewel beetle. Sneaking dumplings to the horses in the stables and making them sick. Getting scolded for swimming in this very fountain . . .' He spun around, as though searching for something. 'And the smell of candied fruit. The kind that the old woman who looked after us used to make. We called her "Grandmother Lu" . . .' He trailed off, his face falling. 'What happened to her?'

'Why the long face, boy?' crowed a new voice. 'Did you think I'd *died*?' A wizened old lady emerged from a side passage and came hobbling towards them with a wooden cane. Her skin was golden brown, and her white hair was pulled into a bun on top of her head. Her face was as wrinkled as a walnut, but her dark brown eyes were bright. 'Now why would I do a stupid thing like that?'

'Grandmother Lu!' cried Shen, with a childlike joy Rose had never heard before. 'I thought I'd never see you again!'

Grandmother Lu wagged her finger as she approached.

'Shen Lo, you naughty boy! You've been away from home for far too long.'

She turned her gaze to Rose, her brows raising. 'But what fine royal company you have kept in the meantime. You look just like your mother, girl. I met Lillith once, many years ago. Eyes like emeralds. A smile as beautiful as an orchid in bloom.'

Grandmother Lu braced both hands on her walking stick and attempted to bow to Rose. She winced as her back cracked. 'I'm afraid that's the best I can do,' she heaved. 'My spine's not as young as my heart.'

'That's quite all right,' said Rose, rushing to steady her.

'So, now you are a queen,' said Grandmother Lu. 'I look forward to seeing you prove yourself worthy of the title.'

Shen's lips quirked. 'Still the same Grandmother Lu I remember.'

Rose smiled, quickly warming to the old woman. 'I hope to do you proud . . . Lady Lu?'

Grandmother Lu cackled. 'Oh, I'm not one for titles. Lady This. Sir That. King Pompom. Pah! Call me Grandmother Lu, like everybody else does.'

'Grandmother Lu is *really* the one in charge here,' said Lei Fan, with a wink. 'She's looked after us since we were children. Father only wears the crown for show.'

Feng glared at his daughter. 'You seem determined to undermine me today, Lei Fan.'

Lei Fan grinned, revealing two neat rows of pearly teeth. 'Someone has to keep you on your toes, Father.'

'Now someone will,' said Kai, under his breath.

Feng's frown deepened.

Shen wasn't listening to them. He was too busy embracing his childhood nanny. 'Grandmother Lu, you are exactly as I remember you. Tell me, do you still make the most delicious candied pears in the Sunkissed Kingdom?'

Grandmother Lu puffed up with pride. 'Try all of Eana, boy. And as a matter of fact, I do! Let's go to the kitchens. I can make some for you now.'

'I'd like that,' said Shen, eagerly. He looked to Feng. 'If it's all right with you, Uncle?'

'Shen Lo, you're the crown prince!' cried Lei Fan. 'You can have all the candied pears you like.'

Feng cleared his throat, summoning a tight smile. 'I'd advise you not to eat too many. Save some room for your welcome banquet this evening.'

Shen clapped his hands in delight. 'I've never had a welcome banquet before.'

Neither have I, thought Rose, hating the sourness she felt.

Shen linked arms with Grandmother Lu as they took off for the kitchens, leaning his head against hers to better hear what she was saying.

Rose watched him go, with a sinking feeling in her gut.

'Shen!' she called out before she could stop herself. He glanced over his shoulder and for a moment he looked at her like he'd never seen her before, like he didn't know what she was doing here.

Rose cleared her throat, worrying her skirt between her

fingers. She wanted him to invite her to the kitchens, not least because she wanted to sample the best candied pears in Eana but mostly so she could feel like she fitted into this new part of his life. Or rather, this old part.

'Oh,' he said, frowning. 'Lei Fan, can you find Rose a room to freshen up in? And she'll want to change for dinner.'

'Yes, I'll need a dress,' said Rose, pretending that was what she was after all along. 'If you wouldn't mind.'

Lei Fan pursed her lips, looking Rose up and down. 'I don't know if I have anything fit for a queen.'

'If it's clean, it will be an improvement,' said Rose, with a warm smile.

Lei Fan grinned, rising to the challenge. 'In that case, come with me, Your Majesty.'

Wren
CHAPTER 29

The day after Alarik had pulled Wren, sopping and shivering from the lake at Grinstad Palace, he sent for her, just as he had promised. After breakfast, Wren was marched through the icy catacombs once more. The mountain creaked overhead, still trying to shake off the deluge of snow as the tunnels grew dark and narrow, winding ever deeper into the earth. And then Alarik was before her, his hands tucked idly behind his back. The king was dressed in black again, his bright eyes shining like diamonds in the dark. His wolves sat either side of him, watching Wren approach with the same keenness.

'Any frostbite?' said Alarik, by way of greeting.

Wren smiled, tightly. 'Who needs all their toes anyway?'

He surrendered a rare chuckle. 'I trust you got my gift the other night.'

'Yes, thank you. I've always wanted a bouquet of dead mice.'

'And people say I'm not thoughtful.'

Wren snorted. 'I can't imagine why.'

'Did you find our furry little friends helpful?' There was

that hunger again – so quick, Wren almost missed it. Alarik was hopeful, even desperate. He wanted this to work just as badly as Wren. Maybe more.

They were standing on either side of the wooden door that led to Ansel's corpse, surrounded by the king's soldiers and, of course, his beasts. Wren was relieved not to see Tor lingering in the shadows. She didn't want to worry about his disapproval when she was already worrying about her spell – and what would come after if she succeeded. Or worse – if she failed.

The king was staring at her.

Wren realized she had forgotten to answer him. 'Very helpful,' she said, thinking of the mouse back in her bedroom, still alive and thriving. 'Though I wouldn't mind a little more freedom.'

'Why? So you can drown yourself in my lake again?'

Wren glared at him. 'That was an accident.'

'What need have you of more freedom? Don't I feed you well?' he countered. 'My cook offers you the same food that I eat.' He gestured to her expensive dress, then the decadent cloak tied around her neck. 'Aren't you wearing the finest garments Gevra has to offer?'

'Just as I am constantly being stalked by its finest soldiers.' Wren pointed to Inga, who was hovering over her shoulder. She had become much stricter since the unfortunate incident at the lake, refusing to make conversation with Wren, and balking at the mere suggestion of going for another walk. 'And locked away in my room, with nothing and no one to entertain me.'

Alarik pretended to pout. 'Shall I send you a wolf for company?'

'I'd prefer the key to my door.'

'You have to earn it, witch,' he said, laying his hand against the door. 'Here is your chance.'

Alarik opened the door and stepped through it, holding it ajar for her. She summoned a breath of courage and stepped inside after him, leaving the soldiers and their beasts to wait for them outside.

The chamber that held Prince Ansel's body was even colder than Wren remembered. She wrapped her arms around herself, fighting the shiver that rattled down her spine.

'It has to be this way,' said Alarik, watching her. In the narrow chamber, they were forced to stand close to each other. Their arms were almost brushing, the king's breath warming the air between them. 'The cold preserves his body.'

Wren dipped her chin. She knew that, and yet, it made the whole affair seem even eerier. A lone sconce flickered on the wall, making shadows dance across Ansel's face. The prince looked serene . . . peaceful, as though he didn't want to be disturbed.

Wren's fingers began to twitch. She swallowed the knot of fear in her throat, trying to ignore the creeping wrongness of this moment.

'You're nervous,' said Alarik.

'No, I'm not.'

'Your hands are trembling.'

Wren curled them into fists. 'Stop looking at my hands.'

'Then hurry up and do something with them.' He reached into his frock coat and removed a small leather pouch, then placed it on the marble slab, by Ansel's left foot. 'This is black sand from the Sundvik shore in the south.'

Wren stared at the pouch but didn't move to take it.

'For your spell,' said Alarik. 'It's the best earth in Gevra.'

Wren turned to look up at him. The king really didn't know the depth of what he was asking of her. He thought it would be simple – that a pinch of sand and a few pretty words would summon his brother's spirit from the afterlife and stuff it back into his body.

Alarik's frown sharpened, deepening the hollows in his cheeks. 'Is it not the right kind? I was under the impression that—'

'Do you have a knife?' Wren interrupted. 'Or your sword. That will do.'

He narrowed his eyes. 'Do you intend to run me through in my own dungeon?'

'No.' Wren paused. 'I mean, I'd consider it if I thought I could get away with it . . .'

'Charming. And barely a day after I saved your meagre little life.'

Wren snorted. 'We both know you would have drowned me yourself if I didn't owe you something.'

He didn't deny it. 'Why the knife?'

'Because your earth – however fancy it is – isn't enough to cast the spell you've asked of me.' She raised her palm, revealing the jagged wound. 'It has to be blood.'

Alarik stared at her hand for a long moment, his expression unreadable. 'How much blood?' he said at last.

'I don't know,' Wren confessed. She had been trying not to dwell on that part. Raising a mouse from the dead was one feat, but she suspected the cost of raising a human would be much higher. 'But we *might* need to draft in one of those wolves out in the—'

'No.' The word was sharp. 'We will not harm the beasts.'

'But—'

'I said *no*.' He bared his teeth – not a smile, but a threat. 'The beasts of Gevra are my brethren. They will not be harmed.'

Wren hesitated. 'I don't know how much blood it's going to take . . .'

'Then we will find out.' Alarik reached into his coat again. He removed a slim silver dagger.

Wren moved to take it, but he snatched his hand back. 'I'd sooner hand it to your grandmother.'

'This spell is going to require *some* trust,' said Wren. 'Unless you want us to freeze to death in here, with your brother.'

Alarik fingered the dagger. 'I confess I have always imagined a more valiant death for myself.'

'I can picture an ice bear eating you,' said Wren. 'How many bites do you think it would take? Two, maybe three?'

'You'd like that, I'm sure,' said Alarik, drolly.

Wren turned her gaze to Prince Ansel, drawn to how his fair lashes cast spidery shadows along his cheeks. 'There's a chance this might go wrong. I've never raised a human from the dead before.'

'I had assumed as much.'

'It's not a good idea,' Wren went on. The more she looked at Prince Ansel, the less sure she became. Why disturb the peace he had found in death? And all just to drag him back to this snow-swept hell, where no one truly appreciated him? 'I mean, morally speaking.'

'You may leave the matter of morality to me.'

She glanced sidelong at him. 'Because you are such a pillar of it.'

The king bristled, and she got the sense that she had finally, *somehow*, offended him. 'I promised I would do everything in my power to bring Ansel back,' he said, curtly. 'And a promise made by a Gevran is cast in iron. It is not easily broken.' A pause, then, his lips twisting. 'Although if Tor Iversen had kept his promise to protect Ansel with his life, then you and I wouldn't find ourselves in this predicament.'

Wren looked at the ground, thinking of the anguish on Tor's face when he had visited her the other night. Ansel's death haunted his every thought, and still he could not bring himself to regret saving her. The memory of those words curled around her heart, squeezing too tightly. 'Then I would be dead.'

'And Gevra would be all the better for it,' said Alarik.

Wren didn't even flinch. 'Who did you promise?'

'My sister,' he said, after a beat. 'It was the only way I could get Anika back on the ship and out of your country before her anger got her killed.'

Wren didn't have to cast her mind back very far to recall the princess's fury, how her rage had erupted from her like a volcano. Even the sight of Wren standing in the throne room the other day had turned Anika rabid.

'But in truth, this endeavour is more for my mother than Anika,' he added, as an afterthought. 'She hasn't been right since my father died. And now this . . .' He gestured at Ansel, without looking at him. 'This loss, I fear, will be the end of her. Ansel was her favourite.'

'I can see why,' said Wren.

She hadn't meant it as a barb. In fact, despite the king's general odiousness and appalling lack of charm, she was beginning to understand that there were some things Alarik did care about. Things beyond war and bloodshed. His loyalty to his family had led him to this moment, shivering in the depths of the Fovarr Mountains, pouring all his hopes out to a witch who would run him through with his own sword if given half the chance.

'I didn't know Ansel very long,' she went on, 'but he was always kind to me. He struck me as thoughtful. Good-natured. Gentle.'

'He will be those things again.'

Wren chewed on her lip. 'I don't know if it's going to be that simple.'

'No act of greatness is ever simple, Wren Greenrock.'

Wren thought of her own journey to the throne, how she had scaled the palace walls and kidnapped her own sister to get her hands on the crown of Eana. 'You would do anything for Ansel,' she murmured, to herself. 'Just as I would do anything for Banba.'

'It appears we have more in common than we thought.'

Wren looked up, sharply. 'We are *nothing* alike.'

'In this moment, we are.' Alarik placed the dagger between his teeth and began to roll up his sleeve.

'What are you doing?' said Wren, warily.

'No sense in ruining another good coat.' He removed the dagger and angled the tip over his palm. 'You need blood, don't you?'

Wren's eyes went wide. 'You want me to use *yours*?'

'I'm hardly afraid of a little bloodshed,' he said. 'Ansel is my brother. It should be my sacrifice.'

Wren stared at the king.

He stared back. 'Is there a problem?'

'No. I don't know.' She frowned. 'We can try it this way.' Using Alarik's blood felt one step closer to what Oonagh had done, twisting the blood of others into her spells. But it was for his brother, after all. And he was giving it willingly. Perhaps it would be easier this way.

Alarik dragged the dagger point along his palm. A pearl of crimson bubbled to the surface and streamed across his fingers. It fell between them with an audible splat.

Wren grabbed his hand and pulled it towards her. 'Don't waste it,' she hissed.

'There's plenty more, I assure you.'

The unexpected warmth of Alarik's hand made Wren realize she was touching him. Skin on skin. The Gevran king wasn't made of ice, after all. 'Still. We don't want to be careless with it.'

Alarik smirked. 'So, you don't want me to suffer.'

'I don't want my *spell* to suffer,' Wren clarified. 'So, you can wipe that irritating smile off your face.'

'Are you planning to get started sometime today? Or is this merely an elaborate excuse to hold my hand?'

Wren dropped his hand and wiped her fingers on her cloak. 'Get over yourself,' she snapped. 'And yes, I'll get started as soon as you stop talking.'

The king raised his eyebrows but said nothing. *Smug bastard.* Wren leaned over Ansel and unlaced the prince's ivory doublet, revealing the pearly sheen of his skin beneath it.

'Come closer.' She carefully placed Alarik's bleeding palm against Ansel's chest. 'Hold it just like that.'

Alarik went as still as a statue. His eyes were closed, a slight dent appearing between his brows. Wren couldn't tell if it was from discomfort or the touch of his brother's dead body, only that his careless demeanour had shifted, and he looked unsettled now . . . almost nervous.

She gingerly laid her hand on top of Alarik's. Their shoulders brushed, and Wren caught a whiff of his scent for the first time. It was subtle, like woodsmoke in winter. Her fingers began to tingle.

'What is that?' he whispered. 'That strange warmth.'

Wren shushed him. 'The magic, you idiot. Now stop distracting me.'

She closed her eyes, inhaling through her nose and

exhaling through her mouth. Alarik slowed his breathing to match hers. The rest of the world fell away, until there was only Wren's magic sparking in her veins, and Alarik's blood guiding it towards Ansel's frozen heart. Just as she had practised last night and the one before it, she focused in on her intention and offered her enchantment. *'With blood for strength, and words for flight, I call your soul back to the light.'*

Wren's voice echoed back at her from every corner of the room, ice water dripping in the silence that followed. Exhaustion tugged at the edges of her senses, and she was seized by the urge to sit down and catch her breath. She didn't know if the spell was working, but *something* was happening. She could feel her magic pouring out of her.

She summoned another breath and raised her voice. 'Ansel,' she called out. *'With blood for strength, and words for flight, I call your soul back to the light.'*

She pressed down on Alarik's hand as her head began to spin. Her magic surged, throbbing like a second heartbeat.

Yes, whispered a voice inside her. *Keep going.*

'With blood for strength, and words for flight, I call your soul back to the light!' cried Wren.

Her shoulders were trembling now, or was that Alarik who was shaking?

A groan seeped out of him.

Wren leaned against him, just as he collapsed against her, both of them holding each other up. Wren just about managed to eke out the enchantment one last time, but when the words left her so did the last of her breath. The final kernel of her energy – her magic – went with it.

She withdrew her hand and opened her eyes. The room was spinning. Alarik had used his free hand to brace himself against the table, the other still pressed to his brother's chest. His eyes were squeezed shut, pain twisting every muscle on his face. His blood was everywhere, the pooling stains glowing like firelight.

Wren reached for his arm as she stumbled backwards, the room spinning faster and faster until she didn't know which way was up.

Alarik raised his head. '*Wren.*'

His voice was so far away. Wren felt like she was falling down a tunnel. She couldn't see straight, couldn't breathe right. She lost her footing, and Alarik lunged, catching her by the waist. He pushed her back against the wall, pinning her between his arms to stop her from cracking her head on the marble slab.

Wren tried to speak, but nothing came out. Her legs were giving way beneath her.

Alarik pressed his forehead into her shoulder, groaning as they slid down to the floor together. They collapsed in a heap, the blackness sweeping in to claim them.

Wren languished in darkness for an eternity, waiting for something to fill the hollow yawning inside her. New breath. Old magic. Anything. The king rested against her shoulder, his head touching hers, their chests rising and falling in perfect unison as the slow drip-drop of ice water gently coaxed them back to consciousness.

Wren woke up first.

A pair of legs swung back and forth in her periphery. Then came a voice, haunting in its familiarity. 'Good morrow, my flower!'

Wren looked up to find Prince Ansel sitting on the edge of the marble slab, waggling his fingers at her. 'I believe it's almost time for our wedding!'

Rose

CHAPTER 30

Rose followed Lei Fan deeper into the Palace of Eternal Sunlight. Light flooded the vaulted hallways, casting pinwheels of colour across the quartz tiles. Shen's cousin paused at one point, lifting her face to the windows and soaking it in, like a flower.

'I've missed the sun's warmth,' she said, quietly. 'I thought I'd never know it again.'

Rose had quickly come to realize that the palace was designed to pour sunlight into every room, every nook and crevice, every forgotten corner. It must have been awful living for so many years without it, so she stood aside and let Lei Fan savour it.

A short while later, they arrived at an ornate door carved with sunbursts. Lei Fan offered Rose a sheepish smile. 'Excuse the mess. I wasn't expecting visitors today. Or ever, really.' She paused. 'And definitely not a queen.'

Rose returned her smile, gesturing to the mud on her sleeve. 'Only if you'll excuse my dress.'

'Deal.' Lei Fan pushed the door open and Rose gaped at

the chamber inside. Tunics of blue and green and red were strewn haphazardly across the floor, gold earrings and ruby hairpins scattered among them like confetti. Even more clothes spilled out of the armoires, which spanned an entire wall. The rest were decorated with breathtaking murals, a blushing desert sunrise to the east, and an amber sunset to the west. In the middle of it all, stood an unmade four-poster bed draped in cerulean silks. Upon it, a black cat was reclining in a shaft of sunlight. It opened one eye in mild interest.

'That's Shadow,' said Lei Fan, as the cat promptly went back to sleep. 'We both thrive in chaos.'

'Hello, Shadow,' said Rose, politely, but the cat was already snoring.

Lei Fan sent out a gust of wind and blasted the river of clothes aside as she crossed the bedroom.

Ah, thought Rose, as she followed her. *That explains the mess.*

Lei Fan flung open a wardrobe and a sea of dresses spilled out. 'There has to be *something* fancy enough in here,' she muttered, as she rummaged through the swell of silks and linens.

'I'm really not that picky,' lied Rose, as she turned to the mirror. She winced at her reflection. Her cheeks were sunburnt, and her hair was a tangled mess. Dark circles pooled under her eyes, betraying her exhaustion.

'Aha!' Lei Fan waded back across her bedroom, clutching a handful of red silk. 'Try this.' She tossed it to Rose before diving into another mountain of clothes. 'Now what should *I* wear?'

While Lei Fan inspected and discarded dress after dress, Rose quickly changed into the red silk gown. Unlike the structured dresses she was used to, this one was loose and flowing, with billowing sleeves and a low neckline. She tugged on it self-consciously. 'Am I wearing this right?'

Lei Fan paused to look up from the mess. 'I'm a genius! I knew the red would suit you.'

Dinner was a small, intimate affair, served in the inner courtyard of the palace, where the walls were hung with yellow marigolds and trailing jasmine. The desert stars danced overhead, the moon casting them in its soft silver glow.

After her hour-long bath, and now wearing Lei Fan's beautiful silk dress, Rose finally felt like herself again. With fresh eyes and a clear head, her focus was shifting. Now that the Sunkissed Kingdom had been found, her thoughts turned back to Barron, and the rebellion taking root in the heart of her country. The sooner she gathered her army and returned to the seat of her power at Anadawn, the safer they would all be.

For now, Rose held her tongue. Tonight was for Shen. The rest would come after. She sat between Lei Fan and Grandmother Lu, while Kai, who looked rather sullen, and Feng, who was impeccably dressed, occupied the seats across from her. Shen, who she hadn't seen since he left for the kitchens with Grandmother Lu that afternoon, was at the head of the table, wearing a new sage tunic and dark trousers.

Much to Rose's disappointment, he barely acknowledged her arrival, and didn't once comment on her dress.

'It feels a bit strange to be sitting at the head of the table,' Shen said, fidgeting and taking a generous slug of wine. 'I'm not used to it.'

'Isn't the seat comfortable?' said Feng. 'I've been keeping it warm for you while you've been gone.' He laughed loudly at his own joke, before tracing the gold band on his head. 'I suppose I should give this back to you as well.'

'It once belonged to your father, Gao,' said Grandmother Lu, with a smile. 'Such a handsome king, he was. And what a smile!'

'It's his sense of humour I miss the most,' said Feng. 'Gao had a knack for making me spit out my wine at family dinners. He used to time his best jokes to catch me out.' He chuckled to himself as he reached for his goblet. 'I never thought I'd miss that, but I do. I miss him every day.'

'I'll have to work on my jokes, then,' said Shen. 'To make him proud.'

Grandmother Lu reached over to pat his hand. 'You already do.'

Rose wanted to tell Shen that his jokes were already funny, that he made her laugh every day, but the moment was passing, and she felt strangely outside it.

'And I know one thing,' added Feng. 'My brother would want his son to wear the Sun Walker's Crown.'

Shen shook his head. 'I don't need a crown, Uncle. I'm just glad to be back.'

'Our people will be expecting to see you in it,' said Feng, exchanging a glance with Kai that was too quick for Rose to read. 'After all, now that the crown prince is back, we cannot hide you.'

'If nobody else wants to wear it, I'll volunteer,' said Lei Fan, conjuring a gust of wind to knock it off her father's head. She grabbed it and placed it lopsidedly on her own. 'Well?' She grinned. 'What do you think?'

Grandmother Lu rubbed her eyes and then widened them in feigned surprise. 'Who is this new queen I see before me?'

Rose giggled. 'It really is quite fetching.'

Shen smiled at Rose across the table and her heart hitched in her chest. But before she could ask him how his afternoon had been – or tell him how good he looked in his new tunic – his gaze slid over her and landed on Lei Fan. 'You used to wear your hair like that when you were little,' he said, gesturing to her two long braids, wrapped with delicate gold twine. 'It still suits you.'

'Lei Fan, the Sun Walker's Crown is not a toy,' Feng interrupted. 'Give it to Shen. Now.'

'I just wanted to try it on,' mumbled Lei Fan, as she removed the crown and handed it to Shen.

Kai took a slug of whisky, watching it pass over the table with a keenness that made Rose uncomfortable.

Shen took the crown, and for a moment Rose thought he was going to put it to the side, but then he placed it on his own head. Something twisted inside her at the sight. She couldn't tell if it was jealousy or fear, only that the thin gold band tied Shen to a place she didn't belong and offered him a future she wasn't part of.

'Do I really need to wear it during a family dinner?' he said. 'I feel a bit ridiculous.'

'No more ridiculous than a prince who has barely set foot inside his own kingdom,' said Kai, between gulps of whisky.

'Such a handsome prince,' said Grandmother Lu, smiling broadly. 'You look just like your father.'

Finally, Shen looked at Rose. 'Well?' he said, his smile sheepish. 'What do you think?'

'It suits you,' she said, even though she still couldn't quite believe she was seeing Shen in a crown.

'Now that that's settled, I'm starving,' said Grandmother Lu, flapping her hands at a passing servant. 'Bring out the food before I salt that crown and eat it.'

Instead of multiple courses, the servants brought everything out on giant platters for sharing. There was a mountain of greens cooked with red chillies, thick hand-pulled noodles swimming in a bone broth, and steamed whole chicken served with ginger and onions, all of it deliciously fragrant and steaming hot.

The greens were so spicy they made Rose's eyes water. She downed her wine to cool her tongue, before reaching for another.

'Too hot for you, Queenie?' Kai smirked as he scooped out another helping.

'It's delicious but quite spicy, isn't it?' said Rose, looking around her. But no one else seemed to be struggling. Shen had already gone back for seconds. 'I've never had anything like it.'

'We grow our chillies in the palace gardens,' said Feng, proudly. 'I've spent years perfecting their spice.'

'With my help,' interjected Grandmother Lu. 'I whisper to the chillies when everyone is asleep. They grow nice and spicy for me.'

'I'm amazed you were able to grow anything at all,' said Rose, trying to catch Shen's eye again so they could share a sliver of conversation, 'living under the desert these past eighteen years.'

'You'll find that like all things in the desert, the Sunkissed Kingdom is resilient. It can thrive where most things wouldn't,' said Feng, a touch defensively. 'We don't need anyone but ourselves.'

Shen fidgeted with the ruby ring around his neck. 'I'm sorry it took me so long to find you. I never knew I had the key.' He frowned, then. 'I didn't know anything.'

'You were very young when we lost our sky,' said Grandmother Lu, heaping more noodles on to his plate. 'You cannot blame yourself.'

'But what happened?' Shen traced the ring like it might whisper to him of the past. 'I can't remember. One moment I was here with my family, and the next, I was all alone in the desert.'

Grandmother Lu set the noodles down and sat back in her chair. 'After the murder of King Keir and Queen Lillith –' she paused to dip her chin at Rose in respect – 'Anadawn went to war against the witches of Eana. Many of the witches welcomed the fight. They were angry. They wanted to take back what the Valharts had stolen from them, what they *continued* to steal from them.'

Rose thought of Banba marching out to face the full cruelty of Rathborne's army, of Thea losing her eye in the battle, and the countless other witches who had perished that day. Not long ago, she had glimpsed their spirits in the Weeping Forest, heard their dying screams in her nightmares.

'But Lillith's War was not our fight,' said Feng, coldly. 'For hundreds of years, we had lived in the desert without the Valhart royals even knowing of our existence. We had our own ruling system, our own king and queen. By then, we had all but seceded from Eana.' He glanced meaningfully at Rose. She held his stare. 'We didn't want Willem Rathborne to know the strength of our warrior witches, the power of our tempests, the quickness of our enchanters. We wanted to be left alone, as we always had been. And so we decided not to join the fight.'

Shen bristled. 'You abandoned the other witches?' He looked between Feng and Grandmother Lu. 'But there are thousands of us here. We could have turned the tide of the war!'

'Or died alongside everyone else,' said Feng.

'You don't know that,' said Shen. He met Rose's gaze – flame on flame – and for a heartbeat, they were united in their anger.

'You sound just like your mother, Shen Lo,' said

Grandmother Lu, sighing. 'Queen Ai Li couldn't bring herself to ignore the witches' cry for help. She and your father argued about what to do. *Ceaselessly*, I might add. In the end, she decided to go on her own. She was one of the most powerful tempests I've ever seen. She believed she could make a difference.'

'And my father?' said Shen, clenching his fists on the table.

'Your father was a formidable warrior. A formidable king,' said Grandmother Lu, her brown eyes softening. 'He stayed here with his people. To protect them. To protect the kingdom. When your mother left, Gao asked her to hide us, as she'd done many times before.'

'Our kingdom has long moved beneath the sands,' said Feng, stepping back into the tale. 'Separate from Eana. Separate from Anadawn.' He glanced meaningfully at Rose, then went on. 'But there has always been a key to unbury it.' He gestured to the ruby ring hanging from Shen's neck. 'Your mother left that key with the person she loved most in the world. The safest place she could think of.'

Shen clutched the ring in his fist, his eyes turning fearful. Rose was seized by the urge to reach for his hand across the table, but this wasn't her story. She was outside the glass bubble again, looking in.

'But you followed her, Shen,' said Grandmother Lu, gently. 'And she never knew. You got lost in the desert, and the key was with you.' She looked down at her hands, and Rose saw they were trembling. 'After your mother died in the war, our only way out disappeared.'

Shen closed his eyes and raised a fist to his mouth, like he was trying to keep himself from crying out for her.

Grandmother Lu went on. 'Your father believed he'd lost both his wife and his son to the war. The grief was too much for him. He barely lasted a year beneath the sands before his heart gave out. He went to join your mother in the stars.' She shook her head, a tear slipping down her cheek. 'All this time, we thought you were there, too. How could a boy so young survive in the desert on his own?'

'Banba found me,' said Shen, numbly. 'She took me to Ortha.' He dropped his head in his hands, his pain muffled by his fingers. 'And I spent eighteen years wearing that damned ruby around my neck.'

'It's not your fault,' said Rose, breaking her silence before it suffocated her. 'How could you have known?'

Kai cleared his throat. 'It sort of *is* his fault.'

'Kai!' snapped Lei Fan.

'What? It's true! If he hadn't chased his mother—'

'He was a child,' Grandmother Lu cut in.

'He grew up, didn't he? And here he is, rubbing shoulders with the queen of Eana.' Kai tipped his empty glass at Rose. 'He could have come to look for us sooner. Looked better. Harder. Everyone thinks the long-lost crown prince, the great and bashful Shen Lo, saved us, but I'm the one who fought my way out of the sands, clawing through the desert until it filled my belly and my lungs to go and save my people, and what thanks do *I* get?' He scowled at Shen's drooped head. 'No fancy crown for Kai.'

'It wouldn't fit you,' said Lei Fan, using a gust of wind to tip his greens on to his lap. 'Your head is too big.'

Kai slammed his fist on the table. 'It's not fair, and you all know it,' he slurred. 'None of this is fair.'

Shen raised his head. 'I didn't ask for any of this.'

Kai barked a laugh. 'And yet you got it, cousin. You got all of it.'

'That's enough, Kai,' said Feng, sharply, and Kai returned to simmering in silence.

For a long moment, nobody spoke. And then a servant rushed in. 'Help!' he said, looking between Feng and Shen, unsure of who to address. 'There's a wolf howling at the gates!'

Rose stood up. 'I'd better see to that.'

'I'm going with you!' said Lei Fan, springing to her feet. 'I've never seen a wolf.'

Rose waited for Shen to stand up, too, but he turned back to the old woman as though he didn't even see Rose, hovering there at his shoulder. 'Tell me more, Grandmother Lu,' he said. 'Tell me everything.'

Wren
CHAPTER 31

Wren stood on top of the Fovarr Mountains, listening to the blizzard scream her name. Her blood glowed underneath her skin, filling her with rippling power. It burst from her like a song, the crimson strands of her magic streaming through the wind. She chased them along the snowy ridge. Before her the magnificent dome of Grinstad Palace glittered like a jewel in the darkness.

You have woken the prince from his eternal slumber, said the wind, in a voice that sounded curiously like her own. Only it was older, darker. *What else can you do, little bird?*

Wren heard the distant roar of the king's beasts and felt her magic stir in answer.

Do you wish to shatter the mountains?

Do you wish to fly to the moon?

Wren took another step, and almost trampled a wolf cub sleeping in the snow. She raised her hand without meaning to. Inside her fist, a blade glinted silver-bright. She stopped herself before she struck the creature. 'No.'

Why not? cajoled the wind. *This life is for the taking.*

This blood will bring you power.

Wren tried to stow the knife and realized it was covered in blood. She looked down, the taste of ash suddenly acrid on her tongue. Instead of the cub, there was a person curled at her feet. Rose looked up at her, blood seeping through her teeth as she clutched at a knife wound in her chest. Wren screamed, but the blizzard swept the sound away. The mountain trembled at her feet, and somewhere over her shoulder an avalanche thundered down the slope towards them. Wren lunged for her sister, but the snow had already swallowed her up.

It careened over Wren, too, a sheet of ice closing around her legs and then her hips. It climbed up to her chest, rooting her to the mountain. Her breath froze inside her and her blood turned to ice in her veins. Her magic snuffed out as her lashes crusted shut. Silence then, the keening wind dying out until there was only that ancient voice whispering to her from a forgotten corner of her mind.

Break the ice to break the curse.

Free me to free yourself.

Wren woke up mid-scream, but the sound of her distress was lost in a deafening rumble. It was barely sunrise, and all the beasts in the palace were roaring. The chandelier was swaying, and the pitcher of water on her bedside table was trembling. She leaped out of bed and rushed to the window, just in time to see a snowdrift slide down the mountain. It crashed through the gates of Grinstad Palace and buried the gardens up to their hedges.

And then everything was still.

Wren gripped the windowsill. 'Hissing seaweed.'

Hours later, when the maid arrived to draw her morning bath, Wren was pacing by the window. 'What was that earlier, Klara? I thought the ceiling was going to cave in.'

'An avalanche.' Klara clutched the jug of hot water to her chest, her grey eyes fearful. 'It's been a long while since we had one like that in Grinstad. The blizzard must have set it off.'

'Is there anything else amiss in the palace today?' Wren fished, thinking of Prince Ansel, who was, as far as she knew, currently undead.

Klara frowned. 'I don't get your meaning.'

'Never mind,' said Wren, surmising the girl knew nothing of the prince. Yet. 'Don't let me keep you.'

Klara bustled into the bathing chamber. 'I'll make sure to set the fire once I've run your bath.'

A few minutes later, Wren sank into her bubble bath, letting the soapy warmth chase away the dregs of her nightmare. Her thoughts turned to Prince Ansel, and where the newly undead prince was at that very moment. After Wren had woken up, near frozen, in the dungeon chamber yesterday morning, she had only managed a brief exchange with Ansel – who had clearly been under the impression that she was Rose – before Alarik had sat up in a daze. The king had leaped at his brother with all the sprightliness of a child, throwing his arms around Ansel and pulling him close as if he was afraid the spell would wear off any second.

Wren had watched the moment unfold with a mixture of

unease and disbelief. While Alarik embraced his brother, she studied Ansel for any lingering signs of . . . well, unnaturalness. Ansel's back was unusually stiff, his smile a touch too wide. And then, of course, there was the matter of him thinking that Rose was his dearly beloved, and that they were about to be married. It was as if he had no memory of their ill-fated wedding or the part where he had ended up dead. But Wren didn't get a chance to voice any of these concerns, because the second she rolled to her feet, Alarik remembered she was in there with them and promptly sent her away.

Wren didn't blame him for it. He wanted to take off his mask of callous indifference and be a brother, not a king. And he could not – *would not* – do that in front of Wren. And so she did as he commanded, stepping out of the room to the curious gazes of the king's soldiers, who had been waiting all that time in the darkness.

'The prince is alive,' she informed them, before swallowing the rest of the truth: *for now.*

Later, when Wren had returned to her bedroom, she threw open the little window and vomited a belly full of ash, retching and heaving over and over until her lungs ached. When her legs gave out, she crawled into bed, and had slept, mired in nightmares, until now. Exhaustion still lingered at the edge of her senses and the strange hollowness in her stomach remained. It felt like someone had reached through her ribcage and snatched a fistful of her organs away.

After her bath, Wren examined herself in the mirror, looking for evidence of what she and Alarik had done in the icy catacombs, but apart from a couple of grey smudges under her eyes, she looked the same. She brushed her hair and applied some face cream, pinching her cheeks to return their colour. She crossed over to the wardrobe, freezing at the sight of a dead mouse, lying in front of it.

'Shit.' Her little miracle was dead all over again. Wren picked up the poor creature and threw it into the fire. She tried not to think of Prince Ansel as she rifled through the wardrobe. If he had met the same fate as her mouse, surely Alarik would be banging on her door, demanding a do-over. Or her head on a platter. But the fourth floor of Grinstad was silent.

Wren chose a dark blue dress with a flowing skirt, slipping it over her head and tying it at the waist. The fire was heating the room quickly, and all this worrying about Ansel was making the back of her neck sweat. Her palms, too.

She opened the window, inhaling a lungful of crisp mountain air as she looked out at miles and miles of jagged peaks and snow-dusted valleys. A single black bird flitted across the ivory sky. It got closer and closer, its silver breast nearly blinding Wren in the morning sun.

She knew it was a starcrest before it landed on her windowsill, but that didn't stop her from backing away from it. 'Rotting carp! What are you doing here?'

She yelped at a sudden banging on the door. Inga poked her head in, waving a card. 'For you, Your Majesty.'

Wren practically sprinted across the room to snatch it from her. Her eyes went wide as she read it. It was an invitation to breakfast . . . from *Anika*. Did the princess know about Ansel? Had she invited Wren downstairs to thank her in person? Or was there something else going on? Wren glanced at the starcrest on the windowsill and swallowed. She didn't exactly relish the thought of sharing her morning meal with the acerbic Gevran princess, but she would take the unpredictability of Anika's temper over the endless monotony of these four walls, where her thoughts were much too loud. And besides she was desperate to find out news of Prince Ansel.

She slipped her shoes on and made for the hallway, letting Inga lead the way down to the dining room. It was a long, narrow chamber with floor-to-ceiling windows that looked out over the gardens of Grinstad, which included an impressive courtyard bordered by winterberry shrubs, a maze of boxwood hedges and the frozen pond that had almost killed Wren. Thanks to this morning's avalanche, it was all covered with a fresh heap of snow.

'Well, that was quick,' came a familiar snide voice. 'You must have flung yourself down the stairs to get here so fast. Are you really so desperate for company?'

Anika was sitting at the end of a frosted-glass table. Her crimson hair was pulled away from her face in an artful chignon that made her cheekbones look even more severe. She was wearing a black dress that hugged her curves, and her pet fox, the same one she had brought with her to Eana, was curled around her neck. But it was not the princess's unusual scarf that caught Wren's attention. It was the person sitting in the chair next to her.

'*Celeste?*' The name came out like a swear word. 'What in rotting hell are you doing here?'

Celeste raised her brows. 'That's hardly any way to greet your friend, is it?'

Wren looked between them, trying to figure out what on earth was going on. Celeste's unexpected presence certainly explained the starcrest on Wren's windowsill, but beyond that she was at a total loss.

'I expect Celeste was worried about you,' supplied Anika. 'She's been sailing on her brother's merchant vessel, and she decided to stop in and say hello. She says she missed me, and while I'm sure that's true – I am a delight, after all – I think, really, she wanted to make sure we hadn't killed you.' She smirked at Celeste. 'I told you she's fine.'

'So I see,' said Celeste, who had been appraising Wren, no doubt searching for signs of injury. 'And well dressed, too.'

'They haven't supplied me with any trousers despite my constant pestering,' said Wren.

Anika pouted. 'Poor little queen.' Her pet fox raised its head and bared its tiny teeth at her.

Wren glowered at both of them. 'So, you invited Celeste in here, like you haven't made it abundantly clear that you hate all Eanans, and then decided to have this fancy breakfast with her?' Wren gestured to the stack of pancakes on the table, which sat next to a jug of maple syrup and a teeming bowl of berries. There was a full platter of bacon, sausages and fried eggs, too. 'Instead of, oh, I don't know, throwing her in a room on the fourth floor and posting a soldier outside to keep her trapped in there.'

Anika laughed like a hyena. 'Your ignorance is hilarious. You see, there is one *crucial* difference between you and Lady Celeste Pegasi.'

Wren sank into the chair opposite Celeste. 'Do tell,' she said, as she nibbled on a strip of bacon.

'Celeste didn't kill my brother.'

Wren's appetite curdled. She put the bacon down. 'I didn't kill your brother, Anika.'

'*And* she's tremendous fun,' Anika went on, as if she hadn't heard her. 'I enjoy her company.'

Celeste smirked at Wren over a stack of pancakes. 'I tend to have that effect on people.'

'Not me,' said Wren, pointedly.

'That's because you have a bad habit of doing stupid things. And I'm the one who ends up having to scold you.'

Wren folded her arms. 'Is that why you've come here, then? To *scold* me?'

Celeste picked at a crumb on the table. 'Of course not. I came to have breakfast with Anika. And to check in on you, I suppose. It was Anika's idea to invite you down here to join us.'

Wren knew Celeste well enough by now to know she was lying. The wrinkle on her nose betrayed her true feelings. She was worried about Wren – and even more so than before.

Celeste reached for a pancake. 'So, Wren, what have you been up to since I last saw you?'

'Oh, a bit of this. A bit of that. Have you ever watched

snow fall for hours on end? It's exceedingly boring.'

'She's made a deal with Alarik,' Anika supplied. 'I was against it at first, but he's persuaded me to give her a chance at redemption.' Wren glanced sidelong at the princess, surmising from her casualness that she mustn't yet know about Ansel. How peculiar.

'Oh?' Celeste popped a berry into her mouth. 'What kind of deal?'

Anika had shoved Wren into dangerous territory. No possible good could come from telling Celeste about the spell. 'Alarik has agreed to set Banba free,' said Wren, vaguely. 'I just have to . . . help him with a task first.'

Celeste set her fork down. 'What kind of task?'

Wren cleared her throat.

'Go on,' needled Anika. 'Or would you like me to do the honours?'

Wren threw her a withering glance. She was about to respond when the door to the dining room flew open and Prince Ansel lurched inside, saving her the trouble. 'Good morrow! Do I detect the sweet smell of maple syrup? Ah! Dear sister, I see you are breakfasting with my future bride.' He grinned widely, his lips stretching and stretching, until Wren could see all the teeth in his head. 'I think you two are going to be the best of friends.'

Anika screamed.

The fox hissed.

Celeste leaped to her feet, brandishing her butter knife.

'That kind of task,' said Wren, slumping back in her chair.

Rose
CHAPTER 32

Rose's footsteps echoed in the darkness as she raced through the abandoned streets of Ellendale. Flames licked her heels, while arrows whistled past her ears. She could hear Barron calling out for her. *Come back, little witch. I've got a special arrow for your rotten heart.*

The air exploded around Rose. Fire rose up from the cobblestones and lashed out at her. She tripped over herself, but when she fell, her knees met snow. A sudden shock of coldness stole through her. She looked up, into a swirling blizzard, to find her sister standing before her.

Wren, Rose cried, with surging relief. *Thank goodness you're here.*

But Wren didn't answer. She smiled as she raised the dagger in her hand, and brought it crashing down, straight towards Rose's heart.

Rose woke with a scream trapped in her throat. She gasped a breath, reaching for the pitcher of water on the nightstand. She drank it down, trying to wash away the image of her sister stabbing her heart, and the slow-burgeoning fear that in the snow-swept wilds of Gevra, Wren was turning into Oonagh, and the twins' curse would find new life in her sister.

Stop that, Rose scolded herself. *It was only a dream.*

And she was no seer. Thankfully.

A quick glance at the clock on the wall told her she had only been asleep for twenty minutes. She was surprised she had managed to nod off at all.

Rose's restlessness had nothing to do with the bedroom she'd been given, which was perfectly luxurious. The bed was piled high with pillows and draped in silks of amber and gold that swayed in the desert breeze. Lei Fan had lent her soft linen pyjamas, and Elske was dozing at the foot of her bed, warming the sheets. It was almost midnight, and the Palace of Eternal Sunlight languished in silence. And yet Rose couldn't seem to settle.

Shen hadn't come by to check on her after dinner. Rose had been so sure he would that she had kept her dress on for hours. She had brushed out her hair while she sat waiting for him at the dresser. Then at the desk. On the window seat. She had paced her room, watching the minutes turn to hours, and still – nothing. She hadn't realized how much she'd grown used to his attentiveness. Back at Anadawn, Shen was always nearby, accompanying her on her garden walks, bringing a book to read beside her in the library, asking how she was, complimenting her, offering support whenever she needed it.

As Rose lay in bed, staring at the ceiling, she scolded herself for taking him for granted. She had been so reluctant to carve out a place for him in her future, and now, here she was, in his kingdom, where there was clearly no place for her.

But then, perhaps it was better this way. What was she doing mooning over a boy anyway? She had far more important things to think about.

Like getting Wren and Banba home from Gevra (because it was clear her sister was in over her head). And dealing with the Arrows (who were proving to be a much bigger problem than Rose had initially thought). And ruling all of Eana, for stars' sake! She was a busy woman. She was a *queen*. Not some lovestruck milkmaid. The sooner she returned to Anadawn, the better.

There was a knock at her door.

Rose sat bolt upright. 'Who is it?'

The door creaked open, and Shen stepped inside, still dressed in his dinner attire. 'I hoped you'd still be up.'

'I was just falling asleep,' Rose lied.

Shen closed the door behind him, and Rose's mouth went dry as she realized they were finally alone together in a bedroom. Far from prying eyes. There were no seers here. No Kai either.

Just Rose and Shen.

She glanced at the slumbering wolf curled up at the foot of her bed.

Make that *almost* alone.

Shen gazed at her for a moment. 'That bed is big enough for you to get lost in.'

'Does it remind you of when you stole me from my bed at Anadawn?' said Rose, biting back a smile. 'Don't get any ideas.'

Shen shook his head as he came towards her. 'I have lots of ideas but stealing you *out* of that bed isn't one of them.'

Rose blushed, furiously. She pulled the blankets higher, grasping for a shred of composure. 'How are you? Today has been . . .'

'A lot.' Shen gestured to the bed. 'May I sit?'

'Of course,' she said, patting the space beside her.

He ran a hand through his hair as he sat down. He was no longer wearing the gold band, and though she didn't know why, Rose felt relieved. 'It's hard to believe any of this is real,' he admitted. 'I keep thinking it's a dream, and that any minute I'm going to wake up back in that forest outside Thornhaven. I feel . . . I don't know . . .'

'What?' said Rose, reading the pain on his face.

He inhaled, sharply. 'I can't stop feeling like it's my fault that everyone was trapped here for so long. I should have figured it out, Rose. I should have done something.'

'You were a child, Shen. You can't blame yourself. The important thing is that you've found them now. You saved them.'

Shen shook his head. 'I'll never get those years back, though. Years I could have been here with my family. And neither will they.' He looked at his hands. 'And they're all being so damn nice about it. We spent the evening playing cards. Feng shared all these funny stories about him and my father when they were our age. And it felt good. It felt *normal*.' Rose tried to keep her face from falling but she was wounded by the fact Shen hadn't thought to invite her. 'Kai threw a few barbs here and there, but I guess that felt normal, too,' he went on. 'And honestly, I'm glad. I think I'd be more uncomfortable if he suddenly started treating me like . . .' He trailed off.

'Like a prince?'

Shen laughed, a little ruefully. 'It still sounds so strange to me. I don't even know what I'm supposed to do with a title like that.' He looked up at her, his eyes shining. 'I guess I'm finally getting some insight into what you and Wren must feel all the time.'

Rose reached out, taking his hand in hers. 'Don't worry. When we're all back home in Anadawn, we'll figure it out together.'

Shen tilted his head. 'Rose,' he said, gently. 'I am home.'

Rose had feared somewhere deep inside her that he would say that, but hearing the words out loud was like being splashed with cold water.

'Well, of course this is your home,' she said, quickly. 'Or at least one of them. A place to visit as often as you like. But it's so far from Anadawn. And we have so much to do there. We need to strategize against Barron and the Arrows before they gain another foothold and we must ensure Wren returns from Gevra in one piece.' She forced a laugh. 'You know how reckless she can be.'

Shen wasn't laughing. He was looking at their hands, entwined on the bed. '*You* need to do all of that, Rose. You're queen of Eana, as you've reminded me so many times.' He untangled his fingers from hers, wearing a smile so sad it chipped her heart. 'I can't sneak around with you forever.

I know I've never been part of your destiny. And that's fine, because now I finally understand my own. I need to be here. This is where I belong.'

You belong with me, thought Rose, but she stopped herself from saying the words out loud. Her eyes prickled and she looked away.

Shen brushed his fingers against her cheek. 'You'll be fine without me. You're stronger than you know, remember?'

Rose's breath caught. She leaned into his touch. The world around them disappeared until there was nothing but the two of them alone in her bed, Shen's hand stroking her face, their breath mingling, their lips about to brush . . .

'I need you with me, Shen,' she whispered. And she meant it a hundred different ways, from every corner of her heart. She closed her eyes, expecting to feel his lips on hers.

Shen pulled back. 'I can't, Rose. I'm sorry.'

She snapped her eyes open, her cheeks flushing violently as she saw the regret simmering in his eyes.

She pulled away from him with as much dignity as she could muster. 'What I meant is that I'll need your help with the Arrows,' she said, clearing her throat. 'I'd welcome any of the Sunkissed witches, but the warriors are of particular interest to me, for obvious reasons.' She summoned a practised smile. 'It will be a brilliant way to bring the Anadawn soldiers and the witches together and empower the entire country, don't you think? And of course, once Barron sees the impressive span of our improved army, he'll stand down at once. Only a fool would move against us now.'

Shen's frown deepened. 'The people of this kingdom have just seen the sun for the first time in eighteen years. There are children here who have never seen the sky until today. I can't rush them into battle.'

'But you said they would help me,' said Rose, recalling their conversation from two days ago, the promises they had made to each other by the river outside Ellendale. It felt like a lifetime ago now. 'You said they would help *us*.'

'Didn't you hear Grandmother Lu tonight? My mother died fighting in a war that wasn't hers to fight.'

'Your mother was a witch,' said Rose, straining to keep her voice under control. 'She wanted to defend her fellow witches. Just like I need you now to help me defend them from the Arrows.'

He was already shaking his head. 'If she had just stayed, the kingdom wouldn't have been lost. She wouldn't have died. Don't you see? My father hid this place to keep our kingdom safe from war.'

'But you're the prince now,' said Rose, desperately. 'Everyone will listen to you.'

'I won't make them fight, Rose.'

Rose balked at Shen as he stood up. 'So, you're just going to sit back and let Edgar Barron whip up an army against Anadawn? Don't you care about me and Wren?' she said, throwing the covers off. 'About the Ortha witches? About your own country?'

Shen paced the length of the room. 'Of course I care. But I need time to figure this all out. It's not that simple any more.

I'm a leader. I have to think about what's best for my kingdom. You of all people must understand that.'

'What I *understand* is that your kingdom resides in *my* desert, Shen,' said Rose, through gritted teeth. 'I understand that I, as your queen, am asking for a pledge of loyalty.'

Shen stopped pacing. 'And I'm telling you as your *friend* –' he paused, the word swelling between them like a thundercloud – 'that I need to be here.'

Rose set aside her hurt feelings. After everything they had gone through, he knew that word would sting her the most. 'Anadawn needs the support of the Sunkissed Kingdom, Shen. That isn't a request. It's an order.' As soon as she'd said the words, she regretted them, but she couldn't take them back. She had made her stance. Now she needed to stick to it.

Shen's eyes flashed. 'I don't answer to you, Rose. And neither does my kingdom. Feng told me about a treaty that was signed between our ancestors a long time ago. One that gives us sovereignty. One that allows me to make my own decisions.'

'What are you talking about?' said Rose, hotly. 'I've never heard of such a treaty.'

'You'd never heard of this kingdom, until you met me,' Shen reminded her. 'Maybe there are some things you don't know.'

'You're being unfair,' snapped Rose.

'And you're being selfish,' he snapped back. 'This kingdom doesn't belong to you. And neither do I.'

Rose reeled backwards, feeling like she had been struck.

Shen stalked out, slamming the door so loudly that Elske woke with a growl. When the echo of his footsteps finally faded, Rose buried her face in her pillow and wept.

In the morning, Rose was resolute. She was going home. She'd done what she had come here to do, and with rebellion stirring in Eana, every minute away from Anadawn was precious. Treacherous. She changed back into her stained dress, packed her satchel with her mirror and her hairbrush, and prepared to leave with Elske.

She'd take Storm for the journey. Shen could at least lend her his horse if not the strength of the Sunkissed Kingdom. *His* kingdom, she reminded herself. According to some long-ago treaty that she had never even laid eyes on, Shen Lo didn't owe her anything. Not his loyalty. Not his heart. What a fool she had been to give hers away.

Elske padded at Rose's side as she stalked down the sun-drenched halls of the palace.

Lei Fan's bedroom door creaked open as she passed and the tempest stepped out, wearing bright yellow pyjamas. 'What are you doing you up so early?'

'I could ask you the same thing,' said Rose, as Shadow slipped out of Lei Fan's room and brushed against her leg.

Lei Fan spread her arms wide and tilted her head back. 'I want to soak up as much of the sun as I can,' she said. 'I forgot how amazing it feels.' As if in agreement, Shadow rolled on to his back, mewling contentedly as he, too, basked in the morning sunlight. He was clearly unbothered by Elske, who for her part simply gave the cat a curious glance.

Rose watched the sunlight dance across Lei Fan's face, the enormity of what had changed for the tempest and the rest of the kingdom sinking in all over again.

'I am glad you can feel the true sun again,' she said. 'I am happy for you, and your cat, and your kingdom. And –' her voice caught, for just a moment – 'and for Shen.' She cleared her throat. 'But I have urgent matters to attend to back in Anadawn. Please thank your father for his hospitality. I really must be on my way.'

Lei Fan's eyes widened. 'You're leaving? Now? But you just got here!'

Rose smiled, tersely. 'Duty calls.'

'But you haven't even seen the city properly!' cried Lei Fan. 'And tonight is the Festival of the Dancing Sun! You must stay for that, at least.'

'I've never heard of that festival . . .' said Rose, curious despite herself. 'But I'm afraid it doesn't matter. My country needs me.'

Lei Fan pulled a face. 'Shen told me about that hideous Barron and his Arrows.'

Rose blinked in surprise.

'We're close,' said Lei Fan. 'Shen knows he can trust me.'

'Well, I'm afraid it's the matter of those Arrows that I must return to, before my country is overrun with them,' said Rose, candidly. 'I thought I might find an ally in Shen, in this place, but his mind is on other matters.'

'He's probably worried about tonight's ceremony,' said Lei Fan, knowingly. 'Which is all the more reason for you to stay a little longer! It's the most magical festival of the year. And now that we have our sky back, we can *finally* celebrate it. Please don't leave on such a sour note, Queen Rose. I know my cousin would hate it.'

Rose fidgeted with the strap of her satchel. If she stayed a little longer, she and Shen might get a chance to speak again. As angry as she was, she knew yesterday *had* been overwhelming for Shen. They had both said things they didn't mean. Perhaps today he would feel differently. Act more like the Shen she knew. And besides, it *was* terribly rude to leave without saying goodbye.

'Stay for one more night,' pleaded Lei Fan. 'You can leave tomorrow if you're not too tired from all the dancing. You won't regret it, I promise.'

Rose glanced down at her wrinkled dress. 'Do you think you could lend me another gown?'

Lei Fan summoned a gust of wind, blasting her bedroom door wide open and startling Shadow, who let out an annoyed meow before darting away down the hallway. 'Step into my emporium.'

Before Rose set aside her myriad of worries, she sent a letter to Thea, assuring the Queensbreath that she would be home soon. And then another to Fathom, to enquire about the treaty Shen had mentioned last night. She knew it wouldn't change anything between them, but as queen of Eana Rose owed it to her people and to the Sunkissed Kingdom to investigate it.

She spent the rest of the day with Lei Fan, trying on dresses and snacking on delicious food. She marvelled at all the rooms inside the palace, including the Hall of Treasures, which contained everything from painted porcelain vases and huge silk tapestries woven with silver and gold to ornate furniture and bejewelled goblets. There was antique jewellery and ancient spell books, rubies the size of Rose's fist and opals of every colour. In the kitchens, she discovered fifty herbs and spices she had never even heard of, and the library was teeming with beautiful books of art and poetry and literature, the reading chairs so exquisitely wrought she didn't dare to perch on them.

'And this is the armoury,' said Lei Fan, parting an entire wall of feathergrass in one of the lower courtyards to reveal a narrow wooden door.

Rose gasped as she stepped inside. Hundreds of axes and swords hung from the ceiling, their blades winking at her in the dimness. There were whips and staffs, too, body armour brushed in gold and silver and bronze, and an entire section for bows and steel-tipped arrows. On a table in the middle of the room, daggers were arranged according to size.

'I never knew weapons could be so beautiful,' said Rose, as she traced the leather hilt of a double-edged sword.

'The blacksmiths of the Sunkissed Kingdom take great pride in their work,' said Lei Fan. 'They believe that in battle, as in death, there must always be respect.' She plucked a diamond-encrusted dagger from the table, dangling it by its tip. 'If you're going to be stabbed in the heart, it might as well be with a sparkly blade, right?'

Rose was seized by the memory of Wren standing over her in the snow, bloodlust flashing in her eyes. She blinked it away. 'I've never thought of it like that. Though I'd rather not be stabbed at all.'

Lei Fan unlocked a hidden drawer and removed two razor-sharp amber hairpins. 'These are my favourite. They belonged to Shen's mother, Queen Ai Li. She was a powerful tempest, but she knew how to fight, too. Gao trained her himself, and when they married, he gifted these to her.' She sighed as she set the pins down. 'She didn't think to take them to war. Though I'm not sure they would have made much of a difference.'

'She sounds very brave,' said Rose, her thoughts turning to Shen, who had clearly inherited his mother's courage. Rose had never known him to shy away from a fight, had never expected that he ever would. It didn't make any sense to her why he was doing so *now*. What was the point in having an armoury filled with the finest weapons in Eana if you weren't willing to fight for your country? Your people?

'Rose?' Lei Fan waved her hand in front of Rose's face. 'Are you all right? You've gone very still.'

Rose shook off her frustration and smiled at Lei Fan. 'Shall we go and get ready for the festival? You were right – I'm already glad I decided to stay for it.'

Wren
CHAPTER 33

'I am positively starving!' declared Prince Ansel as he staggered into the dining room, ignoring the butter knife Celeste was pointing at him. He beamed at Wren. 'Good morning, my flower! You're looking radiant, as ever.'

Wren watched Ansel lumber towards her with a sinking feeling in her gut. His skin was an odd greying hue, and the whites of his eyes were yellow. She was certain he'd looked more human yesterday. 'What a feast! *Oooh*, is that syrup? My favourite!'

He plonked into the chair beside Wren, dunked five pieces of bacon directly into the jug of syrup, and shoved them all in his mouth.

Anika, who was still frozen in shock, managed to eke a word out. 'Ansel?'

'Yes, dear sister?' His head lolled to the side for a moment before snapping back up with a sickening crack.

Anika grasped the back of her breakfast chair. 'I think I'm going to pass out.' Her fox hissed at Ansel, before leaping to the floor and hiding under her skirts.

'Calm down,' said Wren, trying to take her own advice. 'Breathe. Everything is fine.'

'*Fine,*' said Anika, inhaling the word. 'Look at his skin. His smile! I can practically see his tonsils!'

Celeste set down her butter knife and leaned across the table, trying to get a closer look at the prince. 'I don't understand. Where did you *come* from?'

Ansel grinned again, revealing a mouthful of half-chewed bacon. 'Celeste, that really isn't proper breakfast conversation.' He lowered his voice, his head flopping to one side as he spoke. 'My mother and father loved each other very much, and over time, and indeed under covers, that love resulted in Alarik, Anika and me.'

'Why is he being like this?' said Anika.

'Because it isn't really him,' answered Celeste. 'The real Ansel is dead. Whatever this is . . . it isn't natural.' For a moment, she looked like she wanted to leap across the table to throttle Wren, but then she sat back in her chair and folded her arms. 'What the hell did you do, Wren? And *how* on earth did you do it?'

'It's a long story.'

'Then you'd better begin.'

Wren would sooner eat her fist than utter a single word to Celeste about forbidden blood magic. She was not about to admit she was guilty of one of the worst things a witch could do. Or play into those fateful words Glenna had whispered to her back in Anadawn. *Beware the curse of Oonagh Starcrest, the lost witch queen. The curse runs in new blood. It lives in new bones.*

'Time for tea!' Ansel reached for the teapot and poured himself a cup of tea, not stopping as the scalding liquid spilled over the rim of the cup and into his lap. 'Do you remember our tea in Eana, Rose? I told you we could have tea here, too. We have everything you'll ever need.' He held the teapot aloft as steam rose from his lap in curling tendrils. 'That's why we'll be together forever. And ever and ever and—'

'Ansel, put the teapot down.' Wren had to prise the now empty pot from his fingers.

'This is a trick,' said Anika, stepping away from the table. 'This is a curse of some sort. You cursed him!' She brandished an accusing finger at Wren. 'I'll see you hang for this.'

Wren raised her hands. 'Now, Anika, let's not do anything rash.'

Celeste rose from her seat and went to Anika before she could fling herself at Wren. 'Wren didn't trick you, Anika,' she said, planting her hands on the princess's heaving shoulders. 'She just didn't know what she was doing.' Celeste tossed a withering glance over her shoulder. 'She rarely does.'

For once, Wren bit her tongue. It pained her that Celeste was right.

'It doesn't matter,' said Anika. 'I'm going to speak to Alarik about this. *Now*.'

'You must mean King Snoozington!' crowed Ansel. 'He's upstairs slumbering like an ice bear. We stayed up all night, chattering like parakeets, but the esteemed king of beasts couldn't keep up with me in the end. Ha!' His yellow eyes widened, until the irises floated inside them. 'Would you believe I haven't slept a wink?'

'Yes,' said Celeste, flatly.

Anika's fox growled at his feet. Ansel growled back, and the fox scampered away in a fright.

'Naughty fox.' Ansel chuckled as he reached for more syrup, accidentally knocking his pinkie finger against the jug. To Wren's horror, it fell off and landed in the bacon. The prince didn't even blink.

Wren swallowed the bile in her throat and gingerly reached for the finger.

'Leave it,' hissed Celeste. 'It's only going to get worse.'

Anika raked her hands through her hair, tearing her perfect chignon apart. 'You mean Alarik already *knows* about this?' she said, her voice rising dangerously.

Celeste shook her head in disbelief. 'What possessed you to do something so stupid?'

'I did it for Banba,' said Wren, defensively. 'I had no choice. And Alarik promised Anika he would find a way to bring Ansel back. So they could be a family again.'

'But not like this!' shrieked Anika. 'For Great Bernhard's sake, his finger just fell off! If our mother finds out about this – if she sees what her dear Ansel has become, she'll keel over! She's barely coping as it is. She hardly eats or sleeps. She rarely leaves her bedroom. *This* will be the end of her!'

'She won't find out,' said Celeste, quickly. 'We're going to contain this. And then we're going to fix it.'

'But how?' wailed Anika.

Celeste threw Wren a warning look. 'Get him out of here. Fast.'

Wren stood up and grabbed Ansel's arm. 'Come on, Ansel. Let's go for a walk.'

The prince leaped to his feet, sending his chair clattering to the floor. He stuffed a pancake in his pocket as Wren dragged him away from the table and out into the hallway.

She was still trying to figure out what to do with the undead prince when Tor turned the corner and stepped into their path. He froze mid-step, his jaw slackening as he took in the beaming prince.

'Tor! Do my eyes deceive me or have you got even taller?' Ansel prodded Tor in the chest, then pinched his nose. 'Gotcha!'

Tor's gaze narrowed, taking in the rest of Ansel's appearance. His jaw tightened as he looked at Wren over the prince's head, the horror on his face giving way to something much worse. Betrayal. 'I can't believe you did it.'

Wren shifted, awkwardly. 'Honestly, neither can I.'

'Why the stone face, Tor?' Ansel removed the pancake from his pocket and flapped it about. 'Perhaps a little pancake will cheer you up.'

Tor dragged a hand across his jaw, straining to keep his voice steady. 'Does Alarik know about—'

'Yes,' said Wren, tightly. 'But he's sleeping.'

Ansel was still waving the pancake about like a handkerchief. 'When we're married, you *must* wave to the masses just like this, darling! Let's call it the Pancake Salute! The people will love it!'

Wren grabbed his arm and lowered it. 'Ansel, please put down the pancake.' She turned back to Tor. 'I'll explain everything later,' she told him, urgently. 'But right now, I need your help. Queen Valeska could hear of this any minute. Anika is already in there throwing a tantrum. And frankly, I don't blame her.'

Tor cocked his head. 'Who do you blame, Wren?'

Wren hated the accusation in his eyes. 'I'll fix it. Just help me get him up to my room before this gets any worse.'

'What about when Alarik wakes up?'

'I'll cross that crevasse when I come to it,' said Wren, hastily shooing them along the hallway. She shuddered at the thought of what lay ahead for her – and for Banba – if she didn't find a way to make this right. And fast.

Rose
CHAPTER 34

The moon was high in the sky when the desert air began to buzz with excitement. Rose had been surprised by how late the festival began, but Lei Fan said it was customary to start the celebrations at midnight, so the dancing and feasting could carry on until sunrise.

'And then,' said Lei Fan, who was fixing her hair in the mirror, 'when the sun rises, it will surround Shen Lo with its golden rays, marking him as the new Sun Crowned King.'

A king, thought Rose, as she tightened a silk sash around her waist. She had barely got used to Shen as a prince. 'But if everyone thought Shen was dead all this time, why didn't your father ever become king?'

'You can't become king without the sun's blessing.' Lei Fan wrinkled her nose as she twisted one side of her hair into an intricate knot. 'That's why we have the festival in the first place. My father ruled as regent, waiting for the day we would be unburied once more.'

'And then Shen came home. He must not have expected that.'

Lei Fan smiled. 'Our true king returned with the sun. Father's never been a true king here. He likes to think he is, though. He loves bossing everyone around. Especially me.' She rolled her eyes. 'Honestly, I'm surprised at how easily he handed over the Sun Walker's Crown. Grandmother Lu used to joke that he sleeps in it.' Her eyes sparkled as they met Rose's in the mirror.

'No, no!' she said, shaking her head. 'You're tying the top part all wrong! Here, let me help.' She fiddled with the tie on Rose's dress, knotting it into an intricate bow atop her right shoulder. 'There! Now you look like the perfect sun maiden.'

Rose was wearing a dress the colour of flames. As she moved, the gossamer silk shifted – vermillion one moment, and burnt amber the next, turning to ochre and then saffron. Iridescent golden threads were woven throughout, making it shimmer in the candlelight. The material was daringly cut, leaving her left shoulder bare. It tapered in at her waist, the sash securing it, before cascading to the floor in a riot of colour.

Lei Fan had insisted on painting Rose's lips red and had dabbed gold paint on her eyelids, before lining them in black ink. Rose's hair was pinned away from her face by two ruby clips, while the rest tumbled artfully down her back.

Just then, a gong sounded. Rose felt its vibrations under her feet.

'Come on,' said Lei Fan, grabbing her hand. 'It's starting!'

The enchanters of the Sunkissed Kingdom had been busy. The golden statues had been brought to life, the horses whinnying as they reared up, over and over again. The dragon was flapping its metallic wings, while the beetle and scorpion scuttled back and forth, as though they were dancing. Long wooden tables, lit by amber everlights, groaned under heaped platters of food and generous jugs of wine, while on either side of the courtyard, ten pigs roasted on slow-turning spits.

Drummers roamed the courtyard, playing in time with an entire orchestra of stringed instruments Rose had never seen before, and which seemed to be plucking themselves. Tambourines had been passed out to the children, who were laughing and playing with gusto.

'There's so much magic out here I can practically taste it!' said Rose, as they made their way down the steps. Immersed in the splendour of the Sunkissed Kingdom, it was difficult to worry about Edgar Barron and his Arrows, who seemed a world away. In fact, it was hard for Rose to worry about anything at all.

As she passed a blond enchanter tuning a pair of floating flutes, Rose noticed that while most of the people in the Sunkissed Kingdom looked like Shen and his family, with golden-brown skin, dark hair and dark eyes, there were also witches with pale skin like her, as well as ones with skin similar to Thea and Celeste.

None of them were remotely interested in Rose. Either they did not recognize her, or they simply did not care that she was queen of Eana. After all, tonight wasn't about who ruled over Eana. It was about who ruled the Sunkissed Kingdom. And Rose was beginning to understand that those were two very different things.

'Sun dumplings!' Lei Fan chased a passing servant carrying a platter of steamed dumplings. 'These are my favourite!'

Rose bit into one, closing her eyes in pleasure. It was full of spiced meat and a little bit of broth that ran down her chin, but it was so delicious she didn't care.

'So, the festival delicacies are to your liking, Majesty.' Rose's eyes flew open to find Shen standing right next to her. He was wearing the Sun Walker's Crown at a rakish angle, a black high-collared shirt and fitted black trousers. His eyes had been smudged with kohl and the way he was staring at Rose, like *she* was a festival delicacy, made her suddenly feel light-headed.

'Oh, Shen— Hello,' she stammered, quickly wiping broth off her chin.

His gaze roamed. 'I like your dress.'

'Thank you,' said Rose, feeling curiously giddy. 'I like your . . . crown.'

He raised a brow. 'I thought you had complicated feelings about this crown.'

'Oh, please. You know I appreciate beautiful things. And you can't deny that crown is a work of art.'

'Just the crown? Not the person wearing it?' Shen needled.

'You are ridiculous,' said Rose, but she was so relieved that things felt normal between them again, she couldn't stop her smile.

'Is this a truce, then?' said Shen, leaning closer.

She bit her lip, thinking. 'What would you like it to be?'

He moved his lips to her ear to whisper something, and

Rose's breath caught at his sudden closeness. Then the gong sounded again.

'Pay attention, you two,' hissed Lei Fan. 'Here comes Daiyu. She's our master storyteller.'

An ancient-looking woman in a long crimson dress strode to the steps, climbing them until everyone in the courtyard could see her. She clapped her hands, commanding silence.

'I welcome you all to the Festival of the Dancing Sun!' she announced. 'Tonight we gather to rejoice in the return of our crown prince –' she paused as the crowd roared in approval, and Rose smiled at the pride that sparked in Shen's eyes – 'to celebrate the return of the sun, and to honour the origin of our great kingdom.'

The storyteller held her hands out, and two witches came to join her on the steps. Rose watched, mouth slightly ajar, as one created a crack of lightning between her hands and then tossed it into the air, where it became a roaring fire.

'That's my tutor,' whispered Lei Fan, excitedly. 'Her tempest skills are unmatched.'

The other witch, an enchanter, started to manipulate the fire into different shapes.

Daiyu spoke again. 'Our tale begins many thousands of years ago, when Eana the first witch was young and the world still unformed. Eana journeyed from the heavens on her green-tailed hawk, leaving her dearest love, the sun, alone in his sky.' Rose marvelled as the flames turned into a woman riding on the back of a huge bird. 'After years of tireless searching, the hawk landed in the sea and with Eana's magical touch, became the very bones of the country in which we now find ourselves.'

Rose clapped in delight as the flames sprawled, painting the map of Eana in the sky. Beside her, Shen's eyes were shining, just as entranced as she was.

Daiyu's voice grew sombre. 'Heartbroken, the sun watched his lover from afar, waiting for the day she chose to land. And when she did, so moved was he by their love that he floated down to kiss her goodbye.' The flames flared brighter, stinging tears in Rose's eyes. 'But their passion was so great that it scorched the earth itself, creating the Ganyeve Desert. Afterwards, the sun returned to his sky, and Eana gave up her claim on eternity to become a mortal witch in this new land. She knew she would one day die, while the sun would live on.

'Long years passed, and the country grew to welcome others. Eana took on lovers, and had many children, all of whom inherited her magic. She lived and loved freely, the way she had always wanted, but every morning she rose to watch the sun rise. And in those quiet moments when the rest of the world was still in slumber, her heart ached for her greatest love.'

So softly that Rose almost thought she was imagining it, Shen brushed his hand against hers. She glanced sidelong at him, but his eyes were on the storyteller.

'And then one day the sky went dark.' All at once, the flames shrank to the size of a single peppercorn. The courtyard dimmed. 'When Eana looked up, she saw that the moon had passed in front of the sun, blocking its light. It was the first morning of her new life that she had not gazed upon her love, and so she knelt in her garden and wept. Where her tears fell, white orchids bloomed.'

Shen's fingers tangled in Rose's. She closed her eyes, lost to the tale and his touch.

'A man approached Eana and asked why she was weeping. There was something familiar about his voice. When Eana looked up, she cried out, barely able to believe her own eyes. For, standing before her was the sun himself, remade into a man and wearing a band of glimmering gold.'

The flames erupted once more, this time sculpting themselves into the towering figure of a man. And though Rose couldn't trace his face in the firelight, she knew at once that he had been beautiful. Radiant.

'"I could not bear to be away from you a moment longer," said the Sun Walker, lifting Eana from her knees and pulling her into his embrace. "I have come to be with you. And while I am here, there will be no light in the world. My sister, the moon, will hide my absence. And for as long as she does, I will stay."

'Eana rejoiced in the return of her true love. She welcomed the night, and in it showed him the great pleasures of mortality – they feasted and they danced, and when they retired to bed, they loved each other, wholly, in a new way.'

The flames separated, becoming two people, entwined. For a moment, the shape of Eana and her lover was so intimate Rose had to look away. Shen caught her gaze and held it. His fingers brushed the delicate spot inside her wrist, his thumb tracing patterns on her palm.

'For a time, the world was dark. Eana and her lover lived in its shadow, where she bore his children, each one blessed with ancient magic,' Daiyu went on. 'But while love is eternal, so, too, is light. The Sun Walker knew he had to relinquish his human form and return to his home in the heavens. And for the good of the world, and the land she had cultivated, Eana knew she had to let him go. When the sun kissed Eana goodbye for the last time, he left her with a parting gift. A ruby ring that glowed with a heart of fire. A symbol of his everlasting love and the key to what he would give to their children.'

Shen dropped Rose's hand to clasp the ring beneath his shirt, his eyes wide with wonder.

'To his children, the sun gifted a city that would always protect them. One that could move wherever it pleased in the desert and hide itself when under threat. One that would always provide for its people. And so, not long after the land of Eana was made from the enchanted bones of a bird, the Sunkissed Kingdom was born.' The flames arced across the courtyard, becoming a flickering outline of the very kingdom in which they now stood.

The crowd raised their hands as if to touch it.

'The children of Eana and the Sun Walker are our ancestors,' said the storyteller, proudly. 'The sun is in our blood, and so we can survive the restless sands. Live above them, and below them. We have been blessed by the sun's golden light, and tonight we dance and feast in his honour.' She brought her hands together in a steeple and pointed them right at Shen. The crowds parted around him. 'Our crown prince used Eana's ruby to unbury us from the sands, and now that he has returned, he will take his rightful place on the throne as the Sun Crowned King!'

The crowd erupted in cheers. The storyteller crooked her finger and Shen went to her without looking back. He reached the steps and turned to face his people, the fire dancing above his head like a crown.

Rose pressed a hand to her chest to quell her thundering heart.

'In the name of my father, Gao, and my mother, Ai Li, and all the great kings and queens that came before them, I promise to bring honour to our kingdom,' said Shen. 'I promise to protect you from danger and hardship. I promise that you will always sleep under the stars and wake to see the sun risen in the sky.'

Rose stared up at Shen Lo in disbelief. He was speaking like a king. He *looked* like a king.

He *was* a king.

The moment he finished speaking, fireworks exploded in the sky, showering everyone in streams of golden light. And as another cheer went up, Rose knew, with a sudden aching certainty, that Shen Lo would never come back to Anadawn.

The revelry went on for hours. There was little time to broach the topic of Shen's army again. Rose found solace in her food, gobbling up two servings of roasted pork belly with crunchy crackling, a mountain of springy noodles and an entire decadently spiced aubergine.

She was quite certain she couldn't eat another bite, when the servers brought out the candied fruit Shen loved so much. There were pears and apples and bright red hawthorn berries.

'Go on,' urged Grandmother Lu, heaping some on to Rose's plate. 'You must taste my cooking.'

Rose popped a hawthorn berry in her mouth, feeling a rush of giddiness as the hardened sugar cracked between her teeth, before wincing at the sourness of the berry.

'See,' said Grandmother Lu, proudly. 'A symphony of flavour.'

After the feast, there was dancing. Rose had never moved so wildly before. Without a partner, without steps, without propriety, with only the music to lead her. She felt like a spinning top as her skirts swirled around her, changing colours in the flickering firelight. The drums echoed her rioting heartbeat, and she laughed as she threw her head back, feeling like the stars themselves were watching her dance.

But it wasn't only them. Rose felt Shen's gaze before she caught it. He was standing to the side of the courtyard, watching her dance, but instead of making her feeling shy, she felt bold and beautiful. Holding his gaze, she tossed her hair and swung her hips, letting his dark eyes drink her in.

She desperately wanted him to join her, to dance with her until they could no longer stand, but just as she reached out to him, Feng appeared at his side and whispered something in his ear.

Shen glanced up at the sky. It was nearly dawn. Nearly time for him to take his place as the Sun Crowned King

Something shuffled at Rose's skirts, pulling her attention away. She looked down and laughed. 'Elske! Are you trying to join the party?'

But the wolf's tail was low. She tugged on Rose's skirts, as if she was trying to lead her somewhere.

'Elske, stop that! You'll rip my dress!'

Just then, someone jostled past Rose, nearly knocking her over. Elske's hackles rose. It was Kai. Rose frowned. Where was he going in such a rush?

The music stopped, and Shen appeared at the top of the palace steps. As the first brushstrokes of dawn yawned across the desert sky, fireworks exploded once more. Sparks spun off and twirled into sun wheels, dancing in the air around him. The sky glimmered as bright as gold, as the true sun began to rise.

Rose had expected Feng to be the one to anoint Shen, but she couldn't see him anywhere. Instead, Daiyu stepped up. In her hands, she held a golden sceptre.

'Shen Lo, under the light of the rising sun, and surrounded by the love of your people, it is my honour to bestow upon you the Sceptre of the Sun, marking you now and for evermore, as the Sun Crowned King. And so, under the light of a new day, we come together to ask you, do you accept your solemn destiny?'

Shen took the sceptre in his hands and turned to address his people, but whatever he was about to say was drowned out by a scream. One of the fireworks had exploded close to the ground and burst into flames. They took shape, just like they had in the sky, only this time, they were beasts.

And they were multiplying, fast.

Chaos erupted as the fire beasts went wild, lunging through the courtyard and burning anyone in their path. Rose tried to push her way through to Shen, but the crowd surged, pushing her back. Elske let out a thunderous roar, and the people around Rose scattered like marbles.

Just then, she spotted Feng at the bottom of the palace steps. He was standing strangely still, save for his twitching fingers, and he was muttering furiously under his breath. His eyes were trained on Shen.

Rose followed his gaze and cried out in alarm. Most of the beasts were converging on Shen. She watched in horror as he rushed down the steps and leaped over the balustrade, using the Sceptre of the Sun to fight them off, but his warrior magic was no match for the rabid creatures. He yelled as his shirt caught fire, quickly ripping it off. But it wasn't enough. His face twisted in agony as the flames licked his skin, and still more fire beasts came.

'Shen!' Rose screamed, as he ran from the courtyard. The beasts pursued him, chasing him away from the festival and around the back of the palace, to where narrow streets wound their way deeper into the city. Rose picked up her skirts and ran after him, with Elske by her side.

Shen clutched his burning chest as he ducked left, throwing himself into a hidden lane to avoid the flaming stampede. To Rose's relief, the fire beasts roared right past it.

She hurried to catch up with him, her lungs heaving with each step. Shen needed her. She had to get to him, to heal him. At last, she reached the narrow lane. She whirled around the corner, her heart stuttering as she caught sight of Shen's body slumped on the ground.

Before Rose could reach him, Kai stepped out of the shadows and plucked the sceptre from the ground.

'Bad luck, cousin,' he said, as he raised it above his head. 'Your destiny ends here.'

'NO!' shouted Rose.

Elske roared as she lunged at Kai, closing her jaws around his arm. He dropped the sceptre and let out a roar of his own.

His gaze found Rose in the dark, his eyes glowing with hatred. 'Get your wolf off me!'

Rose ignored him and ran to Shen. She knelt on the ground, laying her hands on his burnt chest. 'It's all right,' she murmured. 'I'm here now. I'm going to heal you.'

She loosened a trembling breath, letting her magic unfurl inside her. The chaos around her grew distant as her mind stilled, focusing on nothing but Shen. His burns were deep, already blistering, his heart thudding weakly beneath her hands, but under the gentle thrum of her magic, he began to heal. Slowly, slowly.

Rose didn't know how much time had passed as she tried to knit Shen's skin back together, but when his eyes fluttered open, she nearly collapsed in relief. 'You're awake!'

'Rose?' he croaked.

He tried to sit up, but Rose kept her hand on his chest. 'Shen, I have to tell you something—'

Kai wrenched her off him. 'That damn wolf attacked me when I was trying to save you from those fire beasts!' he said, showing his bloodied arm as proof. It was only then that Rose noticed the three servants behind him. 'I had to shout for help, since *she* wouldn't call it off!'

Rose frowned. 'No, that's not what—'

Kai spoke over her. 'Luckily the fire creatures have been dealt with. Now we need to deal with that menacing wolf.'

Elske yowled as more servants arrived, catching her in a net.

'Stop!' cried Rose, scurrying to help her. 'She saved the king! Leave her be!'

'I think the queen has inhaled too much smoke,' said Kai, loudly. 'She's talking nonsense.'

More and more people crowded into the narrow lane.

'Shen, I have to talk to you!' said Rose, frantically.

'Hush now, everyone. Move out of my way,' said Grandmother Lu, using her cane to push through the fray. Lei Fan followed close behind her, sending out a warning gust.

Rose got lost in the swell of the crowd. They took Shen and Elske away and she was left utterly alone, with nothing but her singed dress and the memory of Kai standing over Shen with hatred burning in his eyes.

Wren
CHAPTER 35

'Do you think he's getting worse?' said Wren anxiously, as she paced her bedroom.

'Yes,' said Tor, who was leaning against her dresser, with his arms folded. 'His thumb just fell off.'

Prince Ansel the Undead, who was sitting cross-legged on her bed, seemed not to notice his missing finger. He was too busy gazing adoringly at Wren.

'My Rose!' he crooned.

'Wren. My name is Wren.'

'What a funny little nickname! If you are a wren, can I be an eagle?' Ansel began to caw.

Wren sighed. 'I really messed this up.'

Tor raised his eyebrows. '*Messed up* is an understatement. You raised Ansel from the dead.'

Wren groaned. After smuggling Ansel up to her room under Tor's coat, they had been working on him all morning, trying to make the prince seem more like himself again. Wren had spent hours trying to enchant Ansel into remembering different parts of his life – even his death – but her magic had little effect on the prince. Tor had even gone down to retrieve a stack of Ansel's favourite poetry books from the library, reciting them in vain to the blank-eyed prince. 'This is a disaster. Alarik's going to wake up soon.'

Tor turned back to the prince. 'Ansel, do you remember the sword-fighting steps I taught you when you were a boy? Do you want to practise them?'

'Muscle memory,' muttered Wren. 'Good idea.'

But Ansel was unmoved by the suggestion. 'I'm afraid there's no time, Tor. I'm about to be married.' He stiffened suddenly, as if he had been set to pause.

Wren looked deep into the prince's blue eyes, ignoring the yellow tinge that lingered around them. 'Do you know where you are, Ansel?'

'I am with my love, at the beginning of our lives together,' said the prince.

'I mean *literally*,' Wren clarified.

'I am *literally* dwelling in a state of pure bliss.'

Tor opened another book. 'Maybe another poem might help . . .'

'Sterling idea!' said Ansel, leaping to his feet and spinning on the heel of his boot. He lost his balance and nearly fell into the fire, but Tor lunged, catching him just in time.

'I will compose a masterpiece this very moment!' Ansel went on, as if nothing had happened. '*Oh, Rose, sweet Rose, of Anadawn, she is as graceful as a swan! My love for her is deep and . . . and . . .*'

'Perilous?' said Wren.

'Perilous!' cried Ansel. 'And her green eyes are like . . .' He paused, searching for another word.

'Asparagus?' said Tor.

'Yes! Brilliant!' said Ansel. 'Her green eyes are like asparagus!'

Wren glared at Tor, who chuckled to himself.

Ansel ploughed on. *'When I look at Rose, my heart swells in size. For her smile . . . her smile . . .'*

'Is like the first rays of sunrise,' suggested Tor.

Ansel turned to Wren. 'Yes,' he said, delightedly. 'That's *exactly* what it's like.'

But Wren was looking at Tor.

He cleared his throat. 'I think that's enough poetry for now.'

Ansel extended his hand to Wren. 'Shall we dance, my sunbeam?'

'You know what? Fine,' said Wren, giving in to the absurdity in the hopes it might lead to a breakthrough. 'Let's dance.' She stood up, all too conscious of Tor's attention as Prince Ansel put his other hand on her waist, and she rested hers on his shoulder.

The prince stood still, staring at her.

Wren raised her eyebrows. 'Aren't we going to dance?'

'We are dancing, my love.'

'Ansel, we're standing still.'

'Ah, my mistake.'

'Come on, let's sway. Here. Just like this. That's nice, isn't it?'

'Oh, yes. Shall I sing a little something?' suggested Ansel. 'Please don't,' said Wren.

Too late. The prince launched into an old Gevran folk song about wolves. It was slow and haunting and woefully out of tune. Wren looked to Tor. 'Please help me.'

Tor couldn't help but chuckle. Wren turned back to Ansel and closed her eyes, trying to come up with some way to make this moment – which felt like it was going to stretch on into eternity – bearable. And then something entirely unexpected happened.

Tor started singing, too, his voice low and lilting as it joined with Ansel's, guiding the melody into a surprisingly pleasing tune. Wren offered him a grateful smile as he sang them into the next verse.

For a while, Wren watched the soldier sing as he watched her dance, all three of them tangled together in this strange moment that, in the end, wasn't so unbearable after all.

Not long after her dance with Ansel, which had no effect on the prince's memory but had bruised more than a few of Wren's toes and sacrificed two of Ansel's entirely, Tor was called away. This morning's avalanche had buried the road into Grinstad with rubble, and he had been tasked with assembling a team of soldiers to clear it.

'I'll come and check on you two later,' he promised, as he pulled the door shut behind him. Wren listened to the rest of his goodbye through the wood. 'Hang in there, Wren.'

'Bring me back a bottle of frostfizz!' she yelled after him. 'Or five!'

'So that we may toast our perfect union!' shouted Ansel.

'Shhh!' Wren turned on the prince. 'Keep your voice down!'

'You cannot silence love, Rose.'

Wren slumped against her dresser. 'I need a miracle.'

'A miracle.' Ansel nodded, sombrely. 'I think I know what you're getting at, my love. And I agree. We *should* have a baby.'

'This isn't working,' said Wren, with a groan. 'I can't fix you, Ansel. You don't even know who I am.'

'Of course I do. You're my darling Rose. And you're so full of beauty and light that you make the very room glow.'

'No, I don't,' said Wren, impatiently.

Ansel pointed at her feet. 'But, look.'

Wren looked down to find that her feet were, in fact, glowing. She sank into a crouch, trying to trace the strange blue light. It was coming from under the dresser. No, not the dresser. The satchel she had stowed underneath it. It was the hand mirror! Wren fished it out to find the sapphires were all alight.

The glass shimmered in her hands, and Rose's face appeared in the mirror. It was smeared with sand and dirt, and her eyes were wide with panic.

Rose

CHAPTER 36

Rose couldn't find Shen anywhere.

As the sun rose over the Ganyeve Desert and the festival came to a close, Rose returned to the Palace of Eternal Sunlight. Morning streamed in through the windows as she wandered the corridors, calling Shen's name. She stopped the servants, demanding they take her to him at once, but they simply bowed and said the newly crowned king was not to be disturbed.

Their refusal to tell Rose where Shen was confirmed what she'd already suspected – that she had no real power here. To the people of the Sunkissed Kingdom, Rose was nothing more than an outsider. The desert truly was its own land, and it did not answer to her.

She stopped by Lei Fan's room, but Shen's cousin was nowhere to be found. There was only Shadow, glaring at her from on top of the wardrobe. Rose had no idea where Kai's bedchamber was, but she wouldn't have dared go there by herself. She couldn't shake the image of him, wild-eyed and seething, as he brandished the golden sceptre high above Shen, ready to strike a killing blow.

She crossed into the east wing of the palace and marched down another gilded corridor, shouting herself hoarse. After what felt like an eternity, a door at the end of the hallway creaked open and Shen's face appeared. 'Rose? Why are you yelling?'

Rose catapulted herself down the hallway and threw her arms around Shen, burying her face in his neck. 'You're alive! Oh, thank the stars!'

Shen chuckled. 'Of course I'm alive. In fact, I've survived much worse. Who knew fire spells could go so wrong? I guess the enchanters were a little out of practice.'

Rose pulled back from him. 'Shen. This isn't funny. You nearly died! If I hadn't been there to heal you—'

Confusion flashed across his face. 'What are you talking about? Kai took me to the palace healer on our way back. He'll tell you himself,' he said, gesturing down the hallway. 'He's just gone to find Feng.'

Rose glanced around, expecting to see Kai's hulking figure stalking down the corridor towards them. 'I have to talk to you. Alone. Can I come in?'

Shen raised his eyebrows as he stepped back into the room, and Rose followed, shutting the door behind her. His bedchamber was even more decadent than the one she'd been sleeping in. The pillows were gilded and strung with tassels, the walls hung with silk tapestries of the desert sun rising and falling over its kingdom.

Rose turned to face Shen. 'You were attacked this morning.

Those fire beasts . . . they weren't an accident. They were an assassination attempt.'

Shen frowned. 'That's a bit overdramatic, don't you think?'

'Kai and Feng tried to kill you. I saw it.' At the look of disbelief on Shen's face, her voice jumped an entire octave. 'Feng was controlling the fire beasts. They herded you into that alley. Kai was waiting there. He knocked you out, Shen. He was about to kill you with your own sceptre when Elske and I arrived.'

Shen's frown only deepened. 'No,' he said, slowly. 'Kai saved me from the fire beasts. But I inhaled too much smoke and passed out.'

'That's not true,' said Rose.

'He carried me back to the palace.'

'Only because he couldn't finish the job.'

Shen's eyes pooled with concern. Not for himself, but for her. 'You're exhausted, Rose. What you're saying doesn't make any sense. Kai is my cousin. If he wanted me dead, why would he take me to the healer?' Before Rose could answer, he pressed on. 'And he had plenty of time to kill me on the way to the desert.'

'But he needed you to unbury the kingdom,' said Rose, desperately. 'You were the key, remember? He couldn't make the map work, and even that made him furious! And remember what Meredia said about him?' Rose grabbed his arms, to try to shake him back into reality. 'She said he had to fight to resist the darkness inside him. Well, he didn't! And his father was the one who set those fire beasts loose!'

Shen placed his hands on hers, gently removing them. He gave her a pitying look. 'Magic is still new to you, Rose. You don't understand how it can escalate sometimes.'

Rose poked him in the chest. 'You're the one who told me it was all about intent, remember? When my healing magic awoke in Balor's Eye, *you* said it was because of how much I wanted to heal you. Well, doesn't that mean that those fire beasts were sent by someone who wanted to hurt you?'

Shen batted the idea away. 'Someone was probably drunk and trying to add to the celebrations.'

'Or someone wanted you dead,' Rose countered. 'Someone who would benefit if you were taken out of the picture. Like . . . Oh, I don't know, the person next in line to the Sunkissed throne!'

Suddenly, Shen's face changed, his concern giving way to suspicion. 'I know what you're doing,' he said, taking a step away from her. 'You want to turn me against them. You want me on your side so we can ride back to Anadawn together. That's all you've wanted since we got here.'

Rose recoiled, like she had been slapped. 'I'm trying to protect you. I healed you.' She resisted the urge to shove him, and instead pressed her hand against his chest. 'Can't you tell it was me?'

For the briefest moment, Shen's face softened, and she thought she had finally got through to him. Then his eyes misted, and he looked away. 'I know you need my army. But trying to come between me and my own family isn't the way to get what you want.'

Rose ripped her hand away from his chest. 'What kind of monster do you think I am? Do you even hear yourself right now?'

Shen was stone-faced. 'I thought I knew you, but maybe Kai was right. Maybe you are a spoilt queen who only thinks about herself. He warned me about this, you know. He said you'd try to turn me against him. And I didn't believe him. I defended you,' he said, ruefully. 'And now all you're doing is proving him right.'

Rose clenched her fists, her nails digging into her palms. 'Of course he told you that! He knows I saw him. He's going to try to stop me from telling you the truth! If you're stupid enough to believe him, then the Sun Walker's Crown won't be on your head for much longer.'

Shen scoffed. 'It's not up to you who wears the crown here, Rose, and you can't stand it, can you? You hate that I'm no longer beholden to you. And you thought that if you told me lies about my family, you could get me to leave this all behind. Go back to being the Shen who serves you, who pines for you. Who will never be your equal.'

'I've always thought you were my equal.'

'Oh, really?' said Shen. 'Then why wouldn't you let us be together?'

'Because I have responsibilities!' she fumed. 'And a kingdom to run!'

'Well, now so do I.'

Rose stamped her foot. 'You sound like a child!'

Shen smirked. 'Says the girl stomping her foot.'

Rose desperately wished for a goblet of wine to throw in his face. 'We can fight about this later. But right now I need you to believe what I'm saying. You're in danger here. We both are. We have to leave immediately.'

'You don't command me here.'

'*Please*, Shen.'

He held her gaze for a moment, his lips twisting as he considered her plea. Then he turned away. 'Go home, Rose.'

'Not without you.'

'I've told you. This is my home now.'

'At least do something to protect yourself against Kai and Feng,' begged Rose. 'They'll try again. Don't let yourself be alone with them. You can't trust them.'

'The only person I can't trust is you.' Shen strode to the door and opened it. 'I think we've both said everything we need to say.'

Blinking back furious tears, Rose returned to the hallway, flinching as the door slammed behind her. Her breath punched out of her as she rushed back to her room on the other side of the palace, looking for Kai around every corner and jumping at her own shadow.

Back in her bedchamber, she locked the door behind her, then threw her slipper at the wall. *Arrogant, stupid Shen*. He was going to get himself killed! Why couldn't he see that she was telling the truth?

She whirled around in a panic, her gaze snagging on her

dusty satchel in the corner of the room. A thought exploded like fireworks in Rose's mind. Maybe there was someone else who could talk some sense into Shen.

With trembling fingers, Rose dug the sapphire mirror out of her satchel and gripped the handle.

'Wren,' she whispered. 'Please, Wren. I need you.'

A minute passed, and then, all at once, the sapphires began to glow.

Wren

CHAPTER 37

Wren listened to her sister in horrified silence as she recounted everything that had happened at the festival, and the argument with Shen that had followed. By the time Rose was done, her cheeks glistening with tears, Wren was fizzing with anger. She was so furious, she forgot all about the undead prince in her bedroom as she pressed her hand against the glass. She let the wind carry her away from Gevra, and into the scorching heart of the desert.

She landed on warm tiles, in a room so shiny it made her wince. There wasn't a minute to waste. She leaped to her feet, mirror in hand, and unlocked the bedroom door. Then she stalked out into the hallway and headed east, following the hurried directions Rose had given her. She stopped in the magnificent entrance hall to pocket a fistful of orchids.

'Hey!' An old woman came pottering over. She was carrying a bowl of sweet-smelling fruit and scowling with her entire face. 'Those are the sacred flowers of the Palace of Eternal Sunlight!'

Wren didn't even blink. 'Well, now they're the sacred flowers of my pocket.'

'Insolent words.' The old woman narrowed her eyes. 'You are not Queen Rose.'

'And you are not Shen Lo,' said Wren, sidestepping her. 'Which means you're no good to me.'

'Shen Lo has been in an accident,' said the woman, stopping her with her cane.

Wren looked down, and briefly considered kicking it away. 'That's not exactly what I heard.'

'What did you hear?' said the woman, warily.

'I'd tell you but apparently it's hard to know who to trust around here.'

The old woman hmm'd. Then, to Wren's surprise, she held out the bowl of fruit. 'Take him these. They are his favourite.'

Wren took the bowl. 'They'd better not be poisonous.'

The old woman barked a laugh. 'Such rudeness from a Gevran!'

Wren stiffened. 'I'm *not* a Gevran.'

'You sure look it.' The old woman picked at the velvet sleeve of Wren's dress. 'Now I know where the beast chained in the courtyard came from.'

'Thanks for the tip,' said Wren, stepping over the cane and continuing on her way. 'I'll make sure to pay her a visit, too.'

The old woman chuckled as she watched her go.

When she reached the east wing, Wren released the bird call she and Shen once used to summon each other back in

Ortha. A moment later, a door at the end of the hallway swung open and Shen Lo stepped out. He was frowning. 'Wren?'

Wren brandished the hand mirror as she came towards him. 'I want a word with you!'

He flung his hands up. 'Don't get involved, Wren. This is between me and Rose. She shouldn't have gone crying to you just because—'

Wren flung the bowl at him.

Shen caught it in mid-air, collecting the pieces of fruit before they landed. 'Was that really necessary?'

Suddenly, Wren was upon him. She knocked the bowl aside and shoved him back against the wall. 'What the hell has got into you? Do you realize your cousin tried to kill you earlier?'

'I'm not having this argument again,' said Shen, flatly.

'Then eat a candy. I'll talk. You listen,' said Wren, furiously. 'My sister has her flaws, but Rose would never exaggerate about something so serious, and deep down you know that.' Shen's face was impenetrable as she went on. 'You're one of the most important people in her world. And she's so worried about you, she could barely get her words out just now. She says that you'd rather cut her out of your life than face the truth about your uncle. Your cousin.'

'Fine. Maybe she didn't lie,' Shen conceded, after a beat. 'But that doesn't mean she was telling the truth either. She's exhausted, Wren. And overwhelmed. She doesn't know what she saw.'

'She knows she healed you. And she wouldn't imagine

something like that.' Wren released him with a sigh. 'I know you've waited your whole life for this moment, Shen. This place, these people. Ortha might have been your salvation once, but it was never your destiny. I would never stand in the way of that. And neither would Rose.' His eyes softened, and so did Wren's voice. 'But just because Kai is the first cousin that came along doesn't mean he's any good at it.'

'Wren—'

'The hard truth is, some people do terrible things for power.'

Shen's nostrils flared. 'Not this, Wren. He's my *cousin*, for stars' sake.'

'I'm Rose's twin sister, and it wasn't that long ago that we scaled the walls of Anadawn to kidnap her,' she reminded him. 'Just look at everything I was prepared to do for the crown. Rotting hell, Shen, I nearly married Ansel!' She flinched as she remembered the undead prince back in her bedroom. Rose's morning was about to get a lot worse.

Shen pressed his lips together. 'I forgot about that.'

'See?' said Wren.

'It still doesn't prove anything.'

'When I came to Amarach a few days ago, I caught Kai trying to sneak into your room,' said Wren. 'I knew there was something off about him then, but I couldn't put my finger on it. The hunger in his eyes, his voice . . . it reminded me of how Banba used to look whenever she talked about Anadawn.' She stepped back. 'If you're determined not to see it for yourself, then let's go to his bedchamber right now. I'll use a truth enchantment on him.'

Shen stared at her.

'What?' she challenged. 'Are you afraid of what you'll find out?'

'No,' he said, a beat too slow.

Wren glanced at the sapphires. Five minutes gone already. 'Then take me to his room.'

'He went to find my uncle,' said Shen. 'We lost him in the fray. He'll be with Feng.'

'The other traitor. Even better.' Wren clapped Shen on the back. 'Lead the way, Your Majesty.'

With some reluctance, Shen turned on his heel and led Wren deeper into the gilded palace, until they came upon another hallway, echoing with the sound of distant voices. Wren lifted a finger to her lips, then reached for the petals in her pocket. With two quick enchantments, she spelled their footsteps, turning them silent on the stone.

With another, she silenced the hinges on Feng's door and eased it open, just a crack. Enough to see the outline of two men standing across from each other.

'. . . been quicker! That moment of hesitation nearly gave the entire game away,' said an older scratchy voice that Wren assumed belonged to Shen's uncle.

'You should have sent the beasts after Rose,' came Kai's voice. 'At least then she wouldn't have got in my way.'

'How was I supposed to know the wolf would be there?' fumed Feng. 'I did my part. Exactly as we discussed.'

Wren and Shen locked eyes in the hallway, his jaw so tight, it looked like it might shatter. Here he was, finally hearing the truth for himself, but instead of feeling triumphant, Wren's heart ached for her best friend.

Kai bit off a curse. 'We won't get another chance like that again.'

'Not until we get rid of the queen,' said Feng. 'So long as he keeps the company of a healer, we won't be able to finish him off.'

'Have you lost your mind?' hissed Kai. 'We can't murder the queen of Eana! Our kingdom lies in her desert!'

'Then get her out of the kingdom,' said Feng, evenly. 'Let the sands take care of her. Or, better still, do it yourself and make it look like an accident.'

Wren removed another fistful of petals, her blood singing with fresh anger. Her mind reeled, searching for a spell that would maim these heartless traitors, but Shen moved like the wind, pulling her away from the door and back down the hallway.

Wren tried to squirm free, but he slammed a hand over her mouth. 'Be silent,' he whispered. 'Kai is a seasoned warrior. And Feng is one of the most powerful enchanters I've ever seen. If they catch us, they'll strike.'

Wren didn't speak again until they returned to the east wing. There were only three sapphires aglow now.

Shen slumped against the wall, scrunching his eyes shut, like he was trying to blink away everything he had just witnessed. 'I've been such a fool.'

'I'm sorry,' said Wren, resting a hand on his shoulder. 'I know what you were hoping.'

Shen looked at his boots, a blush warming his cheeks. 'I called her a liar, Wren.'

'I know.'

'And jealous.'

'She told me.'

'And spoilt.'

Wren hesitated. 'Well, she is a bit spoilt.'

He raked his hands through his hair. 'I put her in danger. I put us both in danger.'

'At least now you know the truth,' said Wren. 'This is your kingdom, Shen. It's beautiful, but there's a poison festering inside it. The sooner you get rid of it, the better.'

He nodded, gravely.

Wren pulled him in for a hug. 'It'll be all right. The ones who matter will stand by you.'

She stood back, then.

He rubbed the back of his neck. 'This king stuff . . .'

Wren smirked. 'It's not all it's cracked up to be, is it?'

'You're still in Gevra, then,' he said, noting her dress. 'How is Banba?'

'Alive.' Wren cleared her throat. 'And . . . so is Prince Ansel.'

'Wait. *What?*'

The second-to-last sapphire winked out. 'I have to go,' said Wren, as she backed down the hallway. She bolted through the entrance hall and out into the courtyard, where she found Elske chained to the wall. There was a girl kneeling in front of her, dangling a thick slab of meat.

She startled at Wren's approach, sending out a gust of wind. 'Rose! I was just looking for you. Your wolf's woken up. I'm afraid father had the servants chain her. But I thought she might be hungry.' Her dark brows knitted. 'Where did you get that dress?'

'There's no time to explain,' said Wren, stepping around the girl and kneeling beside Elske. She crushed the last of the petals in her fist and dissolved one of the chain links. The rest fell away with a clatter.

The girl jumped back. 'That was enchantment magic!'

Wren looked up at her. 'If your father ever comes near my wolf again, I'll make sure she eats him.' She curled an arm around Elske, just as the last sapphire winked out. 'And as for you . . . be careful.'

The girl opened her mouth to respond, but Wren was already gone, the wind tugging her through the looking glass, and back to the snow-swept mountains of Gevra.

Rose

CHAPTER 38

Rose squeezed her eyes shut as she was pulled through the mirror into the icy heart of Grinstad Palace. She crouched on the fur rug in Wren's room, waiting for the wind to stop howling. When it didn't, she cautiously opened one eye. Oh! It was the true wind, keening through the mountains. Rose shivered as she stood up. She was still wearing her festival dress, which was entirely inappropriate for Gevra. And far too flimsy.

She glanced at the glowing sapphires. She was not about to spend the next eleven minutes chattering her teeth off. Especially when there was a wardrobe full of luxurious fur coats, waiting for her. She strode across the room, then paused before it.

The hairs on the back of her neck stood up. But not from the cold. There was magic here . . . strange magic. Rose wrinkled her nose as she scanned the room. And what was that peculiar smell?

Suddenly, the wardrobe flew open and a figure popped out like a jack-in-the-box. 'PEEK-A-BOO!'

Rose shrieked, clutching the mirror to her chest as she stumbled backwards. Was that . . . ? No. It wasn't possible. Wren *couldn't* have. She would never—

'Got you!' crowed Prince Ansel. 'Oh, my flower, don't look so scared! It's just me! Your adoring fiancé!'

Rose swayed on her feet. 'Oh no. No, no, no, no.'

Wren had gone and done it. Against all sense and reason, she'd used forbidden magic to bring Ansel back to life. Or something close to life. The prince's skin was distinctly grey and he reeked. Four flies buzzed around his head. Rose rushed to open a window before she threw up.

She resisted the urge to stick her entire head outside, glancing again at the glowing sapphires. Nine remained. Rose took a steadying breath. Everything was going to be fine. She could manage another nine minutes in this room with an undead Ansel. All she had to do was keep her voice down, remain calm and not cause a scene. She was more than capable of doing that.

As long as he didn't come too close.

Rose shrieked at a tap on her shoulder.

Ansel had crept up behind her. 'Rose, my darling! You are so jumpy! Is it pre-wedding jitters?'

Rose stared at him in alarm. Did he really not remember anything about that day in the Vault? 'Ansel,' she said, gently. 'The wedding was called off. We're not getting married.'

Ansel laughed loudly, the sound like a screeching eagle. 'What jokes! Of course we are. Tomorrow, I believe.' His brow furrowed. 'Or perhaps the day after. Do you know, I'm having the hardest time keeping track of the days? Love has made my mind fuzzy!'

'That must be it,' said Rose, edging away. She glanced at the sapphires. How were there still eight remaining? She felt like she'd been in this room for an eternity already.

'I can think of nothing but our wedding.' Ansel's head lolled to one side. He grabbed it with both hands, barely blinking as it snapped back into place. 'Truly. It is the only thought that occupies my mind.'

'Oh, Ansel.' Rose was seized by a rush of pity for the poor prince, or this strange version of him, stuck pining for a day that would never come. She sat down on the bed, patting the space beside her. 'Why don't you lie down and try to get some rest?'

'Do you know I can't remember the last time I've slept?' Ansel yawned as he crawled on to the bed. A tooth fell out of his mouth and Rose bit back a scream. 'I keep forgetting to close my eyes.'

She reached for the prince's hand and sent a pulse of healing magic into his bloodstream. She didn't know if it would work, since her powers were meant for the living, but then his brow smoothed and he sighed peacefully.

BANG! BANG! BANG!

Rose jumped to her feet as the door swung open, revealing Alarik Felsing, wild-eyed and panting, in its frame. 'I heard you scream,' he said between breaths. 'Where's Ansel? I know he's in here somewhere.'

Rose glanced at the mirror. Five more sapphires to go. She

squeezed her eyes shut, wishing she could disappear. She'd take the company of ten undead Ansels any day over the terrifying king of Gevra.

Alarik stalked into the room, his frown sharpening when he spotted his brother lying on the bed. He turned on Rose. 'What have you done to him?'

Rose reached for a dreg of courage. *Think like Wren. Talk like Wren. Act like Wren.*

She slouched against the desk. 'Calm down,' she said, folding her arms. 'He's just resting.'

The king raked his pale blue gaze over her, noting her scant outfit, which was sun-bright and covered in sand. 'Where did you get that dress?'

'I found it in the wardrobe,' said Rose, forcing a shrug.

Alarik glared at the wardrobe like it had betrayed him, then shook whatever thought was forming out of his head. 'And you thought now was a good time to play dress-up?' He gestured to Ansel, who was staring blankly at the ceiling. 'Are you trying to seduce him back to some kind of normality?'

Rose gasped, before she could stop herself. 'How dare you!'

Alarik narrowed his eyes as he came towards her. 'Something is amiss.'

Stars! Did the king of Gevra always stand so close to Wren? Rose scooted out from under his glare. 'Let me solve the riddle for you,' she said, reaching for Wren's sarcasm. 'Your undead brother is the thing that's amiss.'

'Which is your fault,' he said. 'So, speak, witch. What exactly went wrong?'

'I don't know,' said Rose, frustration making her voice sharp. 'Maybe the fact Wren's never done forbidden magic before!'

The second her sister's name flew out of her mouth, Rose winced. Wren had spent an entire month pretending to be her at Anadawn, and Rose couldn't last three minutes in the company of the Gevran king.

Alarik turned on her, lightning fast. 'Do you often speak in the third person?'

Rose forced a strangled laugh. 'Only when I'm anxious.'

'I've never known you to get anxious.'

'You barely know me,' said Rose, glancing at the sapphires. Two minutes.

Just then, Ansel sat bolt upright. 'Rose? Rooooose? It's almost our wedding day!'

Rose had to get out of here before the switch reversed. In the absence of any sort of plan, she clutched the mirror and bolted through the open door. The king's soldiers caught her in the hallway. Quick as an adder, Alarik grabbed her hand and twisted it.

Rose yelped, trying to pull away, but his grip was like steel. She kicked his shin, but the king didn't even flinch. He was too busy examining her palm.

He raised his brows. 'Your cut has healed.'

'I'm a witch,' said Rose, still trying to shake him off. 'Now unhand me, you wicked beast.'

Alarik's mouth twisted into a savage smile. 'Hello, Rose. I would say welcome to Gevra, but I'm not particularly pleased to see you.'

There was one sapphire left aglow, and no time to run.

Alarik brought his face close to hers. 'Where is your sister? What trick are you two playing?'

'The only trick is the abomination inside that room!' Rose cried out, all her fear and anger rising to the surface. There was no point in pretending to be Wren any more – they were about to get caught. 'Poor Ansel! How could you do this to him? And don't you dare tell me it was Wren's fault. I know you forced her to do it!'

Alarik cocked his head. 'I thought your sister was the mouthy one.'

Rose prodded his chest with the mirror. 'Let my grandmother and my sister go. You've kidnapped a queen of Eana. You know very well that's an act of war.'

'Is that what you've come here for, Rose? To declare war on Gevra?' Alarik flashed his canines. 'Careful what you wish for.'

Just then, the hand mirror began to shimmer. As the wind reached out to claim her, Rose fixed Alarik with her fiercest stare. 'Don't you dare harm my sister, Alarik Felsing, or you will have all of Eana, and its witches, to reckon with.'

In a rush of wind, she was gone, leaving the king of Gevra staring, slack-jawed, at the space where she had just been.

Wren

CHAPTER 39

Wren held tightly to Elske as the wind ferried her home. She felt that sharp tugging sensation again, and then the bottom dropped out of her stomach. The courtyard spun, and she spun with it, the world blurring from streaks of glittering gold to stark white, as a different floor slid underfoot. A wintry chill pricked at Wren's cheeks as she returned to the marbled interior of Grinstad Palace. She blinked to find herself hunkering in the fourth-floor hallway, her arms still fastened around the wolf's neck.

She smiled as she pulled back from Elske. 'We made it, sweetling.'

'Actually, I prefer "Your Majesty",' came Alarik's voice from above. He was standing over her, dressed in a simple navy doublet and black trousers. His pale blue eyes were shot with red and his streaked blond hair was unusually unkempt. He was examining the hand mirror with great suspicion. 'What is this thing?'

'It's a mirror.'

He pressed his lips together. 'Perhaps you'd like Borvil

to interrogate you instead.'

'Fine. If you want specifics, it's a *magic* mirror. It has the power to connect me to Rose. But it doesn't last long.'

'I had assumed from her letters that Rose was the better-behaved queen,' mused Alarik. 'Though after our little run-in just now, I might have to revise that opinion.' He pointed at Elske. 'That beast belongs to Captain Iversen.'

Wren scratched underneath Elske's chin. 'And now she's home. Where she belongs.'

'A happy outcome,' said Alarik, dryly. He handed the mirror to one of his soldiers. 'Enough talk. You have something that belongs to me.' He turned and disappeared into her bedroom.

Wren stood up, resisting the urge to lunge at the soldier and demand her mirror back. Alarik returned presently with Ansel, his arm slung around his little brother to keep him from running off. 'My flower!' cried the prince, and Wren noticed that his front tooth was missing. 'There you are! Every moment away from you feels like an eternity!'

Alarik glared at Wren. 'I didn't give you permission to bring him here.'

'What was I supposed to do? Let him wander around the palace while you were asleep? He already ran into Anika at breakfast.'

'I know. She yelled at me about it. At length.' Alarik's frown sharpened his cheekbones. 'Come. I want to talk where we won't be overheard.' The second the king moved, his soldiers stepped out of every alcove, swarming him like a battalion. Wren scurried after them, glad to have Elske padding alongside her once more. Almost at once, her thoughts turned back to Rose and Shen, and the grand majesty of the Sunkissed Kingdom.

Shen might be a king, but there were enemies within his walls. She hoped he knew what he was doing. Wren had done everything she could in those twelve minutes, but she had a walking corpse and a furious king to deal with now. She couldn't afford to worry about her best friend and her sister, too. She had to trust that they would take care of each other.

To Wren's surprise, Alarik led her into the royal wing on the second floor. It was crawling with soldiers, a new stern face glaring at Wren every ten paces. White tigers and wolves prowled the hallways, while snow foxes snoozed blissfully on the windowsills. Sunlight flooded in through stained glass, illuminating the artwork on the walls. They weren't the usual depictions of great Gevran battles or beast warfare found in the other rooms of the palace – rather, they were landscapes. Oil paintings of snowy sunsets and rushing waterfalls, silver-backed mountain ranges, a glassy sea on a cloudless day, an emerald valley bursting with yellow and violet flowers.

'That must be the Turcah Valley,' murmured Wren. 'It's beautiful.'

Alarik paused mid-step. 'How do you know about the Turcah Valley?'

Once upon a time, Tor had told Wren about it – a place, he said, that was as green as her eyes. A haven that would be her salvation if she married Ansel and came to Gevra. She told him she wouldn't come to Gevra for anything, and yet here she was anyway, brushing her fingertips along a painting of the valley that had – for a fleeting moment – represented hope for both of them. She ignored the sudden ache in her heart at the thought of a life with Tor. A world where they might have visited this valley together.

Alarik, who had braced his hand against a heavy oak door, was watching her too closely. Beside him, Ansel was swatting at the flies buzzing around his head. 'You look like you want to jump inside that painting,' said the king.

'I'd rather be there than here,' admitted Wren.

'That makes two of us,' he muttered, as he pushed the door open. Wren followed him into the chamber, then spluttered in bemusement. 'Wait. Is this your *bedroom*?'

He arched a brow. 'Don't get any ideas.'

'Please. I'd sooner crawl into Borvil's mouth.' The door closed behind them with a thud. There were no soldiers in here, only Alarik's wolves, Luna and Nova, lying on a rug in the middle of the room. The wolves leaped to their feet when they saw Ansel and let out menacing growls. Ansel dropped to his hands and knees and growled back at them.

'Easy, brother.' Alarik pulled Ansel away from the snarling wolves, before silencing the beasts with a sharp command. They sank to the floor while Ansel clambered on to the bed and splayed out like a starfish.

Wren surveyed her surroundings. 'This room is very . . .'

'Tasteful?'

'No.' In fact, it was annoyingly tasteful. The bed was huge yet simple, with a high headboard carved from winterwood and a blanket piled with silver furs. There was a stack of well-thumbed books on the bedside table. Wren had to fight the urge to rifle through them, to figure out what Alarik read at night. For some reason, she couldn't picture it.

Three large windows hung with tawny drapes looked out over the courtyard, while the cream-coloured walls were adorned with portraits that appeared to be mostly of the Felsing family. There was a painting of Alarik and his siblings as bundled-up children skating on an ice rink, one of his father sitting on his throne in full regalia, a youthful Queen Valeska resting a porcelain hand on his shoulder.

Wren swallowed her gasp. The dowager queen was much older now but there was no mistaking her. She recognized those wide grey eyes and that long sweep of pearlescent hair.

She moved on, studying Alarik's official portrait, which hung above an orderly wooden desk. He had been painted standing on top of a snow-swept mountain, dressed in a navy military uniform and wearing his silver-branch crown. There was another older painting of his siblings hanging beside the window. All three of them were laughing. But it was not the sight of Alarik's real smile that had drawn Wren to the picture. It was the sun-brightness of his hair. There was no black streak in the middle of it, and his eyes had not yet acquired their famed sharpness.

'Are you done peering into my childhood?' said Alarik, impatiently. He was at the other side of the room, by an archway that led into another chamber. 'Come.'

He disappeared through the arch. Wren left Ansel lying on the bed and hurried after the king, emerging into another room filled with every colour and style of garment imaginable. Clothing racks climbed all the way to the ceiling, while piles of cashmere sweaters and woollen scarves lined the shelves by the windows. The king had a wardrobe the size of her entire bedroom back at Anadawn.

But Alarik hadn't brought her in here to show off his clothes. His voice dropped to a dangerous whisper. 'Tell me, witch. What the hell have you done to my brother?'

Wren glared at him. '*We* raised him from the dead. Or don't you remember that part?'

A shudder passed through Alarik at the memory.

'I tried to warn you,' she went on. 'I told you I had never done that kind of spell before. Of course there were going to be risks—'

'Enough!' he snapped. 'I don't want to hear warnings or excuses. Turn my brother back into the person he was. Not this . . . ludicrous phantom.'

Wren scowled at the king. 'I'm a witch, not a miracle worker!'

'Then you'd better work on your magic. Unless you've lost interest in saving your grandmother.'

'You manipulative bastard,' said Wren, balling her fists. 'You made me a promise.'

'You made *me* a promise,' he said, just as viciously. 'And *you* have yet to keep it.' He gestured through the archway.

'That *creature* is not my brother. It's some kind of cruel joke.'

'I did my best,' Wren insisted. 'My intentions were good.'

Alarik waved her intentions away. 'You have two days. If you don't find a way to make this right, by blood or by magic, your grandmother will spend the night after tomorrow with my beasts.'

Outside, the wind whipped up in a ragged howl. It whistled through the mountains, casting handfuls of snow against the windows. Alarik cursed. 'And now this. Another damn blizzard. It's unseasonable, even for Gevra.'

Wren felt the same blizzard raging inside herself. Whorls of panic twisted in her gut, her fear blinding her from the way forward. She glared at the king.

He took a step towards her. 'You can hate me all you want. Curse me if you like, but you *will* do what I've ordered, Wren.' He was so close now, Wren could see the stubble on his chin, trace the rings of midnight blue around his irises. 'Is that understood?'

They stared at each other for a long moment, their chests heaving with the same ragged anger, before he suddenly stepped back, and, as if some unspoken command had passed between them, his wolves stalked in, baring their teeth at Wren. 'Now get out of my room.'

Deep in the dungeons of Grinstad Palace, Wren knelt at the bars of her grandmother's cell and called out her name.

Banba was curled up in the shadows, wrapped in the red cloak Wren had given her. She looked up, bleary-eyed, at the sound of her voice.

'Little bird,' she rasped. Her arms were still chained behind her back and her cheeks were gaunt. She came to the bars. 'No,' she whispered, the crevices in her forehead deepening as soon as she saw Wren's face. 'No, Wren. Tell me you didn't do it.'

Wren hesitated. 'Banba, I—'

'I can sense the darkness,' Banba cut in. 'It lingers on you like a second skin. It's the same one that moves in the wind here. That lives in these mountains.' She inhaled through her teeth. 'Now it moves in you, too.'

Wren scrunched her eyes shut. The hollowness inside her yawned, reminding her of what she had done. 'I cast a blood spell,' she said, shame flooding her cheeks. 'Ansel is alive again.'

Her grandmother cursed. 'You foolish child.'

Wren flinched. 'Only he's not the same. He's not as he was. He's convinced that tomorrow is his wedding day, that I'm his bride. His skin is grey and his mouth is too wide, and he's falling apart, bit by bit . . .' She shuddered. 'There's a wrongness to him.'

'What did you expect?' snapped Banba. 'Prince Ansel is supposed to be dead.'

'Well, now I don't know what he is,' said Wren, with rising desperation. 'I just know I have to fix him.'

'Wren. Look at me.'

Wren raised her chin, quailing at the judgement in her

grandmother's eyes. A long time ago, Wren had promised herself she would never let her grandmother down again and here Banba was, looking at Wren like she didn't even know her. 'What you have done cannot be fixed. Not with natural magic or forbidden blood magic. The young prince will never return to who he once was. It is an impossibility far greater than any magic. Greater than the limits of our world. It must be undone.'

Wren frowned. 'What do you mean "undone"?'

Banba levelled her with a hard look. 'Ansel has to die again. And stay dead.'

'Hissing seaweed! I can't kill him, Banba. Alarik will feed us to his beasts.'

'Then you must convince the king that it is the only way forward.' Banba's face was grave, her green eyes haunted. 'So long as blood magic moves within the prince, he will draw darkness down on Grinstad. And not even the king himself will be immune to it.'

Just then, the mountain released a rumbling groan. An icicle dropped from the ceiling and shattered across the stone, nicking them both.

Wren stared at the shards. 'Why do I have a horrible feeling that you're right?'

Banba snorted. 'That is my eternal burden, little bird. To be right. Even when I wish I wasn't.'

Wren sat back on her heels, looking at Banba through the iron bars. The sight of her grandmother, the only family she'd had for most of her life and the strongest witch she'd ever known, now cold and cowed on her knees in the dark, made her want to scream herself hoarse. 'It feels like the world is falling down around us,' she whispered.

'Perhaps it is,' said Banba, with a sigh. Her face crumpled, and for a moment, she looked impossibly old. 'Go home to your throne, Wren. Your sister needs you. Eana needs you.' She rolled to her feet and turned from her granddaughter, the wheeze of her breath filling the silence as she retreated into the darkness. 'Forget about saving the prince. There will be no redemption for us here in Gevra. Not for me. And not for you.'

For the first time in her life, Wren didn't know what to say to her grandmother. And even if she did, Banba was done talking. As the mountains groaned above them, Wren got up and walked out of the dungeon, leaving her grandmother alone in the dark.

There was a time not long ago, before Wren set out for Anadawn to make the switch that would change everything, when she had knelt on the floor of her hut back in Ortha, vomiting until her stomach ached.

What if I can't do it, Banba? she had cried, between retches. *What if I get caught and we never see each other again?*

Her grandmother had knelt on the floor beside her and held her to her chest, her words as warm and sure as the sun. *There is nothing in this world strong enough to keep us apart, little bird. I will rip these cliffs apart if I have to. I will raze the white palace to the ground.* She had squeezed Wren's shoulders then, pressing a morsel of strength into her bones. *No matter what happens, I promise you we will have the future we have been promised. It's you and me, Wren. Always.*

'Always,' said Wren, as she climbed the stairs to her bedroom. 'No matter what.'

And just as Banba had meant it, so, too, did Wren.

Rose

CHAPTER 40

When the wind unravelled around Rose, she was kneeling in the palace courtyard. She looked up to find Lei Fan gaping at her.

'What just happened?' she said, waving around what appeared to be a slab of meat.

Rose retrieved the hand mirror and stood up. 'I take it you met my sister, Wren.'

'She took your wolf.' Lei Fan dropped the meat with a splat. 'Sorry. It all happened so fast.'

'It's probably for the best,' said Rose, with a sigh. She was going to miss that wolf more than she cared to admit, but the desert was becoming more hostile by the moment. Elske would be safer back home in Gevra, where she belonged.

Lei Fan pointed to the mirror. 'I've spent the last eighteen years living under the desert, but I've never seen anything as unsettling as an entire person popping out of that thing.'

'Trust me. It's even more unsettling getting sucked into it.' Rose tucked the mirror into the sash at her waist. 'Please don't mention it to anyone. Kai knows Wren and I are able to switch, but he doesn't know how. And I'd like to keep it that way.'

Lei Fan's brows rose. 'You don't trust my brother, do you?'

Rose hesitated. 'Do you?'

Lei Fan snorted. 'I've known him all my life. Of course I don't.' She slumped on to a nearby bench, absently stroking the carved horse on the armrest. 'I love my brother, but I know how hungry he is. For acceptance. For power. He gets it from our father.' She frowned. 'Sometimes I wonder if things would be different if our mother was still here. If Kai would stop *reaching* for things he doesn't need.'

Rose sank on to the bench next to Lei Fan, trying to figure out just how much she knew about Kai's poisonous ambition. 'Is that why he hates Shen?'

Lei Fan offered no denial. 'It's jealousy, really. You have to understand, we've been trapped under the desert for years. And Kai so desperately wanted to be the hero. He used to talk about it in his sleep.' She lowered her voice and Rose leaned in close. 'He keeps telling everyone about how he dug his way out of here, but who do you think summoned the wind to help him? Who blew mountains of sand out of his way so he could claw his way out?'

'It was you.' Rose's eyes widened with admiration. 'Why didn't you say anything?'

Lei Fan shrugged. 'I don't care about glory. I just wanted to help my kingdom. I think I was the only one who hoped that Shen was still out there somewhere. We were so close when we were little, and I couldn't shake the feeling that he was still alive. That one day he might come back.'

For a fleeting moment, Rose wanted to tell Lei Fan about what she'd seen Kai and Feng do at the festival. But as much as Lei Fan clearly cared for Shen, Rose didn't want to strain her loyalty. Especially after Shen had just turned on her so viciously. 'I'm glad you didn't give up hope,' she said, instead. 'Nothing matters more to Shen than family. Your support means everything to him.'

Lei Fan grinned. 'I'm just glad to have him back. It finally feels like our luck is changing.'

Rose returned her smile. 'I hope you and I can stay friends, Lei Fan. You'll always be welcome at Anadawn.'

'I'd like to visit one day,' said Lei Fan.

Rose snapped her chin up at her name on the breeze. Shen was calling her from inside the palace.

'Excuse me,' she said, rising from the bench and hurrying inside.

Shen was pacing by the Forever Fountain, every muscle in his body coiled with tension.

'Shen!'

He turned at the sound of her voice. He reached her in ten quick strides, taking her hands in his. Relief coursed through Rose at his touch, at the softness in his face. 'I owe you an apology, Rose. I've been an idiot.'

Rose glanced over her shoulder, mindful of the nearby servants. 'We shouldn't talk here,' she said, pulling him away from the fountain. 'Come with me.'

Back in her bedroom, Shen locked the door behind them

and drew the curtains, blocking out the morning sun. He turned around, his face in shadow now. 'You were right, Rose. About everything. Wren and I overheard Feng and Kai talking in my uncle's bedroom. They tried to kill me.'

Rose slumped down on the edge of her bed, the weight of that terrible truth finally leaving her shoulders. Wren had done the impossible. She had got through to Shen. 'I wasn't trying to hurt you.'

He came towards her, his eyes pleading. 'Forgive me, Rose. I should never have doubted you. I'm sorry for the terrible things I said. All I could see was all the things I've wished for since I was a child.'

'You can still have those things,' she said, gently pulling him down beside her. 'Just not with Kai. Or Feng. I'm sorry they aren't the people you hoped they were.'

'At least I know now,' said Shen, steel-eyed. 'I can protect myself and my kingdom. I can protect you.'

Relief blossomed inside Rose at Shen's words, and with it, exhaustion. Goodness, she was tired. She hadn't slept in forever, and she desperately needed to get out of this filthy dress. The knot was digging into her shoulder and it was too tight around her waist.

'Shen?' she said, tentatively. 'Could you help me with my dress?'

He swallowed, thickly, his gaze falling to the hollow of her throat.

Rose offered him a coy smile. 'Lei Fan knotted it so tightly; I'll never wriggle out of it on my own.'

With reverent fingers, Shen began to untie the knot at Rose's shoulder. 'Like this?' he said, his breath tickling her neck.

'Yes, thank you.' Rose closed her eyes, revelling in the sensation of his fingers brushing against her bare skin.

Shen's fingers stilled just above her collarbone. 'I think it's loose enough now.'

Rose's eyes fluttered open. She held his gaze as she unravelled the knot, the fabric slipping down until she caught it just above her chest. Her heart beat wildly against her palm, and suddenly she wasn't tired at all.

Shen's fingers lingered on her skin. He traced the edge of her collarbone and then the column of her neck. Rose's cheeks began to prickle, heat flaring inside her. She closed her eyes and felt herself sway.

'Rose.' He caressed her jaw, brushing his thumb over her lips. 'You need rest.'

'I need *you*, Shen.' The words were out before Rose could regret them. His breath hitched as she tugged him towards her and met his lips with her own.

Shen kissed her back with a hunger that made her gasp. She opened her mouth to him, winding her arms around his neck and letting the bodice of her dress fall between them. His hand skimmed her bare back, sending a shiver down her spine. She moaned into his mouth, and he pulled her closer, kissing her deeper.

In that perfect moment, with Shen Lo in her arms in the darkness, Rose didn't care that she was a queen, that he was the ruler of a long-lost land, or that there were plenty of people who wanted them both dead. All she could think about was Shen's mouth against hers and his strong hands roaming her body.

She broke the kiss, pulling back just enough to stare into his eyes. 'Shen,' she said, her voice ragged. 'I know there's a lot going on right now . . .'

He kissed the shell of her ear. 'There is only this, Rose.'

She pressed her forehead against his. 'Can we pretend we're back in the desert? Just for a little while?'

He smiled. 'We are in the desert.'

'I mean like before . . .' she said, smiling, too. 'Can we be just Rose and Shen?'

'We can be whoever you want us to be,' he murmured, against her skin. 'It's you and me, Rose. No crowns. No kingdoms. Just us.'

'Just us,' said Rose, falling back on to the bed.

Shen leaned down to kiss her, and as their lips met once more, the rest of the world melted away until nothing else mattered but the two of them.

Time, too, slipped away. After an hour that felt like a fleeting moment, Rose sighed as she sprawled out on a mountain of pillows, feeling more at peace than she had in days. Weeks. Months. She was deliciously tired, her skin still tingling from his touch. They still had so much to figure out, but *this* – what she had with Shen – was perfect. She turned on to her side, smiling like a satisfied cat. She'd just close her eyes for a second. And then they would come up with a plan to deal with Kai and Feng. Together.

Shen slung his arm across her waist, hugging her body to his. 'Get some rest,' he said, pressing a kiss to the nape of her neck. 'I'll be here when you wake.'

Rose woke to the sound of torrential rain hitting the roof. Outside, the sun was setting behind a veil of dark thunderclouds. She bolted upright, looking for Shen.

He was standing by the window, studying the heaving sky.

'It's raining,' said Rose, pulling the blanket up to cover herself. 'It never rains in the desert.'

'I asked Lei Fan to brew a storm.'

Rose frowned. 'Why?'

Shen turned around and held up a letter bearing the Anadawn royal seal. 'This arrived for you. The starcrest nearly took my eye out when it barrelled through the window with it.'

Rose crawled across the bed, taking it from him with trembling hands. She ripped it open, immediately recognizing Thea's handwriting.

> *Rose,*
> *I pray this letter finds you. Word has reached*
> *us that Barron is building an army in the south.*
> *He intends to march on Anadawn within the*
> *week. Hurry home. I fear the worst lies ahead*
> *of us.*
> > *Thea*

She looked up, dread draining the heat from her cheeks. 'Shen.'

He took the note from her, his jaw clenching as he read. 'You should get dressed.'

Rose was already braiding her hair away from her face. 'How soon can you ready your horse? We have to leave at once.'

There was an awful beat of silence.

'I'm not going with you, Rose.'

Rose bristled. 'Don't be ridiculous. I can't leave you here with them. What if they attack you again?'

'I've spoken to my Captain of the Guard.' Shen cracked his knuckles, absently. 'We're going to deal with them tonight.'

'Then I'll wait.'

'It'll be safer if you're not here.'

'Safer for who?' Rose demanded. 'You need a healer by your side.'

'I'll be all right. And so will you.' He gestured at the note. 'Anadawn needs its queen, Rose.'

Rose's eyes prickled. 'But you won't be there, and neither will Wren.'

Shen smiled at her. There was such sadness in it Rose had to look away. 'You were always going to rule, with or without us. And Wren will be back soon. I'm sure of it.'

'And what about you?'

He hesitated. 'I'll come to see you when things are more settled here.' Thunder rumbled overhead, drawing his gaze back to the window. 'I'll leave you to get changed.' He nodded to a platter of fluffy buns on the bedside table. 'I've brought you another of Grandmother Lu's specialties. They'll be good for the road.' He stalked across the room, his hands twitching in and out of fists. Rose could tell he was nervous, but whether it was because of their imminent goodbye, the gathering Arrows or the confrontation with Kai and Feng that would come after, she couldn't tell. 'I'll meet you in the courtyard. Don't forget your cloak.'

It was still raining when Rose found her way to the courtyard.

Shen stepped out of the shadows and grabbed her hand. 'Come on. This way,' he said, pulling her after him. 'We're taking the back route out of the city.'

'Why all the secrecy?' she said, hurrying to keep up. 'Nobody here cares what I do. That has been made abundantly clear.'

'I don't want anyone coming after you. Or tipping the Arrows off.' Rose knew he was talking about Kai. Her stomach twisted at the thought of meeting him again in one of these dark lanes. 'He knows I'll do anything to protect you. Which means he could use you against me.'

Lightning flashed overhead, casting shards of silver across the sky. Thunder growled after them as they wound their way through the sodden city. Rose took heart in the rattle and crash of the storm. It meant Lei Fan was helping them. And if the tempest witch knew Rose was in danger, Shen must have trusted her enough to tell her what had happened at the festival.

Finally, they came to a narrow door hidden inside a flowering trellis in the south wall of the city. Shen pushed it open to reveal the wide-open desert beyond. 'Grandmother Lu told me about this place.'

Rose's cheeks prickled with relief. 'Looks like you've got more allies than traitors in the palace.'

'Just about,' said Shen, leading her out into the desert.

Storm was there waiting for them.

Rose smiled as she stroked the horse's muzzle. 'Another ally.'

'She's yours now,' said Shen.

'I'm only borrowing her,' said Rose. 'She'll be waiting for you at Anadawn. We both will.'

Shen's smile was sad, and Rose had the sudden terrible feeling that she'd never see that perfect dimple again. Or those molten eyes. 'Shen,' she said, but she could think of nothing to follow it. She didn't want to say farewell.

Shen cupped her face in his hands and kissed her. Her hood fell as she threw her arms around his neck, the desert storm soaking them both to the bone, but she didn't care. She kissed him back, fiercely, under the lightning-struck sky, her heart as loud as the crashing thunder.

Finally, Shen pulled away.

'This isn't goodbye,' said Rose, clinging on to his cloak 'We'll see each other again. Soon.'

He chuckled, softly. 'Still giving me orders, even though I'm a king now?'

'Some things never change,' she said, as she swung up on

to Storm's back. She twisted to look at him one last time. 'Be careful, Shen.'

'You, too,' he said, flashing his sun-bright smile. 'Go and be the ruler I know you can be.'

He leaned in and whispered a command in Storm's ear, and before Rose could say another word, the horse jolted into a gallop and carried her off into the roiling desert storm.

Wren

CHAPTER 41

Wren wandered listlessly through the halls of Grinstad Palace, at a loss for what to do about Prince Ansel.

She perched on a windowsill on the first floor and looked out at a world spun from silver and white, mesmerized by the savage beauty of Gevra. Even the wind here was hostile, the roaring blizzard a beast all of its own. In its lull, Wren swore she heard a distant shout. Elske bolted upright, her ears sliding back as she tried to trace the sound. Wren recognized it, too.

She pressed her forehead against the window and looked down on the snow-swept courtyard full of snow tigers and wolves. Tor stalked among them, his hands tucked behind his back. His high-collared fur coat might have staved off the worst of the chill, but he still looked like a madman, corralling those animals in the eye of a blizzard.

'What the hell is he doing out there?' muttered Wren. 'The bloody fool will get frostbite.'

Elske released a low whine.

'Come on.' Wren set off for the courtyard, the wolf hurrying at her side. Down in the atrium, the glass dome was covered with a blanket of freshly fallen snow, hiding the evening sky beyond it. Some of the beasts were pacing, nervous. The soldiers looked unsettled, too, like they were afraid the keening wind was a banshee that might come and snatch them away.

Wren had to shove her shoulder against the door to the courtyard and push with all her weight to get it to budge. When it finally flew open, the blizzard yanked her out by her sleeves and shoved her into a snowstorm so icy she had to fight for breath. Elske bounded out after her, weathering the drastic change in temperature with impressive grace.

Tor was still marching up and down the courtyard, commanding the singular attention of twelve untethered beasts. He raised his fist and they dropped to the floor like dominos. A short, sharp whistle brought them back to their feet, while a simple finger snap sent them bulleting across the arena and back again. Watching him in his natural habitat made Wren momentarily forget about the blizzard. He was unerringly calm, fearless in the face of all those dripping fangs. Tor wielded his beasts with the same confidence as his sword, and they respected him for it. No, they *loved* him.

Wren drew her cloak tighter, her body railing against the fierce gale. Tor bristled at her approach, his chin raised as though he had caught her scent on the wind. Or perhaps it was Elske's howl that made him turn around. 'Wren?' he shouted, raising his hand to his brow. 'Is that you?'

Wren waved back. 'THERE'S SOMEONE HERE WHO REALLY WANTS TO SEE YOU!'

Tor turned back to his beasts and barked a command. They sprang up at once and trod back into their pen at the edge of courtyard. He released the stopper and pulled the gate down, sealing them in. He came towards Wren then, moving through the blizzard with unnatural ease. Elske bounded to meet him, and Tor melted around her like a puddle, nuzzling his face into her fur and pressing a kiss to her head.

Watching them, Wren melted a little, too. Then the wind picked up and pummelled her in the face. Tor was on his feet in an instant. He curled a strong arm around her waist, anchoring her body to his as he led them to a wooden hut on the other side of the courtyard.

'In here,' he huffed, guiding her inside. 'This will keep you from blowing away.'

'Would that really be the worst thing?' muttered Wren, as she surveyed the creaking hut – the meagre fireplace in the corner, the empty mugs of tea on the table – surmising that it was a place where soldiers came to rest. The foul weather must have chased them all back inside the palace.

The hut trembled as Wren sat down on a bench by the empty fireplace, wishing for a mug of tea of her own. Elske curled up at her feet, warming her toes. The air in here was laced with ice, but at least they were sheltered from the worst of the blizzard, and they no longer had to scream to be heard.

'What are you doing out in the storm?' said Wren, rubbing her hands together to keep warm. 'You'll catch your death.'

'The blizzard was frightening the beasts. Training distracts them.' Tor hunkered by the fireplace and stacked it with wood.

'Believe it or not, I like the wildness of it. It's the only time I can hear myself think. And it reminds me of home.'

'Sorry for ruining your peace, then.' Wren watched the muscles in his shoulders move under his coat as he built their fire.

'I looked for you earlier,' said Tor. 'You weren't in your bedroom.'

'I know. I was in Alarik's.'

He frowned. 'Why?'

'He came to collect Ansel,' said Wren, quickly. What other reason could Tor *possibly* be entertaining? 'Now he's holed up in the king's wardrobe so he won't be discovered.' She looked at her hands. 'Alarik is furious with me.'

'Well,' said Tor, with a sigh. 'Can you blame him?'

'Yes,' said Wren, crisply. 'The two of us did it together.' She watched the muscles in Tor's neck tighten and went on. 'I didn't mean for Ansel to come back the way he did, Tor. If you believe nothing else, please believe that.' To her horror, her lips began to tremble. 'I just wanted to make it better. For him. For Banba. For *you*. I thought . . . I thought—'

'I know what you thought.' He struck a piece of flint, blowing on the spark until the wood caught fire. 'But some things can't be undone, no matter how badly we wish they could be.' He looked at her over his shoulder, the storm in his eyes just as violent as the one pressing in on them from outside. 'No one can turn back time. Not even you.'

The gentleness in his voice prickled under Wren's skin. At least if he was angry, she could spar with him. She could throw up her walls and lash out with her tongue. But she couldn't rail against the fear in his voice or the dread in his eyes. Dread for her. 'I don't know how to fix it,' she confessed. 'I've made such a terrible mistake and there's no way back. And now Banba has to pay for it. If anything happens to her . . .' She pressed her fists against her eyes, trying to stop her tears, but they wracked her shoulders and streamed down her face. 'I can't bear it, Tor. I just *can't*.'

The bench groaned as he sat down beside her, the heat of his body, the nearness of him, making her heart ache. 'Come here.' He put his arm around her and pulled her close. Wren nuzzled into his collar, inhaling his alpine scent. 'Just breathe.' He pressed his lips against her hair. 'That's all you can do now.'

Wren closed her eyes. His chest rose under her cheek, the steady rhythm of his breath lulling the panic inside her. She wanted to curl up and fall asleep here, to forget all the trouble that lay behind the blizzard, waiting for her. 'Thank you,' she whispered. 'For this moment. This kindness.'

Wren hadn't realized how badly she needed it, but Tor had. And he had given it to her, even though she didn't deserve it. Or him.

He kissed the top of her head. 'Thank you for returning my wolf.'

Wren smiled. 'I bet you're wondering where she came from.'

'I am a little curious.'

'It's quite a story.' Wren sat up and told him all about it, not just the mirror and the wolf but the rest of her day, too – about Alarik's threat, and the grave truth of what Banba had told her down in the dungeon. That to know peace, Ansel would have to die all over again.

'Freezing hell.' Tor dragged a hand through his hair. 'Have you told Alarik?'

'Of course not.'

'Don't,' said Tor, darkly.

Wren traced a button on his coat, wishing the blizzard would snow them in. Wishing she never had to face King Alarik again. 'I've ruined the mood. Let's not talk about it any more.'

Tor laughed, uncomfortably. 'Wren, what else is there to talk about?'

She blew out a breath, looking around the hut for inspiration. 'Tell me about your beasts. Make it something interesting.'

Tor raised his eyebrows, but instead of making fun of her request, he laid his head back against the wall. 'What do you wish to know?'

Wren thought about it for a moment. 'Tell me about the Great Bear. The one on the Gevran crest.'

'Bernhard,' said Tor.

'Good old Bernhard. How come you all worship a bear anyway?'

As the fire crackled to life in the hearth, Tor closed his eyes and launched into his tale. 'For thousands of years, Gevra was ruled by beasts alone. The wolves prowled the rivers and shorelines, while the snow tigers and ice bears lived deep in the mountains. Harmony existed between all creatures – big and small – until a settler tried to conquer the land.'

Wren watched Tor's lips as he spoke, mesmerized by the timbre of his voice.

'The land here was rich in iron. Settlers came often to try to claim it for themselves.'

'Let me guess,' said Wren. 'They were all eaten.'

'Worse,' said Tor, grimly. 'Some stories say the bears learned to tear the flesh from a man's body with their claws, so they could leave it on the shore as a warning to others.'

Wren pulled a face. 'Sorry I asked.'

He chuckled as he tapped her on the nose. 'And now we come to Bernhard. He was the oldest and fiercest of all the animals. Every beast bowed to him. When Bernhard slumbered, his snores were so loud, they echoed through the Fovarr Mountains, and when he was angry, his roar sent fissures through the fjords. Some settlers on the northern continent feared him. Others wanted to capture him. They all failed.'

'Good,' said Wren.

Tor smiled. 'And then one day, a young man without a crown or a jewel to his name journeyed to Gevra in a boat of his own making. His name was Fredegast Felsing. Instead of trying to battle the Great Bernhard, he brought offerings. Salmon, venison.'

'Bribery.' Wren couldn't help but be impressed. 'Nice.'

Tor chuckled. Wren wished she could bottle the sound. 'Against all expectations, Bernhard and Fredegast became friends. Fredegast made a home in the mountains, and, after a time, other settlers came to join him. At Fredegast's request, the beasts made way for them, too, and before long they learned to live in harmony. When Bernhard died of old age, Fredegast wept for ten days and ten nights.'

'Bit overdramatic,' muttered Wren.

Tor shot her an admonishing look. 'He was in mourning.'

'There are better ways to mourn.'

'Such as?'

Wren shrugged. 'I don't know. Repressing your emotions, withdrawing from life and taking up sword-fighting with the eventual goal of revenge.'

Tor chuckled. 'You have quite a way with words.'

'So do you, soldier. Do go on.'

He obliged. 'After that, the beasts bowed to Fredegast and he became the first king of Gevra. At his coronation, he wore Bernhard's skin as his ceremonial cloak.'

'Wait. *What?*' Wren spluttered. 'That's *awful!*'

Tor's eyes crinkled as he broke into laughter. 'It was a mark of honour!'

'Tor!'

He raised his hands. 'I'm being serious.'

'So, if I die in this icy hell, someone's going to go around wearing me like a hat?'

'No one will wear you like a hat,' said Tor, through a grin that nearly knocked Wren sideways. 'We only do it with the beasts.'

'Do you promise?'

That laugh again, as beautiful as a winter sunset. 'Yes, Wren. I promise.'

She folded her arms as she flopped against the wall. 'Because after today, there's a very good chance I *will* die here, and I will *not* have Alarik Felsing wearing me like a bloody cloak.'

'Wren,' said Tor, leaning in until she could see the storm settling in his gaze. 'I'm not going to let you die. I'm afraid I like you too much.'

Wren jutted her chin out, closing the sliver of space between them. 'Prove it.'

He cupped her cheek, his gaze falling to her lips. 'You once told me you'd never kiss me in front of my wolf.'

'I'm prepared to make an exception,' she whispered, as she leaned in. 'And the wolf is asleep.' She smiled as she nipped his earlobe.

Tor hissed through his teeth. He groaned as he kissed her, his tongue sliding into her mouth. Wren kissed him back, gasping, hungry. He fisted his hands in her hair, pulling her to him until there was nothing but heat between them. And still it wasn't close enough. Wren hiked up her skirts, swinging her leg over his to straddle him. Tor stiffened beneath her, holding her so tightly, Wren thought she might shatter. The kiss deepened, her moans drowning out the blizzard as she moved against him.

Wren could have stayed inside that little hut forever, kissing Tor until they both forgot their own names, but the blizzard grew stronger, angrier, and when the fire eventually blew out and Elske woke from her slumber with a howl, they broke apart.

'You should get back inside,' said Tor, catching his breath. 'And I should check on the animals.'

'I have a new-found appreciation for snowstorms,' said Wren, pressing a kiss to his cheek. She lingered a moment, tempted to steal another one, but Tor was right. They both had places to be. She reluctantly clambered off the soldier, and with one last longing glance over her shoulder, Wren returned to the palace to face the hopelessness of her situation. She wasn't surprised when Elske padded inside after her, though Wren suspected it was her master's order and not her loyalty to Wren that made her escort her back to safety.

Wren was on her way up the stairs when she heard jaunty music wafting down the hallway. She followed the sound to a drawing room on the first floor, where she found Anika and Celeste dancing barefoot around a trio of fiddlers. They were laughing raucously as they hoisted their skirts and kicked their legs up. Celeste knocked over a vase, which made Anika howl with glee. The princess was laughing so hard she careened towards the fireplace and singed the bottom of her skirts. Celeste grabbed a pitcher and doused her with water, both girls collapsing on to a couch in a fit of giggles.

The musicians fell out of their melody and looked at each other in alarm.

'Keep playing!' cried Anika, between hiccoughs. 'I don't want to hear that damn blizzard!' She glanced around.

'Diamond! Where are you, darling?' Her white fox leaped up on to her lap and licked her cheek.

Celeste reached for a bottle of frostfizz on a nearby table and nearly drained it in one gulp. There were three more empty bottles rolling around on the carpet.

Celeste went to fling the empty bottle across the room and noticed Wren standing in the doorway. 'Dance on, Anika!' she said, as she scrabbled to her feet. 'I'll be right back!' Anika stood and swayed back and forth, dancing with her fox.

Celeste rushed across the room, shooing Wren out into the hallway. 'There you are!' she said, half breathless. 'Where did you disappear to earlier?'

'Sorry I missed the dance party,' said Wren, dryly. 'I had a little problem with an undead prince.'

Celeste blew a curl out of her eyes. 'I've been looking everywhere for you.'

'Did you fall into a vat of frostfizz on the way?'

'Oh, stop it. Anika drank most of it.' Celeste blinked, noticing the wolf sitting at Wren's side. 'Is that *Elske*?'

'Yes,' said Wren. 'It's a long story.'

'Is Rose all right?'

'She's fine. But Elske belongs here with her master,' said Wren. 'Like I said, it's a long story.'

With great effort, Celeste shook off her curiosity. 'Right. Back to why I'm here.'

'To dance with Anika?'

'You know why, Wren. You're in grave danger.'

Wren rolled her eyes. 'Well, obviously.'

'It's that dream I told you about,' Celeste went on, her dark eyes widening. 'It wasn't just a dream, Wren. The other night, I studied the starcrests. They came to me, and painted the same vision in the sky, only it was clearer. It felt closer, somehow. I saw you trapped in a wall of ice. You were dead, Wren. *Frozen*. Your heart wasn't beating any more.'

Wren tried to swallow the knot of fear in her throat, but it strangled her words. 'Any other dire information I should know?'

'Yes, actually. Barron and his Arrows have advanced their foothold in Eana. Their skirmish with the royal tour down in Ellendale has clearly emboldened them. Thea has sent word that they're trying to raise an army to march on Anadawn. Which means we need to go home. Now.'

Wren balked, a new panic rising inside her. But it did nothing to change the present circumstances. 'Open your eyes, Celeste. Look at what's right in front of you, and not just in the stars. I *can't* go home. After what I did to Prince Ansel, Alarik isn't going to let me waltz out of here. He'll kill me for even trying.'

'CELESTE!' Anika shrieked. 'WHERE IN FREEZING HELL HAVE YOU GONE?'

Wren stepped away from Celeste. 'But *you* can go home. And you should. Rose needs you.'

'She needs both of us!' Celeste grabbed Wren's shoulders and pulled her back, until they were nose to nose. 'Listen to me. Marino's ship will be back at port in two days' time. Steal a horse. Sneak out in a barrel of fish if you have to. But just meet me there. He sails at noon.'

'But Banba—'

'Banba would want this for you, Wren.' Celeste narrowed her eyes, reading the truth in Wren's. 'But you already know that, don't you?'

'CELESTE! I'M STUCK UNDER THE TABLE!' Anika's cackling echoed down the hall.

'I'M COMING!' Celeste shouted.

'Celeste, even if I was willing to leave Banba, getting out of here is not going to be as easy as getting in.'

'Maybe so.' Celeste looked meaningfully at Elske. 'But you and I both know there's someone here who can help you escape. Why don't you ask him?'

That night, after Elske returned to her master, the blizzard rocked Wren to sleep. She woke up on a mountain, the snow rising to her knees as she trekked across its jagged spine. That ancient voice came again, soaring on the wings of a nighthawk. *Welcome to the darkness, little bird. You need not fear it.*

The clouds shifted overhead. A shard of moonlight slipped through, illuminating a figure walking in front of Wren. She had long dark hair and pale skin, and wore a crimson cloak lined in white fur.

'Who are you?' Wren called out.

The young woman's laugh echoed through the mountains.

She turned, skewering Wren with her emerald gaze. *The question is, who are* you?

'Wait. Are you some kind of vision?' Wren quickened her steps, only to stumble. 'Are you . . . me?'

The woman smiled with Wren's teeth. *I am the darkness that lives inside you.*

Wren watched the woman's hands change colour, her skin glowing blood red from the inside out. A thought occurred to her, and she voiced it. 'Do you know how to fix the prince? Is there a way?'

The woman cocked her head. *If there was, what would you do for it?*

'Anything.'

The woman's smile sharpened. *Would you kill for it?*

Snow fell around them, but as the flakes landed on Wren's skin, they turned to drops of blood. When she looked up, the other Wren had disappeared. The night was as black as ink, the moon smothered behind a blanket of clouds.

True power comes from sacrifice, whispered the wind.

Rose

CHAPTER 42

Rose rode through the storm and into the night. The sky flashed, turning the dunes silver as the rain beat down on her, soaking through her cloak. She barely noticed the chill. She was lost in the memory of her last kiss with Shen Lo, wondering why it had felt like so much more than a temporary goodbye. It had felt like forever.

As the Sunkissed Kingdom disappeared into the mist, Rose spied the edge of Lei Fan's storm up ahead, a place where the rain petered out and the sky turned indigo, the first of the desert stars already bright and twinkling. She leaned forward, galloping hard and fast towards it.

Rose heard the unmistakable thrum of hoofbeats behind her. She whipped her head around, squinting into the falling dark. She recognized the horse first, and then its rider.

Kai.

Rose's blood ran cold. Kai was shirtless, his long dark hair streaming in the wind. Every strand was bone dry, just like the rest of him. He must have arced around the storm to catch up with her.

Rose wound her fingers in Storm's mane. 'Faster, girl!'

But Shen's horse was exhausted from riding in the rain, her damp hooves sinking in the shifting sands.

'You spoilt, meddling Valhart!' shouted Kai. 'You ruined everything! You don't just get to go running back to your precious palace. Turn around and face me!'

Rose glanced over her shoulder just in time to see him unfurl his whip with a deafening crack. It lashed through the air, before curling around Rose and yanking her off the horse. She screamed as she fell, landing on her back with a thud. Kai leaped off his horse, a foot landing on either side of her elbows. She tried to sit up, but he crouched down and pressed her face to the sand. Rose flailed in panic, catching a handful of his hair and yanking it, hard. He released her with a curse, and she bolted upright, kneeing him squarely between the legs.

Kai roared in pain.

Rose slid out from under him and scrambled to her feet. She grabbed his whip and flung it behind her, putting as much distance between them as she could.

Kai pulled a dagger from his belt as he leaped to his feet. He ducked his head and charged at her. Rose tried to run, but she was no match for the stampeding warrior. She stumbled on the sand, her hands coming to her head to protect it, just as Storm leaped from the dune and landed between them.

Kai lurched, striking Storm with his dagger. The horse released a terrible squeal as she collapsed on to the sand.

'You spineless coward!' yelled Rose, coming to her

knees beside the quivering horse. 'She was only trying to protect me!'

'Coward?' said Kai, rounding on her. 'Shen Lo is the coward. Hiding out in Ortha all those years when he could have been looking for us!' He spat in the sand. 'He doesn't deserve to be king!' He raised the blade high above Rose. 'If I can't take his crown from him, then I'll take his woman.'

Rose screamed as he brought the dagger down, but at that very same moment, a silver throwing knife whizzed past her, knocking the blade from Kai's grip.

Then came a croaky voice soaring on the desert wind. 'You forget your honour, Kai Lo!'

Grandmother Lu galloped towards them atop a magnificent russet mare. She slashed her cane through the air like a sword, before pointing it accusingly at his forehead. 'You disappoint me.'

Rose blinked, trying to figure out if Grandmother Lu was an apparition. She must be some sort of mirage, because there was simply no way that Shen's old nanny had just appeared out of nowhere, armed to the teeth . . .

All at once, Grandmother Lu vaulted off her horse, somersaulted through the air and kicked Kai in the jaw, knocking him to the ground. She sprang up from her crouch and began to beat him with her cane. 'You. Know. Better. Than. This!' she said between thwacks. 'I trained you myself! I taught you all your fancy moves! But I didn't teach you all MY moves!' With another yell, she used her cane to launch herself into the air, making a cannonball of her body, before hurtling back down at alarming speed. She landed on Kai's chest, winding him so badly, he fell back in the sand, dazed.

'Stop!' he wheezed. 'You know I won't hit you!'

The old woman was back on her feet in a flash. 'Kai Lo, I know what you tried to do to your cousin at the festival,' she said, as she stood over him. 'Don't lie there and pretend you are some goodly man!'

'He also just tried to kill me!' Rose cried, unable to help herself. Beside her, Storm whinnied. 'And also Storm!' she added, quickly. 'He cut her leg!'

'Snitch!' hissed Kai.

Grandmother Lu spun her cane in a blur. She poked him in the cheek. 'You should be ashamed of yourself, attacking Queen Rose. And hurting a desert horse!' She bonked the top of his head. 'Stupid boy.'

Kai tried to bat the cane away, but she was too quick for him.

Grandmother Lu bonked him again. 'I am the master. I make the rules.'

Rose couldn't help but giggle.

Grandmother Lu whipped her head around. 'This isn't a show. Heal that horse and get out of here!'

Rose dipped her chin, quickly doing as she was told. She was not about to get on this old woman's bad side. She closed her eyes and summoned her magic, making quick work of Storm's wound. By the time it was healed, Grandmother Lu was still scolding Kai.

Rose clambered back on to the horse, turning to look

down at the seasoned warrior. 'Will you be all right here by yourself?'

Grandmother Lu barked a laugh. 'I haven't even broken a sweat!' Before Rose could respond, the old woman turned around and whacked Storm on the rump. 'Off with you! Don't stop until you reach Anadawn!'

'Thank you!' cried Rose, as Storm took off in a whirl of sand.

Wren

CHAPTER 43

Wren woke up late and devoured a hearty breakfast of jam pastries and bitter coffee before pocketing two more pastries and heading down to the library, where she listened to the blizzard get angrier.

Fires crackled from two massive fireplaces, flooding the room with delicious heat, and there were more than enough couches to lounge on while she read, each one artfully draped in decadent fur throws. Wren had amassed a stack of books on arrival – everything from a collection of old Gevran folk tales and an encyclopaedia on local medicinal herbs. She hauled it all to a nearby couch, lit a candle on the side table and curled up under a blanket.

She was hoping something in the annals of Grinstad Palace would help her find a way to fix the prince. But as the minutes turned to hours, and day melted into night, Wren began to lose hope. The fires dwindled in their grates. Her lids grew heavy until not even the howling blizzard could keep her awake.

Weary with defeat, she set the books aside. She was

passing through the first floor of the atrium when she spied the dowager queen sitting at her glass piano.

Perhaps it was the late hour or the wildness that desperation brings, but before Wren could talk herself out of it, she went downstairs. Everything was already unravelling around her, what harm could one conversation do now?

'Hello,' Wren called out, waving awkwardly.

Queen Valeska looked up, blinking herself from her stupor.

Wren pointed to the piano. 'I saw you sitting here and I thought you looked like you could use some company. Do you play?'

Valeska looked at her for a long moment, like she couldn't quite figure out who she was. 'No,' she said at last. 'Not any more.'

'Oh. What a shame.'

'Do you?'

Wren shook her head. 'I tried once and it wasn't for me. I'm more of a sea-shanty person.'

The queen's brows rose, intrigue bringing out the beauty in her fine-boned features. 'I'm not sure I've ever heard a sea shanty before.'

'*Really?*' said Wren. 'You've been missing out.'

'Perhaps you might sing one, then?' suggested the queen, like it was a completely reasonable thing to ask.

Wren looked around the dark atrium, noting all the soldiers pretending not to listen from their alcoves, their beasts sleepy-eyed at their feet.

Wren surrendered to her poorer judgement. If tomorrow she was going to hell, then she may as well make the most of tonight. After a full day in the library, she felt strangely giddy, and more than a little hysterical. 'Why not?' she said, hiking her skirts to swing in time with the tune 'Prepare to be dazzled.' She cleared her throat, and launched into her favourite sea shanty.

'*Theeere once was a man called Ned Dupree,*
Who took a barrel of rum to sea,
He left his wife in their little town,
Then drank that barrel all the way dooooown.'

Wren swished her skirts as she sang, coaxing a smile from the dowager queen. She started to prance around the atrium.

'*Weeeeeeeell, poor Ned's head began to spin*
He caught a carp and kissed its fin,
He danced until his heart was full
Then went and fought a seagull.'

The queen burst into laughter, the sound tinkling through the atrium like a bell. Wren grinned at her over her shoulder. 'I could use some musical accompaniment for the next verse. If you're feeling up to it?'

The queen turned back to the piano. Wren hummed her tune, rustling her skirts as she went. '*Da-da-da-da da-da-da-da-da-da-da-da-da-da-daaaaaaa.*'

The queen pressed down on the keys, a single chord erupting like an aria. A nearby soldier poked his head out of an alcove, his eyes widening in disbelief.

Queen Valeska chased that first chord with another, and

then a third, her hands quickening to match Wren, as she leaped into the next verse with gusto.

'*When morning came, Ned's head did ache,*
He rolled from bed, still half awake,
Went up to deck to walk about,
Aaaaaaaand spewed that rum back out!'

The queen threw her head back and laughed, and this time even some of the soldiers joined in. Wren danced a jig around the atrium, bringing the shanty to a close with the help of Valeska's nimble playing. She was still giggling when the song ended. 'That really was quite something!'

Wren sketched a bow. 'Thank you for elevating it.'

The queen stared at the piano. 'I thought music had left me, but perhaps it was simply hiding all along.'

Wren sat down on the bottom step of the grand staircase. 'Can you play something else for me?'

'Nothing that would rival your wonderful sea shanty.'

'Any kind of music will do,' prompted Wren. 'And besides, sea shanties are a bit like rum. If you have too much, you'll get sick.'

The queen chuckled. And then, to Wren's surprise, she turned back to the piano, squaring herself to the keys, like they were a mountain she was about to climb. And so she did. Queen Valeska poured a melody so beautiful into the room that tears pricked the back of Wren's eyes. The notes soared, like a storm cloud swelling in the sky, the crescendo building until it became the thrumming of thunder. Wren's heart beat faster in her chest. The melody turned once more, falling like the first drops of summer rain.

And then it was over, and Wren – to her horror – was crying. She scrubbed her cheeks with her sleeve.

The queen was smiling. 'Careful. Or you'll ruin that beautiful dress.'

'It's not mine,' said Wren.

'I know,' said Valeska. 'They were meant to be for Ansel's bride . . .' She trailed off, her face falling. 'But it seems that was not to be.'

Wren dropped her hand.

Valeska misread the horror on her face. 'It's hard to believe, I suppose. A queen designing dresses. But that was my life once, long before I met Soren.' She smiled, ruefully. 'After my husband died, Alarik encouraged me to return to my passion. He thought it might keep my mind busy. My heart, too.'

Wren stared at the queen. 'The dresses in the room on the fourth floor . . . you designed them?'

The queen nodded.

'They're beautiful,' said Wren.

'I was once very interested in beautiful things.' Valeska looked down at her nightgown, and laughed, sadly. 'Grief can make you feel like you're drowning. All those fancy dresses and furs were my son's attempt at a life raft.' A pause, then. 'One of many.'

The dresses hadn't been for Alarik's sweetheart, after all – they had been for Rose. Each one lovingly designed by his mother. This new information twisted Wren's stomach. She didn't like how it cast Alarik in a different light – not as a brutal king but a worried son. She didn't want to think of him like that.

'Don't look so upset. I'm happy to see them worn,' said the queen, warmly. 'My son tells me you were a friend of Ansel's. That you come from Eana. My husband and I visited there many years ago. We spent a week in Norbrook before Alarik was born.'

'Yes,' said Wren, grasping for a shred of composure. 'My name is Wren. Ansel and I were friends.' She hesitated. 'I'm sorry for what happened to him.'

'Thank you,' said the queen, quietly.

Wren's face fell. She suddenly felt too full, as though a sob was building inside her. There was a heaviness in the air. She had waded into it the moment she had greeted the queen, and as she dwelled in the nearness of Valeska's grief, her own thoughts turned to Banba.

'Why do you look so forlorn?' Valeska's voice interrupted her reverie. The queen smiled, and in the quirk of her lips, Wren saw Alarik. 'You are young yet. The fullness of your life – all that you will love and cherish – is still ahead of you.'

Wren smiled, ruefully. 'I'm grieving someone who hasn't even died yet.'

'Ah.' The queen was silent then, unsettled.

A shadow moved on the first floor. Another soldier peering down on them, no doubt. Wren wondered if it might be Tor.

'Perhaps this person can be saved?' said the queen, hopefully.

Wren almost laughed. 'No,' she said, shaking her head. 'There's nothing left to be done.'

'Then we must be hopeful.' Valeska tipped her head back, her silvery-blond hair brushing the floor as she looked up at the snow-swept dome and the blizzard howling beyond it. 'We must hope for a world beyond this one, where the love we spend in this life will be returned to us tenfold, and the people we gave it to will be waiting for us, with their hearts full of it, when we die.'

Wren frowned. In her experience hoping was easier said than done, and, more often than not, it was dangerous. 'Or we can sing sea shanties. And drink. And dance. And play music while we can.' She gestured at the glass piano. 'Take all the luck we have been given and use it. Before it runs out, too.'

The queen cocked her head. 'I've never thought of it like that before.'

'I find it helps. At least sometimes.' Wren rolled to her feet, conscious of the shadow moving above them. 'It's late. I should go. Thank you for keeping me company.'

'Thank you for the sea shanty,' said the queen. 'And the rest.'

'You're welcome.' Wren made her way up the staircase, smiling at the trill of piano music that wafted after her. She headed towards the hallway where Tor had been skulking, but he was stalking away from her now, trying not to be seen. Well, too late. Wren hurried to catch up with him.

'It's not like you to run away from me,' she huffed, as she

followed him into a room at the end of the hallway. *Especially in dark corridors.*

'I didn't realize we had that kind of rapport,' came a voice Wren was not expecting. Then a pair of pale blue eyes too bright in the darkness.

'Alarik.' Wren took a step backwards. 'I thought you were—' She stopped abruptly, swallowing Tor's name.

'A wise decision,' said the king. 'I'd hate for you to incriminate yourself, or anyone else, any further.' He turned to light a sconce on the wall, the flickering candlelight bringing the room to life. It was full of easels, upon which oil-painted landscapes perched, waiting to be finished.

Wren drifted to one of the Fovarr Mountains. 'The snow looks so real,' she said, raising a finger to touch it.

'Don't.' Alarik flung his hand out to stop her. 'It's not dry.'

Wren turned back to him, fresh horror churning in her gut. 'Please don't tell me these are yours.'

He raised his eyebrows. 'Are they that bad?'

'No. You are not a painter,' said Wren. 'You cannot be a painter.'

'Why not?'

'Because it's way too . . . too . . .'

'Impressive?'

'*Human.*' Wren folded her arms. 'And you are not a human. You are a beast.'

Alarik stepped away from her, his gaze shuttering. For a heartbeat, Wren swore she had wounded him, but then he flashed his canines. 'Even a beast can have a hobby, can they not?'

Wren perched on a stool. 'I liked it better when I didn't know anything about you.'

'I liked it better when you were a speck of nothing back in Ortha,' he shot back. 'But here we are.'

'Why were you spying on me just now?'

'I heard my mother's music.' He paused, frowned. 'I thought it must be a dream.'

Wren relaxed her shoulders. 'You missed the sea shanty, then.'

To her surprise, Alarik chuckled. 'I don't think anyone in Grinstad Palace missed that sea shanty, Wren.'

Wren's cheeks erupted in flames. 'It wasn't meant for you.'

'Nonetheless, I am grateful for it.' To her surprise, Alarik sounded . . . well, *sincere*. 'It's been a long time since I've heard my mother laugh.'

Oh no. The king *was* being sincere. 'Stop,' she said, getting to her feet. 'I don't want to talk about your mother. Your loyalty. Your . . .'

'Humanity?' He cocked a brow. 'Are you afraid it might rub off on you?'

'Oh, please. You don't have any.'

'You're only saying that because you hate me.'

'Of course I hate you!' hissed Wren. 'You made me do blood magic.'

'The blood was mine.'

She jabbed her finger at him. 'You're going to kill my grandmother!'

'Well. Only if you fail.'

Wren briefly considered punching him in the face.

'Go on,' he said, watching her flex her fingers. 'I dare you.'

Wren cracked her knuckles. 'Don't tempt me.'

Alarik turned from her and went to the window, his arms tucked behind his back as he looked out at the raging blizzard. Beyond it, Wren could just make out the frozen pond below. 'When I was a boy and my father was king, he would make time, every week, to come skating with us on that pond,' he said, as though they were in the middle of a perfectly normal conversation. 'It was the best part of my week.' Wren had to stop and look around to make sure he was talking to her. 'I was the worst ice skater you've ever seen, but I've never laughed as hard as I used to laugh back then. I've never felt as free.'

Outside, the blizzard pounded its fists against the window, as if it was trying to break in.

'It seems like something you'd be good at,' said Wren, if only to say something. 'It's cold. Challenging. Dangerous.'

Alarik offered her a pointed look. 'Only to those who drown.'

'*Almost* drown,' Wren corrected him. 'And I was doing pretty well before the ice broke.'

'I know. I was watching you.'

Wren blinked in surprise. She wondered how long he had been watching her before she fell through the ice, and, more importantly, *why* he had been watching her in the first place. 'Why are we talking about ice skating?'

Alarik laid his forehead against the window pane. 'Because you never know how much you'll miss a moment until it's behind you.'

'You still have the pond,' said Wren.

'But I don't have my father.' He ran a hand through his hair, tracing the black line that ran through it. 'The morning after he perished, I woke up with this streak. It matches the one inside me.' He went back to watching the blizzard. 'A hailstorm took my father from me, Wren. An act of nature stronger than any king, any beast. There was nothing I could do about it, nowhere I could channel my rage.' He braced his hands on the window ledge, a breath coming through his nose. Wren noticed he was dressed in black again – another frock coat pristinely cut, with a high collar and buttons of brushed steel. 'But Ansel, my little *brother*, was murdered.'

'By Willem Rathborne,' Wren reminded him.

'In a game that *you* made up,' he said, his voice taking on a dangerous edge. His pale blue eyes were violent and for a fleeting moment, Wren thought he was going to launch off the ledge and tear her apart. 'A game where Ansel was a pawn. You never cared about what would happen to my brother. Heartbreak. Humiliation. *Death.*'

'That's not true,' said Wren, quickly.

'Isn't it?'

She paused, struck by a sudden, horrible realization. It *was* true. She had never considered what would happen to

Ansel after she seized the throne, only what would happen to her. To the witches. Alarik was right. It was her game. And Ansel had been the one to die for it. 'You're right,' she said, quietly, slumping back on to the stool. 'I didn't think about him at all.'

Alarik said nothing, only watched her.

'But that was my rage,' whispered Wren. 'My pain.' She looked up at him, and the rest of it came spilling out. 'Willem Rathborne took my parents from me before I ever knew them. He murdered them in cold blood, took my sister and moulded her into his puppet. And me? I grew up on the edge of the world, where the wind howled me to sleep and the gulls shrieked me awake every morning, without the other half of me. Without Rose. When I came back to Anadawn, all I cared about was the throne. I wanted to seize control of my kingdom and make Rathborne pay for what he'd done. I didn't care about anything else. I didn't *see* anyone else. Not even my own sister.'

Alarik pressed his lips together, considering her words. 'Your loss is what drives you.'

'Not loss,' said Wren. 'Revenge.'

He offered the ghost of a smile. 'We are not so dissimilar.'

This time, Wren didn't argue. 'Maybe not,' she admitted.

'This is the terrible trouble with family. They make you vulnerable.'

'You mean love. It's love that's the problem.'

'A horrible business,' Alarik agreed. 'Just look at my mother.'

Wren nodded, thoughtfully. Then something occurred to her, and it almost made her laugh. 'You know you'll have to marry someone if you want to continue your bloodline?'

'And won't you?'

Wren smirked. 'Twin queens.'

'Ah. Of course.'

'Or you could return Gevra to the ice bears when you're done with it,' said Wren. 'Maybe Borvil would like a go at ruling.'

Alarik glared at her. 'Do you have any idea how ridiculous you sound?'

Wren laughed. 'I'm just trying to be helpful.'

'As ever,' he said, sarcastically. 'I had hoped that Ansel would take care of our bloodline. Anika is too much of a free spirit to commit to anything. Anyone. But my brother was always so eager to marry. So eager to love. Happy to pay the price for it.'

Wren was quiet then, her heart sinking as they returned to Ansel. She had one more truth to surrender, and no matter what happened afterwards, she had to say it. And the king had to hear it. 'I can't save him, Alarik.'

The silence stretched. The blizzard howled. 'I know.'

'I would if I could,' said Wren, and she truly, desperately meant it. 'I *wish* I could.'

'I know that, too.' He stood up, turning his back to her so he could face the blizzard. Or perhaps he was hiding the emotion on his face. 'I'm not ready to let him go,' he said, unable to hide it from his voice. 'Even as he is.'

'I know,' said Wren, coming to her feet. She joined him at the window, afraid to ask the next question, but knowing now she must. 'Are you still going to punish me for it? Are you going to hurt Banba?'

The king turned to look down at her, his icy gaze reflecting the blizzard outside. He opened his mouth to speak – then frowned – as the ground began to tremble.

Wren screamed as the window shattered. Alarik lunged, shoving her away from the exploding shards. They fell to the floor, frantically crawling between toppling easels and falling canvases. They huddled in the corner, their arms thrown around each other for protection as an avalanche came roaring down the Fovarr Mountains and crashed, full force, into Grinstad Palace.

Rose

CHAPTER 44

Sweat dripped down Rose's face and pooled under her dress as she swayed on Storm's back, trying to keep her eyes open. She'd been riding for hours, through the night and into the morning, trusting Storm to lead her home. Finally, just as dawn broke, they had reached the edge of the desert. The sand there petered out into rocky earth, strewn with spiky shrubs and gnarled trees.

They found the Kerrcal Road and followed it east, towards Anadawn.

When the Eshlinn woods appeared in the distance, Rose nearly sagged with relief. She had escaped Kai, and survived the arid desert, and now, at last, she was home. Up ahead, the treetops were shining red and gold. Rose smiled, thinking the rising sun had cast them in its amber glow, but as she drew closer, she began to smell smoke. Charcoal plumes filled the dawning sky, casting ash over the forest like raindrops.

Horror guttered inside Rose as she tasted it on her tongue.

The Eshlinn woods were on fire.

There was no way around the forest – the only way forward was through the trees. Storm trod as far from the flames as possible, but the smoke still found Rose, and her eyes streamed as they galloped, hard and fast, towards the palace.

They passed hundreds of arrows embedded in the trees, some tangled in the branches, while others were still flaming at the tip. Rose's chest tightened as she realized this was no accident. Barron had set fire to her woods. The Arrows were getting close to Anadawn, and he wanted her to know it.

At last, Rose crossed the east perimeter of the Eshlinn woods and spied the golden gates up ahead. A baying crowd had gathered around them. There were at least fifty people, all dressed in red tunics.

She scanned the group as she drew closer. There was no sign of Barron, or the vicious-looking Arrows from Ellendale. These dissenters had come on foot and, mercifully, most appeared to be unarmed.

Rose pushed her hood back. 'Open the gates!'

The Anadawn guards leaped into action. The archers on the ramparts pointed at the crowd. 'Make way for the queen!' shouted the foot soldiers, wielding their swords as they opened the gates. 'Queen Rose has returned!'

'It's the witch queen!' shouted one of the Arrows. 'Look at her snivelling face!'

'Grab her!'

'Pull her down!'

'Shame on you,' Rose cried, as she forced her way through. 'I'm Queen Rose, and you've known me all my life.'

A clump of dirt flew, hitting her cheek.

'Queen Rose, the ragged!' they yelled. 'The soulless!'

'Witches have no place in this kingdom!'

'Barron is coming for you! We will march with him!'

A hand shot out and gripped Rose's ankle.

An archer on the rampart fired, the telltale green feathers streaking through the air before striking her assailant in the shoulder. He dropped to the ground where Storm narrowly avoided trampling him. Rose cleared the rest of the crowd as they fell back, her heart hammering as she vaulted through the golden gates. They slammed shut behind her, but she could still hear the Arrows' cries.

Rose spotted Captain Davers in the fray. 'Davers, where on earth have you been? Disperse those troublemakers before someone else gets hurt!'

'Of course, Your Majesty,' he said, slowly drawing his sword. His eyes darted. 'You should get inside at once.'

'That's exactly what I'm trying to do.' Rose's heart sank as she glanced over her shoulder at the raging crowd and the smoking woods beyond. This was far from the welcome home she had been hoping for.

Rose didn't spare a moment to change out of her filthy dress before rushing to the throne room, where Chapman and Thea were waiting for her.

Thea gathered her into a warm hug. 'Rose, thank the stars you're home!'

'I got your note,' said Rose, pulling back from her. 'Your starcrest found me in the desert.'

'So, that's where you disappeared to after Ellendale,' said Chapman, whose moustache was twitching furiously. 'You nearly gave us all a heart attack. Captain Davers was *distraught* with shame.'

'I sent word as soon as I could,' said Rose. 'I'm sure you understand why I had to be discreet.'

'Well, I do hope your dalliance in the desert was worth it.'

Rose glowered at her steward. 'It was hardly a dalliance, Chapman. Shen Lo and I went to unearth the lost Sunkissed Kingdom. And we succeeded.'

'Oh, some good tidings at last,' said Thea. She glanced at the door. 'Where is Shen? He's never been one to respect the private sanctity of the throne room.'

Rose sighed. 'That's another story entirely.'

Chapman sniffed. 'Well, it will have to wait. We have pressing matters to deal with.'

'I'm aware,' said Rose. 'I just rode through an angry mob.'

'Are you injured?' said Thea, taking her hand. 'I told Captain Davers to frighten them away!'

'He wasn't even at the gates when I arrived. And yes, I'm all right. Just a little shaken.' Rose wrung her hands, the swell of her anxiety rising. 'How bad has it been here? Barron seems to be establishing a firm grip on the south.'

'Our scouts have reported strongholds as far north as Norbrook,' said Thea, grimly. 'The Arrows are few but loud. As you see, they're getting bolder.'

'And the witches here at Anadawn haven't exactly helped matters,' said Chapman, pointedly. 'Your Ortha friends have been throwing their magic around, antagonizing the townspeople of Eshlinn as well as others inside these very palace walls.'

'*Some* of the witches aren't helping,' Thea corrected him.

Rose looked between them. 'Who?'

Thea hesitated. 'Rowena blew Captain Davers off the ramparts when he returned from Ellendale without you.'

'And when the Queensbreath scolded her for it, she went and blew over every stall in the town market!' cried Chapman.

'*What?*'

'Cathal got into a fight with a palace guard yesterday evening,' Thea added. 'Bryony jumped in and enchanted the poor fellow into thinking he was a cat.'

'He nearly drank the kitchen out of milk,' said Chapman, solemnly.

Rose gathered new breath. 'Thea, fetch every tempest out of bed, and tell them to take care of the fire in the woods before it breaches the treeline. Send Rowena to the ramparts. If she wants to terrorize the Arrows, she can use her wind to keep them from climbing the gates.' She raised a finger in warning. 'No harm. No killing.'

'Of course not,' said Thea, both healers seeing eye to eye. She bustled off.

Rose turned back to Chapman. 'Any word from Celeste?'

'She's still in Gevra, trying to corral your wayward sister into coming home, though I gather the Gevran king is proving rather obstinate on the matter,' said the steward, with no small amount of disapproval. 'Captain Pegasi is sailing back there as we speak.'

'Good,' said Rose, with a sigh. 'I don't wish to face this rebellion alone.'

Chapman wrinkled his nose. 'And in the meantime might I suggest you . . . well, bathe?'

Rose looked down at herself, bedraggled and filthy from her journey through the desert. She raked her hands through her tangled hair, feeling a million miles away from the prim and proper queen who had set out on the royal tour barely one week ago.

'I suppose that will take care of one problem, at least.' She would bathe, change and then prepare for the day ahead. For everything to come. With Wren stuck across the Sunless Sea and Shen left behind in the Sunkissed Kingdom, everyone here was looking to Rose to rule. It was just as she had always wanted.

Only she never thought she'd feel so alone.

Wren

CHAPTER 45

Once the avalanche had run its course, and several of the front windows of Grinstad Palace had been smashed to oblivion, Wren and Alarik released each other. They had been huddling in the corner with their arms around each other, waiting – no, *trembling* – for ten endless minutes. Now it was simply a matter of dusting the snow from their shoulders and pretending that it hadn't happened.

The shattered glass had nicked the king's face, drawing a line of blood down his left cheek. He wiped it with his sleeve as he rolled to his feet. 'This is unprecedented,' he muttered, surveying the damage. Snow had piled up everywhere, and there were icicles forming on the ceiling.

Outside the room, soldiers were shouting and running. Alarik snapped his chin up.

'Your mother,' said Wren, but he was already wading across the room. He heaved the door open, pausing to glance at her over his shoulder. 'Go back to your bedroom.'

Wren ran for the dungeons instead, shouting for Banba, but was met by four stone-faced soldiers who swiftly turned her back. The dungeons, at least, had been unharmed by the snowdrift. They were buried so deep under the mountain that not even the wind could get to them.

Reluctantly, Wren returned to the upper floors. She walked the perimeter of the palace looking for Tor, but there was no sign of him anywhere. When she came across Inga, sopping and shivering after crawling out of the avalanche, the guard informed Wren that a group of soldiers had gone out into the mountains. But why she didn't know.

Down in the atrium, the glass piano had been crushed by the snow, but Queen Valeska was safe, if a little shaken. Miraculously, the dome had held, and the blizzard outside had quietened enough for Wren to see the stars. It was a clear night. And yet the air felt heavy. Dark. It was as though the avalanche had left a lingering shadow behind. And though Wren couldn't quite make it out, it raised the hairs on the back of her neck.

Eventually, she returned to her bedchamber. It was at the back of the palace, which meant it was still intact, and someone had even thought to light a fresh fire in the grate. She crawled into bed and buried herself in a mountain of furs, trying to shut out the memory of the avalanche roaring through the palace, and Alarik's arms around her as they had tried to survive it. Sleep found her quickly, but in the darkness of her dreams she saw that woman in the mountains again, the one who wore her face.

This time, she was laughing. Blood dripped from the corners of her mouth as she turned away from Wren and stalked towards the shattered windows of Grinstad Palace, bringing the howling wind with her.

Wren woke to the sound of banging. She sat bolt upright in bed just in time to see Tor poke his head around the door.

'Sorry,' he said, awkwardly. 'I thought you'd be awake by now.'

Wren glanced at the window, where the white sky was wincingly bright. It was well after sunrise. 'So did I,' she croaked, as she threw the covers off and got out of bed. 'Come in.'

Tor closed the door behind him and stood with his back against it. He looked like hell – his hair was a mess and his grey eyes were shot with red. His uniform was askew, the collar crumpled and his shirt untucked from his trousers.

'I take it you haven't slept,' said Wren.

'Not a wink.' He stalked towards the fireplace, which was full of ash, and set about building a fire.

'Leave it,' said Wren.

'You'll freeze.'

'I'm fine.' She laid a hand on his shoulder. 'I looked for you last night, but I couldn't find you.'

Tor fell back on his heels to look up at her. 'The avalanche disturbed the beasts. They scattered into the mountains. They were rabid. *Terrified*. Elske, too. I've never seen her like that before. Even after the snow settled, it was like there was something still chasing her.'

Wren wrung her hands. 'Poor darling. Did you manage to wrangle the others?'

'Most of them,' he said, grimly. 'But this morning, I received word from my sister, Hela. The same thing is happening on Carrig. The animals are turning feral. My sisters are struggling to control them.'

'But Carrig is miles away from here,' said Wren, remembering what the soldier had told her about his home. 'And it's an island. How could they have been affected by the avalanche?'

'I don't know.' Tor rubbed a hand across his jaw. 'But I've got a bad feeling about it.'

That made two of them. But Wren didn't say so as she paced the room, trying to gather her thoughts.

Tor set the fire alight, then stood to face her. 'I have to go home. For a week at least, maybe more.'

'Of course,' said Wren, trying to hide her disappointment. 'You have to be with your sisters. They need you.'

Tor kept his gaze on hers. 'Alarik has released me from service.'

'That was surprisingly good of him.'

'I've served Gevra since I was twelve years old,' Tor went on. 'I've sustained more scratches and broken bones from beasts than you can imagine. Tamed the worst of them. Fought alongside them. For my king and my country. I was ready to die for them.'

Wren listened to the passion in his voice, and secretly wished that all that loyalty – blood-born and bone-deep – belonged to her.

'I've never asked the crown for anything. Not from Alarik,

as a king. Or as the man who was once my closest friend. Until today.' He inhaled deeply. The storm in his gaze had settled, and behind it, there shone such pure and bold affection that Wren's breath caught in her throat. 'I asked him to let you go, Wren. To let your grandmother go.'

'Oh, Tor,' said Wren, quietly. Perhaps she had some of that loyalty after all.

'I'm sorry I can't do better than that,' he went on. 'That all I can offer you is his consideration. But time is better than a noose, Wren. And who knows? Maybe I'll make it back before—'

Wren took his hand in hers, softly tracing the callouses as she laid it against her chest. 'It's enough. It's *more* than enough. Thank you.'

He dipped his head and she rose to her tiptoes, touching her forehead against his. For a moment, the memory of her and Alarik huddling together intruded upon her. 'I'm sorry for everything that got us here. You were right to be angry at me. I was a fool to toy with death.'

Tor raised his chin, their noses almost brushing. 'Forgive yourself.'

'Only if you promise to do the same,' she whispered. 'I know you still punish yourself for Ansel's death.'

He huffed a laugh. 'Forgiveness is a long road, Wren.'

'Perhaps we'll meet at the end of it someday. And finish what we started.'

In another place. Another lifetime, perhaps.

Tor pulled his arms around her and pressed a kiss into the

crown of her head. Wren breathed him in, relishing the scent of alpine and adventure that made her heart sing.

And then, all too soon, Tor was gone, and she was left staring at the door, feeling like the last candle flame inside her had been snuffed out and the darkness was creeping in. Outside, a cold wind blew, making her feel more alone than ever.

Sometime later, Wren was summoned to the throne room. This time, Alarik sent two soldiers to escort her. Nerves pooled in her throat as she descended the staircase in the atrium. It looked strangely empty without the glass piano. The carpets were damp and the windows had been boarded up, but most of the snow had been shovelled away and, outside, the soldiers had managed to plough a road all the way down to the black gates.

The guards deposited Wren outside the doors to the throne room, leaving her to enter alone. She lingered in the doorway of the huge, hollow room.

'Come now, it's not like you to be so timid.' Alarik's voice echoed down the draughty chamber. He was sitting on his throne, wearing an embroidered blue frock coat with silver buttons to match his magnificent silver-branch crown. It seemed to wink at Wren as she approached.

She searched the yawning shadows as she went, scouring the space behind each towering pillar, but there were no soldiers in here. No beasts. Not even Borvil. Only the king, and to his left, perched on the arm of his throne, his sister Anika, wearing a beautiful green velvet gown.

'What's going on?' said Wren, warily. 'Is this some kind of trick?'

At close range, Alarik looked just as exhausted as Tor had been, though his hair was as impeccable as ever.

'No tricks.' He tapped the crown on his head. 'Official Gevran business.'

'Alarik and I have discussed you at length –' Anika took over, the train of her dress trailing after her as she came down the dais towards Wren – 'including what you did to our brother.' A meaningful pause. 'What you did for our mother.' Her face softened fractionally. 'And I'll admit I even discussed you with Celeste, who is a darling, though not as subtle as she might think.' Anika tossed her long crimson hair, looking down at Wren with those laser-bright eyes. 'And for my part, I no longer desire your imminent death.'

Wren raised her brows. 'Well, that feels like an improvement . . .'

'A marginal one,' said Anika, pointedly.

'I'll take it.'

'I suppose you know a certain soldier came to speak on your behalf this morning,' said Alarik, from up on the dais. 'I suspect it's the same one you like to follow down dark hallways.'

Wren's cheeks burned.

Anika smirked. 'You wily witch. How you got Captain Iversen to fall in love with you, I will never know.'

'Must be all that humanity,' said Alarik, mildly. 'Shame you can't spare some for me.'

Wren fought the urge to bite back. 'Get to the point.'

'I have decided to return your grandmother to you.'

Wren blinked. Then stared, waiting for the punchline.

'Under two conditions.'

She forced herself to hold her tongue, as he continued. 'The first is that the witch's hands will be tied until you set sail, so neither of you try anything untoward along the way. We've had enough bad weather to contend with, without the tempest's input.'

'Very well,' said Wren, happy to meet the condition. 'And the second?'

'Your sister is a healer, is she not?' said Anika. 'As I recall, she made quite a speech about her craft on Ansel's ill-fated wedding day.'

'Yes . . .' said Wren, slowly this time. If they thought Rose was ever going to set foot in this hellish place, then they were delusional, but she wasn't about to say as much.

Alarik chuckled.

'What's so funny?'

'That look on your face,' he said, rising to come down the steps. 'We don't expect Queen Rose to make the journey here. Frankly, I wouldn't trust it, even if you offered it. But once things have settled down here, we will come to her. With Ansel. Perhaps she can do what you cannot.'

'And if she can't heal him?' said Wren, knowing already that it was an impossibility. That Rose would never dabble in blood magic even if it was. Wren would sooner spell her sister into a year of slumber.

Alarik shrugged. 'Then we will go to war.'

'Are you kidding?' said Wren.

He flashed a sharp smile. 'Let's hope we don't have to find out.' He extended his hand to her. 'Do we have an accord?'

Wren took his hand, the lie easy on her tongue. 'Yes, we do.'

Alarik made a point of escorting Wren to the dungeons, with his soldiers following close behind him. Though he had insisted on coming, he was unusually silent on the journey, his jaw tight as he stalked ahead of her. When they reached Banba's cell, he stood aside and ordered a guard to open it. Roused by the commotion, Banba lumbered to her feet.

'Wren?' she croaked, as she shuffled into the light. 'What's going on?'

Wren hurtled towards her grandmother, dragging her out of the cell and pulling her into an embrace. 'You're free, Banba,' she said, her voice catching on a sob. 'We're going home.'

'Well, not quite yet,' came Alarik's voice, from behind them.

Wren spun around. 'You lied to me.'

He raised a hand to quell her rising temper. 'My word remains true. But before you leave, I want to show you something that was unearthed in the avalanche.'

'No,' said Banba, drawing back for him. 'Whatever it is, we want no part in it.'

'Banba,' said Wren, trying to calm her. 'It's all right.'

'It's the darkness,' hissed her grandmother. 'It's here. In these tunnels.'

Wren turned back to Alarik. 'What is it?'

He hesitated, a hand coming to the pommel of his sword. 'I don't know,' he said, uneasily. 'I was hoping you could tell me.'

'Fine, then. I'll go with you.' Wren fixed her grandmother's cloak around her shoulders. 'Wait here, Banba. I'll come back for you.'

'You will not,' grunted Banba, as she pushed past her, putting herself between Wren and the king. 'Lead the way, Felsing. Whatever it is, let's get it over with.'

They followed Alarik down the winding tunnel, to a room that was all too familiar to Wren. She glanced around, but there were no beasts skulking in the darkness. No soldiers either. 'Why are we back down here? Is it something to do with Ansel?'

Alarik shook his head. 'Ansel is locked in my bedchamber, where he can't get into any trouble. This is . . . something else.'

The back of Wren's neck began to prickle. She swore her heart was beating slower. The more she walked, the heavier her legs became, like she was wading through quicksand.

'Can you feel it now, little bird?' wheezed Banba.

Alarik paused with his hand on the door. He looked over his shoulder, fear darkening his pale blue eyes. Wren felt the same terror spreading inside her as they followed him into the little room.

'Rotting hell,' cursed Banba.

Wren blinked furiously, trying to make sense of what she was looking at. Before her stood the biggest block of ice she had ever seen. Inside it, floated a girl, frozen to death.

She was wearing Wren's face.

Celeste's vision had come to pass.

Wren stumbled backwards, flattening herself against the wall. 'Who *is* that?'

'My soldiers found her buried deep in the Fovarr Mountains,' whispered Alarik, as though he was afraid he might wake her. 'The avalanche must have loosened the ice.' He looked between them, before settling on Wren. 'You don't know who she is?'

But shock had stolen Wren's words. And her breath. She could only shake her head in horrified confusion.

It was Banba who answered him, with four world-altering words. 'That is Oonagh Starcrest.'

Oonagh Starcrest. The lost witch queen.

The name twisted around Wren like a rope. It tugged her towards the ice, and she went, like a moth drawn to a flame. Alarik tried to pull her back, but she shook him off. She raised her finger to trace the outline of the face that had haunted her dreams. The face she knew she had somehow unburied.

'Wren, no!' shouted Banba, but it was too late.

Wren pressed her finger against the block, and three things happened in quick succession.

An almighty crack fissured across the ice.

Oonagh Starcrest opened her eyes.

And Wren fell to the ground unconscious.

Rose

CHAPTER 46

Rose's first dinner back at Anadawn was almost as stressful as her journey home. Captain Davers had refused to attend, citing the ongoing turmoil in the capital, but Rose suspected it was his dislike of Rowena – and the rest of the witches – that sent him out to the ramparts with his soldiers. Rowena, for her part, had sauntered in late for dinner, looking even smugger than usual.

'Who cares if Davers isn't here?' she said, when Rose informed her of the captain's absence. 'He's about as useful as a sand crab.'

'If you keep telling him that, the less likely he is to protect you,' said Thea, wearily.

'I don't need protection,' Rowena shot back. 'I'm a tempest, remember? I can do whatever I like.'

Chapman harrumphed. 'It's exactly that kind of attitude that brings the Arrows to our gates.'

'And puts out your fires,' said Rowena, sending a gust of wind to ruffle his hair.

'Even so,' said Thea. 'You are not doing us any favours.'

Rowena narrowed her eyes. 'Whose side are you even on?'

'Peace!' said Rose, throwing her hands up. 'We are on the side of peace!'

At the other end of the table, Tilda wouldn't stop asking about Shen, and though Rose had filled the Ortha witches in on the extraordinary events of the Sunkissed Kingdom earlier that afternoon, she couldn't tell them when they might see Shen again. He had his own battles to fight, and Rose had hers.

'But he can't just forget about us,' cried Tilda. 'We're his family, too!'

'I know that,' said Rose. 'But he's a king now.'

'So what?' said Rowena, around a mouthful of roast chicken. 'What does that change?'

'Everything.' Rose reached for her goblet, letting the heady red wine soothe the sting of her worry. 'It changes everything.'

Her anxiety only worsened when conversation turned to Wren. 'When is *she* coming home?' Tilda asked, for the hundredth time that day. 'She's been gone ages.'

'I don't know,' said Rose, skewering a pea with her fork. 'Soon.'

'With Celeste? And Banba?'

Rose exchanged a glance with Thea. 'Of course,' she said, but there was no certainty in her voice.

Thea patted Tilda's hand. 'All we can do now is hope, love.'

Tilda scowled at her mashed potatoes. 'But what if Wren's frozen to death by now? Or what if the snow tigers and the wolves are using her as a chew toy!'

Rose closed her eyes, trying to block out the images Tilda had conjured. She had been checking the hand mirror all day, but the sapphires never glowed, and Wren's face never appeared.

'Or maybe King Alarik fed her to his—'

'Thank you, Tilda,' said Thea, with uncharacteristic sharpness. 'Rose has enough to worry about without you adding nightmares about her sister.'

'It's a shame Wren isn't here,' said Rowena. 'She wouldn't chastise us for defending ourselves against the Arrows. She'd be joining in.'

'You aren't defending yourselves!' Chapman burst out. 'You're going out there to deliberately antagonize them.'

'*They* are the ones antagonizing us!' fumed Rowena. 'Or didn't you hear all that commotion at the gates this morning?'

Rose set her fork down. 'You have to be responsible with your magic, Rowena.'

The tempest snorted. 'Since when?'

Rose glared at her. 'Since I am trying to rule this country, not tear it apart.'

'This country has been broken for centuries,' said Rowena, ripping off a strip of chicken with her teeth. 'If the Arrows want to fear us, then let's give them something to fear.' Her smile turned feral. 'Just wait until Big Bad Edgar Barron finds out about Shen Lo. A warrior, with an entire kingdom of secret witches.'

'The Arrows don't care about the desert,' said Tilda,

sitting up in her chair. 'They only care about fighting against Anadawn.' Her blue eyes flickered fearfully in the candlelight. 'And now I'm the only warrior left to defend us.'

'Nonsense,' said Rowena. 'No matter what happens, the witches of Ortha will band together, like we always have.'

'*And* you'll start getting along with the Anadawn soldiers,' said Rose. 'We must all stand together against the Arrows. They are our shared enemy.'

Rowena took a slug of wine. 'If you couldn't even convince your Captain of the Guard to come to dinner, how the hell are you going to convince him, and his army, to fight alongside us?'

'It's *my* army,' Rose reminded her.

'Well, then you'd better tell them to get ready,' said Rowena. 'Because the next time those Arrows come knocking at our gates, I'm going to show them what true power looks like.'

'Let's hope it doesn't come to that,' said Rose, and for the first time all evening, the table fell silent. In the sudden quiet, the truth was far too loud. She knew in her heart that the time for hope was long past.

Wren
CHAPTER 47

With Oonagh Starcrest's gaze burning into the back of her mind, Wren plummeted into darkness. Down, down, down she fell, through days and months and years, entire centuries flipping past her like pages in a book. And then, at last, the sun dawned, and the ground hardened beneath her feet. She opened her eyes to summer-green grass, and in the distance, a familiar white palace rising towards the clouds. Before her stood two sisters arguing on the banks of the Silvertongue River.

They both wore Wren's face, and so she knew them at once: Ortha and Oonagh Starcrest, the first twin queens of Eana. Somehow, when she placed her hand against the ice that held the frozen body of Oonagh Starcrest, Wren had shattered a wall between them, and fallen into her ancestor's memory. She was a ghost here, in this long-ago place. Watching history unfold before her eyes.

Ortha and Oonagh circled each other like wild animals, twin crowns of golden filigree resting on their heads.

'Your actions have brought shame on yourself, Oonagh,' shouted Ortha. 'You have brought shame on our family. Our ancestors. On all the witches of Eana.' She flung her arms wide, a gust of wind rising with her anger. 'For the good of our noble country, I cast you out. From the throne. From the palace. From this kingdom.' Her voice broke, pain shining in her emerald eyes. 'Don't you see, Oonagh? You've given me no choice. You cannot come back from this.'

Wren moved around the twins until she could make out Oonagh's face. It was twisted in hatred.

'Go now before the soldiers come,' said Ortha. 'Don't make this any harder than it already is, sister.'

'*Sister!*' Oonagh recoiled from the word. 'You are no sister of mine, Ortha,' she sneered. 'You have stolen my crown and my kingdom! I curse you for your disloyalty. For your cowardice.' She pointed a finger at her sister as she backed towards the river and began to mutter under her breath. Even in memory, Wren felt the wrongness of the spell. It swelled between them, like a cloud of ash.

'*With my blood and these words spoken, let Eana's magic now be broken!*'

Ortha's hands came around her middle. 'Stop,' she heaved, but it was already too late. The wind died as her magic splintered. The tempest strand was leaving her. 'Oonagh, *no*. Don't do this!'

Oonagh smiled as she teetered on the edge of the river. Blood poured from her mouth, her nose . . . and then her eyes. She had used it all to curse her sister; the spell so powerful it was killing her. 'If I can't have the throne, then neither can you.'

'NO!' Ortha lunged at her sister.

Oonagh's eyes went wide as Ortha slammed into her, her arms pinwheeling as she fought for balance on the edge of the Silvertongue.

'Oonagh!' Ortha reached for her sister's skirts, but she was too weak to pull her back.

Wren lunged for Oonagh at the same moment, but she was just a ghost here, her hands passing through her ancestor like the wind. She could only watch in horror as Oonagh fell into the Silvertongue River, her teeth bared in a dying scream, blood still glistening on her teeth.

The memory changed, then – rushing, moving like the river, and Wren went with it. Below her, she watched Oonagh's body sink down into the Silvertongue. And then, suddenly, it changed. One minute, she was a young woman, flailing – *drowning* – and the next, she was disappearing, one more drop of blood magic twisting her into a writhing merrow, six gaping gills slashed into the column of her neck.

Oonagh Starcrest stopped drowning and began to swim. The vision got further and further away, Wren floating into the sky like a cloud. She looked down on the world and saw her ancestor like a streak of silver arcing across the map.

And then Wren was standing on the shores of Gevra, watching Oonagh emerge from the icy water as a woman once more, with frost in her hair and icicles dangling from her sleeves. She walked on bare feet, the shape of her getting smaller as she passed into the snow-swept mountains. Wren tried to follow her but the vision faded, until all she could hear was Oonagh's ancient voice ringing in the wind.

'*I bind the witches' curse inside me until my bones are free. As long as my blood is frozen, so too will it be.*'

Wren woke with a gasp. She was lying on the dungeon floor, in a freezing pool of water. A blade flashed above her. Alarik's sword was drawn, the king standing over Wren's body as he pointed it at Oonagh Starcrest.

The block of ice had melted. Oonagh stood – alive – in the space where it had just been, baring her bloodstained teeth. Wren's mind reeled, as the threads of the past came apart around her. Oonagh Starcrest wasn't dead. Although Ortha had pushed her sister into the Silvertongue River, she had not drowned. Instead, Oonagh had fled to Gevra, where she had been all along, not dead but frozen deep in the Fovarr Mountains, sustained by blood magic.

'Get back, you cursed creature!' shouted Banba. 'You have no power here!'

Oonagh flexed her fingers. 'Move or die, witch.'

Banba didn't flinch. 'This is a new world, Oonagh. You are not welcome here.'

Oonagh threw her head back and laughed. 'I am power incarnate, old woman. All these years, my curse has slumbered inside me. But now it is broken. The five strands of magic, once frozen, are now whole again. And I will use them to take revenge on Eana. To tear your new world apart and remake it as my own. With magic the likes of which you've never seen.'

Alarik raised his sword. 'You will not leave this room alive.'

Oonagh smiled as she took a step towards him.

Banba turned on the king. 'Free me,' she hissed. 'Quickly!'

Wren scrambled to her feet as Alarik brought his sword down, slashing the binds around Banba's wrists in one clean swipe. Her grandmother flung her arms out and fired a sharp gust at Oonagh's chest. 'I said, get back!'

Oonagh slammed into the wall, cracking her head against the stone. Banba gritted her teeth, using every ounce of her magic to keep her pinned there. Her knees began to tremble. Wren could tell her time in the dungeons had weakened her magic.

Blood streamed from the fresh wound in Oonagh's head. She turned her cheek to the wall and tasted it, her skin glowing as she swallowed.

A rush of panic coursed through Wren. She lunged for the door and wrenched it open. 'Alarik, call your soldiers! Now!'

Oonagh raised her palm and slammed it shut before the king loosed the command. She came towards them, pushing against Banba's waning wind.

Banba shut her eyes, every ounce of her magic straining to keep Oonagh at bay. 'Run!' she heaved. 'Wren, go!'

Oonagh looked between them. 'I've never sacrificed a witch before.'

Wren whirled around, desperate, searching. There were no weapons in sight, no sand, or earth. No time. Only Alarik's sword. In a fit of desperation, she opened her hand and slashed her palm across it. Alarik leaped backwards. 'What are you doing?'

Wren ignored him, trying desperately to come up with a blood spell that would stop Oonagh. Something that would cut her at the knees, give them time to get away.

Banba whipped her head around. 'Wren! Don't!'

Her grandmother's concentration faltered, allowing Oonagh to close the gap between them. She grabbed Banba by the throat, using her free hand to send out her own howling gust. Wren screamed as she was thrown backwards. Alarik landed on top of her, his sword spinning across the floor.

The wind became a wall. Wren beat her fists against it, shouting for her grandmother. 'BANBA!'

Oonagh picked up the king's sword. Banba flailed in her grip, out of magic and out of breath. With the last of her strength, she turned her head, her emerald gaze finding Wren's. There was no fear in it, only love, as fierce and bright as Wren had ever seen. And then the sword came down in a flash of silver, and Banba's body was slumped on the floor and Wren was screaming again, her grandmother's blood racing towards her in crimson ribbons.

Oonagh knelt and soaked her palms in the blood, her skin glowing as she absorbed it. Her lips moved, and the wind got stronger. The walls trembled as she gathered new power, the strands of her magic knitting themselves together until lightning blazed behind her eyes. She turned away from Banba's broken body and stalked through the wind, dragging Alarik up by his collar to yank the crown off his head. She settled it on her own. 'There,' she purred, as she flung him across the room. 'That's better.'

She looked down on Wren. 'I'll spare you once, little witch, for casting blood magic and waking me from my slumber. But do not cross me again.' Wren was trembling too hard to speak, pain and rage and fear making a knot in her throat. Oonagh crouched down, until Wren could see the shadows moving beneath her skin. Something inside Wren writhed in answer.

'You look just like my sister.' Oonagh dropped her gaze to Wren's bleeding palm, a smirk tugging at her lips. 'But you remind me of myself.'

And then she was gone, sweeping through the door like a wraith and making the mountain tremble as she went. Icicles fell from the ceiling and shattered around Wren as she crawled towards her grandmother and cradled her head in her lap.

'Banba,' she sobbed. 'Banba, wake up.' Her grandmother's eyes stared unseeing at the ceiling, the last wash of colour fading from her cheeks. 'Banba, *please*,' she begged. 'Please, don't leave me.'

An icicle shattered by Wren's foot, cutting her ankle. Another nicked her cheek, but she barely noticed. She was looking into her grandmother's eyes, praying for a spark. The ceiling began to crumble, plumes of dust and shale stinging her eyes.

A hand closed around Wren's arm. 'Move,' said Alarik. 'The mountain's coming down.'

Wren shook him off. 'I'm not leaving her.'

'Wren, she's gone. We have to go.'

'I don't care! Leave me be.'

The mountain rumbled, the crash and thud of falling rock

getting closer and closer. There was dust everywhere. Wren's eyes were so blurry she couldn't see anything beyond the shape of her grandmother dead in her arms, and her blood painting the stones red. She thought the king had left her, but then she felt his hands under her arms, pulling her away. She tried to fight but grief was in her bones now, making them heavy. Banba slid from her lap, as she was lifted to her feet.

'*Move*,' growled Alarik.

Wren stumbled as he pushed her towards the door. He grabbed her waist and carried her over the threshold, just as the ceiling caved in. Wren turned to go back, but Alarik tightened his grip, dragging her down the narrow passageway as rocks thundered to the ground behind them.

'Stop fighting me!' he shouted. 'Come on, witch, save yourself!' He dragged her on, weathering her punches. 'That's what she would want. She told you to run!'

Alarik's words jolted something inside of Wren. She remembered her grandmother's plea, and the last spark of her determination kindled to life. She picked up her feet, stumbling into a run. The king hurried alongside her, both of them matching each other stride for stride as Oonagh tore the mountain down, burying the catacombs with rubble and ice.

Wren fought for every breath, but she didn't allow herself to slow down, or to think about what she was leaving behind her. She reached the end of the tunnel and flung herself at the staircase, the steps trembling underneath her as she scrabbled on her hands and knees, climbing for the palace.

Alarik was behind her, his hand pressed to her back, urging her higher, faster.

And then marbled ground was before them and they were on their feet again, staggering into the sunlit atrium. The dome had shattered, the fallen glass glistening across the floor like diamonds. Soldiers and beasts lay scattered among them, some groaning. Some dead.

The doors were swinging on their hinges, revealing the snow-swept gardens beyond.

Oonagh Starcrest was gone. She had blasted her way through Grinstad Palace, leaving a trail of destruction in her wake. The mountain had finally settled, but the wind was picking up again. Pieces of glass lifted into the air and swirled into a tornado, gathering speed at an alarming rate. Wren stood frozen in the centre of it, watching the shards get bigger and faster and—

'Wren.' Alarik's hand fell heavy on her shoulder. 'Stop doing that.'

Wren blinked. 'Doing what?'

The wind faltered. The glass hovered in mid-air, casting tiny rainbows along the ivory walls.

'It's you,' said Alarik. 'You're making the storm.'

Wren stared down at her fists. She uncurled them, and the wind died. The glass fell, and all was still. 'Oh,' she whispered, swaying on her feet. 'That's new.'

This time, when she passed out, the king caught her.

Rose

CHAPTER 48

Rose stood on the banks of the Silvertongue, watching Ortha Starcrest circle her sister, Oonagh. The air rang with the sound of their anger. When Oonagh raised her finger to cast her curse, Rose felt the words guttering through her soul. She cried out, begging to be free of this strange nightmare, but it pulled her closer, until she was standing on the edge of the river, watching blood pour from Oonagh's mouth.

Ortha lunged, shoving her sister. Oonagh screamed as she fell, pulling Rose down with her. And yet, in those endless seconds before she hit the water, Rose could have sworn it was Wren who had gripped her skirts and dragged her down, down, down, into that unforgiving darkness . . .

'Rose, love? Can you hear me?'

Rose woke with a gasp. She blinked, trying to remember where she was. Her heart was hammering in her throat, but she was safe in her bed at Anadawn Palace, cast in a warm shaft of morning sunlight.

Thea was sitting beside her, a gentle hand resting on her arm. 'You were crying in your sleep.'

'It's Wren.' Rose winced as she sat up. Her head was throbbing awfully. She reached for the hand mirror under her pillow, but the sapphires were dim. There was still no sign of her sister. 'I think she's in trouble.'

Rose couldn't make sense of the rest of the nightmare, but the part about her sister was so troubling, so *real*, that she was sure it must be a sign. An ill omen.

Thea grimaced. 'I'm afraid we can't worry about Wren right now, Rose.' She looked to the window. 'Barron's army have reached Eshlinn sooner than expected.'

'Goodness.' Rose threw the covers off and ran to the window. Beyond the golden gates, half the Eshlinn woods had been reduced to blackened stumps. But the air was still hazy, fresh smoke blowing in from across the Silvertongue. She stuck her head out, a cry gathering in her chest when she saw that the streets of Eshlinn were lit up in an amber blaze.

'What on earth is Barron doing?'

'He's laying siege to the capital,' said Thea, coming to her side. 'And punishing anyone who doesn't join his cause.'

The distant sound of screaming reached them on the wind. The ordinary people of Eshlinn were fleeing their homes in terror. Rose drew back from her window and bolted across the room. She slung on her dressing gown before wrenching the door open. She took the stairwell two steps at a time, shouting for her soldiers, her witches.

Chapman met her in the hallway. His hair was mussed and his eyes were glazed as though he, too, had just been startled from sleep.

'Call the tempests! Send them down to the river, at once. Eshlinn is burning!' said Rose, in a bluster. 'And where on earth is Captain Davers? Tell him to evacuate the city, to bring as many people as he can to Anadawn. They may shelter here while we mount our defence of the palace.'

She spun around, her eyes wild and darting. The hallway was full of guards, rushing to and fro. 'Wake the witches!' she shouted, scattering them in every direction. 'Wake everyone!'

'Rose, love.' Thea tugged her aside, her voice low and urgent. 'You should send word to Shen Lo. We don't know how many Arrows Barron has tempted to his cause, but we do know they do not fight fairly. We must use every soldier and witch at our disposal to make sure Anadawn doesn't fall.'

Rose was already shaking her head. 'Shen won't make his people fight, Thea. And I won't ask him to. And besides, he has his own battle to fight back in the Sunkissed Kingdom.'

A battle that Shen might well have lost. Rose pushed that worry from her mind. She couldn't afford to think of Shen or Wren right now. Not while Eshlinn was burning under her watch.

Thea frowned. 'He would want to know about this.'

'I can't think about what Shen Lo wants right now,' said Rose, stepping away from her. 'I have to defend my kingdom.'

Already the screams from Eshlinn were getting louder, each one burrowing into her heart. Rose's magic flared, thrumming like a drumbeat inside her. She wished her healing power was strong enough to reach across the river and blanket the entire city, to protect all those terrified people as they fled their homes. But the fire raged on, and all Rose could do was watch her city burn, as Barron and his Arrows drew ever closer.

Wren

CHAPTER 49

When Wren awoke, scared and shivering in Alarik Felsing's arms, she desperately wished she could go back to sleep. In the darkness, there had been no pain, no memory of what had happened in Grinstad Palace or what she had lost in the mountain underneath it. Now she was back in the atrium, surrounded by shards of broken glass, and staring up at the king of Gevra.

He was frowning at her. 'Can you stop passing out? It's highly inconvenient.'

Wren sat bolt upright, nearly smashing her forehead into his nose. Her skin flared white-hot, and for a heartbeat, it felt like the sun had melted into her bloodstream. She turned her hands over, looking for a telltale glow, but they were pale and trembling. Magic pooled in her stomach and her throat, like it was trying to burst its way out. *What the hell?*

She leaped to her feet and began to pace, trying to walk off the strange fizzing sensation inside her. The wind began to pick up.

'Stop doing that!' said Alarik. He looked wretched, his

once pristine frock coat now ripped at the shoulder and covered in dust. His hair was a sopping mess, and there was a bruise blooming on his jaw from where a falling rock had hit him. He stalked towards Wren. 'Control your magic before you tear the rest of my palace down.'

'I don't know how.' Wren squeezed her fingers in and out of fists. 'But Oonagh broke the witches' curse,' she said, more to herself than him. 'She must have done something to me.' Wren could feel the strands of her magic writhing inside her, the crafts of seeing, healing, fighting, tempesting and enchanting, all trying to braid themselves together. She wondered if somewhere across the Sunless Sea, this was happening to Rose and the other witches, too.

But beneath the five strands of witchcraft, Wren was dimly aware of another darker strand weaving itself inside her. *Blood sacrifice*. 'Shit,' she hissed. 'Shit, shit, *shit*.'

The wind howled.

The walls shook.

'I SAID THAT'S ENOUGH!' bellowed Alarik.

'Don't you dare yell at me!' Wren whirled on him, her anger rising like a maelstrom. The wind rose with it, her tempest strand riding the swell of her emotions. 'This is your fault! You took Oonagh Starcrest out of the mountain! You unburied her! You brought her here!'

'*Me?*' Alarik's eyes flashed. 'You're the one who woke her up! She *said* that. I heard her.' He raked his hands through his hair, losing the dregs of his composure. 'And how was I to know you had some *other* twin secretly living in my mountains?'

'She's not my twin,' Wren snapped. 'She's my ancestor. And she's supposed to have died over a thousand years ago.'

Alarik barked a mirthless laugh. 'That's *much* better! She's just a wrathful undead magical ancestor hell-bent on destroying my palace!'

'Who cares about your stupid palace,' heaved Wren. 'My grandmother is *dead*.' Those four words cut a jagged line right through Wren's heart, the pain of Banba's death making her breath shallow. She clutched her chest, trying to breathe, but more pain swept in, and she realized with dawning horror that she was dangerously close to breaking down. 'I can't stand another minute in this cursed place!' She spun on her heel and stalked towards the doors, bringing the wind with her.

'Get back here!' Alarik marched after her into the courtyard. 'You made this mess and you're going to fix it!'

'This is *your* mess,' spat Wren. It was snowing again but she barely noticed. 'You're the one who made me use blood magic in the first place. That's what woke Oonagh up.'

'You said you could do the spell,' Alarik reminded her. 'You *volunteered* yourself. You never told me how big the risk was. How bad it could end up.'

'It's *forbidden blood magic*,' hissed Wren. 'Use your brain. The clue is in the name!'

Alarik gritted his teeth. 'Watch that viper's tongue when you speak to me, witch. You're still in my kingdom.'

'Don't you mean Oonagh's kingdom?' Wren shot back.

'Say that again,' he said, coming towards her. 'I dare you.'

'I'm done with your dares, Alarik.' It was only then that Wren noticed the white wall that surrounded them. She was so angry she had accidentally brewed a blizzard. It howled in her ears, spat snow in her hair. 'In the end, it was all for nothing.' Her shoulders sagged under the weight of Banba's death. Hot tears prickled in her eyes. 'My grandmother is dead. And I can't even retrieve her broken body.' She cut her eyes at Alarik. 'Are you happy now?'

'You tell me, Wren.' He took another step towards her. 'My little brother is an undead corpse stuck in an endless time-loop.' Then another. 'And my palace is all but wrecked thanks to your unhinged ancestor.'

'Good,' said Wren, shouting over the wind. 'You deserve it.'

'Drop your blizzard!'

'No!'

He grabbed her shoulders. '*Enough*,' he growled.

Wren twisted her fingers in his collar, threatening to choke him. The blizzard roiled, shoving them closer. There was snow in Alarik's hair, on his face. A single white flake on his bottom lip. 'I hate you,' she hissed. 'I hate you more than anyone I've ever met.'

'And you think I care?' he sneered. 'I hate you, too.'

'Tyrant,' said Wren, rising to her tiptoes.

'*Brat*,' he shot back.

She jutted her chin out. 'Wretch.'

He dipped his head. '*Witch*.'

'So what?' she said, her gaze falling to that single snowflake on his lip.

He moved his hands up her neck, trapping her face between them. 'Wren.' His fingers slid into her hair, holding her still. 'Stop. It.'

'Make. Me.'

And then they were kissing. Wren didn't know why she licked the snowflake from his bottom lip, or why he opened his mouth to her, seizing the kiss. But now, it was too late. The spark had been ignited, and they stood in its fire, letting it consume them.

Alarik Felsing knew how to kiss. There was a quiet ferocity to his passion, the way he held her tightly against him, how he angled her head to claim her mouth. And Wren let him, melting as his tongue found hers. She nipped his bottom lip with her teeth, chasing the movement with her tongue until he groaned into her mouth. They kissed again – harder, hungrier – both of them gasping and clinging to each other like they were drowning, and this one kiss, made out of pain and anger, was their only salvation.

The storm grew as the kiss deepened. Wren's magic erupted inside her, as bright and golden as a flare. Alarik smiled as he tasted it, not afraid of the witch in his arms or the wind at his back. The blizzard curled around them, shutting out the world, until there was only the king of Gevra and the queen of Eana pouring themselves into each other, looking for release from their grief, and finding it, in the snow-swept embrace of an enemy.

Rose

CHAPTER 50

The day after the Arrows set the city of Eshlinn alight, the palace was teeming with people who had lost their homes in the fire. Under Rose's command, they had been rescued by Captain Davers and his soldiers, and ushered through the golden gates. By nightfall, the great hall was packed to the rafters, servants rushing about with food and water and warm blankets, while Chapman questioned the townspeople about what they had seen. What they might know.

Hundreds of men, women and children had fled their homes without looking back. They offered Chapman the same truth over and over again. The Arrows had come to offer them a choice: join the uprising or burn like the witches. When they had refused to fight, Barron's men had returned to their homes and made good on their threat.

Against the advice of Captain Davers, Rose had gone down to the great hall herself. She sat for hours with those who trembled and healed whoever asked for her touch. When Thea took over from her, allowing her magic to rest, Rose still lingered, passing out Cam's special jam tarts to the frightened children and promising them, repeatedly, that all would be well.

The lie was sour on her tongue.

After the Arrows ransacked the capital of Eshlinn, they staked their claim on it, hoisting blood-red banners and tattered flags from the charred rooftops, while more bands of rebels streamed in from the south.

Barron's bloody rising would soon come to pass, and with Wren stuck in Gevra, and no luck with the enchanted hand mirror, Rose was preparing to face it all by herself. In a last-ditch attempt at getting through to her sister, she sent word to Marino and Celeste, warning them of the impending war, and begging them to try to get through to Wren, using whatever means they could.

In the meantime, all Rose could do was wait inside the walls of her palace, hoping the uneasy alliance between the Ortha witches and the Anadawn soldiers would hold long enough for them to defend it. If luck was on their side, the battle against the Arrows would be swift, and the threat of civil war would soon be behind them, but there was no telling just how far Barron's hateful rhetoric had travelled, or how many people he had convinced to join his rebellion.

Three days after the burning of Eshlinn, when Rose was down in the great hall, sharing breakfast with her people, Chapman came to fetch her. The steward's face was grave. The news even worse. The Arrows were on the move. Hundreds were marching across the Silvertongue towards the palace. Rose rushed to the balcony, where she quailed at the sight of their bloodied flags and hefty weapons, which included everything from longswords and knives to chains and axes.

And there at the very front, marched Edgar Barron himself. Steel-eyed and ready for war.

Barron's past life in the army had served him well. This was no angry, baying mob. This was a regiment of soldiers, determined, focused. And they were coming straight for her.

Wren

CHAPTER 51

The day after Wren kissed the king of Gevra, she sat alone in her bedroom, picking at the stitches of her grief. Her new-found magic thrummed inside her, reminding her it was there. Not for the first time, she wondered if the same power had taken root in her sister across the sea. Maybe a witch over there had accidentally brewed a blizzard, too. Though Wren doubted any of them were foolish enough to kiss their mortal enemy inside it. Guilt stirred within her. She kept thinking of Tor, his spectre looming over the memory of that moment of weakness.

And then there was her throne to worry about.

If only Alarik hadn't confiscated her hand mirror – then she could know for sure what was happening back in Anadawn. And yet part of Wren was relieved not to have to deliver the bleak news about Banba's passing just yet. She couldn't quite find the words.

Food arrived at regular intervals, and she picked at that, too. Soldiers knocked, before sticking their heads around the door to check on her. She waved them away. Soon, the sun was setting. The wind was unusually quiet. The mountains were still. The flames crackled in their hearth. Wren sent out a breeze, making them dance. The pain in her heart eased, if only a little. She liked how easily tempest magic had come to her. It made her feel closer to Banba.

Downstairs, the palace was bustling with activity. The bodies of nineteen soldiers and twenty-seven dead beasts had been removed and buried since Oonagh's rampage. The servants were still trawling through the shattered glass and fallen beams, trying to rebuild what Wren's ancestor had torn down on her way out, while five hundred soldiers had been dispatched to the mountains to start clearing away the rubble.

And all the while, Wren sat inside, staring at nothing. 'I have to go home,' she told herself for the twentieth time that day. 'There's nothing left for me here.'

Except Banba, said a voice in her head. *If you leave now, you'll still be leaving her.*

There came another knock at the door. It was Inga. 'The king is waiting for you down at the pond.'

'I have no interest in ice skating,' said Wren.

Inga hesitated. 'It's about your grandmother.'

Wren was on her feet in a heartbeat.

Alarik Felsing was standing alone at the edge of the pond, with his hands tucked behind his back, waiting for Wren. His wolves, Luna and Nova, paced the frost-laden grass, watching Wren as she marched through it. She kept her fists clenched, the blizzard of her emotions at bay. For now.

'This'd better be important,' she called out.

Alarik raised his brows. 'Everything I do is important.'

'Don't,' said Wren, raggedly. 'I'm not in the mood.'

'For kissing?'

'For talking to you. To anyone.'

His face changed, the joviality seeping from his voice. 'I gathered.' He stood aside, revealing the sled he had been blocking. The one Wren had been too busy staring at his bruises to notice. She saw it now, and it took her breath away. Upon it, lay her grandmother's body. Her face was pale but peaceful. There was no blood in her white hair, no dirt matted to her cheeks. Someone had cleaned her up.

Wren's eyes burned as she stumbled towards the sled. 'But the mountain . . . the rocks . . . I don't understand.'

'My soldiers excavated the catacombs this afternoon.'

'But why? There was nothing down there . . .'

Nothing but Banba.

Alarik was silent.

She looked at him. 'Alarik, why?'

He frowned, examining the cuff of his sleeve. Wren understood, then. Alarik wasn't going to tell her that he did it for her, that he had been moved by sympathy. It was an emotion the king of Gevra was not supposed to feel. 'You may decide what you wish to do with her,' he said, instead.

Wren reached for Banba's hand, shuddering at the coldness of her touch. Her skin was waxen, and even in death, her mouth was set into a hard line.

She doesn't have to be dead, whispered a voice in Wren's head. The one that came from that dark and primal place. Whispering through a forbidden doorway she had already opened.

Wren's fingertips began to tingle. She closed her eyes, trying to imagine her grandmother alive once more. She could *try*, at the very least. She could try to bring her back. But there was so much fear inside her, it threatened to choke her. She knew Banba wouldn't want it. Banba would *hate* it.

And if it did work, who knew what version of her would even come back?

Wren's frown deepened as she wavered.

But still . . . just to hold her grandmother one last time. To hug her. To tell her how sorry she was . . .

'I know what you're thinking,' said Alarik.

Wren could feel him watching her. 'Would you stop me?'

A long beat. 'No,' he said at last. 'But it won't be the same. You know that.'

She turned back to him. 'You have Ansel.'

'Not as he was.'

'But would you give him up?' said Wren, though she knew the answer already. It was knitted into Alarik's grimace. He would rather have the mind-addled version of his little brother than none at all.

'Perhaps, if I was selfless.' He smiled, ruefully. 'But I am a selfish man, Wren.'

Wren nodded. The trouble was, she was selfish, too. She didn't care what Banba would have wanted. All she cared about was seeing her grandmother open her eyes, her cheeks flush with colour once more.

Alarik raised his chin to the mountains, in the direction Oonagh had disappeared. 'If you do it, won't it make you more like her?'

'I'm already like her,' said Wren, bitterly. 'Why not make it count?'

He inhaled through his teeth.

Wren snorted. 'What? Are you afraid of me now?'

'No. But aren't you a little afraid of yourself?'

Wren's hands twitched in and out of fists. An old magic was rising inside her, desperate to be used. To be twisted to her every whim. The trouble was, she knew it would twist her soul, too. It had already begun to.

She stepped away from her grandmother's body, trying to fight it.

Banba would hate it. And she would hate me for doing it.

And worse than that. *I would hate myself.*

'Wren?' Alarik interrupted her thoughts. The sun had set, and now darkness was yawning across the skies of Gevra. 'What do you want to do with the body?'

Wren loosed a breath and, with it, two soul-wrenching words. 'Burn it.'

Back in Ortha, whenever one of their own died, the witches would burn their body in a glorious bonfire, dancing and drinking and singing all night to celebrate the fullness of their lives. Banba would brew a fierce wind, making it roar with their collective grief as it carried the spirit back to the Mother Tree.

The pyre in Grinstad was higher than Wren was expecting, piled in the gardens beside the pond, where Banba's body lay, wrapped in fur blankets. Wren watched the flames take hold of her grandmother, and prayed she would find her peace. They were a long way from the Mother Tree now.

The courtyard was deserted. Even the beasts had been taken in. There was only Wren, standing alone before the flames. She flicked her wrist, turning them a bright, blazing silver. They roared as they grew, climbing higher and higher, as if to lick the moon.

Wren's chest heaved, tears streaming down her face until the world turned to streaks of silver and black. 'Goodbye, Banba,' she whispered, as she sent out one final gust of wind. It curled around her grandmother's body, lifting her spirit away from the earth and carrying it off into the night, like a silver ribbon. Back home, to the Mother Tree.

Wren stood at the pyre until the flames burned out. And when it was done, and Banba was at peace, she turned back to the palace. Alarik was standing out on his balcony, his hands braced on the balustrade as he watched her trudge across the courtyard. She pulled her hood up and pretended not to see him.

There were others, too, watching the spectacle of her grief from the windows. The dowager queen was standing in the atrium. She held her hand out to Wren as she passed, squeezing once, before letting go. Wren drifted onward, up the stairs to the fourth floor and on down the hallway, where a new fire crackled in her bedroom. She put it out with a gust of wind, then crawled underneath the covers and cried herself to sleep.

Rose

CHAPTER 52

Rose stood on the balcony of Anadawn Palace, where barely one moon ago, she and her sister had waved to thousands of well-wishers who had come to celebrate their royal coronation. Now a sea of Anadawn soldiers swarmed the courtyard, building barricades to enforce the outer walls while Barron's army marched towards the palace.

Beside her, Thea worried the edge of her eye patch. It was a nervous habit Rose had noticed more and more in recent days. 'They'll be here within the hour.'

'Are the tempests—'

'On the way out to the ramparts, with the enchanters.'

'Good,' said Rose. 'Any word from Celeste?'

'Not yet. But with any luck, she got your letter.'

'Or maybe all my starcrests have drowned in the Sunless Sea,' muttered Rose.

'Celeste is a seer,' said Thea. 'Letter or not, she'll figure something out.'

'I hope you're right, Thea.'

They turned at the sound of shouting. Tilda had burst into

the throne room and was causing a commotion. The young redhead vaulted out of one guard's reach, then ducked another's on her way to reach Rose. 'I want to fight,' she burst out. 'But no one will let me go outside!'

'And with good reason,' said Rose, shooing her back inside. 'You're still a child.'

Tilda jutted out her chin. 'I'm a warrior. Shen trained me. And now I'm the only one we've got.'

Rose smiled, taking heart in the girl's courage. 'You're very brave to want to go out there, but if Shen was here, he'd tell you the same thing. It's too dangerous.'

'But—'

'I'm sorry, Tilda,' said Rose, cutting her off. 'My decision is final.'

Tilda stormed off, just as a horn blared outside. The Royal Anadawn cavalry – fifteen hundred impeccably trained soldiers – came riding around the east wall, with their swords drawn.

The Arrows who had made it over the bridge began to charge, their shouts rising on the morning wind. Though she had lost sight of him, Rose knew Barron was somewhere in the fray.

'Even numbers,' she muttered, looking between her soldiers and the advancing Arrows. 'How are there so *many* of them?'

'We have witches up our sleeve,' Thea reminded her. 'The balance is still in our favour.'

Rose glanced sidelong at the Queensbreath. 'Then why do you look so nervous?'

'Because I care so much. About this queendom, and everything it stands for.'

Rose counted the witches gathering out on the ramparts. There were around fifty tempests and enchanters, including Rowena, Bryony, Grady and Cathal, all of whom had forgone the traditional Eana uniform in favour of dark leathers and hooded cloaks. The rest of the witches were either too young or too old to fight and were sheltering inside the entrance hall with the townspeople.

Barron's army struck first. A volley of steel-tipped arrows whizzed through the air, knocking a soldier from his horse.

Rose rushed to the balustrade. 'RAISE THE WIND!' she shouted, drowning out whatever order Captain Davers was barking down in the courtyard. 'BLOW THEM BACK TO THE RIVER!'

Rowena twirled like a dancer, savouring her moment. She flung her hands out, and the other tempests followed suit, sending out a burst of wind so strong it howled. The gust thundered towards the Arrows, but to Rose's horror, they turned sideways, raising a wall of shields. The wind pushed against it, but it couldn't break through. The Arrows gritted their teeth, driving onward in perfect formation.

'That is annoyingly clever,' muttered Rose.

'We still have our enchanters,' said Thea, calmly.

'They're not close enough yet.' Rose didn't *want* them to be close enough. She had been hoping not to have to use the enchanters at all.

Within minutes, the cavalry were upon the Arrows. They

met in a clash of steel and fire, the horses rearing up as flames snaked across the grass and burned their hooves.

'How are they doing that?' said Rose, leaning over the balustrade to get a closer look.

'Oil,' said Thea, uneasily. 'They're firing it with the arrows.'

Soldiers were thrown to the ground, their own horses trampling them in panic, while the Arrows seized the upper hand, slashing at them from above.

Over the next few hours, Rose watched in silent horror as a fierce and bloody battle surrounded Anadawn Palace. The Arrows fought with a savagery she had never seen before, diving into the fray without care for each other or their own safety. They burned the earth and struck the animals, screaming themselves hoarse as they swung their weapons, cutting down anyone who got in their way.

'Where is their honour?' fumed Rose. 'There's supposed to be an order to these things!'

A burning arrow sailed through the air and struck the balustrade. Rose yelped as she leaped backwards, pulling Thea with her.

Down on the ramparts, Rowena tipped her head back. 'Sorry! Missed that one!'

Rose could see the tempest's magic was waning. She needed to rest. They all did. Another arrow whizzed past her ear. Grady used a whip of wind to spin it around and fire it back at the Arrows. 'I wish I had a hundred more tempests,' muttered Rose. 'No. Make that a thousand.'

Down on the battlefield, her soldiers were barely holding

the line. The Arrows were prepared to fight dirty, and for every ten of them that fell, twenty more seemed to come running over the Silvertongue.

The balcony doors burst open and Chapman appeared, ashen-faced. 'Stars above, Queen Rose. What on earth are you doing out here?' He grabbed her wrist, tugging her away from the balustrade. 'The Arrows are within firing range. You'll be struck!'

But Rose couldn't tear her gaze from her fallen soldiers. 'They need a healer, Chapman. I should be down there, helping them.'

'Absolutely not!' Chapman seized her other arm, as though he was afraid she would launch herself off the balcony. 'You'll only be a liability. You have to stay inside the palace, where it's safe.'

'Chapman is right,' said Thea. 'I'll go down instead.'

'No,' said Rose, at once. It was far too dangerous. 'I need you here.'

At Chapman's insistence, they retreated into the throne room where they watched the battle for Anadawn go from bad to worse.

The Arrows eventually fought their way through the cavalry and pushed north. Soon, their shouts reached Rose on the wind.

She pressed her nose against the glass. 'They're climbing the barricades! Don't they see the spikes?'

Thea exhaled through her teeth. Her calm demeanour had begun to slip. 'They see them. They just don't care.

That's what makes them so dangerous.'

Captain Davers opened the gates, sending out six hundred foot soldiers to beat the advancing Arrows back. The tempests brewed another gust, but after hours of casting, their power was all but spent. Rowena swayed on her feet, Grady narrowly catching her before she hit the ground. A volley of arrows sailed over the wall, striking the balcony where Rose had been standing. Another narrowly missed Bryony, while one fell into the fountain, its flame going out in a curl of smoke.

Rose was so busy watching the Arrows wound themselves on the barricades that she almost missed the small red-haired girl who burst out of the palace and went scurrying across the courtyard.

'Tilda!' she shouted, but she was too far from Rose, and on a mission of her own. As the Arrows hurled themselves over the barricades and ran straight into another thicket of soldiers, Tilda clambered up on to the ramparts and went to Rowena.

'What on earth is she doing?' said Thea. 'She's not a tempest!'

Tilda was lugging a sack with her. She set it down beside Rowena, then reached in and pulled out a potato, before firing it straight at the Arrows.

Rowena braced herself on the stone wall, laughing as Tilda fired another. And then another and another.

'TILDA!' screamed Rose. 'FALL BACK THIS INSTANT!'

But the young witch wound her arm round and round, firing another potato.

Rowena crowed in delight as it soared over the wall.

Rose crushed her fingernails into her palms. Tilda's aim was impeccable but Cam's old potatoes were no match for the ferocious anger of the Arrows, especially considering the speed with which they were running through her poor foot soldiers.

Some had already broken through the fray and managed to reach the outer wall of the palace. The enchanters leaped into action, close enough now to cast their spells. The first two Arrows to reach the wall fell back from it and began to fight each other.

'Clever,' muttered Rose, as the next group turned on each other, too. Another man fell to the ground and began furiously licking the grass, while the woman beside him flung her sword away and started doing cartwheels.

Yet still more arrows flew higher, brighter.

Rose stiffened as a rippling scream rang out.

Time seemed to slow as she watched the young girl collapse, an arrow embedded in her shoulder. It was still flaming. Rowena stood over her, shouting for help, but the rest of the tempests were too spent to move. The enchanters were overrun with Arrows climbing up the walls, and down in the courtyard, not a single soldier broke rank to fetch the stricken young witch.

But that didn't matter. Tilda didn't need a soldier; she needed a healer.

Rose fled the throne room at once.

She was glad to be wearing a pair of Wren's trousers as

she took the stairs three at a time, sprinting down one hallway and then another, until the courtyard was before her. The palace guards tried to stop her, but she ordered them aside.

She hurried towards the ramparts as a chorus of cries filled the air. It was underpinned by the clash of steel on steel, and the crack and whistle of burning arrows soaring overhead. They rained down on Rose like amber tears, but she paid them no mind. If she started worrying about herself, she'd never get to Tilda.

When Rose reached the ramparts, the other witches pulled her up. She crawled to Tilda.

The young witch was curled into a ball at Rowena's feet, the tempest using the last drop of her magic to cast a protective wind around her. Tilda's face was as white as a sheet, her heart barely fluttering beneath Rose's hands. Rose carefully removed the arrow, shivering at the slick of blood on the tip. She pressed down on the wound and closed her eyes, letting her magic flicker to life inside her.

She found the thread of Tilda's life, short and golden, in the centre of her mind, and reached for it. Her blood began to thrum, healing magic filtering through her and into the young witch, until, finally, after what felt like an age, Tilda opened her eyes.

Rose smiled as the rest of the wild, angry world rushed back in. 'Are you all right?'

Tilda's bottom lip quivered. 'I'm scared.'

'Come now,' said Rose, ignoring her own light-headedness as she helped the girl sit up. 'Let's get you back inside.'

Just then, Rowena shrieked as she was yanked over the wall by a climbing Arrow. She lost her footing, and without anyone to anchor her, she fell to the ground on the other side.

'Got one!' screamed the triumphant Arrow. 'She's one of the stormy witches!'

Rose leaped to her feet. 'LEAVE HER BE!' she shouted. 'On pain of death, I order you not to—' Then she cried out, as someone grabbed the bottom of her trousers. Another Arrow scaling the wall had decided to seize his opportunity. She wobbled for an agonizing heartbeat, but Tilda was too dazed to catch her and Rose too dizzy to steady herself. By the time she thought to try, she was already falling . . .

The world whizzed by in terror and flame, the ground rising far too quickly. Rose landed on the grass with a rattling *thud!* Vaguely, she was aware of heavy footsteps, then frenzied voices.

'Burning stars, it's the bloody queen!'

'Kill her, quick!'

'No! Grab her. Barron wants to do the honours himself.'

Rose tried to sit up, but there was a boot on her chest. A man loomed over her, and before she could kick out at him, he brought the hilt of his sword down. Rose groaned as it connected with her head. Stars exploded in her vision before giving way to a familiar darkness.

Wren
CHAPTER 53

The following morning, before the sun was up, Alarik sent for Wren. Still half asleep and too tired to be curious, she rolled out of bed and shrugged on the first dress she could find. To her surprise, it was Anika who opened the door to the king's bedroom. There were shadows underneath her eyes. Shadows behind them, too.

'What is it?' said Wren, uneasily.

'Come in. Shut the door behind you.'

Wren followed her across the room, to where Alarik was standing sentry by the bed. Below him, Ansel was staring at the ceiling, and moaning softly. Wren's heart clenched as she stared down at the prince's face. It was almost green now, his cheeks so hollow, the bones above them looked like scythes.

'My brother says you've got your power back,' said Anika, hoarsely. 'You can make storms now. Like a tempest.'

Wren nodded, absently.

'Then you must be able to heal, too.'

Wren looked up, frowning. 'I don't know. I haven't tried it.'

'So, try it now,' said Anika, impatiently. 'We can't live like this any more.'

Wren looked at Alarik. 'I don't understand.'

'Ansel is suffering,' he said, tightly.

'You know I can't heal him,' said Wren. 'Not with magic. Or time.'

He nodded, stiffly, and Wren realized he had already come to that conclusion. He was asking her for something else. 'We wish to let him rest.' He looked to his sister, the knot in his throat bobbing. 'To let him go.'

'Oh,' said Wren, as realization dawned. The Felsings hadn't summoned her to save Ansel, but to put his soul back to sleep. To heal him, by releasing him from this world. They wanted her to let him die. Again. 'I'll . . . try.'

Wren sat down on the edge of the bed, trying to remember everything Thea had ever told her about healing. She knew it came from the blood and drew on the healer's natural energy, that each spell was guided by intention. She took Ansel's hand. It was trembling, slightly. Or perhaps that was her own. She closed her eyes, and saw the thread of his life writhing inside her mind. Once golden, it was tarnished now, and hopelessly tangled. She reached out to unknot it, but it slipped from her grasp.

Come back. Let me help you.

But the thread was getting further away. A shadow swept in, hiding it from her. Wren's head began to pound. She was dimly aware of her body swaying on the bed, a groan seeping through her teeth. Then came that awful voice again, rising from deep within her.

Blood that takes can no longer heal, it said, mockingly. *You have chosen the darkness, little bird. It is here you must dwell.*

There came a sudden *thud!* Pain lanced through Wren's shoulder, jolting her back to the bedroom. She opened her eyes to find herself on the ground.

'What are you doing, you stupid witch?' hissed Anika, from above. 'Now is not the time to pass out!'

Wren sat up, the warmth draining from her cheeks in prickles as she peered over the bed. Ansel was still alive and muttering feverishly to himself. Alarik's hand was steady on his shoulder, but his hawkish gaze was trained on Wren. 'What just happened?'

'I . . . I'm sorry. I have to go.' Wren scrambled to her feet and bolted for the door. Her eyes blurred as she thundered down the hallway, searching blindly for the stairs. She climbed away from the twitching prince and the grieving king, away from the anger blazing in Anika's eyes, but no matter how fast she ran or how hard she cried, Wren couldn't outrun the voice inside her.

You have chosen the darkness, little bird. It is here you must dwell.

Wren had barely reached her bedroom, when Alarik caught up with her. He slammed the door shut behind him. 'What in freezing hell was that about?'

Wren turned around, tears still streaming down her face. 'I can't do it,' she said, between hiccoughs. 'There was a price for what I did to your brother. I can't heal him. I'm broken.'

She pressed her fists against her eyes. 'I'm just like her. And this is the proof.'

Alarik was silent for a moment, then he sighed. 'You are not broken, Wren.'

'Yes, I am!' she shouted. 'Just get out!'

Alarik didn't move. 'You're not broken,' he said, again.

She dropped her hands to glare at him. 'What the hell do you know?'

He crossed the room in three strides. 'I know that if you can bring yourself to care about something beyond yourself, then *you are not broken*.' The final words came out in a growl. Rough, insistent. He raised his hand, curling a strand of her hair around his finger. When he lifted it, Wren saw that it was bright silver. 'See how much you care, Wren?'

Wren turned to the mirror. She had been in such a rush this morning that she had missed her own reflection, but she saw it clearly now. There was a new streak of silver in her hair, right at the front. She looked to Alarik, who was standing behind her.

He traced the blackness in his own hair. 'My father once told me that to know grief is to know love,' he said, quietly. 'And you cannot love something if you are irretrievably broken.'

Wren stared at the king in the mirror, trying to figure out where on earth this version of him had come from, or if perhaps it had been there all along, hiding beneath his icy facade. 'You once told me love is a horrible business.'

'It is,' said Alarik. 'But why does that have to change anything?'

For a heartbeat, Wren almost laughed. Then her shoulders sagged under the weight of the truth. 'I can't fix Ansel,' she whispered. 'I can't even fix myself.'

'You don't need to be fixed. You just need time to heal.'

Wren closed her eyes, feeling his grief as her own. A small, wayward part of her wanted to reach for him, to curl herself into his embrace and distract herself from the crack in her heart.

He stood back then, and the moment slipped away.

'Go home.' He turned to leave, his smile soft and fleeting. 'Find your healing, witch.'

It was only after Alarik had left that Wren thought to ask him for her hand mirror back. She needed to speak to her sister, to find out what was going on in Eana and hopefully arrange safe passage to get back there. She went to find the king, but the instant she stepped into the hallway, she heard someone shouting her name.

Wren followed it all the way down to the atrium, where Celeste was pacing. Dressed in a fur-lined burgundy coat, grey winter boots and a matching woolly hat, she looked like a Gevran.

'You're back,' said Wren, hurrying down the stairs.

Celeste spun around. 'There you are!' she said, relief trilling in her voice. 'Of course I'm back. You hardly thought I'd leave you in this awful place, did you?' She gestured around them. 'What the hell happened here anyway? I swore

I heard the mountains come down. And I had that vision again. It's been haunting me these past few days. I thought you were dead, Wren.'

Wren stalled on the bottom step. There was so much to say, and she didn't know where to begin. 'That wasn't me in your vision, Celeste. It was Oonagh.'

Celeste stared at her. '*Stars above.*'

'And, er, speaking of my undead evil ancestor,' Wren went on. 'How is your magic these days?'

'Confusing,' said Celeste. 'The same as always.'

'Have you . . . oh, I don't know . . . brewed any storms lately?'

'I'm not a tempest. You know that.' A pause, then. Celeste narrowed her eyes. 'What's going on with you? What happened here the other day?'

'A lot, actually,' said Wren, and to her horror, before she could even broach the topic of her grandmother, her voice broke.

Celeste's face softened. She reached out to trace the streak of silver in Wren's hair. Then she did something utterly unexpected. She grabbed her by the shoulders and pulled her close, the hug so unexpected a sob burst out of Wren. 'I already know about Banba,' she murmured. 'And I'm sorry, Wren. I really am.'

Wren pulled back, wiping her cheeks on her sleeve. 'Did the starcrests show you that, too?'

Celeste pressed her lips together. '*He* told me.'

Wren blinked. 'Who?'

'Alarik,' said Celeste, in a low voice, as though the name itself was dangerous. 'He sent an escort to fetch me down at the docks. I was waiting on Marino's ship, trying to figure out a way to get you out of here. I suppose the king had his spics on us all along.'

'I don't understand.'

Celeste sighed. 'Neither do I. But we can muddle it out on the way home. We've wasted enough time already. There are things I have to tell you, too.'

The king's royal sled was waiting for them in front of the palace. Queen Valeska, who was taking her morning walk, smiled at Wren as she passed by. Wren waved at the dowager queen, before climbing on to the sled. Celeste noticed the exchange but said nothing.

This time, Wren rode up front, the winter wind feathering her cheeks as the wolves pulled them away from King Alarik and the rest of his deadly beasts.

And yet, as they rode down the long driveway of Grinstad Palace, Wren swore she could feel the king's eyes on them. Only when they reached the black gates did she glance over her shoulder to see a distant shadow standing on the balcony.

Celeste noticed that, too.

Wren ignored her look of disapproval. She traced the silver streak in her hair, then pulled her hood up, setting her mind on home. 'Tell me about Eana, Celeste.'

'Very well.' Celeste cleared her throat. 'But fair warning, Wren, you're not going to like it . . .'

Wren sat back and listened, her anger burning brighter with every word.

Marino Pegasi's ship was already in the dock when they arrived at midnight. If the captain was surprised by their royal mode of transport, he didn't show it. He simply threw his arms out in welcome as they climbed on board. 'Welcome back, Miss Tilda. Better late than never!'

'Your darling Lessie came to my rescue,' said Wren, summoning a smile for the genial captain. 'Thanks for waiting for me.'

Celeste rolled her eyes. 'I forgot how annoying you both are when you're together. I'm going below deck to find some food. I'm famished.'

Wren waved her off, falling into step with Marino as they crossed the deck. The *Siren's Secret* was a hive of activity, the crew hoisting the sails and unmooring the ship as they prepared to set sail. 'Got any rum on board?'

Marino chuckled. 'Does it snow in Gevra?'

'Good,' said Wren. 'I could use a strong drink right now.'

'I gather it's been a rough few weeks,' said Marino.

Wren nodded, absently. 'Though I expect the worst is still ahead.'

Marino sent a swabbie below deck to fetch a bottle of his finest rum. When she returned to the bow, Wren took the bottle and untwisted the cap, pouring a shot out for Banba. Then she took a generous swig for herself.

'Aren't you going to share that?' said Marino, coming to join her once they had cleared the Death Crevasse.

Wren passed him the bottle. 'Any luck with your mermaid yet?'

The captain shook his head, before drinking deeply. 'No matter. I'm a patient man.'

'And a fool for love.'

'Everyone's a fool for something, Wren. Why not let it be love?'

Wren stared out at the glassy sea, letting her mind turn to Tor, and the kindness in his eyes, in his spirit. She tried not to think of Alarik – that fierce gaze and dauntless soul – but they arrived on the same thought now, the king and his captain, entwined in her memory.

'I know that look,' said Marino. 'You're thinking of your Gevran sweetheart.'

'I don't have a sweetheart,' said Wren, quickly. 'And I don't want one.'

Marino's brown eyes filled with pity. 'Then what do you want, Wren?'

Wren turned back to the water. It had been a long time since anyone had asked her that. Without Banba's guiding hand and Rose's voice in her ear, Wren didn't know what she wanted. Only this. 'Take me home, Marino. I've got a date with Edgar Barron, and I'm already late.'

Marino dipped his chin. 'So long as the wind cooperates,

I expect we'll make good time.'

Wren looked at him over her shoulder. 'Mind if I give it a little nudge?'

With the captain's blessing, she raised her hands and brewed a gale so strong, she swore she heard Banba's laugh inside it. The sails billowed, full and straining, and the *Siren's Secret* lurched, picking up speed at such an alarming rate Marino had to sprint back to the wheel to keep the ship from capsizing.

Wren smiled as she stood out on the bow with the wind in her hair and a storm in her fists and chartered them home, all the way across the Sunless Sea, to where the war was waiting.

Rose

CHAPTER 54

When Rose awoke, she was far from her palace. She blinked away her haze, trying to think past the throbbing pain in her skull. The world shifted into focus, just enough that she could tell she was in a burnt clearing at the edge of the woods. Everything smelled like ash and smoke. Her hands were bound in her lap, and her body was tied to a charred tree trunk.

Before her stood Edgar Barron. Despite the battle raging nearby, he looked immaculate, with perfectly coiffed hair. He was wearing a fine crimson doublet under sleek black armour and was leaning lazily on the hilt of his sword.

'Queen Rose.' He sketched a bow. 'We meet again.'

Rose glared at the leader of the Arrows, with all the hatred she could muster. 'This is high treason, Barron. Release me, at once.'

Barron's blue eyes danced. 'You are hardly in a position to negotiate.'

'The queen of Eana is always in a position to negotiate.'

Barron came to his knees. 'Here is my first and final offer, witch. You may beg for your life.'

Rose closed her eyes, summoning the last of her courage. And with the rage of all the witches burning inside her, she did something she had never done before in her life.

She spat at Edgar Barron.

He reeled backwards. 'You filthy witch,' he said, leaping to his feet. He angled his sword below her chin. 'You'll pay for that.'

This time, Rose kept her eyes open. If she was going to die, she would at least look her murderer in the eye. Her heart thundered. She felt the press of steel against the hollow of her throat, the warm trickle of her own blood as her skin broke.

Suddenly, the wind howled. There came a gust so strong, it cast her hair skyward and ripped Barron's sword from his grip. Rose gasped as the leader of the Arrows stumbled backwards, losing his footing in the eye of the storm.

It ceased just as quickly as it had come, a swift silence falling over the clearing.

Then Wren's voice rang out. 'Big Bad Edgar Barron. Didn't my sister and I warn you to play nice?'

She appeared through a break in the trees. Wren looked utterly unlike herself, dressed in a decadent Gevran gown, her hair, now streaked with silver, braided into two long fishtail braids. She glanced at Rose.

'Are you all right?'

Rose's lips trembled as she nodded. 'I knew you'd come back.'

Barron scrambled to his feet. But Wren flung her hand

out, knocking him over with another fierce gust. 'Stay on your knees, traitor.'

Rose whipped her head around, looking for Banba, but it was just the three of them inside the clearing. Somehow, the storm had come from Wren.

'You're supposed to be an enchanter,' said Barron, looking between them. For the first time since Rose had met the unflappable leader of the Arrows, she noticed, with a sliver of satisfaction, that he looked frightened.

'And you're supposed to be behaving yourself,' Wren countered. 'But since you're here, trying to murder my sister, do you want to see another demonstration of my new power?'

'No!' said Barron.

'Yes!' said Rose.

Wren swept her arm around, creating a roaring wind. It thundered towards Barron, lifting him off the forest floor, and casting him into the air, where he was flung like a twig over the burnt treetops. He screamed as he flew, but Wren didn't stand still to watch him go.

She whirled on Rose, removing a dagger from up her sleeve as she fell to her knees. She made quick work of the binds around her wrists and the rope at her waist. 'I'm sorry I'm late,' she said. 'I came as soon as—'

Rose flung herself at Wren, throwing her arms around her sister and squeezing her so tightly, Wren fell out of her sentence. 'You're here now,' she said, pressing her face into her shoulder. 'That's all that matters.'

Rose was so lost in the joy of her reunion, she didn't

realize her fingers were tingling until she pulled back from Wren. A strange warmth was spreading out inside her. No, not warmth. This was magic, and somehow, it felt both now and ancient.

Rose looked up at her sister. 'Something's happening to me.'

Wren smiled. 'It's the twins' curse, Rose,' she said, reaching for her hand. The heat inside Rose flared. 'Now that we're together again, I think it's finally breaking. The five strands of witchcraft are reuniting. Our power is returning.'

With those words came a flood of power so warm and bright, Rose felt like her blood had caught fire. By the time she stood up, her fingers were crackling. She could feel a storm brewing inside her and was seized by the urge to fling her hands out and set it loose. 'Goodness,' she said, breathlessly. She felt somehow as though her soul had swelled, that parts of herself she had yet to learn were creeping out of her bones and knitting themselves together. 'Now what?'

Wren took her hand, pulling Rose away from the woods. 'Now we fight.'

Wren

CHAPTER 55

Wren had never felt as close to Rose as she did then, both of them leaving the shelter of the forest and marching back towards Anadawn Palace, where chaos and bloodshed awaited them. But they were not the same people they had been barely one moon ago. The witches' curse was breaking, the five strands of Eana's magic flowing from Wren into Rose and mending a thousand-year-old wrong.

And yet, deep down, there was part of Wren that feared her sister would sense the darkness inside her, the broken strand of healing magic that refused to work. She would have to tell Rose about Oonagh sooner or later, confess what she had accidentally set loose in the bowels of Grinstad Palace, and what it had cost them. Or, rather, who.

'Wren, you're trembling.' Rose squeezed her hand. 'Do you need a moment?'

Wren shook her nerves off. 'No.' The sun was setting, the last of its golden rays bleeding across the white towers of Anadawn. Darkness was sweeping in, and, with it, a pale and distant moon. 'Let's show these Arrows who they're up against.'

The twins stalked across the battlefield, bringing a howling gale with them. There were hundreds of soldiers lying on the grass, some groaning, while others were still. The barricades around the palace walls had been destroyed, and the golden gates were beginning to cave in.

Wren channelled her rage into her magic, summoning the fullness of her power from the very depths of her soul. Beside her, she could tell Rose was doing the same. The wind shrieked around them, the earth trembling at their feet, as they bore down on the Arrows.

'Shields up!' yelled one of the rebels. 'It's only wind! Advance and seize the queens.'

As one, the Arrows charged.

Rose tensed. 'I didn't wait eighteen years to go to war. I waited eighteen years to lead my people in peace and prosperity.'

'Then let's end this.' Wren balled her fist until it crackled with lightning. The sky above Anadawn Palace split open, and a fork of lightning leaped down from the clouds, burning a jagged line into the earth.

The Arrows froze mid-charge.

'THERE WILL BE PEACE!' cried Rose, as Wren pulled down another bolt, singing the earth around them. 'PLEASE, JUST LET THERE BE PEACE!'

Across the battlefield, Wren spied Rowena in the fray. Rowena picked up a discarded sword and spun it in the air, before catching it by the blade tip. She flung it, with expert aim, into the back of an axe-wielding Arrow. Then she looked at her hands, as if she had never seen them before and began to laugh. 'The curse! It's broken!'

Tilda leaped off the ramparts and landed in her own whorl of wind. 'Look! I have tempest powers now!'

The Arrows whipped their heads around, horror-stricken, as more witches poured out of Anadawn Palace, flinging their hands to the sky, and finding new power rising inside themselves. The twins stalked on, bringing the lightning with them.

'Fall back!' Rose called to their soldiers. 'Get behind us!'

Rowena rushed to meet them. 'Finish them!' she shouted, calling down her own jagged lightning. 'Every single one!'

Wren flexed her fingers.

'No!' said Rose, grabbing her wrist. 'We'll push them back to the river. Block them off at the bridge. That will give us time to tend to the injured. There must be hundreds of healers among us now.'

Rowena curled her lip. 'All this new power and you're still gutless.'

Rose shoved her aside. '*Move.*'

Wren shot a warning look at Rowena as she marched after her sister.

Many of the Arrows were fleeing now, but a foolish hundred or so were still pushing forward, trying to breach the golden gates. To Wren's surprise, they swung open, as though to welcome them.

Rose whipped her head around. 'The gates have been breached!'

'Not breached,' said Wren, uneasily. 'They've been opened, Rose. I think we've been betrayed.'

Wren hoped she was mistaken but as they made their way towards the palace, her worry only grew. Inside the courtyard, some of the guards had turned their swords on the witches. And worse than that, Captain Davers was standing at the gates, ushering more Arrows inside.

Wren broke into a run. 'You filthy traitor! I'll have your head for this!'

'Wren, the children!' Rose pointed to the rose garden, where a group of young witches were cowering behind Celeste, who was wildly swinging a longsword at anyone who dared come near them.

'Seize them!' shouted Captain Davers. 'Take out as many witches as you can!'

To Wren's mounting horror, more guards turned on the witches, but whether it was from fear of their new-found power or some pre-concocted plan, she didn't know. Before Rowena could cast a deadly strike, Davers knocked her out with the hilt of his sword. Grady and Cathal went down next, while Tilda ducked to narrowly avoid a flying axe. Even with the witches' new-found powers, they were hopelessly outnumbered.

By the garden, Thea had commandeered a sword and had managed to reach Celeste, but they were under siege, both of them struggling to protect the young witches in their charge. Wren and Rose split up by the fountain, Rose rushing to help the children, while Wren went after Davers, who in the absence of Edgar Barron, had assumed the role of traitorous ringleader. Wren had never liked the man, and now she knew why.

The Captain of the Anadawn Guard was expecting her. They met by the ramparts, where he raised his shield, blocking her tempest magic while twelve of his best soldiers surrounded him. Traitors, every last one of them. But Wren kept her eyes on Davers.

It was like Banba always said. Take out the leader, and the rest will fall.

'No wonder Barron made it so far with a turncoat like you to help him,' hissed Wren.

Davers jabbed his sword, pressing her back against the ramparts. Wren flexed her fingers, willing her warrior strand to kick in so she could swipe it from him. 'The old ways were working just fine,' he said, as though this was a conversation and not a fight to the death. 'Anadawn was safe. Peaceful.'

'Not for us,' said Wren, slinging another ball of wind.

Davers ducked to avoid it. 'Barron is right. No one should have this much power. It's not natural. It's not right.'

Wren's fists crackled. 'If you truly cared about what's right, you would have given us a chance to rule.'

He made a noise of derision. 'How can you rule a kingdom when you can't even control the guests in your own palace?'

Wren raised her fist, but when she looked up to summon a bolt of lightning, she found herself pinned by a familiar seething gaze. She barely had time to think before Edgar Barron leaped from the ramparts and came down on her like a ton of bricks. Wren collapsed underneath him, her head connecting with the stone ground in a sickening crack.

Stars swarmed her vision, and for a brief, crucial moment, she slipped from consciousness. When she came to, she was limp on her feet, with a dirty rag stuffed in her mouth. Barron held her hands behind her back as he dragged her across the courtyard. The Arrows parted around them, clearing a pathway to the fountain.

'Here's a tip from me to you,' Barron hissed in her ear. 'When you attack an enemy, *always* make sure you finish the job.'

Wren spat the rag from her mouth, but her head was swimming and she couldn't think straight, let alone summon a morsel of magic. She struggled feebly as she was shoved into the fountain. As death lapped at her knees, Wren was dimly aware of her sister shouting her name. Celeste was screaming. And Thea, too. But no one came to help her.

They were all going to die here, on the precipice of possibility, the last of the witches lost to the pages of a soon-to-be forgotten history.

Wren scrabbled backwards in the fountain, cold water lacing her chest as she tried to escape from Barron's grasp. But he crawled in after her, his blue eyes alight with violence.

'You're the know-it-all, Wren,' he sneered. 'Did you know you can drown in just a cup of water?'

Wren rasped a laugh. 'All the better for me to kill you.'

'Arrogant, as ever, witch. Even at the hour of your death.'

There were Arrows all around them now, every leering face more hostile than the last. Rose tried to fight her way through, but she was hauled away by Davers, her hands pinned behind her back. And then Celeste was there, only she didn't try to push her way through. Her gaze met Wren's in the crowd, and just as a guard came to capture her, too, she drew her arm back and flung a red rose into the fountain. It landed in the water, beside Wren.

Barron saw it and laughed. 'A flower for your grave. Even your allies know there is no hope for you.' A lone petal floated towards Wren, and she closed her fist around it.

'You die today, witch, and your sister will be next.'

Wren curled the petal in her fist as Barron grabbed the back of her hair and shoved her face first into the water. He held her there, his grip twined in her hair as she flailed for new breath.

Wren heard him laugh as she fell still, heard the Arrows cheer his name. After three long minutes, Barron released her, so bloated by his own triumph that he didn't notice the enchantment working its way through her body, nor the merrow gills in her neck.

He stood up in the fountain, and summoned Rose. She was dragged towards him, kicking and shouting. Wren caught the moment her sister saw her floating lifelessly in the fountain, Rose's primal scream so heart-wrenching that Wren almost raised her head.

Barron stepped over her. This time, he called for his bow and arrow. Someone scurried out of the crowd to hand it to him. His garbled words echoed in the water as Wren reached, ever so slowly, for her dagger.

'Your sister is dead. It is time for you to join her.' Wren heard him nock his arrow to his bow, and pictured him aiming it at Rose's heart. 'Here we find ourselves, under the Great Protector's eye. There is no truer arrow than this one,' he announced. 'No better death than yours.'

Wren struck, driving her dagger into Barron's calf. He fell to his knees with a ragged shout as she leaped up from the water.

With her hair plastered to her face, she could just make out her sister struggling in Davers' grasp. Rose seized upon the captain's shock, slamming her elbow into his side and bounding away from him. She lunged for Wren, but Barron intercepted her. He pulled Rose against him, ripping Wren's dagger from his calf and holding it to her neck.

'Don't move another muscle,' he said, through gritted teeth. Wren froze, her frightened gaze meeting Rose's across the water. 'Let's try this again, shall we?'

Dread rippled down Wren's spine. She had failed her sister. She hadn't been quick enough, or smart enough, to save her. To save any of them. And now here it was – the moment that would separate them forever. And to make it worse, Rose would die first.

I'm sorry, she mouthed.

Rose smiled, forgiving Wren. Forgiving herself. *I love you*.

Then she squeezed her eyes shut, readying herself for death. Wren shut her eyes, too, but instead of the sinking sound of steel meeting skin and bone, she heard the unmistakable whistle of flying steel.

And then a telltale *thwack*!

Rose cried out.

Wren's eyes flew open. Over her sister's shoulder, Barron's face had frozen mid-grin, the hilt of a familiar golden dagger sticking out of his neck. His fingers slackened, the knife tumbling from his grasp. He fell backwards, landing with an almighty splash.

'Sorry we're late,' came a voice from above. 'We were dusting off our weapons.'

Wren and Rose looked up at the same time to see Shen Lo standing on the ramparts. He was wearing his golden crown and brandishing the biggest sabre Wren had ever seen. Lei Fan stood on one side of him, holding her own gilded bow and arrow, with Grandmother Lu on the other spinning her staff. All along the rest of the ramparts, as far as Wren could see, stood an unbroken line of witches dressed in glittering black armour and brandishing their own menacing weapons.

'All you witch-hating cowards probably haven't heard of the Sunkissed Kingdom,' said Shen Lo, as he stepped off the wall, dropped twenty feet and landed in a perfect crouch. 'Why don't we introduce ourselves?'

With a rallying cry, the rest of the Sunkissed army leaped off the wall and descended on the Arrows.

Rose

CHAPTER 56

Moonlight bounced off the weapons of Shen's army as they roared into battle, swarming the courtyard in a mass of steel. The Arrows relinquished their hold on the Ortha witches and ran for the gates, but they were no match for the strength and speed of the Sunkissed Kingdom. They flung gusts like throwing knives, their bodies spinning through the air with deadly grace.

The soldiers who had betrayed Wren and Rose raised their weapons, only to have them kicked from their trembling hands. They took one look at each other and ran for the river. Wren joined the Sunkissed witches and ran after them, trying to stop as many as she could.

Rose stood up in the fountain, sopping wet from head to toe, and watched them all flee. *Let them run*, she thought, an unfamiliar bitterness coursing through her. After eighteen years, her own guards had turned on her. Even Captain Davers, whom she had known all her life, had been so afraid of her magic that he had bound her hands and tried to drag her to her death.

Shen sloshed through the water, his dark eyes assessing her. 'Are you hurt?'

Rose shook her head, but tears prickled in her eyes. She couldn't shake the image of her sister floating dead in the water. The fight had gone out of her in that horrifying moment, the last of her hope extinguished. And yet here she stood, alive. Saved. 'I can't believe you came.'

'I couldn't let you face this battle alone, Rose.' Shen came towards her, making a shield of his body as he pulled her close. 'I never thought Barron would get this far, so soon.'

Rose looked up into his molten eyes. 'I didn't want to drag you into this, Shen.'

His brow furrowed as he traced the wound on her neck. 'It's a good thing Thea sent a note.'

'She did?'

'And so did Rowena.'

'*What?*'

'And also Tilda.' Shen paused. 'Did you know her penmanship is terrible?'

Rose gaped at him. 'I didn't ask any of them to—'

'I know,' he said, seriously. 'But I'm glad they did. I had no idea it was this bad.'

'Even so,' said Rose, with a sigh. 'I know you didn't want to march your people to war.'

'I didn't have to,' he said, with a shrug. 'I just said I was going to fight and gave them the choice to follow.' His lips curled, revealing his dimple. 'Turns out being trapped under the desert for eighteen years can get pretty boring.

Most of them were up for a bit of action.'

They climbed out of the fountain. Rose's throat tightened as Shen retrieved his dagger from Barron's neck and cleaned it on the hem of his cloak. She avoided the Arrow's unseeing gaze as she stepped over his dead body, but she couldn't stop the shiver that crawled up her spine.

Death, no matter whose it was, didn't sit right with her. It made her heart ache.

'It's good timing, too. Considering all this extra power we've got to play around with.' Shen twisted his hand, lifting a nearby pear tree up by its roots. 'Any idea where it came from?'

'Wren,' said Rose, craning her neck to see where her sister was. 'She found a way to break Oonagh Starcrest's ancient curse. It seems the strands of our magic are uniting once more.' Rose frowned. 'But as to how she did it . . . That is another question entirely.'

Shen lifted the pear tree higher, angling it at a fleeing soldier. 'If the Arrows didn't like us before . . .'

'No,' said Rose, bracing her hand on his arm. 'There is no *us* and *them*. We must be a united Eana. It's the only way forward.'

They looked out at the carnage beyond the gates, listening to the screams on the wind. Grandmother Lu had corralled a bunch of fleeing soldiers and was making them twirl round and round in an endless dance. Tilda was using sharp bursts of wind to spring higher in the air, only to somersault back down on unsuspecting Arrows. And even Celeste had picked up her discarded sword and was spinning it through the air, her delighted laughter soaring from her like a song.

'It might be a little late for that,' said Shen. 'The witches want to explore their new power. They want to teach the Arrows a lesson. And who can blame them?'

Rose didn't want to talk about blame. She wanted to talk about peace. She knew, in her heart, it was the only pathway to the future. But how could she get the others to see that?

Most of the Arrows were almost at the river now, slipping in the fresh mud as they looked fearfully over their shoulders. The rest had fallen, dead or groaning somewhere along the way. Rose knew if they fled now, they would only come back stronger and angrier to avenge Barron.

'This has to end,' she said, striding out past the gates.

Shen fell into step with her, idly spinning his sabre in case a last-minute defector charged at them. 'Looks like Wren and Lei Fan are hitting it off,' he said, gesturing to where the two witches stood down on the banks of the Silvertongue, their heads bent together. Rose regarded their matching smirks with rising apprehension. Wren as an enchanter was one thing. But Wren with all five strands of her magic and a rising thirst for revenge would be quite another.

Rose broke into a run, but long before she reached them, Wren and Lei Fan raised their hands in unison. There was an almighty *crack!* as they pulled a fork of lightning out of thin air. Lei Fan used it to set a discarded flag alight, the flames twisting and growing until they became a ball in the sky. More witches joined in, holding it steady, as Wren cast a fistful of earth and began to manipulate it.

In less than a minute, the flames had become a huge, writhing snake.

The Arrows screamed.

The witches roared in triumph.

'No!' cried Rose, running faster. She watched in horror as the snake opened its jaws and released a hiss of sparks and smoke. The Arrows fell back from the bridge, shrieking in fear. The snake dived at them, snapping at their ankles.

The witches laughed as they fed their power to the blaze, the serpent growing ever larger as it herded the Arrows, its tail twisting around them in a mighty circle.

And then, suddenly, they were trapped. With nothing between them and death but a wall of hissing, spitting flames. They cowered together. Some passed out in fear, while others tried to leap through the fire, only to fall, burnt and howling, to the ground.

Rose skidded to a stop on the riverbank. 'Wren!' Even from here, the heat was relentless. She couldn't imagine what it felt like to be trapped inside the blaze. 'WREN!'

Reluctantly, Wren turned from the flames and jogged towards her. 'Why do you look so scared? We're winning!'

'At what cost?' demanded Rose. 'For goodness' sake, what were you thinking making that awful creature?'

Wren jutted her chin out. 'They'll never rise up against us again, Rose. Not after this.'

Rose's hands were trembling. Her heart, too. 'I don't want

to rule with fear, Wren. Fear leads to hatred, to *this*. We're no better than they are.'

'Maybe not, but at least we're stronger.'

Rose grabbed her sister by the shoulders. 'A just ruler shows mercy. There is a better way than this. A smarter way.'

'This is the smart way,' said Wren.

'No. This is the way of Oonagh Starcrest.'

Wren recoiled from the name, from what it meant.

'We promised ourselves we wouldn't be like them,' Rose went on. 'That we would lead with unity. With *peace*. This is our kingdom, Wren. What good is it if it's built on fear?'

Wren hesitated. Rose could see the war behind her sister's eyes – the old ways that Banba had taught her battling with the new, the thirst for revenge slowly giving way to thoughtfulness. She glanced at the fire, then back at Rose. 'All right,' she said, on a breath. 'What do you need me to do?'

'Just follow my lead.'

Rose threw her hands to the heavens and walked on, towards the flames. *Eana, wherever you are, please send us your strength*, she begged her ancestor. *We need it now more than ever.*

'What are you doing?' said Shen. 'You'll get hurt.'

Rose closed her eyes, channelling every drop of her magic into summoning a new storm. Beside her, Wren did the same. The wind came first, kissing their cheeks as it toyed with their hair. Then thunder rolled across the sky, bringing a heavy grey cloud with it. It was the biggest rain cloud Rose had ever seen, and still it swelled, casting Anadawn in its shadow.

The wind picked up as it rumbled through the sky, until Rose could feel static on her skin, in her hair. The cloud stopped above the riverbank, and for a moment, everyone looked up.

'NO!' shouted Rowena. 'Don't spoil all the fun!'

The snake lashed out, burning another group of Arrows. They screamed as they dropped to the grass.

Wren grabbed Rose's hand. 'Let's end this.'

'Together,' said Rose, squeezing her sister's hand.

With an almighty sigh, the heavens opened. Sheets of freezing water poured from the storm cloud, drenching everything and everyone below it.

The snake hissed as it burned out, its tongue turning to putrid black smoke before their eyes. The twins walked on, into their storm, calling down another hail of rain until it hung from Rose's lashes and turned the world blurry. She was soaked to the bone, her clothes sticking to her skin, but with her sister at her side and their magic flowing in perfect unison, she had never felt so powerful.

As the last of the fire snake curled up in a plume of grey smoke, the Arrows fell to their knees, looking to the sky with wonder as though the Protector himself had come to deliver them from death.

That would not do.

Rose summoned a gust of wind and used it to cast her voice across the riverbank until every witch and every Arrow, and all her soldiers – the good and the traitorous – could hear her.

'Put down your weapons! Call back your power!' she cried. 'Stow your fear and your anger. This battle is finished.'

'There will be no more blood spilled on this soil today,' shouted Wren. 'No more lives lost.'

They came to a stop before the quivering Arrows, this once righteous mass of bloodthirsty insurgents now sopping and shivering at their feet.

'Today, you have proven yourselves traitors to the throne,' said Wren. 'You burned our city, and for that alone, we should let you burn, too.'

A cheer went up from the witches.

Rose lifted her hand to silence them. 'But we believe that will only light another dangerous spark. If we show you the same hatred that you carry in your hearts, we will only be adding to the poison festering in this country.'

'We believe in a better Eana,' said Wren. 'A stronger Eana. A united Eana.'

The rain began to peter out.

'We believe in an Eana where witches and non-witches live side by side,' Rose went on. 'Where you can take your sick child to a healer witch and know they will get better. Where you can sleep soundly in winter knowing your crops will still flourish, where our warriors will fight for you and not against you.' Wren squeezed her hand, strengthening her words, as she continued.

'We believe in an Eana where witches can walk freely in the streets, without having to mark their doors in fear or hide who they really are. We believe a peaceful Eana is a more powerful Eana.' The storm cloud was breaking apart, silver strands of moonlight filtering through the grey. 'Today, my sister and I choose to show mercy. To offer an olive branch instead of a noose, so you will know it was not the Protector who saved you. It was the witch queens of this kingdom.'

Wren raised her chin, a challenge in her voice. 'Now we ask you to show us that you are worth saving. Stake your loyalty to this country, and let it flourish, as it was always meant to.'

Silence.

The Arrows stared at the twins, like they were only just seeing them for the first time. The witches were silent, too, waiting. Wary.

And then, from the sopping masses, Captain Davers stepped forward, fear and regret warring in his eyes. He dropped his sword and fell to his knees. 'Queen Rose, the Merciful. Queen Wren, the Gracious. Forgive me.'

One by one, the Arrows cast their weapons aside, and knelt.

The full moon broke through the clouds, casting the twins in its silver light. Rose closed her eyes, taking courage in their ancestor's closeness. *Thank you, Eana.*

'Nice speech,' said Wren, under her breath. 'But please tell me we're still going to punish Davers for that mutiny.'

Rose snapped her eyes open. 'I may be merciful, but I'm not an idiot.'

Afterwards, when the wind had retreated into the trees, and the moon was holding court in a clear sky, Rose invited any witches who were willing, to walk the battlefield with her and tend to the injured. Not all of them were happy to help the fallen Arrows, and Wren had disappeared entirely, but Rose made it her mission to stay out until every last drop of her magic was exhausted. Only then, did she retire to the bustling great hall.

'Now you truly are a queen,' said Grandmother Lu, winking at Rose over a generous goblet of wine. 'I had a good feeling about you.'

'I think I need to work on my healing strand,' said Shen, as he wandered over to her. 'I'm too easily distracted.'

'It will come,' said Rose, letting her hand brush against his as they stood in the middle of the hall. 'Give it time.'

He smiled at her. 'Queen Rose, the Merciful. It suits you.'

'And what about you, King Shen?' she asked. 'What ever happened to Feng and Kai?'

His gaze flitted towards the desert. 'They're stewing in my dungeon, as we speak. I suppose they're waiting to find out what kind of king I'll be . . . Shen, the Vengeful . . . Shen, the Lenient . . . Shen, the Handsome . . .'

'Shen, the Modest,' teased Rose.

'Shen, the Ravenous.'

Rose giggled. 'Well, that makes two of us.'

'Come on,' he said, pulling her away from the crowd. 'Let's go to the kitchens. Celeste's got a bottle of wine down there with our names on it.'

Rose went gladly, smiling at the buzz of chatter in the air. Anadawn had never been so full before. The trill of conversation, mixed with the smell of Cam's chicken soup and freshly baked bread, filled her with a rush of joy. It felt hopeful, this moment, where peace dwelled, as new and fragile as a baby bird.

It felt like a promise for the future.

Wren

CHAPTER 57

Just after midnight, Thea found Wren sitting alone in the west tower. She was still dressed in her damp Gevran dress, the fine velvet skirts now bloodstained and spattered with mud.

Thea pushed the door open, letting the music from below waft inside with her.

'There you are, little bird,' she said, as she padded over to her. 'Shouldn't you be downstairs, celebrating?'

Wren lifted her head from the crook of her arms. At the sight of her grandmother's wife, soft-eyed and smiling, her face crumpled. 'Thea,' she began, but the words left her. In their place, tears came. She had been holed up here for hours, hiding from the truth. But there was no escaping it now. 'It's Banba.'

Thea pressed a hand to her chest, and Wren knew that she had been steeling herself for this moment. 'She's gone, isn't she?'

Wren tried to tell her the awful truth of what had happened back in Gevra, but to her horror, a sob burst out instead. It wracked her shoulders and sent more tears streaming down her face, until she could only bear to nod.

'Come here, my love.' Thea's knees creaked as she lowered herself to the floor. She gathered Wren into a warm hug. 'It's going to be all right,' she murmured. 'We're going to be all right.'

'I t-t-ried m-my b-b-best,' said Wren, between hiccoughs. 'I p-p-promise.'

'I know you did, love.' Thea pulled back, wiping Wren's tears with the pads of her thumbs. Then she closed her eye and offered a healing pulse. It trickled into Wren's bloodstream, and she felt suddenly able to breathe again.

'Thank you, Thea.' Wren's heart ached, knowing she could do nothing for the healer's pain. That no matter how strong her magic became, she would never be able to access her healing strand.

'I swear part of me already knew,' whispered Thea. 'I woke to a peculiar feeling some days ago. It was like a pinprick in my heart. It took my breath from me. For some time now, it's felt as though a flame inside me has gone out. That I am only half as bright as I was.'

'I'm so sorry, Thea.' She squeezed her hand. 'Please forgive me.'

'There is nothing to forgive, little bird. Surviving loss is the great sacrifice of our mortality.' Thea's smile was watery. 'But while Banba is gone, our love will forever remain. It is one of the few things on this earth stronger than magic. I will take comfort in that. And so should you.'

They hugged again, anchoring each other in their love for

Banba, and their grief at her passing, until new footsteps sounded.

Wren looked up to find her sister standing in the doorway.

'Ah! My seer strand must be kicking in,' said Rose, swishing her skirts in triumph. 'I had a feeling I'd find you up here. Don't be so mopey. Come downstairs and dance!'

Rose looked resplendent in a magnificent pink gown. Her hair had been freshly braided into a crown on her head, and her cheeks were flushed. She was dressed for celebrating, not grief.

And yet when she saw Wren's face, her own fell. 'What is it?'

Wren shook her head, trying to find the right words. Any words. 'I'm sorry I didn't tell you before.'

Rose looked to Thea. 'It's Banba, isn't it?'

'Yes, love,' said Thea, sadly. 'She didn't make it, after all.'

Rose closed her eyes. 'That awful, ice-hearted king.'

'It wasn't Alarik.' Wren looked between Thea and Rose, offering the truth in three terrible words. 'It was Oonagh.'

Thea frowned. 'It can't be.'

Rose quailed. '*Starcrest?*'

'The one and only,' said Wren. 'Oonagh Starcrest isn't dead. She's the one who killed our grandmother. Celeste's vision was correct. She saw a queen frozen in Gevran ice, only it wasn't me she was seeing. It was Oonagh.'

'What are you saying?' said Rose, coming towards her.

Wren did her best to explain, sketching out the moment of Banba's death, and how Oonagh Starcrest had pulled the mountain down on top of them, shattering the windows of Grinstad Palace as she strode out into the mountains.

'She's back,' Wren finished. 'And something tells me we haven't seen the last of her.' She looked to Thea, who was silent with shock. Then to Rose, wringing her hands as she stood by the window.

'Goodness,' she murmured. 'What do we do now?'

Wren tipped her head back. The trouble was, there was nothing to do but wait. Strands of music floated up from the great hall. 'I suppose we might as well dance.'

Rose

CHAPTER 58

When Rose woke up the morning after the battle, cocooned in silk sheets beside her snoring sister, she felt at peace. It wasn't because she'd slept well, although she had, or that she was wearing her favourite blue nightgown, which she was. Or even that she had spent last night dancing with Shen Lo, listening to his easy laugh and falling into his night-dark eyes. It was because she knew, with an unerring, bone-deep certainty, that for the first time since she had become queen, she had done something *right*.

She had put aside her fear and anger and been the ruler she'd always wanted to be, the one she knew she could be. The Arrows had laid down their weapons and listened to her and Wren. And although Rose knew this peace was fragile, and much too early to stake the future on, she felt like the pieces of their destiny were finally falling into place.

And yet there had been great loss, too. Hundreds had died during the battle for Anadawn, and then there was Banba. The grandmother she'd never truly known, the grandmother who'd left her in Anadawn all those years, who'd plotted against her, even used her as a pawn, was gone. The fiercest witch Rose had ever known, the one she had been learning to know, to love, was dead.

Rose was still struggling to believe it. Though it explained why Wren had looked so hollow yesterday, why her dark hair was now streaked with silver. She had loved Banba with a ferocity that had sometimes frightened Rose and she had the kind of reckless loyalty that had sent her running into the icy maw of Gevra. Wren had risked her life to save their grandmother, and she had failed. Rose knew it would be a long time before her sister forgave herself for it.

A tap at the window startled her from her thoughts. She slipped out of bed, careful not to wake her sister. There was a starcrest sitting on her windowsill. She reached out and untied the scroll from around its foot. It was tattered and ancient-looking and wrapped in a handwritten note.

Queen Rose,
Felicitations! The skies have whispered to us of your victory in battle.
    Ever since your letter arrived, we have spent all our time tirelessly searching for the scroll you requested. Pog found it hiding underneath a stack of old maps. Perhaps that boy is not such a lost cause after all!
    Yours mystically,
    Fathom

Sometime later, down in the warm kitchen at Anadawn

Palace, with mugs of hot tea to drink and a plate of fresh cookies to nibble on, Rose sat with Thea and Shen, discussing Banba.

'As far as I'm concerned, Alarik Felsing is still to blame,' said Shen, scowling into his mug as though he could see the Gevran king floating inside it. 'If he hadn't taken Banba, none of this would have happened.'

'There is no point in dwelling on *what ifs*, Shen Lo,' said Thea. 'The winds of destiny blow in a thousand different directions. We do not always get to choose the ones that carry us.'

Rose picked absently at a crumb. She was thinking of Wren, who, despite the advancing hour, was still in bed. Despite what she had told them about Oonagh, Rose had a feeling that she didn't yet know the full story, only the blurry edges of what Wren had told her, and what she had gleaned for herself on her brief visits there. She wondered if she would ever learn the rest.

'I'm sure Alarik thinks if his brother had never come to Eana that he would still be alive,' she offered into the silence. 'We've all lost people we love. Revenge won't bring any of them back.'

'Maybe not,' said Shen. 'But it provides a nice distraction from grief.'

Thea chuckled. 'I'd say Banba wouldn't want you to speak like that, but we both know nobody harboured a grudge like her.'

Shen's mouth quirked. 'Do you remember when she took

up against old Gideon back in Ortha because she was convinced he was giving her the smallest carrots from the vegetable patch?'

'Do I remember? Who do you think she complained to all winter long? Every time I made soup she swore she could taste the size of the carrot!' Thea released a wheezing laugh. 'She was so angry she went outside and blew every one of his prized pumpkins off the cliff.'

'And right before Samhain!' Shen recalled, his eyes crinkling with laughter.

Thea shook her head, smiling at the memory. 'I had to swim into the sea to get them back.'

'No one did petty like Banba,' said Shen, fondly. 'It was one of Wren's favourite things about her.'

'I'm not sure she even cared for carrots in the first place,' Thea confided. 'But she loved the drama of it.'

'What about when Grady broke her favourite jug?' said Shen.

'Oh, the uproar!' crowed Thea, both of them grinning as they launched into another story, and then another, and another, until the kitchen echoed with the sound of their laughter.

Rose leaned in to listen, feeling as warmed by the stories as the tea in her hands.

After a while, Thea set her mug down. 'Thank you both for spending your morning with me. Memories really do possess their own kind of magic. But my heart is tired. I think I'll go and lie down for a bit.'

'Will you be all right?' asked Rose, as Shen helped Thea to her feet. 'I wish there was something more I could do.'

'Time is the only healer for wounds of the soul,' said Thea, sagely. 'If I need company, I'll call for Tilda. She's always cheering, isn't she?'

'Yes, she is,' said Rose. 'In fact, I caught her cartwheeling through the lower hallway on my way down here.'

'That must have been after the rain cloud she made in the great hall,' said Shen. 'She soaked six of Cam's breakfast pies before Lei Fan put it out. But the townspeople seemed to enjoy the spectacle.'

'The more they experience magic, the less afraid of it they'll be,' said Thea. 'Though I'll be sure to caution Tilda about wasting food.' She smiled at them as she shuffled out of the kitchen, leaving them alone. 'I'm sure you two young rulers have a lot to talk about.'

Shen sat down next to Rose on the bench. His thigh brushed against her leg, and she was overcome by the sudden, desperate urge to climb on to his lap. She shook it off. They were in the kitchen in the middle of the day, after all. It would be entirely inappropriate.

'So, Rose, the Merciful, how long much longer will you be harbouring half the population of Eshlinn in your palace? If you're not careful, they'll drink all your wine.'

'They're welcome to it for as long as it takes the soldiers to repair their homes,' said Rose. 'Although Chapman says some of the Arrows went down there last night to help and are already making good progress.'

Shen's eyes shone with admiration. 'I could certainly learn a thing or two from you about ruling.'

'That reminds me,' said Rose, reaching into the pocket of her skirts. 'Now that we're alone, I have something to show you. Or, rather, to give you.'

Shen raised his brows. 'Tell me, before my mind wanders . . .'

'This arrived this morning,' said Rose, as she unfurled Fathom's scroll. 'After what you told me in the desert about your kingdom's sovereignty, I asked Fathom to look for it. It's an official declaration from over a thousand years ago, signed by Ortha Starcrest and the Sun Crowned Queen Jing. You were right, Shen. The Sunkissed Kingdom doesn't belong to Anadawn. It's yours.' She bit her lip, her cheeks heating in shame. 'It's always been yours.'

Shen took the parchment, barely blinking as he read the words. 'Of all the things I was expecting you to say . . .'

'Feng was right about one thing,' Rose went on. 'But I was too insecure to see it at the time. Too frightened about what it would mean for the fate of Eana, for my fate as its ruler, for *us* . . . The Sunkissed Kingdom has always been its own dominion. I had no right to try to command it. To command you.'

Shen flashed his dimple. 'Isn't being bossy your thing, though?'

Rose buried her face in her hands. 'I'm afraid it's as much a part of me as my fingernails.'

He chuckled then, and Rose found herself laughing, too.

Shen returned his gaze to the parchment. 'Our ancestors were allies.'

'They fought side by side. Just like us.'

'Perhaps we can be allies, too.' He cleared his throat. 'Officially.'

Rose's heart hammered in her chest. 'And what are the terms of this . . . alliance?'

Shen's eyes danced. 'You're a queen. I'm a king. I'm sure we can figure something out.' But his smile faded, and he turned serious, then. 'I just need to figure out how to be a good king first. I want to make my people proud of me.'

Rose laid her hand on his leg. 'You'll make a wonderful king, Shen. You have a good heart. All you have to do is lead with it.'

He stilled beneath her touch. 'Tell me, Rose,' he said, his voice rough. 'Can I rule with my heart if I've given it away?'

Rose bit her bottom lip. 'I'm afraid I'm facing the same dilemma.'

He cupped her cheek, leaning closer. 'About this alliance . . .'

'Yes . . .'

He gently slid his hand into her hair. 'I think we're going to need a lot of late-night meetings . . .'

'One would think,' said Rose, driven to distraction by his fingers.

'All very official, of course,' he said, tracing her bottom lip with his thumb.

'Of course,' Rose murmured, pressing a kiss to it.

'*Rose*,' he whispered. 'My Rose.' And then his mouth was

on hers and Rose couldn't think about anything else. She wound her fingers in his hair, pulling him closer, until every part of her was pressed against him, their moans slipping from them in perfect harmony. Shen pressed her back against the workbench, and accidentally upended a bowl of limes.

As they toppled to the floor, reality crashed back in.

They were in the kitchen! In the middle of the day! When *anyone* could walk in.

She pulled back from Shen. 'Oh,' she said, breathless. 'I'm afraid the moment ran away with me.'

He swept a hand through his hair. 'I've forgotten what we were talking about.'

Rose tried to be serious, but her lips twitched into a smile. 'I'm afraid we should return to our duties.'

'Right. Yes. Our duties,' said Shen, his gaze on her swollen lips. 'What are those again?'

'I have a country to fix,' said Rose, laughing as she prodded him. 'And *you* have a kingdom to return to.'

He smirked at her. 'Are you still ordering me around?'

She returned his smirk. 'Not everything has to change, you know.'

Wren

CHAPTER 59

Wren sat on the bow of Marino Pegasi's ship, with her feet dangling above the water, and smiled as the wind nipped at her cheeks. She didn't realize how much she had been missing the sea until she returned to it. There was something soothing about the wind out here. It made her feel closer to Banba, closer to herself.

'Do you *have* to sit so precariously?' said Rose, who was standing behind Wren, dressed in a lavish fur coat and a matching ivory hat. Her arms were pulled tightly around her, the chill chattering through her teeth. 'I'm anxious enough already without having to worry about you falling overboard.'

Wren swung around to face her sister. 'I already told you: you don't need to be anxious.'

Rose's gaze darted. 'What if this whole thing is a trap?'

Wren flexed her fingers, reminding her sister of the magic that flowed through their veins. 'Then it will be the Gevrans who suffer, not us.'

'Don't worry, my fair queens.' Marino's voice rang out as he came striding over, dressed impeccably in a cobalt frock coat and dark leathers, his tricorn hat tipped roguishly to one side. Rose looked him up and down, appreciatively, and Wren got the sudden sense that he was once her childhood crush. Or perhaps her adult crush, though not even the swashbuckling captain could hold a candle to Shen Lo now.

Even so, Wren suspected that if Shen knew *quite* how handsome and charming Marino Pegasi was, he might have forsaken his return to the Sunkissed Kingdom to accompany Rose on this journey.

'If Alarik Felsing even so much as looks at either of you the wrong way, I'll run him through with my cutlass.'

Rose squeezed his arm. 'Heroic as ever, Marino. And just as good as battling real foes as the imaginary villains of our childhood games. As I recall, you were particularly good at defeating dragons.'

He flashed his teeth. 'Don't make me blush. And you'll find I'm much better with a sword of steel than a stick of wood. '

'I don't remember you two flirting this much when we were younger,' grumbled Celeste, who was following close behind him. 'And don't get any ideas, Marino. Rose is all but spoken for.'

'Celeste!' said Rose, dropping Marino's arm as if she'd been scalded. 'We are *not* flirting, and as for the other thing, that's hardly something to be discussed here. In public.' Her cheeks turned bright pink, though Wren knew it had nothing to do with the biting sea wind.

'You *were* flirting,' she teased her sister. 'Although that's only because Marino flirts every time he draws breath.'

The captain assumed a look of mock offence, and Wren winked at him.

'Stop that,' warned Celeste. 'I'm not getting saddled with trouble incarnate as a sister-in-law.'

Wren stuck her tongue out. 'You wound me, Lessie. I'll have you know I'm a delightful sister. Just ask Rose.'

'Only when she behaves herself,' needled Rose.

'Which, of course, is hardly ever,' said Celeste. 'And *please* stop calling me "Lessie".'

'Fine,' said Wren. 'And to further prove my graciousness, I won't marry your brother.'

'We'll settle on firm friends,' said Marino, with a laugh. 'We all know my heart belongs to the sea anyway.'

'And what a fine captain you make,' said Wren. 'In fact, this is the third time you've made this treacherous journey for me, Marino, which means you have more than earned your knighthood.' She smirked. 'Don't worry, I haven't forgotten our deal.'

Rose looked between them. 'I really wish you wouldn't make royal deals without me.'

'It was only a small one,' said Wren, defensively.

'Last week you promised to knight Tilda.'

'In my defence, she told a *very* funny joke. I had to reward her.'

'She also promised me a mermaid,' said Marino.

'Wren!' Rose shook her head at her sister, but a smile danced on her lips. 'I suppose I can support that one, actually. I would quite like to meet a mermaid.'

Celeste chuckled. 'You really shouldn't indulge him.'

Marino pouted. 'Leave me be, Lessie. I'm heartsick.'

'Aren't we all?' said Rose, touching her head against his shoulder, as her thoughts no doubt turned to Shen. Wren cast her gaze out to the sea, trying not to think of Tor, and the mess she had made back in Gevra. She had a bad feeling she was going to have to face at least some of it today.

The sea was flat and grey, veiled by a low-hanging mist that hid its true expanse. It was so silent Wren couldn't hear the waves, but the wind nudged them onward, into the silvery abyss.

'So, this is the famous Sunless Sea.' Rose came to her side, her nose wrinkling. 'It seems so . . . *dead*.'

'That's because it's deep,' said Wren. 'And full of secrets. Who knows what kind of creatures are moving below us right now . . .'

'Thank you for that calming thought.' Rose blew out a breath. 'I wish your healing strand would hurry up and kick in. Then I wouldn't have to face that dreadful king again.'

Wren felt a jolt of unease at the word 'dreadful'. The truth was, Alarik Felsing was far more complex than that. So, too, were her feelings about the Gevran king. And then there was the matter of Wren's healing magic. She forced an easy smile. Her healing strand wasn't just late, it was non-existent. Wren would never possess the most noble strand of the witches' power because of what she had done at Grinstad. 'It'll be over before you know it, Rose. There's nothing to fear. I'll be right here.'

As though the twins had willed its arrival with their thoughts, a mighty ship with silver sails appeared in the distance, like it had formed from the mist itself. It seemed much larger than Wren remembered, and yet it moved towards them with the gracefulness of a swan.

Wren's heart began to hammer in her chest. She strained to make out the figures standing out on deck, but the creeping fog made ghosts of them.

Rose stiffened. 'Alarik'd better not have brought his beasts.'

'Pay them no mind,' said Wren, thinking of the king's wolves, and that great hulking bear. 'They're well trained.'

Thanks to Tor. Her pulse quickened.

'That's precisely what I'm worried about. How do you know Alarik isn't going to order one of them to tear us to pieces?'

'Please try to trust him, Rose. Trust *me*.'

Rose sighed. 'I'll do my best.'

Within minutes, the king of Gevra's ship was before them. Marino's crew leaped into action, dropping the anchor and securing the gangway.

Celeste climbed up first, flinging her arms out for balance as she began the walk to the other side.

Wren went next, tapping the pouch of sand at her waist for luck, then the dagger at her hip for courage, before climbing on to the gangway. She was dressed in her favourite trousers and leather boots, which she had paired with a fur-lined crimson coat that reached all the way up to her chin. She pulled it tighter as she inched across the plank, keeping her gaze on the back of Celeste's head.

Celeste swung down from the gangway, showcasing her newly honed warrior magic as she landed on deck with a triumphant thud. Wren hesitated. A soldier stepped forward, his hand outstretched to help her. She knew him at once.

Wren's breath hitched as she took Tor's hand, her legs trembling as she came to the end of the walkway. She was so distracted by his presence that she made a misstep and nearly tumbled into the sea. He lunged forward, catching her by the waist and pulling her against him.

'Careful,' he said, his warm breath ruffling her hair. He swung her around, lowering her gently to the deck.

Wren found her footing, but she was slow to step away from the soldier. She didn't want to lose the feeling of his hands on her body, or that stormy gaze pouring into hers. The air crackled between them, a familiar flare heating her cheeks.

'You're back,' she said.

He smiled. 'I didn't think we'd—'

'Excuse me! I also require some assistance!' Rose called out from the gangway. 'I'm the one you called for, am I not?'

Tor stepped away from Wren and turned back to the gangplank to help Rose.

'Queen Rose,' he said, in an entirely different voice. Formal. Stiff. 'The king is in his cabin, waiting for you.'

'Lead the way, soldier,' said Rose, shooing him on. 'Let's get this over with.'

Rose
CHAPTER 60

Rose followed Tor across the deck, pausing when she realized Wren wasn't by her side. She turned back to her sister. 'Wren?'

Tor cleared his throat. 'King Alarik has requested that you come on your own.'

A strange expression flashed across Wren's face so fast Rose nearly missed it. It looked almost like hurt. And yet she made no move to follow Rose. She truly trusted the king of Gevra.

Well, that made one of them.

Rose wrung her hands. 'Must I go alone into the cabin of the man who very recently kidnapped my grandmother and kept my own sister locked up against her will?'

Tor's hand came to the pommel of his sword. 'I give you my word, Queen Rose, that no harm will befall you while you are on this ship.'

Rose assessed the soldier and found that she trusted him. But, more than that, she trusted his loyalty, not to her but to her sister, who had survived the icy maw of Gevra, thanks in large part to him, and who was now staring after them like a lovesick paramour.

'If Rose isn't back up here in ten minutes, I'm telling my brother to ram this ship,' Celeste called after them.

'You'll do no such thing!' said Rose, but she felt the warmth of her friend's chuckle through the gathering mist.

Wren summoned a smile, waving her onward. 'We'll be right here waiting for you. You can do this, Rose. It has to be you.'

And with her sister's belief in her bolstering her confidence and quickening her steps, Rose followed Tor below deck.

Downstairs, they paused before a heavy wooden door, the intricate carving of a silver ice bear marking it as the king's cabin.

Tor knocked, and when the door opened, a tendril of icy mist seeped out. Rose shivered as the strange chill settled underneath her thick furs.

King Alarik stood before her. 'Rose.' He nodded his head, his expression absent of his usual simmering arrogance. 'Please come in.'

'You've certainly changed your tune,' said Rose, as she stepped into the cabin. 'I suppose you're capable of being at least somewhat polite when you want something. And it's *Queen* Rose.'

'Forgive me, Queen Rose.' The king stepped to one side, revealing the figure of his brother, lying on the four-poster bed in the middle of the cabin. 'I am most grateful for your help.'

The sight of Prince Ansel pierced Rose's heart. She suddenly remembered that she had come today not as a queen but as a healer. 'I'll do my best,' she said, softly.

'I hope your best is better than what your sister could do,' said Anika, who was sitting on a chair by the bed, keeping watch over her brother and wearing what looked to Rose like a fur-lined dressing gown. The Gevran princess glanced at the soldier hovering in the doorway. 'I don't want you in here, Tor. Alarik may have forgiven you, but I have not. I won't have these final minutes with my brother sullied by your presence.'

For a heartbeat, Tor looked guilt-stricken, but then he stiffened, his expression returning to that of an obedient soldier.

'You may go,' said Rose, deftly navigating the delicacy of the moment, not to mention the storm of emotions already clouding the little cabin. 'I can take it from here.'

Tor closed the door behind him, leaving Rose alone with the Felsing siblings. She approached the bed, her hand coming to her mouth to trap her horror. Ansel looked even worse than the last time she'd seen him. He stared blankly at her, then slowly juddered to life.

'My bride,' he croaked. 'Do you know, you look even more beautiful than I remember?'

Rose moved closer and perched on the edge of the bed and took his hand in hers. It was cold. Deathly cold. 'Thank you, Ansel.'

'You must excuse me for not getting up. I'm so tired. More tired than I've ever been.'

'Ansel, my love, I think you need to sleep.' She offered him a gentle pulse of magic to ease his addled mind. 'And when you wake . . .'

She trailed off as her voice broke. She hovered on the verge of tears for Ansel and the life he would never get to live, the future he had so desperately wanted.

'When I wake?' he prompted.

'When you wake, it will be our wedding day,' she whispered. 'And it will be wonderful.'

Ansel smiled, settling back into the pillows. 'It will be, won't it?'

Rose nodded, not trusting herself to speak. Anika stifled a sob.

Rose glanced over her shoulder. 'It's time,' she said.

Anika flung herself on the bed, burying her face in Ansel's chest.

Ansel tried to stroke her hair, but his arm was too heavy. 'Ani, don't cry. Weddings are supposed to be happy occasions.' He rolled his head around, towards Alarik. 'I hope you've prepared a speech, dear brother. You are so very good at speeches . . . so very . . . very . . .'

Rose glanced Alarik. But the Gevran king remained where he was, his jaw so tight it looked painful.

'Don't drag it out,' he said, turning his face away.

Anika drew back from her little brother. 'And be gentle,' she sobbed.

Ansel yawned, his lids growing heavy. 'Will there by dancing at our wedding, my flower?'

'As much as you like,' said Rose, squeezing his hand.

Ansel began to hum a waltz. Rose closed her eyes and reached for the thread of his life. It was tarnished and tangled, far beyond the talents of any healer. But she wasn't here to mend it. She was here to set it free. She sent another pulse of magic into his bloodstream.

Ansel fell out of his song with a sigh. His lids began to flutter.

'Regarding the speech for your wedding,' said Alarik, into the silence. 'I was thinking I'd tell everyone what a fine brother you are, Ansel. Better than any man could ask for. I'll tell them how you have always been the best of us.' His voice hitched just a little. 'And that we are lucky to know you. To love you.'

Ansel smiled, his body relaxing as Rose's magic spread. 'I feel happy,' he said, his voice growing distant. 'So very happy.'

'Rest now,' said Rose, gently.

She held on to the thread in her mind, her magic deftly untying it, knot by knot. It trembled beneath her touch, slowly turning golden once more. With a final breath, Rose let go of it. For the briefest moment, it glowed, as bright as the sun, and then shimmered away, into nothing.

Sleep well, sweet Ansel.

When Rose opened her eyes, they were filled with tears. Below her, Ansel went very still, the last of his breath leaving him. His skin was pale once more, his eyes the bright blue of a winter sky. His blond hair fell like a halo around his head, and he was still smiling, just a little. She reached up and brushed his eyes closed, and then very gently, leaned down and pressed a kiss to his lips. 'Goodbye, Ansel.'

With a sob swelling in her chest, Rose staggered to her

feet. She felt more spent than she had on the day of the battle with the Arrows. Anika was slumped in a chair beside the bed, weeping into her hands. Alarik had gone to the cabin window, his shoulders so stiff he looked carved from stone. He pulled back the curtains, a shaft of winter sunlight streaming into the bedroom and casting its glow upon Ansel's face. Alarik closed his eyes against the light, and as Rose slipped from the cabin, she could have sworn she saw a tear roll down the king's cheek.

When Rose closed the door of the cabin, she was trembling all over. A small piece of her heart had been left below deck with the young prince, along with the life she had once imagined with Ansel. He was a good man, cheerful and kind and full of hope for the future. He hadn't deserved the fate that had befallen him but at least he was at peace now. Rose had given him that if nothing else.

Wren

CHAPTER 61

Wren paced the upper deck of Alarik's warship, trying to soothe the rattle of her nerves. Soldiers watched her in the mist, their chins tipped to the pallid sky. Though there were no beasts prowling about up here, every inch of the king's vessel was under armed protection.

It was not that which unsettled Wren. She couldn't quite fathom the strange prickling inside herself. The rush of desire she had felt at Tor's touch had curdled into something sharp and thorny. It felt a lot like guilt.

'What's got into you?' said Celeste. 'An hour ago, you thought this was a great idea.'

'Helping Ansel is a good idea,' said Wren. 'Not to mention it will go a long way to establishing good relations with Gevra.'

'Then why are you acting all . . . twitchy?'

'I'm not acting twitchy.'

Celeste snorted. 'Who are you trying to fool? Me or you?'

'Wren?' said Tor, returning from below deck. 'Can we talk?'

'Mystery solved,' said Celeste, with a wry grin. 'Don't let me keep you.'

Wren tugged her hood up to hide the sudden flush in her cheeks.

Celeste's chuckle echoed after Wren as she fell into step with Tor. Under the watchful gaze of his fellow soldiers, he kept his hands by his side, but as they ambled towards the back of the ship, he pressed closer, letting his arm brush against hers.

'Why did you come back up?' she said.

'Anika wanted it to be a private moment,' said Tor, in a pained voice. 'And your sister seemed more than capable of taking care of herself.' He paused, glancing at her. 'How are you?'

'I don't know,' said Wren, honestly. 'It's all been such a whirlwind.' She blinked away the sudden flash of her blizzard kiss with Alarik. 'The battle at Anadawn took its toll on all of us. It's been weeks and yet I still dream of it. And losing Banba . . .' She trailed off.

'I'm sorry, Wren. I heard about what happened when I returned from Carrig. I wish I could have been there.'

Wren looked up at him, struck by the sympathy in his eyes. She was glad Tor hadn't been there to face her unhinged ancestor or witness her reckless kiss with Alarik. She couldn't even bear to imagine it. 'How are things back on Carrig?'

'Carrig was unrelenting.' His sigh was heavy. 'We've corralled most of the beasts, but there's a strangeness to them, even now. It's as if they're aware of something that we are not. Like a storm brewing over the horizon.'

Wren had a bad feeling she knew what that storm was.

Or rather, who. 'And there's been no sign of Oonagh since her wrecking spree back at Grinstad?'

Tor shook his head, but his expression was grim. 'The king's scouts continue to scour the country. The entire kingdom is on edge. No one more so than Alarik.'

Wren didn't want to talk about Alarik, to even *think* about Alarik. How he had held her in the eye of the blizzard, devouring her kiss and her pain along with it. It set her mind spinning, and filled her with a guilt so fierce, she half considered chucking herself overboard, if only to outswim it.

They reached the back of the ship, the mist falling like a veil around them, until it felt like they were the only two people on the entire Sunless Sea.

'Wren.' Tor turned towards her. 'You're trembling.'

Wren didn't realize she was shaking, until he lifted her hands to his lips and pressed a kiss against her fingers. She squeezed her eyes shut. 'I don't deserve your kindness.'

Tor chuckled, softly. 'Don't you always take what you want?'

'I'm serious, Tor.' She stepped away from him, her back flush against the ship's railings. 'I've made so many mistakes. I've done stupid things. I've *hurt* people.'

'To survive.'

Wren shook her head. 'Sometimes when I look in the mirror, I don't even know who I am any more.'

Tor held her gaze, his voice unerringly sure. 'I know you, Wren.'

'No, you don't.' She pulled her arms around herself to hold the awful truth of what she had done inside. The blood spells and the sacrifice, the way she had thrown herself at Alarik, how sometimes, in the dead of night, she still dreamed of that blizzard, that frenzied kiss. 'I'm not a good person, Tor.'

'So, what is it that you want, Wren?' Tor stepped towards her, and she let him. He braced his hands on the railings, blocking out the rest of the world. 'Absolution?'

Wren swallowed, thickly. 'Don't you want to know what I've done first?'

'I want to know what you need, Wren.' He tilted his chin down, until they shared the same breath. 'And I want to be the one to give it to you.'

She looked up, losing herself in the storm of his eyes. Desire nudged her closer, until her hands were on the lapels of his coat, tugging him in.

He leaned down, kissing the sensitive spot beneath her ear. 'I wish we were a hundred miles from here.'

Wren smiled against him. 'In the Turcah Valley?'

Another kiss, his breath feathering her cheek. 'Yes,' he whispered. 'All day. All night.'

'Tor.' She rose to her tiptoes.

He brushed his nose against hers. '*Wren.*'

'WREN!' shouted Rose, her voice echoing all around them. 'Where are you?'

Tor pulled back from Wren just as her sister came stalking through the mist. Rose's eyes were glassy and her cheeks were pale.

Celeste was with her. 'Rose is finished. It's done. Whatever this is, wrap it up.'

'We were just talking about . . . Elske,' said Wren, knowing nobody believed her and not really caring. She went to her sister, taking her elbow to steady her. 'Are you all right? How did it go?'

'I'm fine. And Ansel is at peace.' Rose's smile was shaky. 'I'd like to go home now.'

'Of course.'

They made their way back to the gangway, with Tor following close behind. This time, Rose went first, supported by Celeste. Tor helped Wren climb up last, his hands lingering on her waist, his eyes saying the goodbye that he couldn't voice out loud.

Wren wanted to say something, too – to tell him that she would write, that they would see each other again, but she couldn't make a promise without merit. Not with him. She had no idea what the future held, or whether they might ever see each other again. So, instead, she smiled, saying nothing as she stepped on to the narrow wooden bridge.

It was then that she saw him, a figure taking shape in the silver mist. King Alarik had appeared on deck. His blue eyes were rimmed in red and his face was drawn, as if he hadn't slept in days. As if he might never sleep again. She could tell he had been crying and hated how something inside her lurched at the thought.

'It seems our bargain is finally at an end.' He offered the ghost of a smile, but his voice was ragged. She hated that, too. He came to stand beside Tor. Wren's cheeks burned under the spotlight of their gazes. The moment was so acutely awkward that a small part of her wanted to laugh. The rest of her wanted to fling herself into the sea, where the cold water would soothe the sting of her guilt and destroy the twin flames of her desire.

She didn't trust herself to speak, so instead she waved a clumsy goodbye, before turning abruptly on her heel and scurrying back towards the *Siren's Secret*.

The king's voice followed her through the mist. 'Until next time, Wren.'

Rose

CHAPTER 62

Rose perched on the velvet bench of the royal tour carriage, carefully adjusting her crown.

'It is straight?' she asked her sister. 'I don't know why but it feels heavier.'

'Must be all the responsibility,' said Wren, brushing a stray curl off her sister's forehead. 'You look perfect.'

Rose smoothed her skirts, trying to settle the flutter of nerves in her stomach. 'I just want the tour to go well this time.'

'It will go well,' Wren assured her. 'And we'll both be thoroughly bored by the end of it.'

Six weeks had passed since the battle at Anadawn Palace, where the witches had inherited the fullness of their power and the people of the Sunkissed Kingdom had come to their aid. Since then word had spread throughout Eana of the lost desert kingdom, as well as the twins' mercy at the golden gates, how they had spared the frightened soldiers and repentant Arrows who had turned against the witches, in the hope of forging a future where they could all live together in harmony.

Afterwards, the twin queens and Shen Lo had officially pledged to defend each other and the land of Eana from anyone who sought to attack it, either from within or without. Now Shen and Rose were not only equals but allies, as fiercely protective of each other as they were of their kingdoms.

Shen had invited them to visit him on the final stop of the tour, and Rose had gratefully accepted, vowing to make the most of their time together.

'You're blushing,' said Wren. 'You must be thinking about Shen.'

Rose swatted her arm. 'Don't be so uncouth.'

'Just get married already,' said Wren, through a sprawling yawn. 'Put yourselves – and the rest of us – out of our misery.'

'I'm far too busy to even consider such a thing,' said Rose, quickly. 'And besides, he hasn't *asked* me.'

'So, ask him.'

'And forgo my ring? Now you really are trying to rile me.'

The carriage slowed. Wren drew the curtain back to peek out of the window. 'We're almost at Ellendale,' she said. 'I can see the banners up ahead.'

'So, there are townspeople?' said Rose, anxiously.

'Lots.' Wren sighed. 'We'll be shaking hands for hours.'

Rose smiled. Now that Edgar Barron was dead and his rebellion had been stamped out, mistrust of Rose and Wren was finally petering out.

'I'm starving.' Wren kicked her feet up. 'When can we eat?'

'You just ate an entire bowl of candied fruit,' said Rose. 'Which were Grandmother Lu's gift to *me*, by the way.'

'Next time, tell her to make double.' Wren closed her eyes, a furrow appearing between her brows.

'What are you thinking about?'

'How much Banba would hate this.'

'It's strategy. She'd understand.'

Wren hmm'd. 'I'm thinking about Gevra, too.'

Rose stiffened. The thought of Gevra still sent a chill down her spine. Not just because it was the place where Banba had died, but because she couldn't bring herself to trust its frost-hearted king or his strange hold over Wren. Rose couldn't quite figure out how or when it had happened, but there seemed to have developed a kind of bond between Alarik and Wren, which made her more than a little uneasy. And then there was the matter of Oonagh Starcrest.

Wren must have sensed her sister's discomfort. 'I'm just wondering what's going on in Gevra. *Generally*. That's all.'

In an effort to keep her sister's mind on Eana, Rose pulled back the carriage's privacy curtain. 'Do you hear that, Wren? They're cheering for us.'

Wren snapped her eyes open. 'If anyone tries anything untoward, I'm blowing them away in a hurricane.'

Rose sighed as the road turned to cobbles beneath them, the golden carriage trundling onward into the town of Ellendale. 'Mind the children, at least. They might throw a few roses at us.'

'So long as they're not on fire,' muttered Wren.

Rose knocked twice on the roof of the carriage. 'Ramsey, lower the roof, please!'

There came the sudden sound of cranking as metal wheels shifted somewhere behind Rose. The roof groaned as it was peeled away from the carriage, like the skin of an apple. The sky yawned overhead, revealing the crisp autumn sun.

'Nice trick,' said Wren.

Rose smiled. 'Why, thank you. It was rather fun to design.'

'We have very different ideas of fun.'

Rose rolled her eyes and swatted her sister on the knee.

Outside, the main street was lined with crowds of people all dressed in their finest clothes. Some of the children were even wearing paper crowns. They were waving flowers and flags and calling out to the sisters by name.

'Queen Rose! We love you! You're so brave!'

'Over here, Queen Wren! Please wave at me!'

'Did you see that, Marcel? I swear she looked right at me!'

'Lena, look, there's Queen Rose! Blow her a kiss!'

Rose turned back to Wren, raising her voice over the clamorous welcome. 'Why don't we show them a little magic?'

Wren smirked. 'I like your thinking.'

She clicked her fingers, drawing a flicker of lightning that soon erupted into a ball of fire. A chorus of gasps rang out as she tossed it back and forth, between her hands. Rose removed a pinch of earth from the pouch at her waist and uttered a spell she had been working on all night. She would always be a healer, at heart, but after a little practice, she had taken to the enchantment strand of her magic with remarkable quickness. Perhaps it was because her mother had been an enchanter, too.

Within minutes, a hundred flaming wrens were flying in circles above the carriage. The children surged forward to get a closer look. Wren laughed as she blew the birds over the rooftops and into the clouds, while Rose crafted an entire kaleidoscope of butterflies from one of the bouquets in the carriage. Red and yellow, pink and violet petals all took flight and fluttered into the crowd, the children hollering in delight as they landed on their shoulders.

Wren chuckled as she watched the floral butterflies. 'You know, in all my years as an enchanter, I never once thought to do that.' She spotted a teenager rudely jostling his way through the crowds, and idly sent out a gust of wind to knock him over.

Rose pursed her lips. 'Somehow I'm not surprised.'

They rode on, through the streets of Ellendale, where the air was buzzing with excitement. There wasn't a single Arrow in sight. As another bouquet of butterflies fluttered their way through the town, Rose felt a gentle peace stirring around her, and took it as a sign of good things to come.

Beside her, Wren was blowing kisses with gusto, basking in that same ray of hope for the future. In a rare moment of quiet, when the carriage was trundling between one winding street and the next, she turned to say something to Rose.

Rose watched the smile on her sister's face falter as the world dimmed around its edges. She reached for Wren's hand. And then everything went black.

Rose blinked to find herself floating above the world, on the wings of an ancient hawk. Below her, sprawled a white mountain range glistening with ice. She was in Gevra. The bird swooped, and Rose went with it, until she hovered above a sparse pine forest.

There was a woman standing in the middle of it. For a heartbeat, Rose swore it was Wren, but then the woman smiled, revealing her bloodied teeth. A gasp stuck in Rose's throat.

She knew with sudden chilling certainty that it was Oonagh Starcrest.

Oonagh flung her arms wide. The ground began to rumble. Trees cleaved in two and crashed to the earth, while beasts howled from the snowy mountains. Oonagh spat a glob of blood on to the earth, and a rotting hand burst up from the ground, as if to catch it.

Rose screamed as the rest of the corpse emerged, but the hawk was carrying her away. The wind whipped up, and in its howl, she heard Glenna the seer's voice. '*You broke the ice and freed the curse. Now kill one twin to save the other.*'

A rousing cheer brought Rose back to herself. She was on a street in Ellendale, listening to the whoops and hollers of its townspeople. She turned to Wren to find her staring, her eyes so wide Rose could see her own reflection in them.

'Did you see that, too?' Wren whispered.

Rose nodded, suddenly too frightened to speak.

'Oonagh *will* return to Eana.' Wren turned her face north, her eyes darting. 'This was her kingdom, Rose. Her throne. I don't think she's done with it.'

In the absence of her voice, Rose squeezed her sister's

hand. Wren squeezed back. And for the rest of their tour of Ellendale neither of them uttered another word, though Rose knew they were both thinking the same thing.

They would do whatever it took to protect Eana and each other. No matter what the seer said. They would defy the stars themselves if they had to.

And they would do it together.

Acknowledgements

Thank you to everyone who read *Twin Crowns* and wanted to continue the journey with us in *Cursed Crowns*. We hope you have as much fun reading these books as we did writing them.

This book is dedicated to our agent Claire Wilson, AKA Princess Claire, and we are forever grateful to have her as our steadfast champion.

And in the US, we are lucky enough to have the amazing Pete Knapp on our side. Pete, thank you for your excellent insights and continued enthusiasm.

We would also like to thank the wider team at RCW, especially Sam Coates for selling *Twin Crowns* and *Cursed Crowns* to many wonderful publishers around the world. Thank you as well to Safae El-Ouahabi at RCW, and to Stuti Tevidevara at Park & Fine.

Thank you to our film agents Michelle Kroes, Berni Barta, and Emily Hayward-Whitlock.

Huge thank you to Lindsey Heaven and Sarah Levison at Farshore in the UK, and Kristin Daly Rens at Balzer&Bray in the US, for making the editorial process such a joyous one.

We love working with all of you and look forward to future adventures in the *Twin Crowns* world.

Everyone who has worked on the book deserves their own crown, but we are especially grateful to Pippa Poole on the PR team, Jasveen Bansal and Ellie Bavester in marketing, and Brogan Furey in sales. And of course, we have to thank the King of Design, Ryan Hammond, for creating another stunning book cover featuring the incomparable Charlie Bowater's art. We love it!

We are very grateful to all the retailers and bookshops for their support in the UK, Ireland, the US, and beyond! We would also like to thank the teams at FairyLoot and LitJoy Crate.

A heartfelt thank you to our fantastic street team, the Twin Crowns 22, for going above and beyond with their support for the book. Aamna, Abi, Angie, Angelina, Courtney, Diana, Divya, Emily, Gigi, Georgia, Holly, Katelin, Kayla, Kelly, Kellie, Kimberly, Maha, Pawan, Rosa, Samantha, Sarah, and Stacey – thank you all! And we are delighted to welcome all the new additions to our Cursed Crowns Crew.

Thank you, thank you, thank you to all of the readers who have taken Rose and Wren (and Shen and Tor) into their hearts and shared their love for these characters. It means so much to us.

And of course, thank you to all of our wonderful friends and family across the globe for their continued support, with special thanks and love to the Webber, Doyle, and Tsang families.

COMING SOON . . .

TWIN CROWNS 3

CATHERINE DOYLE & KATHERINE WEBBER are both bestselling and award-winning writers of YA and children's books. In addition to co-writing the *Twin Crowns* series, they are sisters-in-law.

Catherine grew up beside the Atlantic Ocean, where her love of reading began with great Irish myths and legends. She is the author of the YA *Blood for Blood* trilogy and several magical middle grade books, including the award-winning *Storm Keeper* trilogy. She lives in the west of Ireland with her husband Jack and their dog Cali.

Katherine is from Southern California and spent much of her childhood in the Palm Springs desert. She is the author of *Only Love Can Break Your Heart* and *The Revelry*. For younger readers, she also co-writes the *Sam Wu is Not Afraid*, *Space Blasters*, and *Dragon Realm* series with her husband, Kevin Tsang. She is currently based in London with her husband and young daughters.